JENNIFER BLAKE
BETINA KRAHN
GLENDA SANDERS
JODI THOMAS

Love blooms beneath the stars—in that magical time when restless, lovelorn spirits follow their dreams to undreamed-of places ... and whispered wishes of impossible romance are gloriously answered. Explore this breathtaking realm of hearts and wonders with four accomplished and admired authors of romantic fiction in timeless and unforgettable stories of sensuous, mystical, breathless passions born in the silver moonlight ... and nurtured by STARDUST.

Avon Books Presents

Stardust

JENNIFER BLAKE
BETINA KRAHN
GLENDA SANDERS
JODI THOMAS

AVON BOOKS ◆ NEW YORK

AVON BOOKS PRESENTS: STARDUST is an original publication of Avon Books. This work is a collection of fiction. Any similarity to actual persons or events is purely coincidental.

AVON BOOKS
A division of
The Hearst Corporation
1350 Avenue of the Americas
New York, New York 10019

The Warlock's Daughter © 1994 by Patricia Maxwell
A Touch of Warmth © 1994 by Betina M. Krahn
Sweet Cream and Irish Whiskey © 1994 by Glenda Sanders Kachelmeier
Shadows Bend © 1994 by Jodi Koumalats

Published by arrangement with the authors
Library of Congress Catalog Card Number: 94-94076
ISBN: 0-380-77692-8

First Avon Books Printing: September 1994

AVON TRADEMARK REG. U.S. PAT. OFF. AND IN OTHER COUNTRIES, MARCA REGISTRADA, HECHO EN U.S.A.

Printed in the U.S.A.

RA 10 9 8 7 6 5 4 3 2 1

Contents

Avon Books Presents

Stardust

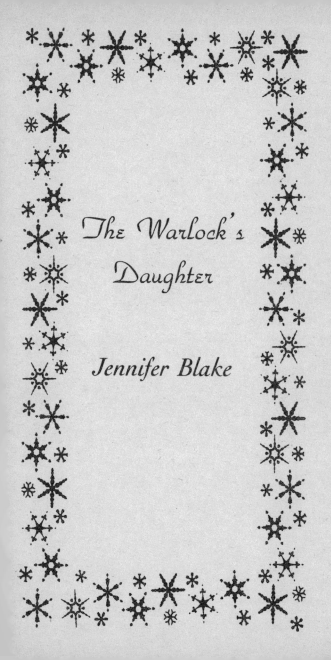

The Warlock's Daughter

Jennifer Blake

1

Carita Grey was not afraid of ghosts or goblins or any other creature of darkness, real or imagined. That was why she was always given the evening errands, such as taking the vicious boxer dog belonging to the widowed aunt with whom she lived for his walk before bedtime or going for the doctor when there was illness in the house. It was why she was out tonight, collecting the flower vase left behind after the decoration of the cemetery for All Saints' Day. It was also the reason she failed to retreat when she saw the stranger sitting on the raised family tomb.

The gentleman was not particularly threatening. He was, in fact, immensely polite, rising to his feet with lithe grace, sweeping off his high silk hat, executing his bow with all the polish of a courtier before a queen. Nor was there anything to distress her in the way he looked: his handsome features and tall, broad form were too pleasing, if anything. Still, there was something about him, as he stood there in the light of the rising moon with the white marble sepulchres of New Orleans' City of the Dead gleaming around him, that set alarm bells clanging in her mind. That was even before he spoke.

"What kept you, *chère*?" he said. "I've been waiting for hours."

Carita felt the rich tone of his voice, with its shading of familiarity and wry humor, vibrate deep inside her. It set off a rush of fierce longing that expanded, crowding out thought, heating her heart, weighting her lower body while her mind swam with euphoric intoxication. The sensation was like nothing she had ever known, a consuming flame of purest desire. Startled, unbelieving, she was defenseless against it.

The man's rigorously sculpted features softened. He transferred his hat to the same hand that held his cane, then reached out to her. As he moved forward, his long cape billowed to expose the red silk lining inside the dark folds. It made him look, for an instant, like a hawk swooping down on its prey.

"No!" she said on a quick gasp. Shuddering at the effort, she stepped backward beyond any possibility of physical contact.

He stopped and let his hand drop to his side. A waiting stillness settled over him while he regarded her with distracted care, as if listening to her panicked breathing, absorbing her reluctance. Beyond the brick and wrought-iron cemetery fence, a carriage rattled past at a slow pace and faded into the night.

As quiet closed in on them once more, he said simply, "Why?"

"You—you must be mistaken in who I am, sir." She clasped her hands tightly together at her waist under the slits of her short velvet cloak.

His mouth, sensual in its chiseled curves, exquisitely tender in the tucked corners, curled in amusement. He said, "Oh, I don't think so."

"Well, I certainly don't know you! And if you will permit me to pass, I have to retrieve—"

"Renfrey."

"I beg your pardon?"

"My name. You did not know it."

The tenderness of his voice was like a caress. Carita did her best to ignore it. With great firmness, she said, "Yes, well, but your saying so can hardly be called an acceptable introduction, can it? As I was saying, there is a vase behind you left by my Aunt Berthe that I must—"

"It's worthless. I wouldn't trouble myself over it." The words were judicious and dismissive. He paused, said in intent demand, "How are you called?"

"Carita. It's odd, I know, but it was an endearment my father used, so it had special meaning to my mother before—" She halted, amazed at herself for saying so much when she had meant to say nothing at all.

"Before she died?" he finished gently. "I was reading the engraving on her tomb, I think, just now."

Carita looked beyond him to where a bouquet of wilting chrysanthemums and wild ageratum tied with black ribbon streamers lay on the couchlike foundation of the family resting place. There were roses there, also, a huge mass of late-fall blooms. How fresh they looked, as if just cut. She didn't remember her aunt bringing them. Who had?

She gave the man before her an inquiring frown. At that moment, a luna moth of enormous size fluttered from the ranks of tombs. Pale green, ethereal, it drifted about their heads, then settled on Renfrey's broad, black-clad shoulder like a gentle, moon-dusted ghost.

And abruptly Carita's every sense was exquisitely alive.

How delightful the night was; she had hardly noticed before. Moonlight glinting on the dark and shiny leaves of the evergreen magnolia just beyond where they stood gave them the look of black crystal. The marble mausoleums and memorials that surrounded them were smoothly graceful and touched with peace, while the planes and angles of their shadows were velvet-edged and inviting.

She could smell the delicious scent of the roses on her mother's tomb, and from some nearby garden sweet olive drenched the air with its honeyed seduction. She identified the mustiness of decay on the withering seedpods of the magnolia, caught the dry herbal mustiness of the lantana where it grew against a headstone. The scents of parched grass and old bones hovered near.

In the mausoleum just over there, a mouse scuffled, making a nest. At the wrought-iron fence, a stray cat, gray with night, wove in and out between the palings; he had not yet detected the mouse.

The wind on her face had currents of coolness and warmth, of spice and sweetness, as if some portions of it had traveled from the snowcapped Andes while others had last drifted through nutmeg groves or over the heated sugarcane fields of a Caribbean isle. The brush of it against her skin was a languid, inciting caress. The breeze sighed through the row of cedars not far away and clattered in the magnolia leaves. It tinkled a wind chime left hanging in a distant marble tomb's doorway, and the faint, minor sound was like the passing of a soul.

A wisp of pale hair, turned platinum-and-gilt by moonlight, loosened from her chignon and blew around her face in shining filaments. As Carita caught it back with one hand, holding it, she wondered if her eyes were as night black as those of the man who watched her.

"Your mother," he said softly. "How did she die?"

"How?" she answered almost at random in her distraction. "She was killed by an excess of loving."

"You mean she met death in childbirth?" He tilted

his head as he waited for her answer. At the movement, the great luna moth lifted from his cape and
fluttered into the darkness. Without its soft presence,
they were incredibly alone.

"So many do, don't they?" she answered. "They
are here, lying all around us so quiet and still, many
with the tiny babe at their side or enclosed within
their bones. But no. My mother was loved too well.
Her heart could not sustain it; it just—stopped."

"Is there such a thing as too much love?"

Renfrey's words had the sound of quiet contemplation. Hearing it, Carita's tingling senses expanded
still further. It seemed, as she looked into the fathomless depths of his gaze, that she knew him. She
had intimate knowledge of his body: the powerful
bands of muscle that encased it, the strong skeleton
beneath, the heart that beat so fiercely inside. And
knowing him, she ached for his touch as she might
for food after an eternity of fasting.

On a quick-drawn breath, she said, "My Aunt Berthe, my mother's older sister, certainly thinks so. She
claims my mother was too frail in body and spirit
for physical closeness. She says my father knew it
would be so, must have guessed in the beginning
that his passions were too strong, his needs too demanding. Therefore, he killed her."

"And you believe it?"

She faced him squarely. "I have no reason to
doubt it."

He was silent while the blowing hem of his cape
brushed the diamond-glitter of dust from his boots.
He set the ferrule of his cane on the toe of one and
rested both hands on the silver handle. At last he
said, "She must have been a woman of uncommon
beauty."

"They say so; I never knew her." She heard the

regret in her own voice, something else she had never noted before.

"I expect you are her image."

The flush that rose at the compliment was painful in its intensity. Her vanity, however, was untouched. "My aunt says not, though the resemblance is there. I am more like my father, which is unforgivable. I have his strength."

"You would, of course," he said, and smiled to himself.

Carita watched him, and she wondered. But no, it was unlikely that he could know anything of her situation. He was only a chance-met stranger, and perhaps an accomplished trifler with the female sex. He might be—was without doubt—good at reading the desires of a woman's heart. But that was all.

Or was it? The warmth of his smile seemed for her alone; the look in his eyes caressed her. She was encompassed, held prisoner, by the sheer male force emanating from him. With these things was something more that was like mystic recognition. And possibly the handiwork of fate.

"What of your mother?" he asked, delicately probing. "Did she regret the loving?"

It was a personal question, like his personal comments. She should not answer, should not stay to exchange another word. Yet the compulsion was strong. She said, "There is nothing to show that she did. My aunt regrets it enough for both of them."

"And has accomplished her revenge against your father by transferring it to you?"

A frown drew her brows together. "Why should you think so?"

"She has made the memory of your mother bitter with regret and turned you, with her claims, into the daughter of a murderer. Encouraging you to despise

your father, she has taught you to disavow the part
of yourself that is like him."

"Not—intentionally."

"No? But you can't deny she has proved her lack
of concern for your well-being. After all, she has sent
you here alone, unchaperoned, on All Hallows' Eve,
the one night in the year when anything can happen."

She had never thought of it like that. Still, she said,
"Perhaps I came of my own choice."

"I salute your loyalty; it is a lovely virtue. But
does your aunt deserve it?"

Between confusion over the compliment and recognition of her own doubts, her protest was weak.
"She must be given some consideration for caring
for me since I was born."

"But if she can't or won't protect you, now that
you are a young woman, it could be time for you to
seek the safety of a gold band."

"Hardly," she said, "if you mean the kind that
comes with a husband attached."

Laughter flashed like lightning across the darkness of his eyes, then vanished. "You sound so certain. Perhaps you've been married?"

The violent shake of her head threatened to loosen
her small hat of feather-trimmed felt. "No, thank
goodness. Rather, I've seen the husbands chosen by
my aunt for her daughters."

"You weren't impressed?"

The solicitation in his voice was, she thought,
completely spurious. "One of them drinks all day
and falls asleep at dinner with his face in his soup.
The other sleeps during the daylight hours and
drinks all night with his male friends."

"And on the strength of their example you shun
matrimony."

"I haven't the temperament for it." Her face was

without expression. He could not know the subject was distressing to her.

Renfrey was thoughtful. "I will grant that I have little experience with the cool and pallid passions of the church, but you don't have the look of a nun."

"The problem," she said in stringent tones, "is not a lack of heat."

"What an intriguing admission—" he began with a wicked smile, then stopped. "No," he corrected himself. "That was a statement of information, I think, not an invitation to dalliance. The question is, then: What are you afraid of?"

The night wind shifted the fullness of her wide skirts so they brushed the tombs on either side. The friction crumbled old lichen from the surfaces into black flakes which sprinkled down onto the worn gray silk, catching on the circular bones of the hoop underneath. Above them in the night sky, a trio of bats swooped in silent delirium on brown velvet wings, mouths open to catch the mosquitoes which danced in the air. Voracious, the small flying animals combed the air with their teeth for what they needed in order to live. As did all creatures, each in its own way.

Releasing the breath she had caught, Carita said in stark denial, "I'm not afraid of you."

"Indeed not; why should you be?" he said. "I am no threat."

But he was, and she knew it. Before this night, there had been no one who might have answered the need inside her, no image to use for a hook on which to hang her dreams. She would not have believed there was someone who could fill the aching void in her heart, yet this man was pushing his way inside and settling there, bit by bit, like a homing night owl in a hollow tree.

She said, "Some fears cannot be explained."

He was not to be put off with ambiguity. "You aren't afraid of the dark, or even the unknown, or you wouldn't be here. You obviously aren't timid of the opposite sex, and we have settled that you don't have the disposition of a nun. I don't understand. Can it be you are afraid of dying like your mother?"

"You might put it that way," she answered in tight evasion.

His eyes narrowed at the corners. "No, I don't think I would, after all. Perhaps it's living that is your secret horror? And loving?"

"No." The word was stark.

"No, but something very close to it," he mused, relentless. "Is your aunt also to blame for that?"

He was far too acute for comfort. "Really, I don't believe it's—"

"Any of my affair? Agreed." He paused. "It's one thing to be ruled by your own terrors, you know, but something else again to yield to the fears of others."

"Or the persuasions?" she suggested, with an edge to her voice. Her gaze was direct if a little defensive.

He laughed, a sound resonant with warm and accepting humor. "Especially the persuasions. Or worse, their overweening passions. Unless you don't know your own mind—or prefer to pretend you don't."

"Letting someone else take the blame for whatever may happen then?"

"Or the credit," he said with audacity.

She watched him and wondered again exactly what was in his mind. And she wished she knew what had brought him there and what he intended, but was afraid he might tell her if she asked. It would never do to be certain, for then she would be forced to go. Which was, she discovered, not at all what she wanted. Not yet.

"Walk with me," he said abruptly, his gaze intent on her face. "For just a little while?"

It felt as if he had read her mind; there had been a momentary and incredible sense of invasion followed by warm unison. No, impossible. She must have initiated that small merging herself, must have failed to guard her thoughts because she was too absorbed in guarding her emotions.

His invitation should be refused; she knew that beyond doubting. All the reasons that made acceptance futile and unwise clamored in her head along with the certain consequences. Louder still, however, was the urging of instinct.

Her manner withdrawn, she said, "Walk where?"

"Anywhere. Nowhere. Must there be a destination?"

"It's usual." She added, "Also more prudent."

"I thought," he said with astringency, "that we had dispensed with prudence along with fear?"

Her gaze was calm. "Did you? I was not aware of it. But I must return to my aunt's house. If you care to walk in that direction, I have no way of stopping you."

He inclined his head with a trace of irony. Replacing his silk hat at a jaunty angle, he moved toward her, offering his arm for her support. As she reached out to take it, however, he snapped his fingers and whirled away. Stepping toward the family tomb with fluid grace, he returned with the vase she had been sent to find.

"You wanted this, I think."

How could she have forgotten? The answer was in the form of the man before her. Foolish, so foolish. She murmured her thanks, not quite meeting his gaze as she accepted the piece of white porcelain.

To stroll at Renfrey's side along the rows of tombs toward where the gate stood open had all the tremulous excitement of the forbidden. Carita salved her conscience with the knowledge that it would be for only a few short minutes. At the same time, she savored, carefully, the close company; it was so very rare.

Her aunt had done her duty by taking an orphaned babe into her home, but Carita never felt as if she belonged; there was always a sense of being there on sufferance. As she grew older and her cousins, her aunt's daughters, married, she had been left the sole companion of her aunt. The two of them had sadly little in common, however, as Carita had no liking for gossip and handwork such as funeral jewelry made from human hair, and her Aunt Berthe cared nothing for books or ideas.

Taught from an early age to make herself useful around the house, Carita had discovered only after she came of age that the household subsisted on money left behind by her father for her care. By then, service, like isolation, had become a habit.

Renfrey matched his pace to hers without apparent effort. He was an able escort as they wove in and out among the tombs, steering her clear of entanglements and around obstacles. She could feel the warmth of his body, sense the taut muscles and sinews under the broadcloth of his sleeve beneath her grasp.

He had thrown back his cape so that the lining had a bloodlike sheen as it dipped and swirled behind his shoulders. In his free hand he swung his cane, batting at the dusty heads of weeds. Well balanced, it seemed rather heavy, as if it might have a sword concealed in its glinting, silver-tipped length.

The night flowed, timeless and lavender-gray around them, shutting out all else. Behind them, the gray cat followed at a distance, a soft-slipping shadow leaping from tomb to tomb with insouciance, mincing down the gravel walk, starting at shadows to streak ahead then sit waiting for them.

Conversation being an accomplishment expected of a lady, Carita said after a moment, "You are not from New Orleans, I think? Are you visiting relatives or friends?"

"What makes you think this isn't my home?" The words were accompanied by a quick downward glance.

"The way you speak, for one thing," she said. "You have an accent I find hard to place. Then you appear a gentleman, yet I've never seen you at the theater or any of the balls of the winter season. The social circle here is small; we should have met at some time or other."

"Actually, I arrived only recently," he said.

"From Europe, perhaps?"

"Among other places, from Turkey to Taipei."

"A world traveler," she said dryly.

"In a fashion. I am thinking of staying, though whether I will . . . depends."

"On what?" It seemed a natural question.

"Developments." He went on with hardly a pause. "You enjoy your life here? You never think of leaving?"

"Often," she said. "There is so much beyond this one place that I would like to see."

"Then you aren't happy?"

"Oh, who would not wish for some change, however small? No matter. I am resigned if not content." The understanding in his voice was addictive; she must beware of it.

His glance was skeptical. "What do you do with your days?"

"Very little you would consider of interest," she said in even tones.

"Permit me to guess. You direct your aunt's servants in their cleaning; you order the meals, see to the shopping. You mend and sew and embroider linens. Yes, and you fetch and carry and run the small errands your aunt finds inconvenient."

"How did you—" she began, then stopped as she saw the answer.

"Yes, the usual life of a spinster living with a relative. Only you are far too young and lovely to deserve the name, much less be resigned."

"You consider I should be doing all those things for a husband, I imagine."

"For yourself, in your own home, though the man you may choose to join you would also benefit."

"And have legal right to my services, not to mention ownership of the house?" There was a waspish edge to her tone.

"The house may or may not belong to the man," he said, "but the home is always the woman's province where a man is only a guest. She can make him as comfortable or uncomfortable as she pleases."

"But not be easily rid of him?" She gave him a steely look.

He halted and a frown appeared between his dark brows. "Does that mean that you want me to leave you? You have only to say the words and I will be gone."

"We were not," she said with acid satisfaction, "speaking of you." She kept her steady pace.

Renfrey made no reply. Catching up with her in two strides, he walked on a few steps before he said, "What of your father? Have you seen him recently?"

"I've not seen him at all," she answered. "He went away when I was a few weeks old."

"You never knew him, then. A pity."

"So I've often thought. My aunt, of course, feels otherwise."

His words measured, he said, "I believe he did what he thought was best in leaving you with her."

It was Carita who stopped this time, forcing him to come to a halt beside her. Her voice compressed, she said, "You speak as if— Can it be you know him?"

Renfrey's gaze was considering. "I met him once."

"Where? How did he look? Was he well?" Excitement made the words tumble from her in near incoherence.

"It was in Paris, I think," he answered, taking her questions in turn. "Or was it Rome? A distinguished gentleman, cosmopolitan, learned. He had a great interest in antiquities. And he seemed in robust health."

She moistened her lips. "It was he who told you about me, wasn't it?"

"We talked of your mother, of her death and how much he missed her. He had received reports of you which worried him. There was a suggestion that I might seek you out if ever I found myself in New Orleans."

She digested that and found it disquieting. She said, "For what purpose?"

"The meeting? No purpose was given. I should think, however," he went on deliberately, "that it would be for the usual reason—the thing which most concerns a man with a daughter who is a beauty with independent ways."

"Courtship? Marriage?" The words were tight as she turned her head to stare straight ahead.

"If it should come to that. There is, of course, no obligation. On either side."

"That's all that passed between you?" She could

not help looking at him again, searching for she knew not what. There was nothing in his face that should not have been there. Delicately and in silent trepidation, she sent out a mental probe for more.

Odd. There seemed to be a barrier which prevented her from penetrating his thoughts. She had never encountered such a thing before.

His features hardened momentarily before an ironic smile tugged at his lips. He said in answer to her question, "What else should there be?"

"A great deal. My father might, if he had been fair, have given you a warning." She inhaled on a small gasp. The words had been in her mind, but she had not meant to say them aloud.

"Of what kind?"

Should she speak? Was it at all wise? She had never given herself away before, but then she had never been in a position where she felt it might be required.

Controlling her breathing with valiant effort, she said, "He might have told you it was dangerous to know me."

"Dangerous," he said as if he had never heard the word.

"Even deadly," she added. "Especially if you should—presume to love me."

"There is a reason, I suppose?" The inquiry was tentative, almost reluctant.

"Indeed," she answered with her head held high. "The man who spoke to you of me happens to be a warlock."

"Ah," he said, a soft sound it was impossible to interpret.

"And I," she said with mingled pride and despair, "I am the warlock's daughter."

2

Renfrey surveyed her slowly from the shining silver-gilt hair under her small hat of felt and feathers, to the beautifully symmetrical shape of her body, to the gray-silver hem of her skirt that swept the ground. In the moonlight, her features were pale perfection, as remote as the carved angel on the tomb behind her. The wind shifted his cape, brushed it against her so the silk-on-silk made a soft, whispering sigh. It seemed he felt the contact with every last fiber of his body.

"If you are the daughter of a warlock," he said in trenchant admiration, "what does that make you? A witch?"

"I wouldn't call myself so." Her gaze met his without evasion.

"But you are not like other women?"

"No, I have never been as they are." The moon sailed behind a gray wraith of cloud, leaving her face in shadow. The light faded, as if with the dulling of her spirit.

He summoned a smile. "If you are trying to engage my attention, Carita, you have succeeded. Though I should tell you, since we are being fair, that you already had it."

"You don't believe me?" A small frown pleated the skin between her delicately arched brows. From some distance away there came a low rumble o thunder. A rise in the wind shivered the leaves of the live oak that guarded the cemetery gate.

"Is it likely, do you think?" he asked. "You are lovely and intelligent, and I admire you. Still, you are plainly just a woman, no more."

The wind gusted as if with some elemental annoyance. The rush of it carried the tall silk hat from his head and sent it bowling along the path.

She said, "I promise it's so."

"Promises aren't necessary; all I require is honesty." He glanced at his hat but made no attempt to chase it. Standing straight and tall, he watched her while the rising wind whipped his dark hair into ruffled waves and tore at the ends of his white silk cravat.

Thunder grumbled closer. Black clouds boiled upward into the night sky from the southern quadrant. She said, "You don't seem to recognize the truth when you hear it."

"I recognize that you think you are something apart. But that isn't the same thing, is it?"

Directly above his head, lightning crackled in silver pitchforks, striking earthward to outline the tombs around them in blue fire. Marching toward the cemetery fence, it sparkled along its iron length with a sound like ten thousand angry bees.

"What will it take to convince you?" she said in musical tones, while her cloak lifted like wild wings around her and lightning shimmered in the fathomless deep-sea darkness of her eyes.

"You claim to be the cause of all this?" he said on a reckless laugh. "Then give me rain. No, wait. Give me sleet here where it's seldom seen."

"If you like," she said, and smiled with hard purpose.

The sleet pelted down in balls of silver ice so cold they shattered on the ground like crystal. They filled the air until it was white with their mass. Frozen white marbles, the balls pounded his uncovered head and his shoulders, crackled around his feet, mounted in piles against the nearest tombs.

Opposite him, within reach of his arms, Carita stood untouched. The hailing ice parted above her head, rolled harmlessly down the bell of her skirt. She held his gaze, and so clear and purposeful was the look in her eyes that he was forced to steel himself to sustain it.

At the same time, he ignored the stinging, bruising punishment, letting it roll over him. Gathering his strength, he concentrated it while his smile remained affable and admiring.

The balls of ice turned to smaller beads, then began to lose their chill. They splattered into slush against the ground. Melting, they became cool raindrops. Warmer they grew, and warmer still. Hissing as they slanted down, they dissolved the ice on the ground, turned the earth to mud.

The rain began to dampen Carita's wide skirts in huge, wet splatters. It puddled in the mud at her feet, dashing it onto her hem until her gown sagged with the weight. The feathers of her hat grew sopping and drooped over one eye, while the dye that colored it dissolved to ooze in a silver-gray streak down her face.

Abruptly, the rain stopped. Around them, the air steamed with the change of temperature so they stood in a seething white cloud shot with clear light from the returning moon.

Renfrey watched Carita's face. He waited.

Puzzlement hovered in a frown between her brows. Then some explanation must have occurred to her—some error she had made or fault within herself—for her self-possession returned. Her tone even, she said, "Shall I give you the sun to dry you?"

"A pleasant thought," he replied. "But we

wouldn't want to wake the populace or alarm them, now would we? Do you think you could manage a small fire?"

She nodded, a brief gesture of disdain.

It was a bonfire, licking skyward in hungry orange tongues of flame. The smoke was acrid in the lungs, its pinewood smell pervasive. Crackling, roiling in its red heart a few feet from where they stood, it washed their faces with color and flared brightly in the black pupils of their eyes.

"Very nice," he said in tones of congratulation as he reached to take her hand and lead her a few steps closer to the flames. "It should dry us both out if anything will."

She glanced down at her bedraggled gown, then met his gaze with a species of shock moving over her features. "I never—" she began, then stopped.

"You never get wet when you indulge in a temper tantrum of the elements?" he said with sympathy. "What happened this time to your powers as a witch?"

"I told you I'm not a witch!" she snapped as she dashed the dye from her face. Reaching to catch her skirts with both hands, she gave them a furious shake that sent water droplets flying around her in every direction. It effectively dried her gown, returning her miraculously to her former appearance.

He stood watching a moment before giving a wry shake of his head. "What are you then? Goddess? Grace? Fury? Nymph? Sprite? Fairy? What?"

"Nothing. I'm simply—"

"I know. Daughter of a warlock. A woman it is hazardous to touch, to hold, to desire, to love." The leap of confusion into her eyes was a potent combination with her unhappiness. Recognizing it, he went on with a shading of regret. "You do realize that it's a challenge no man can resist? I'm afraid it has made a kiss, at least, inevitable."

Her eyes widened, grew darker. "No," she said on the edge of panic. "You can't!"

But he could. Taller, stronger, more determined, he swept her into his arms and pressed his mouth to her parted lips.

The force of the contact stunned thought, routed complacency, jolted his heart to a violent rhythm. His blood crashed through his veins like storm surf, while his skin radiated such intense heat his clothing took on the smells of wet and scorched linen, silk and wool. His breath stopped. His brain felt as if it were simmering in the cauldron of his skull. Behind his eyes was the bloodred haze of a desire more compelling than any he had ever dreamed.

The only coolness, the only anchor for his sanity, was the honeyed sweetness of her mouth. The only thing that stopped him from seeking deeper nectar, searching for deeper quenching, was a crashing pain across the toe of his boot.

He wrenched backward with the chill tinkle of breaking porcelain in his ears. The vase Carita had been holding lay in pieces at his feet. She had dropped it, perhaps, or possibly she had thrown it down with purpose. Either way, it was effective. The throbbing pain brought the self-control he so desperately needed.

Bending in haste, he reached for the shards of porcelain. His cape slid forward, covering his hands for fleeting seconds before he threw the heavy cloth back out of the way.

Straightening, he summoned his most profound bow as he presented the vase, whole once more, to the lady. "Forgive my clumsiness," he said softly "but at least some things are not easily demolished." He waited expectantly for her response to his double apology, double meaning.

"But I thought—" she began, then stopped. Veil

ing her gaze with her lashes, she took the unblemished porcelain, turning it in her hands as if searching for cracks. He saw the tremor in her fingers, saw the way she stilled it by pressing against the vase's sides until her fingertips were the same glassy white.

She lifted her gaze, moistened her lips with the tip of her tongue. She opened her mouth to speak.

"Yes?" Renfrey said when she made no sound.

Her lips clamped shut and she closed her eyes, then opened them again. "Never mind," she said. "I don't know why I'm lingering here, can't imagine what possessed me to bandy words with you. There is no purpose in it, can never be any."

Swinging from him in a silken whirl of skirts, she moved swiftly off through the tombs. He watched with appreciation. She might leave him, but she would never escape him, not now.

His smile was rueful, but he erased any trace of amusement from his voice before he called after her, "Running away?"

"It's far better," she said over her shoulder, "than becoming an unintentional murderess."

Swift, mocking, he pressed his offensive. "What would it take to make it intentional?"

She halted, turned slowly. "You want to die?"

"There are worse ways than from an excess of love." The words were low and carrying. He meant them.

"No doubt," she said, her gaze stark, "but what of the one left to live with the guilt and sorrow?" Putting her head down, she swung once more and moved quickly to the gate. She slipped through it and started down the street.

Renfrey followed her with his gaze while he breathed slowly in and out against the pain inside him. It was her pain, readily assumed, deeply felt, in the instant when she had allowed him to see it. He had that gift, at least.

He had also seen days and nights set apart. He knew, because he had assimilated her desolation. He saw her future with no one and nothing to love because human beings were too fragile, too mortal.

She faced it with such courage, was so unwilling to inflict the consequences of her wayward passions on someone else. She made him ashamed. She made him ache somewhere deep inside where nothing and no one had ever touched.

He wanted her as he had never wanted anything in all the long, eventful days of his life. Regardless of the consequences. Or possibly because of them.

And yet, he was not without his own loneliness, or his own expectations. He required something more than merely to become the answer to another person's need.

Love, freely given, was essential. He needed to be wanted for himself alone, not for what he could withstand or perhaps give, especially not for who and what he was by an accident of birth.

Obtaining what he needed might be something more of a challenge than stealing a kiss. Giving what she required could tax his strength to the limit.

She was magnificent. It had been underhanded to provoke her to such a display of temper; still he would not have missed it. There had been a practical purpose; he had wanted to see what forces she could rally against him, what methods she would descend to using in order to prove a point or gain a victory.

Magnificent, but a lady even then. Yes, it would be a challenge, but one worth winning.

He glanced at the fire. It flared high and hot, but he gave a single negligent nod and it settled into sizzling black ash. He shot the cuffs of his shirt, settled his cape, and returned his clothing to dry per fection again. Retrieving his hat without effort, he swung immediately in the direction Carita had taken. His footsteps were silent, but they were sure.

Overhead, the moon sailed at treetop level, following them. There were no streetlamps here; the only illumination was faint glimmers from houses closed up behind shutters, fences, and gates. The leaves of the oaks overhanging the uneven wooden sidewalk spoke in sibilant undertones while crickets and peeper frogs sang from damp garden corners and amid tangles of waning fall flowers. Somewhere a dog barked and was shouted into abeyance.

Ahead of Renfrey, Carita moved with the agitated rustling of skirts that came from haste. Sometimes she glanced back, or else broke into a run for a few steps, as if she knew she was being pursued. She was paying little attention to where she put her feet, none to what lay ahead of her.

Until she stopped with a sudden, bell-like sway of skirts. Renfrey saw the two men at the same time, and broke into a run.

Carita was not frightened so much as startled. She was usually more aware of her surroundings; it was a sign of the dazed condition of her mind that she had not noticed the thugs bearing down on her.

They were out of place, those two, bullies who had wandered away from the wharves along the river, or else from around Gallatin Street or the Irish Channel. She could smell the liquor on their breaths, see the glaze of drunkenness and lust in their eyes. There was also the avid gloating of the hunter in their faces; they thought she was defenseless, at their mercy.

"Well, now, look what we got here," the bigger of the two growled as he swaggered closer. "Nice bit of tail as I ever seen. Think you can hold her, Jack, whiles I tears me off a piece?"

"Hol' her," Jack said with an owlish leer, " 'en have her, too."

Carita had been walking alongside a wrought-iron fence with the palings formed like ornamental arrows. She glanced at them with speculation. The barking dog heard minutes ago also sprang to mind; if summoned, it might be a deterrent.

Then she heard the soft thud of running feet. There was a flash of movement and Renfrey appeared at her side. Hard fingers fastened on her arm, dragging her behind him.

"No!" she said sharply. She fought his grasp for an instant, but it was strong and would take too long to break. Subsiding, she stood in strained readiness.

"Here now," the leader of the two thugs said with a crude oath. "We'uns seen her first!"

"She's mine," Renfrey said with quiet precision. "Move on while you can."

Carita gave Renfrey a swift glance. At the same time, she saw the leader of the thugs grope at his waist. Light flashed silver along a blade.

The burly man gave a coarse laugh. "Your'n, is she? We'll just be seeing about that."

"Yeah," the other man echoed. Half-drunk, he fumbled for a moment before bringing another long knife into view.

They were crude but vicious weapons, honed to a razor's edge and measuring more than fifteen inches from welded hilt to tapered tip. The two men held them with ease shaded by eagerness, as if they had used them before against flesh and bone and enjoyed the feel of it.

"What you think of this, my fine buck?" the first man growled, lifting his lips in a hard grin marked by missing teeth. He swept his weapon from side to side, feinting with quick, hard jabs.

"Not a great deal, actually." Renfrey's reply was

without heat. Hard on it came the slicing hiss of a drawn sword. It was followed by a hollow clatter as he discarded the useless portion of what had been his sword cane.

Moonlight tested the limber blade in his hand for sharpness with a silver glimmer, then winked at the tip. Eyeing it, the leader let out an oath. "You got yourself a fine frog-sticker there, friend, but we still be two agin one."

"My favorite odds." Renfrey released Carita, gave her a small thrust farther behind him. The swordsman position he assumed was easy, classic.

"We'll see about that. Now, Jack!" Hard on the yell, the first thug plunged into an attack.

Carita gave the men only a small portion of her attention. Staring at the iron fence, she issued a mental order.

Arrows of iron strained, snapped with the dry showering of paint and rust. They broke free, hurling themselves with hard purpose on a direct and driving course toward the pair of thugs.

The thin and narrow blade in Renfrey's hand flashed with the moon's cool silver light. It struck twice, faster than the eye could follow, a meteor's explosion of fire in its trailing tail. The thugs howled as the knives flew from their hands to clank away into the darkness.

Before the two could draw breath, the fence palings, with their blunt arrowheads, took them in belly and chest, thigh and groin. The two were flung back while the heavy bars of iron clanked and clattered around them. Hoarse screams tore from their throats as they wallowed on the ground, clutching their bruises.

Renfrey advanced a step. Carita moved at his side.

The thugs heaved away from them, clawing, scrambling to their feet. Staring wild-eyed back over their shoulders, they plunged away across the street and down an alley.

Renfrey lowered his sword point until it touched the broken stone of the walk. His voice musing, he said, "Just think of the tales those two will tell."

"Sotted ramblings," Carita answered shortly as she knelt in a settling island of skirts to retrieve his cane cover before rising and handing it to him. "Who will listen?"

He put out his hand to take the cover. Clasping it, he paused. His gaze sharpened, and he transferred his grip to her fingers. "You're trembling."

"My usual reaction to brutality. Pay no mind," she said in brittle tones. Dragging her hand away, she pulled her shawl tightly around her shoulders.

"You were afraid for me," he corrected her with amazement in his voice.

"I was enraged that you would risk so much." She stopped while appalled consideration rose in her eyes. "But that's the same thing, isn't it? Never mind. I am not yours. And now it's over."

She backed away from him for several steps before she spun around and began to walk again. Her skirts and her hair reflected moonlight with pearllike sheens that danced away, ghostlike, into the dimness. They had not quite vanished when Renfrey sheathed his sword with a sharp click.

"Oh, no," he said in grim resolution as he began to follow her once more. "It's just begun."

3

It was not far from the cemetery to her aunt's house. Carita walked the remaining distance with swift steps. Renfrey was behind her; she knew it with certainty. She was as attuned to his presence now as to her own inner self.

She opened the gate before the plain, narrow, two-storied house, then paused. She had meant to go inside without looking back. Somehow, she could not bring herself to do so.

She would just say good-bye. It was such a small thing; surely there could be no harm in it. It was perhaps natural to feel the urge for a final gesture, an end to all the things that might have been.

Or perhaps it was merely an excuse; she didn't know. She didn't understand herself tonight. Her powers inherited from her father had never failed her before. The fault must lie within herself; she had been unable to maintain her concentration back in the cemetery because she had been unclear in her mind as to what she wanted to accomplish. She had not, in fact, wanted to send Renfrey away. Still didn't.

She closed her eyes, resting her head against the tall arched top of the gate. Why did it have to be so hard? Why?

He was coming. She could hear his quiet treads, the silken swish of his cape. She lifted her head and waited for him to emerge from the street shadows.

The gray cat came first, stepping as light and proud as the most pampered of house pets, though he was an old tom and skittishly wild. It was odd that he had abandoned his cemetery haunt to escort Renfrey; he was usually wary of both familiar visitors and strangers alike. He might have felt the call to prowl, of course, and recognized in Renfrey a source of protection.

There was little doubt that Renfrey could provide it. He had been alert back there, and valiant and strong—all the things expected in a man, yet so seldom found. She could admit that much, if only to herself.

Behind her, there came a low growl. Her aunt's boxer dog must be out of the house. Aunt Berthe had probably released him into the fenced yard thinking Carita would let him back inside when she returned. No doubt he had seen the cat; she could hear his toenails clicking on the walk as he trotted toward the open gate.

The gate! Carita stepped back and gave it a hard swing, trying to slam it closed.

It was too late. The burly dog barreled through the opening. Tearing past her skirts with the ruff on his neck standing high and a threat rumbling in his throat, he charged the cat.

The old stray feline leaped high and came down on all fours with a savage hiss of warning. The boxer skidded to a stop.

"Down, boy!" Carita shouted. "Stay!"

The boxer gave no sign of hearing. Feet planted, lips drawn back in a snarl, he watched his adversary. His chest rumbled and saliva dripped from his muzzle.

Bow-backed, the cat faced the dog with its fur in wild spikes, with fangs bared and fierce challenge in its yellow eyes. Abruptly there was only a blurred tangle of legs and claws. Frenzied yowls and dust rose from it.

The fight was furious, but the boxer was heavier and more powerful. With a hoarse growl, he lunged. The cat twisted away, spitting, but was caught by the scruff of the neck. The boxer shook the soft, limber body and prepared to toss it high, ready to seize a killing hold.

Carita gave a cry of pity. It had happened so fast; she could not think what to do. There were only seconds left in which to make the dog drop the cat.

Then Renfrey was there, striking the boxer a smart blow across the back with his cane. The dog's jaws opened as he yelped. The cat sprang free. Renfrey bent swiftly to scoop the feline up.

The boxer, recovering, snarled and sprang to snap. Glistening white teeth closed on Renfrey's wrist. The cat squirmed out of his grasp, clawing its way up to a shoulder, where it perched with a baleful stare.

Grim-faced, Carita plunged forward to touch the dog with the tips of her fingers. The boxer shuddered at the familiar yet electrifyingly painful contact. Releasing his grip, he whined and dropped to his belly. With lowered ears and dragging tail, he rolled his eyes upward to her face. Finding no forgiveness there, he whimpered and lay still.

Carita straightened, swung immediately toward Renfrey, and reached for his wrist. "Let me see."

She thought for an instant that he would refuse. Then he thrust out his hand with the palm uppermost and his wrist exposed below the bloodied cuff of his shirt. She reached to push the cloth higher while she cradled his hand in hers.

The dog's teeth had torn the skin, but the lacerations were not deep and no veins had been severed. She could feel a faint quivering in his fingers. The cause might be from pain or even shock, but she didn't think so.

She looked up, and her gaze was snared by the darkness of his eyes. Their surfaces were so still, held such patience, so much understanding, that she felt something shift, achingly, inside of her.

An impulse fluttered over her, gathered strength. It was so small a thing, yet a part of all that had passed unspoken between them. Before it could be banished by propriety or sanity, she acted.

Bending her head, she pressed her lips to his injured wrist. She closed her eyes while purpose guided her. An instant later, she smoothed her fingertips in benediction over his healed, unblemished skin, then let go of his hand.

"Thank you," he said, the words a husky whisper.

"You believe me now?" It was asked with care, with exactitude and finality.

"What does it matter?" he said. "You will still be gone."

"I prefer that you know it's not you I am denying."

"You cherish my immortal spirit, but not my mortal flesh. Is that what you're saying?"

"Something like that." Her face was colorless.

"Then if we were mere disembodied vapor, we could make merry and passionate love until the cows wind their way homeward and trumpets play?"

"I suppose so. Yes."

His smile was wry. "You will forgive me, but it sounds as if something would be lacking."

"Very likely."

"But you have no means of being sure, never having sampled the alternative?" The tilt of his head was alert.

A flush rose to her cheekbones. "You mean—No,

I've never made love to a man. Never."

"Then how in infernal blazes," he said with compressed heat, "do you know it's lethal for your partner?"

She made a gesture between anger and despair. "If it's evidence you want, go back and look at my mother's grave."

"What does her death, as tragic as it may have been, have to do with me?" He braced his hands on his hips, a gesture that almost dislodged the cat on his shoulder. "Do I look frail? Do I seem at all likely to die of loving or being loved?"

Her lips tightened. "You don't, no, but do you really want to put it to the test?"

"There are many things I desire," he said without hesitation, "but none more than this: that you would come to me willingly and seek pleasure in my arms."

Rising moisture glimmered in the darkness of her eyes. "I can't."

"Why?" he said with strain cracking his voice. "I cannot imagine even your mother died of a single night of passion."

Her eyes widened as her thoughts tumbled through her mind. Why had she never considered it? Because she thought of love in terms of forever, that was why. Yet, he was right. If forever was forbidden, what was wrong with one night, one chance, one brief plunge of the heart?

"Listen to me, Carita, *ma chère*," he went on, his voice dropping to a new, richer register. "Love doesn't come with safeguards, nor does living. There is always risk, always the chance that this moment, this night will be the last. It's a part of the mystery, something you accept and forget. You do it, because otherwise you shut yourself into a cramped and miserable prison of your own making. And that, you may discover one day, is only another death, the death of everything that makes you unique and valuable."

"I'm not afraid for myself," she answered steadily. "If it was only my own safety, I would take the risk and never look back."

"Commendable," he said, "but also unbearably righteous. You cannot decide the fate of another person; you have no right. We each have to find our own joy, our own manner and time of loving. And dying."

"Yes, but what of the consequences?" she began.

It was then that a shaft of light, dirty yellow, sharp-edged, fell across the bars of the gate and onto the sidewalk. A querulous voice called out, "Carita? Is that you?"

It was her aunt. Carita drew breath to answer. Before she could make a sound, Renfrey reached to place a finger across her lips. Taking her arm, he drew her deeper into the shadows. She went with him, unresisting, though her muscles were stiff and she could remember no decision to move.

"Carita? Did you hear me? Come in, girl, and lock the gate behind you."

Close to her ear, Renfrey whispered, "She is afraid of you. Did you know it?"

He was right; Carita could hear the wariness and the doubt that verged on distrust. How had she missed it before now?

She could also hear, however, the age and the anger of unwanted dependence. It was sad beyond imagining.

Now her aunt had discovered the dog. Her voice sharpened with anxiety even as it dropped to a croon. "What are you doing lying there like that, boy? What happened to my Bruno? Let me look at you."

The fear and concern in that familiar voice were more than Carita could bear. She pulled away from Renfrey, stepped forward into the light. "Nothing is wrong with him, Aunt Berthe. He just had a scare, that's all."

Her aunt straightened. "You did it, I know. How could you, when you're his favorite."

It was a sore point between them, one of many. It wasn't surprising the dog preferred her, Carita knew, since she was the one who fed and walked him, but her aunt could never see that. She moved closer. Holding out the vase she carried, she said, "He was after a cemetery cat who followed us home."

"Why didn't you just let him have it? Poor Bruno." Her voice was crooning as she accepted the worthless porcelain and bent to pat the dog that crowded against her skirts. Then she stiffened, came upright. "Us, you said? Someone is with you?"

"This gentleman and myself." Carita gestured toward where Renfrey stood watching.

The older woman's voice sharpened as she peered into the shadows. "Who is he?"

A flush rose to Carita's face at the suspicious undertone of her aunt's question. She barely glanced at Renfrey as he stepped to her side, into the light. "Only an acquaintance of my father's whom I happened to—"

Renfrey's voice cut across her explanation. "Someone who took it upon himself to escort your niece home. It seemed she was in need of protection."

"Indeed?" Aunt Berthe's head came up. She folded her arms across her thick waist, standing as tall as her squat figure allowed. Her small, pale eyes were cold. "And what else did you take?"

"Aunt Berthe!"

"I know his kind," her aunt said in bitter condemnation. "Handsome womanizers ready to snatch an advantage; it's no great wonder to me he is acquainted with your father. You will have no more to do with him, do you hear me?"

"It was never my intention—" she began.

"Young women do a lot of things they never intend. Go into the house. I will send this gentleman about his business."

"No, really, Aunt Berthe," Carita said. "He has been most kind and not at all—encroaching." Her voice trailed away as she recalled, belatedly, his kiss.

"Just as I thought," her aunt said with grim acceptance. "You will wind up like your mother—or worse, cause destruction that will haunt you all your days. I said go into the—"

"You prefer," Renfrey said to the older woman, "that her days be haunted by regret? Are you quite sure you are protecting her? Or are you punishing her?"

"I'm trying to save her!" Aunt Berthe said.

"From what? Love? Life? Knowledge of the wide world beyond your narrow little household. Or perhaps the joy your sister found?"

A spasm of disgust, or perhaps pain, crossed the older woman's face. "You can know nothing of the matter, nothing at all! I would advise you to leave us while you still can."

"But there you have the trouble," Renfrey said with a faint smile. "It's too late; it was always too late. Some things, once begun, cannot be ended."

"You mean—" Her aunt stopped. Then her gaze flitted over his features that, seen in the lamplight, were touched with the wildness of a hawk's, over his frame with its power and careless elegance. Her eyes blared open with horror. She retreated a hasty step, then swung on Carita. "Get into the house! Now!"

"There is no need to be rude to someone who has been of service," Carita said stiffly. "I will say goodnight, then join you."

"If you stay, you will be damned as surely as if you philandered with the devil. You must come with me, now, this minute."

"Be reasonable," Carita said with a trace of pleading. "I only ask for a moment."

Her aunt swung away, marching in stiff-backed haste through the gate. Over her shoulder, she cried, "Come inside, or I wash my hands of you."

Mulish anger made Carita lift her chin. "I will be there when I am ready."

"Then don't bother to come at all!" her aunt shouted.

Facing forward, the older woman snapped her fingers at the dog, then sailed up the narrow walk. The boxer heaved himself up and trotted behind her. The door of the house closed behind them, shutting in the light.

Carita was stunned. She had never felt her aunt loved her, but she had thought there was at least mild affection between them. To discover that it could be discarded so easily was a loss.

"Walk with me," Renfrey said quietly at her side, as he had once before.

Carita recalled the words but knew that this time they meant so much more.

She could go or stay. If she went inside at once and was sufficiently contrite, her aunt would relent. Surely, she would relent.

Staying, she could have peace and safety. She could accept the things she had discovered and use them to rearrange her life, to make her personal prison more bearable.

Going, she would gain the freedom to be her father's daughter. Yet she would also in some degree be consenting to the intimacy Renfrey had asked of her. She must decide how far she would go to attain her desires, how much of herself she could give and still live with the results.

Carita raised her troubled gaze to Renfrey's. His eyes were dark, opaque with his refusal to force her decision. She prized that in him.

On his shoulder, the old cat watched her also, its yellow stare unblinking, wondering.

Decision was a difficult thing. So was capitulation. However, neither necessarily required words to make them plain.

She forced her lips to curve in a tremulous smile. Reaching up, she took the cat in her hands and brought it against her breast where she stroked it gently, reassuringly. Turning, she began to walk away from her aunt's house.

Renfrey was still for a moment, then she heard the soft, sudden release of his breath. In a moment, he reached her side. Together, they strolled down the moonlit street. They did not look back.

The air was softer, warmer, as they drew near the river. The moisture in it caused the pores of the skin to expand to fullness. A smell of mud and fecundity was carried on it, along with the pervasive aroma of ripe pears from over a garden wall and just a hint of open drains. Somewhere there was a jasmine vine pouring its prodigal sweetness into the night.

The cadence of their footsteps was slow and deliberate. Their way led into the French Quarter, where the measured click of their heels on the slate ballast stones carried ahead of them under the overhanging balconies. The shadows here in these narrow ways were sometimes black and crude, sometimes ornate and curling silhouettes of hand-worked wrought iron. They passed them all with hardly a glance.

It was later now, and there was mystery in the deeper night stillness. Or perhaps it was only within herself; Carita could not remember a time when she had been less certain of who and what she was.

"When was it," Renfrey said as they strolled, "that you first knew you were different?"

She considered the question. Over the purring of the cat she held, she said, "I'm not sure. At the age of three or possibly four—or maybe my aunt only began to treat me differently then. It was because of a doll I was playing with at the time. I made it talk to me."

"That would do it, I would imagine," he said.

"I was punished for it, of course. I cried, but felt a secret pride for what I could do that my older cousins, her daughters, could not. After a while, the pride was gone. I only wanted to be exactly like them, exactly like everyone else."

His tone thoughtful, gaze straight ahead, Renfrey quoted softly:

> *From childhood's hour I have not been*
> *As others were—I have not seen*
> *As others saw—I could not bring*
> *My passions from a common spring.*

Her voice, calm, reflective, picked up the lines.

> *From the same source I have not taken*
> *My sorrow; I could not awaken*
> *My heart to joy at the same tone;*
> *And all I lov'd, I lov'd alone.*

"Poe, of course," she said. "And yes. Yes, that's the way it was."

The tragedy of being different through no fault of her own was plain in her voice. Behind it, Renfrey suspected, were a hundred small slights, a thousand sneers and slurs. He wished that he could take them from her. He wished that he could change the circumstances of her life, could force open all the closed little minds around her and cause tolerance to be the accepted standard for daily existence. It was impossible.

"And now?" he asked, his voice rigorously impassive.

The cat, attuned to the undercurrents Renfrey would not permit to sound, came alert and stared at him. He reached to take the animal, to smooth its fur in reassurance, then set it on the sidewalk. It followed them, lightly stepping, watching the shadows.

"And now," Carita was saying in answer, "there are times when I enjoy who I am." She paused, then went on with the strained ache of yearning in her voice. "And there are others when I would give the world and all there is in it to be someone else, anyone else."

He stopped. "I expect that will always be the way of it, and for that I have no remedy. But for the rest—"

"Yes?" Halting beside him, Carita looked up inquiringly into his face. His expression was serious, his eyes shaded with compassion. He moved not a muscle, yet there crept slowly in upon her a sense of encompassment, as if she were being gathered into a close embrace. The hold was warm, strong, yet without constriction. It offered consolation and, most of all, abiding understanding.

Tears rose inside her, the tears that spring up because of sympathy freely offered, help and comfort given without expectation of return. She had not known she needed those things, yet she accepted them now with gratitude. A frisson of relaxation moved over her, and she shivered with it while she accepted his mental support, savored his nearness, his enfolding solace. Standing perfectly still, she yet eased more fully against him in her mind, resting her head upon the firm strength of his chest. He did not move, yet his arms closed around her.

It was a total accord, passionless, generous, infinite. Until the warmth became a steady heat. Until the shivering drove deep. Until the closeness became a delicate blending of spirits, the instinctive merging of nerves and imaginations, responses and minds. Until the pleasure of it rippled through them and caught them, unprepared, with its splendor.

Carita almost retreated a step, but caught herself. That would do no good; she knew the truth now, as she had suspected from the moment she faced this man across the fire in the cemetery. As she had surmised when she accepted from him an unbroken vase which she knew had been shattered. As her aunt must have guessed. It had, of course, been impossible to be certain.

Watching the emotions flitting across his face, she thought he intended to ask forgiveness for the intrusion of his nonphysical embrace. She did not want that. Tipping her head, she said with unsteady irony, "Some remedies are more effective than others."

Laughter leaped into his face, and something more that softened the darkness of his eyes. "There are additional cures," he said, "some of which may be applied either here or elsewhere."

"Here?"

He indicated the tall, handsomely painted door beside him with its knocker of silver in the shape of a Pan with pipe. "This is my home, the place where I am staying while in New Orleans."

Hard on his words, as if at a silent summons, the door opened to reveal a manservant. He was as dark as the night with a grizzled head of silver and a white jacket over black livery. He bowed them inside, took their outer wraps and Renfrey's hat and cane, then stood back for them to precede him along a tunnellike entranceway.

To enter required no conflict of conscience; Carita had come this far, so might as well go on. She moved ahead of Renfrey along this passage that led underneath the house. Passing through pools of light falling from lamps of hammered silver, walking alongside Italian frescoes in jewel colors highlighted with gold and silver, they emerged in a courtyard.

In that space open only to the sky, Carita discovered the source of the jasmine she had noticed earlier. Its scent permeated the air, along with that of roses and tuberoses, sweet olive and gardenia. The combined perfumes were a mind-swimming assault on the senses.

The walls and columns of the house were warm and golden even in the cool light of the moon. French windows in arches looked down on them with shining squares of lamplight. The stones of the courtyard floor were a mosaic of garnet and turquoise, jade and amethyst in geometric patterns edged with gold. In the center was a porphyry fountain where the splattering water played a soft, Andalusian melody and droplets glittered like falling diamonds. Under the house eaves at one corner, in the deep shade of a great sheltering live oak, turtledoves chortled softly in the darkness.

Their pathway led through the center of the courtyard toward where double doors stood open to the night. Renfrey took her hand and put it on his arm, holding it with a warm clasp as he urged her forward. With the cat following, they skirted the fountain, trod lightly up the low and wide entrance steps, and entered.

There was a vestibule with a floor of rich green

malachite and Greek vases on bronze plinths. Beyond was a dining room hung with cloth of gold, and velvet the color and texture of spring moss. The floors glowed with an intricate inlay of light and dark woods, while enormous Renaissance mirrors on opposite walls reflected the table laid for a late supper, the food set out on a sideboard, and also repeated the crystal and bronze d'or chandeliers into infinity.

Round, intimately small, the table was centered with roses and sweet peas and lilac. The napery was the finest damask, the serving plates of Aztec gold, the utensils of heavy and deeply engraved coin silver. The crystal glasses had been handblown in Venice and were chased and rimmed in gold. Poured into them, waiting, was a vintage wine like liquid rubies, which breathed the delicate and astringent perfume of grape flowers.

Carita came to a halt. Her fingers on Renfrey's arm tightened before she forced them to unclench. The cat circled her skirts and sat down among them at her side, where it began to wash its face. The manservant soft-footed his way to a door leading into a butler's pantry and disappeared inside.

Carita moistened her lips. "Lovely," she said, "and I am impressed, but I fear I'm not dressed for such a sumptuous residence or grand repast."

"You have no need of further adornment," Renfrey answered in low tones. "You are the one perfect jewel that has always been needed to give the rest purpose."

"Nevertheless," she said.

Inclining his head, he moved with her toward one of the tall mirrors. For an instant, the silvery surface was dark, then it cleared.

Gone was her dull little hat and drab gown. Her hair was dressed high, the silver-gold strands entwined with pearls and diamonds. The creation she wore was of shimmering tissue silk in iridescent blue and gold, exquisitely cut, perfectly fitted; an airy confection piled in layers over a hoop of enormous size. Under it, she could feel the most fragile of silk pantalettes and no more than a wisp of ivory-boned corset.

She stared at herself in fascination. Removing her hand from his arm, she lifted it to touch the fortune in pearls, sapphires, and diamonds that sparkled in her ears, at her neck, on her wrists.

Turning slowly from the mirror, she looked up at the man beside her. Her mouth curved into a smile that did not quite reach her eyes.

"Presumptuous for a man I hardly know," she said. "Also paltry. For a warlock."

4

"I should have told you at once," Renfrey said. "My only excuse is—"

"Arrogance?" she supplied.

"Vanity, rather, which I like to think isn't quite the same thing. I didn't want you to fall into my arms simply because I was suitable."

"What," she said in trenchant inquiry, "made you so certain I was going to fall into your arms at all?"

Exasperation shifted across his face. He thrust his fingers through the dark waves of his hair and clasped the back of his neck. "It was not a foregone conclusion, of course—but, as with royalty, the choice of our kind is not wide."

"Royalty," she repeated, diverted momentarily by the comparison.

He turned from her, walking to the window where he stood staring out at nothing. "You yourself pointed out to me one of the possible consequences of looking for a mate who is not as we are."

He was referring to the fate of her mother. "Yes, certainly. So it was all neatly arranged and our meeting set. I take it you yourself had no expectation of becoming enamored, even if I developed an affection for you."

"It wasn't necessary. The match seemed appropriate."

"How very convenient for you, a doting consort of the correct lineage."

"It didn't turn out that way," he said, clenching his hand on the heavy draperies as he rested his forehead on the cool glass of the window. "I saw you, spoke to you, and was enchanted—more than that, entranced. The future seemed perfectly cloudless. At least for a few short minutes."

She considered what he had said while watching the portion of his set face that she could see from where she stood. "And what happened to change it?"

A short laugh shook him. "I realized exactly who and what you are, how you think and feel and the depths of love you are capable of giving. And I was consumed by terror."

"I don't think I understand." She had an inkling, but could not bring herself to accept it without confirmation.

"We have spoken of your origins, but not of mine," he said without turning. "As it happens, both my mother and father have the power. You, on the other hand, are only—"

"Only a warlock's daughter. A half-breed, you might say."

"It's possible that it matters."

"A case, I perceive, of correct lineage and royal protocol." Her voice was constricted.

"You know better!" he said in savage denial. He paused. When he spoke again, he was calm once more. "You should understand it perfectly, since you pointed out the problem. I saw it from your side earlier, and found it amusing. It never occurred to me to turn it around until just now when—"

"When you took me in your arms." She was growing used to finishing his sentences for him, and having her own finished. It was one of the many consequences of overacute perception.

"In a manner of speaking," he agreed with the wraith of a smile.

"I am not like my mother," she said, because it seemed that he might not go on.

"No. And yet, how much difference is there? You were concerned enough for me when you thought that your strength might be a danger to me. You are a potent force, made more so by intelligence and imagination. But I know—without arrogance if you please—that my power can overcome yours. It has been proved."

"And because of that," she said slowly, "you are afraid that you are a danger to me."

"The possibility exists. It is too dire to be ignored."

The tension between them had teeth and vibrancy. She said against it, "It could be given an ultimate test."

He turned with careful control. There was a sheen of perspiration across his forehead. "No."

"Don't you think your concern is excessive? You

said yourself that a single night of love could hardly be fatal."

His laugh was mirthless. "I said a great many things, but—no."

"Why?" she asked, and let the single word stand as a bald demand.

"I don't want or need the pain of something that must end so soon."

"It would pain you to end it?" she said softly.

"Rather, such a temporary joining is useless to me. I prefer forever."

"Forever," she repeated, with light rising in her eyes and the soft sweet echo of the word ringing in her mind.

"A permanent union being clearly impossible," he said, "a few hours of pleasure is a risk for which the penalty may be too dear."

His eyes, she saw in the brightness of the many candles, were not actually black but a dark and mysterious green. Across them was a near-mortal wash of pain and distress. It gave her courage.

"Only," she said in quiet certainty, "if you value the thing you will lose too—dearly."

Renfrey watched her from across the room while his mind raced in cogent thought. He knew he had shown momentary weakness, knew it must be corrected. His decision was made and accepted between one breath and the next.

The words even, he said, "You think I am concerned because I love you? I have admitted to being entranced, and might have been more, given time. But there is none available and my emotions are, in keeping with my kind, eminently controllable. I have a care for you now, but no more than I would take with any moderately pretty lady of the evening who happened to be weak, silly, and supplicating."

The verbal blow was devastating, and meant to

be. She had expected something of the kind, however, so did not permit him to see her flinch. Her eyes clear, her tone acid-edged, she said, "It's just as well then, don't you think, that I'm none of those things?"

He tested that declaration, accepted it. When he spoke it was in answer to her thought rather than her words. "You are feeling combative? This is a duel no one can win, a challenge I must refuse. If you will change your clothes again, I will take you home to your aunt."

"Change?" she said with a lifted brow. "Oh, but I believe I've grown fond of this ensemble; it makes me feel quite—regal. In any case, it was chosen especially for me and I am convinced that it flatters."

"Keep it, then," he said shortly. "Shall we go?"

He was anxious to be rid of her. That was promising.

"You know," she said judiciously, "I don't think we shall. All these exertions have made me hungry, and it would be shameful to waste the midnight supper you so thoughtfully ordered."

He watched her for long, unblinking moments before he said in pleasantly conversational tones, "I could send you on a whirlwind."

"No doubt," she answered at once. "Then who would be throwing a—what was the phrase?—temper tantrum of the elements?"

"Carita—"

The word, ragged at the edges, ground to a halt. He looked down at his hand that was curled into a fist. By slow degrees, he opened it, forced a gesture of graceful acquiescence. "Yes. Well. By all means let us be adult and mannerly and civilized, at least insofar as we are able. You are hungry. So am I. Shall we dine?"

"Sup," she corrected him. "It's too late for anything else." She paused, watching him, but if he rec-ognized the allusion to his own declaration, he did not show it.

They took their places at the table. Polite to a fault, stiff with decorum, they began their meal. Renfrey drank too much. It did not make him drunk, of course, but did incline him to morose self-judgment.

He should have forced her to go. She might have fought him, but he had no doubt that he could have prevailed. To be constrained to sit and watch her, knowing that he had only to reach out his hand for her to come to him, was indescribable torture. It was perverse of him to be grateful for every minute of it.

He loved the proud tilt of her chin, the determined set of her lips, the light of battle in the deep and rich sea-blue of her eyes. She had not given up; he knew that. He must and would counter every wile and stratagem she concocted. Still he saluted her fiery spirit. Even as it gave him cold chills.

By all the saints of this hallowed eve, but he wanted her. She knew it, because he himself had told her. Exerting himself to convince her that the glory of loving was possible between them, he had succeeded far too well. Now he was determined to convince her otherwise, and all her powers were arrayed against him.

He had, ordinarily, a penchant for irony. This particular example of it did not entertain him.

Still, this time could be used for the accumulation of memories. The gleam of the candlelight on her skin. The imperious sweetness of her smile. The perfection of the gown of his choosing. He would not remember, if he could help it, the pleasure of dressing her in it.

Mental perception could sometimes be more vivid than bodily experience. Such as the moment when he had embraced her out on the street. That rare accord had, of course, been shared.

He looked up, startled, to find her watching him. She lowered her lashes at once, but he had seen the dazed satisfaction there. She had, for an instant, slipped into his mind as he had penetrated hers. It had felt like a wondrous completion. Something more to guard against.

It was also, he thought, the first foray in the battle. As such, it was an indication of the tactics she might use. He wondered how strong his defenses were against that kind of insidious invasion.

It did not help, of course, to realize that he had shown her the maneuver himself.

There were methods in her repertoire, he discovered, that he had certainly not taught her. The way she drank her wine, wetting her lips with it and licking the drops with small, delicate strokes of the tip of her tongue. The manner in which she curled her fingers around a breadstick, buttered it with care on one end, then ate it with tender precision. Her deliberate movements as she chose a small ripe peach, rolled it between her hands while breathing the aroma, then bit into it with white, sharp teeth.

Wincing, Renfrey swallowed hard and reached for his wineglass. The wine tasted, he found, of peach juice and the fresh sweetness of her lips. Damn her.

How had she known? How had she discovered his most fevered fantasies? She was an innocent. Unless . . .

Unless she was following the lead of his own licentious thoughts and impulses. No one else, ever, had been able to do that to him. He felt the tops of his ears grow hot.

He was—had meant to be—a gentleman: impassive, correct, forbearing. This was too much. He focused his attention on her peach.

She exclaimed and spat out the next bite, that had become a virulent, poisonous green. Screwing up her mouth, she reached for her water glass.

She drank deep, slowed, tilted the glass at a slight angle. A single, pure drop fell from the base of the crystal stem. It caught the candlelight in a prism of fire as it struck her chest above her décolleté and rolled, unerringly, over the blue-veined curve of her breast and into the shadowed valley between them.

Renfrey's eyes burned as he watched. The inside of his mouth was desiccated, parched for the taste of that life-giving drop of water. He could feel it on his tongue. He could also feel his tongue on her skin, circling the satin firmness of her breasts, tasting the taut nipples. She was a fountain, bounteous, endlessly flowing, life for the taking.

She had done it to him again. Incredibly. Anger smoldered, rising to heat the top of his brain. He glanced at her fingers on the glass, tipped his head a bare inch.

Her hold on the piece of crystal slipped. Water cascaded. The front of her gown was drenched with icy cold wetness.

She gasped, a sound of shock. She reached for her napkin. Stopped.

Her eyes, as she raised them to his own limpid gaze, were bright with fury. An instant later, they turned fluid, piteous yet rueful. "Oh, dear," she said. "It seems I'll have to change after all."

It was a fascinating transfiguration. The gown dissolved into a delicate mist; the jewels disappeared. For an instant, there was a glimpse of rose nipples, a narrow span of waist compressed by a miniscule corset, the slender turn of shapely thighs under pantalettes. The vision evolved, became one of sentient ivory nakedness behind drifting folds of tissue silk. Then she was covered by swirling material forming a simple oriental robe of robin's-egg blue edged at the low-dipping neckline with the icy sparkle of perfect diamonds.

He should have looked away, but could not find the will. "Mesmerizing," he said, and meant it. God help him.

Something must be done to counter the effect of her ploy. Hot, he was so hot; he had to cool off. Yes, of course; that should help. He added with false concern as the temperature in the room began to drop precipitously, "But I hope you won't be too chilly in your light draperies."

She was apt, inconceivably so, in her intuition. And she had no hesitation in the attack.

"It's doubtful I will freeze," she answered as log fires laid in the marble-faced fireplaces under the mirrors at either end of the room burst into flames. "But a fire is so much more enjoyable on a rainy night. Think how lovely it would be to lie before it, even to make love there to the music of the rain."

Outside, a slow and steady downpour began. It pattered and drummed into the garden, releasing the fragrances captured there so that they penetrated into the closed house. The rhythm of the rain was hypnotic and infinitely inciting. Renfrey listened in stony silence while he conquered the tightening in his groin.

When he spoke at last, his voice had a much lower note. "Rain as an aphrodisiac? To my mind, it has no power unless you can see and hear it without impediment."

The windows along the far side of the room swung open, along with the doors leading from the vestibule. Chill, wet air swept inside on a gust of wind.

"Very nice," she said, without a shred of truth. "But you derided my storm earlier. Perhaps you have discovered that the elements can be exciting, after all. Who knows what thrilling effects we might create if we join forces."

Hard on her words, thunder rolled, cracking in the distance with a mighty roar. The wind picked up speed and power. Rain splattered in at the windows and splashed onto the marble of the vestibule.

He should stop it. He would in a moment, when he could tear his gaze away from her as she sat opposite him with her perfect skin beaded with chill while her face was flushed with angry desire. God, but he did not know whether he wanted most to subdue her with force or with tenderness.

As if in answer to his thought, the wind rose to a tempest. Somewhere a priceless antique vase smashed and scattered across marble. The lusters of the chandelier overhead chimed, sending bits of smashed crystal sparkling downward. A picture frame bumped against the wall, then fell with a jolting impact.

She wanted him to stop her, he saw, for that would be an admission that she could affect him. She would see, then, what a storm could be with his greater aid.

The wind whipped into the house, carrying lashing torrents of rain. The water flooded across the floor, wetting the Turkish carpet and pushing it into crumpled folds. It boiled into the fireplace and doused the leaping flames, extinguishing all warmth. Cold, drenching, it soaked the tablecloth and sent silver rattling to the floor. Carita's wineglass overturned, so that rainwater-diluted burgundy poured across the table, dripping to the floor like fresh blood.

And the wind and wet molded her oriental robe against her slim form with utmost fidelity, making the silk quite transparent. Renfrey, retrieving his own wineglass, isolated himself from the storm in a protective cocoon of air and leaned back to watch the spectacle.

Carita made a brief, abortive gesture with one hand as if to cover herself, then desisted. Abruptly, her hair came loose and its pins tinkled on the marble floor like silver bells. The thick lustrous swath of her hair slid downward to become a silver curtain that enticed more than concealed. The wind caught it then. Her smile, as the silver-gold cloud of it blew around her in a wild tangle, grew diabolical.

The cat, drawn up in a bow and hissing, emerged from where he had been begging under the table. He looked at Carita, then streaked for cover beneath a china closet.

"You enjoy nakedness?" she asked in musical tones that carried easily above the clamor. "That seems bizarre under the circumstances, but it is easily arranged."

He felt the cold, wet wind on his bare skin even as he looked down. His coat, shirt, and trousers were parting at the seams, falling away to lie in a tailor's puzzle of pieces in the water that washed across the floor. Even his evening shoes disintegrated, along with his braces and underclothing. His watch, chain, and fob rattled into his lap. He was left with nothing by way of concealment, or dignity.

Renfrey surged to his feet in a blaze of temper. The table, unbalanced by the rising wind, overturned with a horrendous crash of china and crystal. The broken pieces and dented silver scattered over the floor, spinning into the far corners.

"Oh, by all means," she shouted at him as she leaped up also and backed away, "destroy this nest of seduction. That's all it is, all it ever was. What a jest, to call it a home. How would someone of *your* *kind* know what a home is or what a half-morta woman might do there, or feel about it? You're only a misfit, an oddity, a mere creature with no more idea of love and home than a beast in the field!''

The bestial Minotaur, half-bull, half-man, came to him, summoned with the rage of denied desire and vanished hope. Its fearsome strength was his, and its brutish instincts. He advanced on her, inflamed, out of control, as intent as ever a mythological being had been on rapine and destruction.

She saw it in his face and alarm sprang into her eyes. Whirling away from him, she sprinted toward the open vestibule and the dark tempest in the courtyard beyond.

She was fleet, but he was faster. He caught her halfway along the path to the fountain. Snatching a wrist, he wrenched her to a halt and dragged her into his arms. He leaned over her, letting her feel his hot breath in her face while she twisted in his hold and pounded at his chest.

"No!" she cried. "No, not like this!"

But he hardly heard for the boil of the blood in his veins and the sweet thunder in his heart and soul. He was as wild as the wind that swayed the creaking limbs of the oak above them, as fierce as the lightning that lit the sky. He wanted the woman he held and there was nothing to stop him from taking her. The principles and restraints that had once guided him had been abandoned as he divested himself of his normal body. Though they lingered, silently clamoring, somewhere in the depths of his mind, they had no power to deflect his half-crazed lust.

The colored stones of the courtyard floor were wet and matted with torn leaves and tree limbs and crushed flower petals. Still, he forced her downward with inexorable strength while tearing away, with fiendish joy, the last thin, wet layer of silk over her delectable body.

"No. Renfrey, please," she said again, a whisper of unimagined grief. "I never meant to do this to you."

He heard, oh, he heard, and something cried out in pain inside him. Still, it was not loud enough to compete with the bestial growling he made. Leaning over her, he reached for the cool, firm globe of her breast and closed his hand around it with mindless rapture.

And abruptly he felt a tearing agony in his nose. Wetness flowed, hot and brilliant vermilion in the lightning. He bellowed, roaring with the pain. Releasing her, he staggered back, off-balance. As he lifted his hands to clutch at his face, they fastened on the huge brass ring that pierced his nostrils.

Carita struggled to her feet. In her hand was the nose ring's chain. She held him while the wind whipped her hair into glittering witch's locks and her eyes reflected the fire of the lightning. There was no victory in her gaze.

The punishing anguish cleared his head. He drew a deep breath, fought instinct and atavistic compulsion. Clamping down on his will with determination, he banished the Minotaur. But he could not rid himself of the hard core of his anger. As the head of the bull evolved once more into his own features, he took the brass ring and the chain and fashioned them into shackles of purest gold. Fastening them to her wrists, he bound her to him.

They stood for endless moments while the storm pummeled them with stinging debris and the rain sluiced down their bodies. Chest to breast, groin to pelvis, they absorbed each other. The gooseflesh of their chilled skin meshed while their blood poured in torrents through the creaking chambers of their hearts and their harsh breathing shuddered through them with the force of a gale.

Then Carita lifted her bound wrists, which were caught between them. The shackles blurred, shrank, became bracelets of gold.

Shaking back her hair, she said in low and anguished tones, "All I ever wanted was to be loved for what I am, as I am—"

It was, he recognized, the voicing of his own tormented need. She was once more ensconced within his most sequestered self. From that source, she had mined and refined, with generosity and sure intuition, the single thing that united them, the shared longing that might make them whole.

It was also, of course, the one thing he could never give her.

"No," he said. "If loving is death, then it's impossible." His face set, his heart locked, he withdrew his spirit from her with quiet finality.

It wasn't enough, of course. He had to remove temptation, wrench free of her and retreat step-by-step. She was left alone, her pale shape buffeted by wind and rain and his own inexorable power of will. Alone in her defeat.

Except that, standing there in the windswept night, she lifted her arms, holding them out to him. And the wind whirled around her in a savage tornado.

It drew every leaf and petal in the courtyard into its vortex, sucking the draperies, flapping, through the open windows of the house, sending every free bit of paper and bric-a-brac whirling in her direction. It tore the vines from the walls, whipped the water from the fountain, made the great oak that shaded the open space thrash and groan as if in agony.

It was the expression of her need and a demonstration that she was more his equal than he had known. It was also an illustration of the clash inside him, his fervent desire, against all odds, to go to her and be the center of the tumult in her heart. More, to make her the warm, sweet core of his own.

He stood against it. Immobile.

It was not enough. He had to stop her before it was too late, before he succumbed to her anguished appeal. He raised his gaze to the tree above her.

The huge oak uprooted with a rending explosion. The earth rumbled and the tree swayed. There was a splintering roar. Leaves showered down. The oak toppled, began to fall, gaining speed.

Carita squared her shoulders, lifted her chin, closed her eyes. The tree's shadow fell across her still face. Its darkness covered her, crashing down, down upon her.

She made no move to avoid it.

She did not attempt to resist.

5

Feathers, white, swirling like snow. The leaves, the branches, the bark and body of the oak tree were transformed so they drifted down, windblown, to cloak Carita in their softness.

Renfrey stood panting with the effort of that final, wrenching metamorphosis. Then he clenched his fist and thrust it high above his head.

The storm stopped.

Yet he stood there, with sweat and acid grief burning his eyes. He dared not move. It was terror that held him, the terror of what else he might do if he released even a fraction of the lock he had clamped on his supernatural powers.

Carita, seeing his fear, felt the despairing madness leave her. Tears welled into her eyes.

"Don't," she said in distress. "It doesn't matter. I'm all right, you haven't hurt me, and—nothing has changed, nothing will change."

Still he did not move.

Stepping lightly through the feathers, she swept them toward her with graceful gestures, collecting them in a pile. In seconds, they formed a plump mattress covered by buff satin sewn with gold cord and caught with gold tassels at the corners. She was tired, so tired from her exertions that she wanted only to rest.

Yet the destruction around her was an irritant that made it impossible to relax. With housewifely thoroughness, she began to set it to rights. After a moment, she felt her purpose reinforced as Renfrey lent his effort.

In a short time, the courtyard was clear. Flowers bloomed and the fountain played once more in the darkness. The draperies in the house hung dry and straight. The vases and chandeliers and picture frames were renewed and in their appointed places. The supper table sat with its crystal and silver restored and food ready, awaiting anyone with appetite enough to enjoy it.

Carita could not even begin to consider eating. She returned to the mattress and sank down upon its softness. Drawing up her legs, she clasped them with her arms and rested her head on her knees. Her hair spilled around her in a glowing cloak, sliding forward to screen her face.

After a moment, she felt the great feathered cushion give to another weight. It was Renfrey settling beside her.

Time passed. The doves under the eaves cooed sleepily. A pair of moths circled a great white moonflower and each other in delirious hunger and wooing. A toad hopped with deliberation toward a station under the fountain. The night breeze, somnolent with tropic warmth, brought the scent of mint and sage and bay from a garden bed nearby.

"I almost killed you," Renfrey said at last.

She heard the tightness in his voice and replied to that as much as to his words. "We almost destroyed each other, in one way or another."

"You would have allowed yourself to die. You made no effort to prevent it."

"I wasn't thinking too clearly at the time," she said in weary assent.

"Yes, but why? It would have been so easy for you to move, to alter the threat, change yourself. Something. Anything."

She lifted her head, thrust her fingers into her hair as she supported her head. "Insofar as I can tell you, I think I meant to demonstrate that it's something more than merely righteous to choose how another person will or will not die."

"Yet you let me stop it."

Her smile was brief. "It seemed a more acceptable alternative. Besides, somewhere inside I knew you could, and would, if forced to it."

The imprecation he whispered was creative and virulent as he gazed, unseeing, into the darkness.

"I know," she said quietly. "It wasn't a fair tactic."

His laugh was short. "It was effective" After a second, he added, "I didn't mean to hurt you—it was the last thing I had in mind when I brought you here."

"The very last; I know. But don't you see that you can't always control what you do?"

"If we are back to the dangers of loving," he said

in rough protest, "then I will remind you that you intended to make the choice for me before you realized I was not a mortal. How is my choice for you any different?"

She frowned in concentration. "For a woman to be a threat to a man is rare, while with women it's quite otherwise. Millions of us have died from the effects of being loved, giving up our lives because of complications in childbearing."

"And millions of men have lived with the guilt of it," he said.

"Yes, but women don't choose to forego the loving because of it, nor do men cease to love them. If either happened, the race, all races, would come to an end."

"It isn't the same," he said, with strain in his voice.

"Isn't it? Only a woman can know how much she needs love. Only a woman has the right to decide whether she will take the risk."

"And what does she use," he said, "to make the decision?"

Carita shook her head. "Nothing very weighty, I'm afraid. Only her emotions, her desires."

"That is how you would make your choice again?" The words were almost inaudible.

She turned her head and drew back her hair to look at him. Trying to smile, not quite successful, she said, "My need for love is strong. As was my mother's."

He sighed. "Darling Carita, there is so much that is good and pure and proud in you. I am not worthy."

"And how worthy am I?" she said painfully. "Only a half-breed."

"You are everything I've ever wanted, all I will ever need. When I look at you, my will, unlike yours, is weak when it should be strong. If I could turn back the clock, if I returned the two of us to the cemetery where we met, would it help? Do you think that if we lived the last few hours again we could find a different ending?"

"No," she said, and shuddered.

He drew back. "I understand."

Exasperation touched her. "I doubt it. Why should we take the chance that it will all be done over again? I don't want to oppose you; it hurts too much. All I want is—"

He smiled, finishing for her. "To be loved as you are."

"Yes." It was a whisper as she met his black-green gaze.

"Then be loved," he said in low supplication, "and love me in return. For I know now the only sure way to defeat you is by loving you."

"Yes," she whispered. "It's the only choice."

He reached out to her then, and opened his mind to her like swinging wide a barred gate. She came to him with grace and giving, drawing aside her every defense, allowing access to who and what she was to the utmost corner of her being.

They moved as one in transcendent communion. There was no awkwardness, no doubt. Guided by instinct and certain knowledge, they gave to each other what was most desired, most necessary.

There were no physical barriers. Naked and magnificent with it, they matched pore to pore, muscle to muscle, sinew to quivering sinew. The proud globes of her breasts pressed into the firm planes of his chest; his hard loins cradled, nudging, her soft and delicate folds. She smoothed the powerful spread of his shoulders while he tested the slender turn of her waist and resilient softness of her hips.

She thought, lapping the tight, dried-peach brown

of his pap, that he needed a gold medallion to nestle in the soft pelting of his chest. Ancient, priceless, it appeared.

He thought that her skin in the valley between her breasts had a maddening perfume. It intensified in strength and distraction.

She felt a fleeting, half-drugged desire that he suckle her breast gently as he spread his fingers over her abdomen. The heat of his mouth covered her nipple. She had her answer, with variations.

He needed to feel her hand on his male hardness, and her cool, nimble fingers found it, stroking with perfect firmness and care. And additional creativity.

Inflamed by the compelling caresses and sensitive incursion of his long, flexible fingers, she longed to have him press deeper inside her. His breathing hoarse, he complied.

Tasting the sweet tenderness between her thighs in delectable, delirious questing, he longed to feel the heat of her mouth in similar exploration. With flawless affinity, supple as a mythical nymph, she moved to do so.

Their hearts pulsed with silent thunder; their skin glowed with lightning's heat. Breaths mingling, gusting, they melded with interlacing, licking tongues, drinking each other. Ecstasy, vibrant as life, imperious as death, raced along their veins, blending into a rampage that stunned thought and banished inhibition.

As one, in absolute communion, they came together. Pulsing hardness, entreating softness, they merged body and spirit. And paused, dazed, at the violent perfection of the consummation.

Then they were caught in the whirlwind, for its power and ferocity was in them. Tempered by caring, harnessed by discipline and desire, they rode it.

Carita took the lunging force of his movements

against her and felt her heart expand. Strong, vital, she thrust upward, needing, wanting his jolting power. He gave it, and more.

Turning with her, he drew her above him, allowing, following her pace. She sank upon him, taking him deep, deep, absorbing him even as she dipped and swung to her own throbbing rhythm. Her hair flailed him, stroked him, shielding them in silver-gold glory. And her strength, her endurance, were without end. Beyond fear.

Immortal, they strove, assaulting in concert the constrictions of time and space. Surmounting them. Sweeping with windblown fury toward violent surcease, supreme victory.

It burst over them, a thunderous cementing of mind and soul, the ultimate immortality. And they took it as a gift, and gave it as a benediction, each to the other. Sealed in rapture, immutable, they held each other with aching tightness, and did not let go. Even afterward, when the grandeur passed and the rapture faded to a sweet and sensual memory.

"Did I tell you," he said long moments later, "that I love you desperately, forever and without end."

She shifted a little, burying her face deeper in the strong curve of his neck. "I think so; I can't remember."

"I will, or will again, then," he said on a low laugh, "when I catch my breath."

"Would you like me to say the same?"

"No," he answered, lifting a strand of her hair and letting it fall, glittering, back onto his chest. "I can hear it in my heart."

"That isn't possible," she objected, though merely for form.

"Listen," he said, and gathered her even nearer, physically and mentally, merging his being with hers.

Nothing moved for some time then. The fountain played, the flowers waited, pale in the moonlight, breathing perfume. A soft breeze meandered over the mosaic floor and, finding them, cooled their skin, swung the tassels of their cushion, and departed.

Then a wide square of light was flung toward them and across their entwined forms, as the doors to the house opened. The gray cat stepped out and padded softly to the steps. It sat down, observing them with unblinking concern.

The cat's shadow moved, stretched, elongated. In the next instant, the animal was gone and in its place was a distinguished gray-haired gentleman in evening clothes. He regarded the pair on the cushion with relaxed complacency.

"I knew," he said in deep and cultured tones, "that you two were suited, and would find it out if thrown together."

Renfrey made a quick, sweeping gesture and a white silk sheet billowed above them, settling to cover their nakedness. Carita clutched it as she sat up.

"Father!"

"My love," the older gentleman said, inclining his head. "Are you well—but no, don't answer. I can see you are blooming."

"You—you've been watching us," she said.

He held up a strong, yet elegant hand in negation. "Acquit me, if you please, of anything so depraved. I was merely keeping an eye on your welfare from a discreet distance."

Renfrey, supporting himself on his elbow, spoke then. His voice carried a hint of menace. "And are you satisfied now that she will come to no harm?"

The elder warlock smiled. "Quite. Though you will admit I have had reason for concern. The two of you have turned my hair quite white."

"I'm surprised you didn't feel compelled to intervene."

"How do you know," Carita's father said gently, "that I didn't?"

She leaned forward to say in low tones, "Did you? Really?"

His gaze was benign as he shook his head. "No, but I would have if there had been the need. You are very dear to me, my Carita."

She hesitated, then said, because there might never be another chance, "My mother—"

"Your mother was a woman of rare bravery. Her heart was strong in spirit but weak in fiber, something we did not discover until it was too late. I loved her. The rest," he said quietly, "is none of your affair. But you need never fear loving, or being loved."

She glanced up at Renfrey, and he down at her. They smiled together.

"Yes, well," the older man said and cleared his throat of some apparent obstruction. "There is a manservant inside who needs occupation to calm his nerves. And I rather thought you might both be in need of sustenance to repair your strength. There is, you will remember, an excellent supper inside which should take care of both problems. Will you join me?"

Renfrey looked down at Carita. "Shall we?"

"If you like," she answered, "though not, I think, in our current state of dress."

"Undress, I would have said," her father corrected with a wicked twinkle in his eye as he rose to his feet. "I shall see you two in the dining room, then."

They were not particularly prompt, in spite of their manifold advantages. They decided to dress each other, and their mood, turning a little giddy, ran through several varieties of uniforms and national costumes, fabrics and modes of decoration. And it was necessary, naturally, to snatch a kiss or a touch between each change—or to change in order to have an excuse for it. They settled at last, however, on the same clothing they had so rashly discarded earlier.

They were mounting the steps toward the vestibule, hand in hand, when Renfrey stopped. His face serious, though his eyes were not, he said, "Pity the poor mortals. They can never know what we have found."

She looked into his mind, caressed it, left her own half-mortal impression. Her smile was generous, tantalizing.

"Can't they?" she said.

Jennifer Blake

JENNIFER BLAKE was married at 15, began writing at 21, and sold her first book six years later at the age of 27. Since then, she has written 37 other novels, including *Fierce Eden*, *Wildest Dreams*, and her most recent, *Shameless*. Her first novel to make the *New York Times* best-seller list was *Love's Wild Desire*. Three more Blake books have appeared on the *Times* list in the intervening years, and others have shown up regularly on the *Publisher's Weekly* best-seller list and the lists of national book chains. She has received numerous awards for writing, but the one she prizes most is the Golden Treasure Award for lifetime achievement in the romance genre, the highest honor extended by Romance Writers of America.

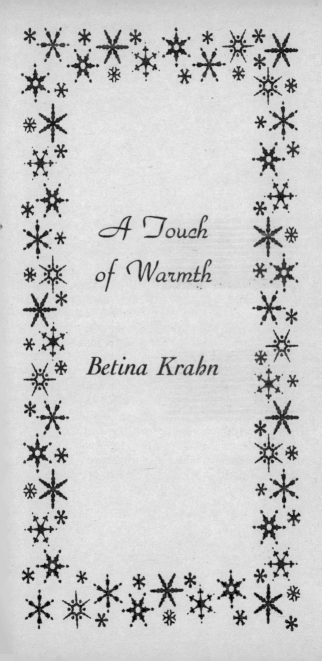

*A Touch
of Warmth*

Betina Krahn

1

April, 1879
A meadow in Devonshire, England

"**Y**ou were acting like a fool," came an angry voice.

"Like a brazen little hussy!" came another, shriller one.

"Ye put us all in danger . . . pullin' your hide out of trouble again," came a harsh third.

"Tamsin, you must stop doing things like this!" The rounded, white-haired patriarch of the band stepped in front of the irate group and stood looking down at her in the moonlight. "Forever dancing on the edge of the circle and staying out until the rays of dawn are peeping through the grass. Look at you. Your wings are crumpled and your hair is a mass of twists and tangles." Argo clasped his hands behind his back and looked stern, very stern indeed. "Worst of all is this dangerous game you play, lingering too long at the edge of the humans' vision—*flirting* with them—"

"Well, you do it, too," Tamsin said, drawing her willowy legs up under her chin and wrapping her arms around them. Huddling back on the pebble where she was seated, she cast a resentful look all around her at the glowering faces of the members of her band. "All fairies do. It's part of *the fun*."

A murmur went through the group gathered

around her. It was indeed part of *the fun*, a long-standing fairy tradition of baiting and dallying with human consciousness.

"Yea, but there are rules to the game. *The fun* is seeing how far you can tease and confuse without being seen," a wizened old fellow with a silver beard down to his knees declared indignantly. "And tonight you were *seen*."

"I was not!" She straightened from her huddled posture in a wink and stuck her chin up at them. "I'm too quick for that. That human didn't see me— he was just dew-drunk and snatching at things inside his own head."

"Silly nymph," snapped a mature, matronly fairy with white hair that reached all the way to her heels. "Too stubborn to listen to your elders. Mark my words—you'll be *caught* by a human someday!" Hespera's dire prediction drew gasps of horror from the fairies. She shook a finger and her pale eyes glowed pink with heat. "And when you're stuck in a jar somewhere, being tormented by ugly human creatures with hot hands and huge flapping ears, you'll regret not listening to us!"

"I won't get caught," Tamsin said with a frantic edge to her voice. "Humans are much too big and slow ever to lay a hand on me."

"That is exactly what my great uncle Rosemount thought," Hespera said, rustling her wings in indignation. Her voice lowered ominously. "He was caught by a human and carried to one of their hovels in a *pocket*." She glanced around at the others' pale eyes and even paler faces. "By the time they found him and pulled him out, the heat of that human had shriveled him like a salamander stuck in the sun. Nothing was left but a wrinkled brown husk. That's what happens to fairies who get captured by humans."

There was a general intake of breath, and all over the band, wings fluttered in distress and eyes darted over shoulders toward the moon-drenched meadow and the massive old trees looming at the edges. They all knew the tale, and it never failed to send a hot chill down their spines. Humans were not only huge and slow-moving, their bodies were appallingly hot. And human heat, fairy children were taught before their first wings sprouted, had been responsible for the demise of many a hapless fairy.

"That's what'll come of you flaunting yourself before humans, girl," the wizened old elder declared. "Yes, *flaunting* yourself. You're entirely too interested in humans, I say."

"I am not," Tamsin denied, sliding off her pebble and spreading her wings behind her, trying to look more formidable. "It's just that I'm not *afraid* of humans, like the rest of you." Following their disapproving gazes over her shoulder, she stiffened at the sight of her disheveled wings, with their crumpled ribs and dull, lackluster surface. With her face nearly pink with humiliation, she struck off through the grass around the trampled ring where the band had been dancing only moments before her fateful encounter with the human.

She strode through the clover patch, through the taller grasses, and into the valley of the lilies, where the sweetness of the tall spikes of white bell-shaped flowers permeated her senses and soothed her battered spirits. Plopping down in the middle of the broad lily leaves, she tried to straighten her wings, rubbing them gently between her hands.

It was hopeless, she realized moments later. She would just have to wait for them to straighten on their own, and it would take more than a little work to restore their iridescent luster. Her shoulders sagged and her chin quivered. Dismally, she lay back on the soft cushion of leaves and stared up at the star-littered sky.

It was true, she admitted reluctantly. She possessed a consuming and increasingly reckless curiosity toward humans. What was it about them she found so fascinating? They had no wings, they chopped off their hair so that their round ears stuck out, they weighed down their bodies with clothes, and their voices rumbled and crashed like thunder. They were clumsy and easily confused—the antithesis of everything fairies found desirable.

And tonight her wretched curiosity had almost led her into disaster. She had been determined to touch a whisker on that old fellow's face, and had almost reached it when he turned his head and caught sight of her. His bellow of surprise had knocked her back, head over heels, into a downward spiral that landed her in the grass with her wings crumpled beneath her. Her cry had alerted the others and they had come to her rescue, flitting about so fast that the old human got confused and lost track of her.

High above, a shooting star streaked across the sky, and she sighed, thinking of how close she had come to that whisker and to the human's raging heat. The elder fairies always described *the heat* as suffocating, searing, and shriveling. But it hadn't felt that way to her. It had made her skin tingle and her heart beat faster and her wings tremble.

She scowled and turned over onto her stomach, laying her pale cheek against the cool waxy surface of the leaf, spreading her wings over her like a rumpled blanket. The memory of that wicked warmth washed through her again and her eyes began to glow pink, then sultry red. She rubbed one wing slowly across the other. *The heat* felt curiously akin to excitement . . . or pleasure.

Had any of the elders actually felt human heat? If

they had, how could they describe it as suffocating, scorching, burning? Or did it feel pleasurable just to her?

The thought was alarming. Owls and dogs aside, what a fairy feared most was being different from the others in his or her band, for it was always the "different" fairies that came to a bad end in the tales and legends.

Out of the depths of her memory a long-ago story-feast rose into her mind. As the band sat in the great circle, after dancing, the elders had recounted lurid tales of human heat and cruelty, setting her and the other fairy children quaking with fear. Her Aunt Clytie had leaned down beside her, wrapped her in a protective cloak of hair, and whispered that she mustn't be afraid. It was just a tale, Aunt Clytie said; human heat didn't really hurt at all. There was a twinkle in her eye as she said it, a light that might have been reassurance or mischief . . . or knowing.

But then, Aunt Clytie had always been a bit "different." Not long after that she had disappeared from the band, and all assumed she had met some dire fate. Had Aunt Clytie felt the pleasure of human heat? And had it proved her undoing? Tamsin sat up and shoved those disturbing thoughts away.

From a distance came the muffled sounds of other young nymphs and sprites lying entwined on lily leaves. It had been a long time since she had lain in the lilies with a handsome young fairy, tickling, giggling, and making pleasure. She thought of Artemis, the cocky young sprite who was always catching her up in his wings and trying to carry her off to the lilies. The prospect of lying in his arms wasn't at all appealing. The realization jolted her, for fairies lived to have fun. Making sport and pleasure was their whole reason for being!

She did want pleasure, she told herself. It was just

that the pleasure she wanted was ... A surge of re-membered sensation took her breath. She tried to hold on to the tantalizing swirl of excitation it caused in her, but after a moment it dissipated, leaving her with only an ache of longing.

She wanted another wicked, hot thrill. She wanted to feel another forbidden wave of heat. She wanted to *touch* a human.

Shocked by her thoughts and fleeing those worrisome yearnings, she slid to the edge of the leaves and then to the ground, testing her wings. They seemed airworthy and she set her jaw and lifted skyward on a powerful downstroke.

As she flew low over the lily beds, she spotted the handsome young sprite, Artemis, lying in the lily leaves with a silly young nymph. Irritably, Tamsin soared up and away through the trees. She slowed to look back at the meadow, then felt a spurt of daring and pressed on into the forest, flying farther than she had ever gone before.

After a long while, she came to the edge of the woods and glimpsed a broad, treeless field. Lighting on a high limb to survey the moon-drenched landscape, she spotted a patch of light. It seemed to be coming from a human-built structure—one of their houses! The yellow glow shining from that window seemed to call to her. Her heart beat faster, and her limbs tingled with excitement.

Unused to stifling her urges, she took a deep breath, flew toward the light, and hovered, shielding her eyes to peer into the brightness. There was the old human she had encountered earlier that night. She gasped and covered her eyes and mouth—then gradually peeled her fingers away.

As she watched him moving about and scratching his head, her fear began to fade. Her gaze fell to the old human's beard and the temptation of an even greater excitement grew in her. Soon she was developing a new plan to snatch a whisker from that beard . . . and once again to feel that lush, forbidden heat.

Forrest Reed swung down from his horse and glanced around the yard of the stone and half-timbered cottage that nestled at the edge of the woods. It hadn't looked so bad from a distance, but as he approached he saw that chunks of the wattle and daub were missing from the walls, the timbers were in sad need of repair and paint, and the stones of the lower walls and foundation were tumbling from their bed of mortar. Grass and weeds had reclaimed much of the small yard, and the wooden shed at the back was still negotiating a precarious balance with gravity.

"Hello?" Forrest called toward the half-open door. "Uncle, are you here?"

"Who's there?" a gravelly voice replied from the dim interior of the cottage.

"It is Forrest—Forrest Reed," he called back. "Your sister Elaine's son."

The old man hurried out the door and halted, squinting against the bright sunlight. Old Grovenor Tredwell was the very picture of dishevelment; unshaven, and wearing a rumpled coat, a shirt hanging open at the neck, and trousers that looked as though they hadn't seen a pressing iron in years.

"Forrest, boy . . . that you?" He scratched his graying whiskers and ran a hand through his unkempt hair. There was no mistaking the impeccably clad younger man for anyone other than Elaine Tredwell Reed's son. He was the very image of his well-bred mother: tall, clean-limbed, with strong patrician features and thick, dark hair. "Well"—the old man grunted—"ain't you a sight?"

"I must be. I've had rather a long ride." Forrest brushed his dusty breeches with one gloved hand. "I've come to pay you a visit, Uncle—"

Just then a huge, rawboned hound raced around the corner of the cottage and launched itself at Grovenor. The old man staggered back, fending off the beast's attack, and Forrest jolted forward to help . . . then halted when he saw that the dog's teeth weren't bared. It was climbing the old man in order to lick him; the attack was one of mere exuberance.

"Not now—damn yer mangy eyes! Get off me!" Grovenor snarled. The mottled gray hound dropped to his feet, spotted Forrest, and rushed to give him a good sniffing instead.

"The family—" Forrest continued, eyeing the creature who was assessing his boots as if they might be edible, "have been most concerned about you."

"Concerned, eh? *Humph!*" Uncle Grovenor tugged his rumpled coat square on his shoulders and produced a defiant expression. "That fancy family of mine has never given two tiddly-dams whether I was even alive . . . not since I lost my money." He paced this way and that, then turned a scorching look on Forrest. "What do they want from me? Whatever it is, it won't do 'em any good—I ain't got nothing left."

That last part, Forrest knew, was no exaggeration. His uncle had long ago drunk and gambled away the fortune he had inherited as a youth, and in his advancing years had landed here, in this ramshackle cottage, living on a pittance of a military pension.

"They—we don't want anything from you, Uncle. In fact, I have come to render *you* a bit of service," Forrest said, reaching for his reins and wishing he could just climb back onto his mount and ride straight back to London.

"Ahhh." Grovenor's face lit with angry comprehension. "Come to straighten me up an' dry me out, have you?" He huddled back with a glower. "Well, you're wastin' your time. I ain't about to change, boy. I live the way I want, with nobody pullin' or peckin' at me . . . nobody tellin' me what's proper or decent or godly."

"But surely you could use—"

"See here, boy, stay or go as you please—it don't matter to me!" The old man advanced on him, growing steadily more agitated. "But don't expect me to feed you—or look after you—or *talk* to you. That's why I come here—to get away from all that *talkin'*." He jabbed a finger at Forrest. "You're on your own! Come on, Boxer!"

Forrest watched his crotchety old uncle barrel off down the path through the woods with the dog at his heels. Expelling a heavy breath, he tethered his mount and pushed open the cottage door.

The sour, musty smell of the place made him think again of fleeing straight back to London. Unfortunately, that was not an option. He hadn't been sent here to rescue Uncle Grovenor, so much as to endure a sort of personal exile. His mother and aunts wanted him out of sight and out of mind, at least until the furor surrounding his broken engagement faded.

"Dearest Heaven, Forrest, you might at least have *said* something!" His mother's voice was still ringing in his ears. "You just stood there like a stump while she insulted you in front of half of London!"

He had indeed just stood there while the beautiful and high-spirited Adele Barstow declared he was as stiff as a shirtboard and had no wit, no *joie de vivre*, and not a single drop of warmth in his blood.

The worst of it was, it was all perfectly true.

He was the most hopelessly correct, boring, and colorless man in all the Inns of Court. He did everything according to the book and by procedure . . . so much so that he always seemed to be citing chapter and verse while making small talk and to be doggedly following some mental diagram while dancing with a woman in his arms. Even his Head of Chambers had called him an insufferable dry stick, and declared that his greatest virtue as a solicitor was that he hadn't a scrap of imagination with which to muck up the facts.

Adele, his gorgeous, raven-haired fiancée, had been his complete opposite. That was what he had adored most about her; her vivaciousness, her easy social grace, her impetuous outbursts of humor. Unfortunately, it was those very things that had led her to cry off from their betrothal in the midst of a crowded dance floor, and in the next breath to announce that she was engaging herself to a dashing cavalry officer.

The hurt and anger he had denied for the last three days finally erupted in him. It wasn't his fault he had no imagination! He tried to think of wonderful and witty things to say . . . it was just that he always managed to do so *after* the situation was past. He did have ideas, interests, and opinions . . . it was just that he could never seem to put them into words. In social situations, he grew stiff and terse and insufferably proper. And in private, he found it almost as difficult to break through the wall that imprisoned his inner self.

Now, with the one chance for warmth and color in his life gone, the chill of inadequacy extended into the deepest regions of his heart as well. He was reduced to exile in a filthy, tumbledown cottage in the middle of nowhere . . . foisting himself upon a cantankerous old rummy of an uncle who clearly didn't want him around. As he looked about, he felt a great weight settling on his heart. He would probably end up just like irascible old Grovenor. Only instead of drowning himself in rum as Grovenor did, he would probably just dry up and blow away.

Work was the only thing he knew to keep despair at bay, and he removed his gloves and coat, rolled up his sleeves, and vehemently attacked the piles of clothes on the chairs and the crusty dishes strewn over the table and dry sink.

It was nightfall before he sat down to rest on the settle by the stone fireplace. The cottage was at least livable now; the two rooms were dusted and swept, and the dishes and kettles had been scoured and stored. He had found a braided rug on the bed in the small sleeping room, beaten it, and placed it by the fire. He had aired the blankets and mattresses and made plans to find a laundress in the nearby village. He had even put together a dried-meat stew for supper and found some edible bread and cheese in the cool well. When his uncle didn't come home at sunset, he ate alone, cleared away the dishes, and built up the fire for the evening.

Deep into the night, Forrest came awake, snapping bolt upright with his heart pounding and his senses searching for what had disturbed him. He shoved to his feet and scoured the main room of the cottage, finding all as it had been; tidy, quiet, and lighted only by the glow of reddened coals. Then he heard it—a muffled groan from outside the door, then a thudding against the door itself.

The weathered oaken panels slammed back with a loud bang, and through the opening stumbled Uncle Grovenor—wild-eyed and roaring drunk—carrying a young girl in his arms. A *naked* girl.

"I got me one!" The old man staggered, as much

from the rum in his head as from the weight of his burden. "I'm rich!" he crowed.

"Good God!" Forrest choked out, staring at the limp form in his uncle's arms.

"Caught me a f-fairy! Alwus knew I'd get me one o' the little devils. Just a matter o' time—and here she is!"

"Uncle—what have you done?" Forrest rushed to take the poor girl from his uncle's drooping grasp, but the old man pulled back with a pugnacious look.

"She's mine—*all mine*—an' the wishes is mine, too!"

The old man had gone completely around the bend! Forrest rushed to light the small lamp and to pull a blanket from the bed in the sleeping room. Over his uncle's drunken ranting and raving, he finally managed to cover the girl and pry her from the old man's arms. She weighed almost nothing, and as he pulled her against him, he realized she was cold.

Quickly, he carried her to the fire and laid her on the rug in front of the glowing hearth. As he hurried up the steps to the sleeping loft to retrieve his own blankets, Uncle Grovenor closed the door and bolted it, then shuffled heavily to the settle and collapsed on it. By the time Forrest returned, he found the old man and his young victim unconscious.

"Crazy old sot," he ground out, dropping to his knees by the young girl and wrapping her securely in a cocoon of additional blankets. "Rampaging round the countryside, abducting young girls—it's an outrage!"

He laid more logs on the fire and stoked it to a fierce blaze, then settled back on his heels to get a better look at his uncle's victim. And he stopped dead.

She was breathtaking. Her unbound hair was such a light blond that it seemed almost white, and her face was a work of delicate and classical beauty ... exquisite cheekbones, straight little nose, and full Cupid's bow mouth. Feeling guilty at such unseemly thoughts, he averted his eyes from that stunning face, telling himself she was just a child ... a very pretty, very ill used child. But something drew his gaze back to her face, and it was a moment before he realized with alarm that there was a blue tinge to her pale perfect skin. Her cheek felt like cold, smooth marble.

"Damn it—she's half-frozen!" He wrung his hands and tried to think what to do. In desperation, he peeled the blankets back to feel her feet. They were icy and he sat down instantly, pulled them onto his lap, and began to rub. He stroked and massaged them until his own hands ached with cold and he had to hold them out to warm by the fire before he could continue. Her feet drew the heat from his hands again and again, until at last he felt a hint of warmth in her toes and ankles, and moved upward toward her knees.

Ingrained decency forbade him to go farther than mid-thigh, though—Lord knew—he had already seen enough of the little thing to compromise her forever in the eyes of decent society. Tucking her legs back under the covers, he proceeded to rub her body through the rough blankets—her slim hips, her small waist, her delicate shoulders. Then he fished her arms from the blankets and spent a long while trying to rub some blood back into them. It worried him that she hadn't awakened and wasn't even shivering or quaking. What if she was already too far gone? The thought spurred him to even greater effort.

Somewhere in the middle of the night, fatigue and

resignation overwhelmed him, and he ceased rubbing. Then he recalled what his nanny and the upstairs maid had done for him when he had fallen through the ice on the pond as a boy. They had stripped to their shifts and pressed him between their ample bodies to warm him . . . and saved his life. He quickly built up the fire again, rolled the girl onto her side, and lay down behind her, pulling her body against his and awkwardly wrapping himself around her.

She seemed so small, frail, and helpless. He could feel the cold of her through both the blankets and his clothes, and shivered as his body lost heat to hers. Gradually, with the fire on one side and him on the other, she began to warm.

"A mere slip of a girl," he muttered from between teeth that were clenched to keep them from chattering. "The old fool ought to be horsewhipped." Laying his head on his arm, he realized that he had trapped a bit of her hair beneath his cheek. It was as soft as spun silk. Rather than disturb his carefully settled position, he left it there. He didn't mean to fall sleep, but before long, he had closed his eyes and surrendered to both the growing warmth and the exertions of the day.

Tamsin awakened to a general discomfort and a panicky feeling that something was wrong—terribly wrong. She was hot . . . smotheringly, stiflingly hot . . . and tingling all over. Opening her eyes, she was greeted by the ominous red glow of burning coals. Try as she might, she couldn't seem to distance herself from that terrifying sight. She seemed to be caught in something. A spiderweb? But when she glanced down and saw the pile of woven blankets over her, she realized she was caught in a *human* bit of spinning and weaving!

Panicking, she squirmed and tried to beat her wings to break free, but something was weighing her down. Looking over her shoulder, she saw a face with a huge pair of odd-colored eyes set in a frame of *dark* hair. Sweet Minerva—a human face! She struggled to free her arms, but everything was happening so slowly, she felt as if she was immersed in pine pitch!

The human spoke and her eyes flew wide with terror. She turned her head and found him staring at her with a ferocious scowl, saying something. To her horror, his voice didn't sound like thunder anymore; she could actually make out the words!

"Are you all right?"

"Let me go!" Her voice was lower and slower than she had ever heard it before. To her surprise, the weight on her lifted and the human withdrew.

She pushed up to a sitting position and found that she was on the floor of a human habitation, beside one of the stone places they built to contain their fires. It looked just like the place she had spied the other night. The hewn wood, beams, stone fireplace, bench, and table . . . it was the old human's cottage!

"Who are you, miss—what is your name? Where do you live?" The human's voice assailed her again, tolling like a giant bell in her head.

Her only thought was escape. She began tearing at the cocoon of blankets, feeling heavy and clumsy as her thoughts raced far ahead of her actions. She made it onto her knees, then her feet, searching frantically for a means of escape. As she threw off the last layer, the human gasped and lunged at her with yet another covering.

"You're not dressed—you'll catch your death," he declared. She stumbled backward over the blankets still tangled around her feet, lost her balance, and would have fallen into the fire's place if he hadn't caught her. She cried out as the heat of his hands burned into her bare shoulders.

"I won't harm you," he said, struggling to cover her, "but you have to stay warm. You nearly froze to death last night, and I'll not have you dying of exposure now—not after all I went through to warm you."

Last night. Tamsin slowed her struggles as the memory of what had happened began to assemble in her head. She had her hands on the old human's whisker, then, out of nowhere, a massive hand came down on her, and she was—Galvanized, she wriggled and twisted with everything in her, trying to escape those scorching hands! But the human was shockingly fast, and she was appallingly slow. What was the matter with her? Why couldn't she just duck and dart and escape him?

Panic seized her as he grabbed her by the waist and pulled her back against him, trapping her arms at her sides. She could feel him pressed against her back and tried to flutter her wings to shove him away, but she couldn't even feel them.

"See here!" Every time she managed to shove the blanket from her top half, he made a growling noise and dragged it back over her. "I know you've had a terrible shock, but you cannot run about stark naked."

It was no use, she realized. She was caught hard in the human's grip, held tight against his huge, hot body. This was the long-predicted outcome of her youthful rebellion and perilous desires, and there was no escaping it. She shut her eyes and stilled, feeling her body heat rising . . . certain that she would soon be a husk or a cinder, as the tales and legends said.

She poised with her heart racing, alive to every nuance of her fatal predicament . . . the feel of the human's arms around her, the hot shivers caused by that unthinkable contact, the dread anticipation as she waited for her poor body to either wither or combust. But as moment followed moment, steamy silence reigned.

"Wha-a—what's going on?" came a rusty bellow from nearby.

The human holding her captive shifted, turning her toward the source of the sound. There, rising from the bench, was the grizzled old human. His face was nearly purple and his eyes were fairly bulging from his head as he stared at her.

"What have you done to 'er?" he roared.

"I haven't done a bloody thing to her," a deep, powerful voice rumbled just above her ear. "Except possibly save her life—"

"You must 'ave done something—she ain't the same!" the old man charged, searching her face and blanket-clad form with genuine distress. "She's *grown!*"

As Tamsin faced her grizzled captor, she was shocked to realize that she was nearly equal in stature to him. The old man was right! She looked down at herself and saw her bare leg beside the human's. She was nearly as big as he was!

The human's heat hadn't caused her to shrink; it had caused her to *grow!*

Forrest looked down at the girl in his arms and was surprised to find that she did indeed seem larger than he remembered. His gaze trailed down her side and encountered a shockingly bare leg and curvaceous hip visible where the edges of the blanket didn't meet. Reddening, he jerked his head up and discovered that the top of her head met the top of his shoulder. Confusion boiled up in him. Last night she had seemed no more than a child; this morning she was clearly a young woman.

As she swooned and sagged, he caught her and dragged her to the settle, depositing her there and sinking onto one knee beside her. He had to drag his eyes from the sight of her pale, perfect breasts as he released her and readjusted the cover. Raising his gaze to her face, he caught his breath at the sight of her light eyes and the tousled fall of silvery white hair around her bare shoulders. He'd never seen hair so long, thick, and luxurious. It hung to her hips at least. . . .

"See here, I don't want to hurt you, miss," he said in low, soothing tones, bringing her alert once more. "My uncle has treated you abominably and if you'll just tell me who you are and where your family is, I'll see that you're returned home safely."

"The bloody hell you will!" Grovenor declared, rushing to the settle to lean over the girl. "She ain't goin' anywhere 'til I get my three wishes. This is a trick of some kind. I don't know how she done it—growin' like that—but fairies are plumb full of tricks. Listen here, Twinkle-toes"—he shoved his grizzled face toward hers—"I caught ye fair and square. I want my three wishes, an' I want 'em now!"

"I can't give you any wishes," she declared, huddling back with a petulant look, folding her arms protectively over her chest. "My wings aren't fully grown yet, so I don't have any dust. And even if I did, I couldn't make *wishes* come tr—" She halted abruptly, her eyes widened, and she jerked away from the back of the settle to stare over her shoulder at her bare back. "My wings! They're gone!"

"Wings?" Forrest stared at her in disbelief. "What wings?"

"My *wings*," she wailed, her eyes stark with horror as she wriggled her shoulders and caught a glimpse of smooth, flat skin where her wings used to be attached. She turned on him. "What's happened to them?"

Forrest's jaw sagged and he sank abruptly back onto his heels. They were daft—the pair of them! His drink-crazed uncle thought he'd captured a *fairy*, and the poor creature he had abducted thought she'd misplaced a pair of *wings*!

"Give them back to me!" She turned on Uncle Grovenor, then raked the cottage with a frantic gaze.

Grovenor's eyes narrowed in calculation as he seized the advantage. "Not 'til I get my three wishes," he said, sticking out his chin. "You'll get your wings back after I get my youth back . . . and my palace filled with servants . . . and my bottomless bucket of gold."

"Bucket of gol—" She sprang to her feet in a flash, leaving it to Forrest to catch the sliding blanket and fumble to wrap it about her bare body again. "Fairies can't grant wishes. We don't have that kind of magic," she said hotly. "Wicked old human— pulling the wings off fairies! That's about as low and mean as a creature can sink!"

"Pulling the—You cannot actually believe you're a fairy," Forrest said, trying to interject reason into this bizarre encounter, while wrapping her up and tucking the corner of the blanket to secure it. In the process his knuckles raked the cool, silky valley between her breasts, and she shrank as if he'd burned her. He jerked back, too, unnerved by the cool, pleasurable shock that contact had sent through his body. When she glared up at him, he had the odd, distracting thought that the centers of her extraordinary eyes looked pale and delicate, almost like . . . snowflakes.

"Of course I'm a fairy," she said irritably, crossing her arms and skittering back.

Forrest swung a glowering look between his wild-eyed uncle and the strange young woman whose beauty, rare coloring, and abhorrence of clothing were nothing short of unnerving. Was this some shared delusion? some contagious lunacy?

"This has gone quite far enough," he declared. "There are no such things as fairies, Uncle, and no such things as wishes either. And you, young woman"—he struck his most authoritative solicitor pose—"you've undoubtedly sustained a knock on the head that has rendered you temporarily confused."

"I'm not confused," she protested, edging away, eyeing the door. "Old 'Whiskers' over there caught me last night and pulled off my wings. Make him give them back to me, so I can go back to my—" She halted, swallowed hard, and looked down in horror at her greatly enlarged self. "I have to go!"

She was around them both in a blink and tugging at the door handle by the time they lurched into motion. When the door didn't open, she darted for the window, where she smacked her hands on the glass. Her panic rising visibly, she began to dart in and out, up and down, searching for an escape route.

Forrest and his Uncle Grovenor stumbled after her from door to window to loft stairs. But her movements were so quick that, time and again, they were left colliding with each other and snatching at air. She flitted around the cottage, easily avoiding both of them, but bumping into the table, "Owww!" tripping on the blankets left on the floor, "Ohhh!" and smacking into a doorframe with her shoulder, "Ufff."

"Where are they?" she said with a groan, digging through the pile of soiled clothes and linen Forrest had placed by the door to be taken to a laundress. Then she stopped stock-still and turned a tumultuous look on him that caused his heart to stop. "My wings—I can't go back without them." Desperation crept into her voice. "Please, tell me what you've done with them!"

In the morning light streaming through the window, her magnificent hair took on the glow of spun silver and her fair skin seemed translucent. He stood mesmerized, drinking in her delicate features, tempting curves, and exotic textures that he could somehow feel with his eyes. There was an air of the pristine and untouched about her, something that gave him goose bumps and made him feel both feverish and shivery.

Uncle Grovenor watched irritably. He glimpsed the fascination on Forrest's face and the female sorcery on his captive's . . . that helpless, fetching look that had mesmerized and ensnared the human male since the Garden of Eden. . . .

"Don't look square at her, boy!" Grovenor warned, thrusting himself between them to disrupt whatever spell she might be casting on his nephew. "Don't you know any better? Fairy females are dangerous. Worse'n women. Full of lies and tricks an' such."

Forrest came abruptly back to his senses, and was annoyed to find his uncle staring at him as if *he* were the one with a few loose rungs in his ladder.

"Don't be absurd, Uncle," he snarled. Then he decided to try another tack entirely. "I assure you, miss, we'll do whatever we can to help you. Forgive me—I am Forrest Reed, of the London firm of Sterling, Torrence, Darcy, and Reed. And this is my uncle, Grovenor Tredwell, Royal Army, Retired. And your name is?" He coaxed a response with a hand motion, and after a suspicious look, she gave him one.

"Tamsin."

"Ahhh." Forrest nodded. "Lovely name. Certainly

unusual. Tamsin what?" She scowled at him for a moment before a quick bit of deduction told her what he wanted.

"Not Tamsin What. Just Tamsin," she said irritably. "Fairy folk have no need of more than one name."

"Of course not," he said with strained indulgence. "And you live ...?"

"In the meadow," she answered, hoping she wasn't giving too much away. As long as she didn't mention the mound next to the old log, it was probably safe. "And I want to go back there."

His determined smile thinned a bit. "Which ... meadow?"

"Which?" Her eyes widened in alarm. "There's more than one?"

Forrest lost all pretense of humor. He advanced on her, sending her scurrying back so quickly that he could scarcely follow the movement with his eyes.

"Enough of this!" He shot an irritable look at his uncle, then at her. The pair was a study in lunacy; one drink-addled and the other moonstruck. He hadn't a prayer of untangling this mess until one or both of them came to their senses. It was a small mercy that the young woman wasn't charging his uncle with anything more depraved than "wing-napping."

"I want the truth, the whole truth, and nothing but the truth, young lady. And until you're ready to tell me who you are and where you live, I have no choice but to keep you here. I will not be responsible for turning you out into the forest, clad only in a blanket." She huddled back with her arms folded adamantly, and he turned to Grovenor with a hard look. "And you, Uncle, unless I hear a full and rational explanation from you by tomorrow, I intend to go to the local constabulary and see you brought up on charges. Do I make myself clear?"

Grovenor's lips moved mutinously as he turned on his heel and headed for the door. Just as the door closed, his voice drifted back: "I need some rum."

Forrest watched him go, dragged his hands down his face, and headed for the battered pots and tins on the shelves.

"I need some coffee."

2

Tamsin watched the old man slide back the metal bolt, jerk the door open, and storm outside. She was at the door in a flash. So, unfortunately, was Forrest Reed . . . blocking the way. He rebolted the door with a glare of warning, then turned back to take some things down from the shelf.

She retreated to the stack of wood in the corner by the hearth and sat down, drawing her knees up under her chin, feeling utterly miserable. Caught by humans and held against her will . . . shriveling in a pocket would have been a mercy compared with this! Look at her! She held up her hands. They were huge. And pink. *Ugh.*

She'd grown to the size of a human, and the quicksilver movements on which she had always prided herself had completely deserted her. Now she misjudged size and distance, lumbered and stumbled like a lame mole. She rubbed the red spot on her thigh where she had smacked into the edge of the table earlier. It was humiliating.

And with every passing moment she seemed to be getting larger. What if she didn't stop at human size? What if she kept on growing? She pulled open the top of the blanket and looked down at herself. It was worse than she thought. She wasn't only getting pink, she was getting *lumpy*! The two little buds on her chest now lay atop mounds of flesh, and her slender hips had broadened noticeably. What was happening to her? Was she turning *human* or just *hideous*?

She sat huddled on the woodpile, watching Forrest Reed move about the cottage, mixing things and setting a kettle over the flames he stirred to life in the hearth. When the old one he called uncle returned, Forrest let him in and they sat down at the table to eat. They offered her food and drink, but when she saw what it was, she declined with a shiver of horror. On the platter were small, shriveled, brown things, and she couldn't help but wonder . . .

Later that morning, after the old man had left once more, the one called Forrest dragged a comb through his dark hair and pulled a coat on over the other garments he wore. Clothes upon clothes, she thought, it was a wonder humans didn't suffocate altogether. Then he disappeared up the steps and returned with a huge white garment, which he held out to her, saying that it wouldn't be as scratchy as the blanket she had wrapped around her. With surprise she realized that the blanket did feel prickly and uncomfortable. When she reached for the shirt, her hand brushed his. The contact felt like the kiss of a flame. She jerked back, rubbing her skin.

She glanced up in time to see the door close and then looked down at her hand again. The human's touch was hot . . . like firebrands . . . quiet lightning . . . smoldering stars. And yet that scorching heat left no mark, only the intriguing tingles that caused an odd ache to settle in her middle. She let the blanket drop, then experimentally pushed her arms into the sleeves of the shirt. It felt cool and smooth, and she realized her skin had become more sensitive.

But she had no time to explore that discovery. All she could think about was getting back to the meadow. Perhaps wise old Argo or the learned Hespera could help her turn back into her fairy self.

With her mind set on escape, she tried the door and found it blocked from the outside. She pressed against the front window to no avail. Squinting hard against the light coming through the dusty panes of glass, she ran her fingers around the edges of the wooden frame and smiled when she discovered a bit of metal that was shaped like the bolt on the door. It slid to one side with a click, and when she pushed, the window swung open in a haze of dust. Through the opening, trees and sky and fresh air beckoned. The terrors of the morning were temporarily eclipsed by the prospect of freedom.

Trembling with eagerness, she climbed up on a stool beneath the window and launched herself through the narrow window with her arms extended, anticipating that first exhilarating tug of buoancy as her wings caught the air. . . .

But she had no wings, and she had seriously misjudged the relative sizes of the window opening and her newly expanded lower half. The impact that halted her forward motion caught her totally by surprise. Her hips were lodged in the window frame and, with a shocked cry, she tumbled down the side of the cottage.

Grovenor's hound, Boxer, was frisking around Forrest's feet as he tried to saddle his horse in the pole shed at the back. The hound suddenly perked up his ears and shot around the corner of the cottage to investigate.

Forrest heard Tamsin's scream mingle with the dog's frantic barking and came at a dead run. "What's happened?" he shouted, rounding the corner to find her hanging down the front of the cottage, flailing in terror at the dog. Everything in his chest contracted sharply at the sight of her dangling helplessly while the dog lunged at her, and he rushed to help.

"Down, you hell-hound! Get away—go!" he shouted, shoving the animal away. "Are you all right?" He had to counter her panicky struggles in order to lift and examine her.

"Don't let it get me!" she wailed.

"Don't be frightened—I've got you. The dog won't hurt you—I promise," he assured her, glancing over his shoulder at Boxer, who was prancing back and forth, panting and eyeing them with interest. Forrest looked her over and didn't see any blood; she seemed more frightened than damaged. Turning his attention to the window, he realized she had been climbing out and gotten her bottom wedged in the narrow opening. He tried to turn her so he could tug her the rest of the way through the window, but he couldn't manage that maneuver without help.

"Brace yourself," he ordered. "I'll go inside and pull you back through the opening."

"No—don't leave—" she begged, but he was already halfway to the door.

Forrest's plan seemed like the logical thing to do, until he raced inside and found himself faced with a set of lithesome legs and a rounded bottom that were catastrophically exposed beneath the tail of his shirt.

Pale, shapely limbs writhing . . . bare, curvaceous

bottom wriggling . . . the sight sent a spear of excitement through his loins. With a will of their own, his eyes fastened hungrily on that erotic vision. The muscles of his belly contracted, his shoulders tightened, and his breath came faster. There didn't seem to be anywhere he could grasp her within the bounds of propriety . . . or sanity.

Fighting the unexpected seduction of his senses, he stepped onto the stool behind her, set his hands on her hips, and braced himself against the wall. Once, twice, he hoisted and hauled. On the third tug, she came hurtling back through the window with a cry. The force knocked him off the stool and he crashed to the floor with her atop him.

For a stunned moment, neither moved. Then Tamsin recovered her breath and pushed up on her arms—and found herself nose-to-nose with Boxer's grinning maw. She screamed and shrank back, but Boxer lunged after her, scrambling on top of Forrest's prone body. Finding her back against a wall, she took a deep breath and blew full force on the beast's nose. Boxer flinched, looked startled, then began to bark for all he was worth.

Forrest bolted upright, grappling with Boxer. The dog apparently thought wrestling with a human was great fun, and began to paw him, slobber, and bark all the more. "Damned mongrel! What's the matter with you?" Forrest fended him off enough to scramble onto one knee and gain the leverage to give him a mighty shove. "Out! Get out of here—*out!*"

The dog skidded and scrambled out and, his ears still ringing, Forrest rolled to his knees and staggered up to close the door. When he turned back, Tamsin was on her feet, weaving and holding her midsection. Her face was ashen and her eyes were huge with fright.

"He was going to eat me!"

"Boxer? Hardly," Forrest said, brushing himself off, scowling. "Your screams got him worked up, that's all. Dogs get frantic when they hear screams."

And they get hungry when they see fairies, she thought. She blew on her fingers and looked alarmed, then blew again. "My frost-breath is gone...." No wonder the dog hadn't turned tail and run—her breath was too warm to frost his nose! Her prime fairy defense against dogs was gone!

"What was that?" he asked, watching the strange look on her face and the way she held her middle. "Are you all right?"

"I—this feels awful," she gasped, pressing her ribs and stomach gingerly. "I can hardly get my breath."

"It serves you right for trying to escape," he declared, running a hand through his hair and edging closer. "You'll likely have a good bruise or two. Let that be a reminder—" He halted, sensing that something about her had changed and trying to identify what it was. "Are you ... getting taller? I could have sworn you were only up to my ... "

The top of her head was now even with his chin. She had seemed larger that morning than when Uncle Grovenor had carried her through the door last night, but Forrest had put it down to his own fatigue and the dim light. But there was no denying it this time; she was definitely larger than she had been at sunrise. When she looked up at him, he could see new color spiraling through her light eyes ... like the swirling blue from a paintbrush plunged into a glass of clear water.

"And your eyes ... they were ... " He swallowed hard, unnerved by what he was witnessing. It was as if the snowflakes he had seen earlier had melted and turned into clear azure pools. What sort of female was this, who grew by the hour and whose eye color changed even as he watched? He was unable to keep his gaze from sliding to the open shirt pulled tight across her breasts. Whatever else, she was an exquisitely sensual, artlessly enticing creature... one utterly without modesty or shame.

"The least you can do is button that shirt, young woman," he said irritably.

"B-button?" Tamsin said in a whisper, looking down at her body as if seeing both it and the shirt for the first time. She *was* bigger. From the corner of her eye, she caught sight of her hair and picked up a lock of it. Her hair was losing its silvery cast and taking on a golden sheen. Everything about her was changing.

"Yes, button it. Fasten it up."

Floundering in rising panic, she unfolded her arms and touched her eyes. How bad was it? Was she getting warty, red-eyed, and horrible?

"For God's sake," he growled, reaching for the shirt and buttoning it himself. "These little round things, remember? They go in the holes... and hold the front together so that you don't go around with your—your—" He clamped his jaw shut and scowled furiously.

She looked up at him in desperation. "Please let me go. The longer I stay, the uglier and more hideous I become. I don't know anything about granting wishes, I swear. If I could do magic, believe me ... I wouldn't still be here."

He searched her face. "You needn't be afraid." His voice softened. "I won't let anything hurt you. And you're not at all ugly. You're—" He halted, but his eyes said it for him. *Beautiful.* And something in the quiet earnestness of that visual compliment reached through her panic.

She felt an odd but pleasing tingle of warmth that caused her fear to subside. She settled her gaze on his long, supple fingers as they continued buttoning.

They moved with surprising grace over the bits of shell that hung in a row down the front of the garment. As she watched, her plight, her peril, and even the ache in her ribs began to fade from her mind. She had never imagined hair could be so dark, like the sky on a clear winter night. And his unusual eyes were fringed with long feathery lashes that sometimes shaded and sometimes enhanced them. He wasn't pretty by fairy standards, but his face had a bold attraction, a distinctive male angularity that drew her gaze and caused a soft flutter in her stomach.

Her body began to tingle in curious places and she wondered what the rest of him looked like beneath those stifling clothes.

"Wha—what's happened?" Uncle Grovenor came rushing into the cabin just then, out of breath. He caught sight of them, standing close and staring into each other's eyes, and glowered. "What's goin' on, boy?"

Forrest dropped her shirttail and stepped back, while she darted across the room to perch again on the woodpile. Neither met the old man's gaze.

"She tried to climb out the window and got stuck," Forrest muttered, as he headed for the stairs to the loft.

Moments later, he returned with a pair of trousers and ordered her to wear them, at least until he could ride into the village to obtain more suitable female clothing. But she didn't seem to have the faintest idea how to put on a pair of pants, much less what to do with the braces that were meant to hold them up. Forrest clenched his jaw, muttered to himself, and helped her.

Uncle Grovenor rambled off into the woods again with his dog, vowing to be back at sunset and warning Tamsin that she'd better start working on his wishes if she ever expected to see her fairy folk again. When Grovenor was out of sight, Forrest apologized for his uncle's uncouth behavior, then promptly locked her in the cottage and spent the afternoon outside, doing badly needed chores.

As he repaired the pole shed, carried water, and chopped wood for the fire, he thought about the strange lapses in Tamsin's mental functioning. She seemed to have forgotten a number of very ordinary things, like how to button buttons. And even the greenest of virgins knew that men wore braces to keep their trousers up.

The bump on her head had obviously affected her memory. He'd heard of such things. But that didn't explain her bizarre conviction that she was a fairy or his uncle's even more absurd notion that her involuntary presence in his house entitled him to a palace, a fortune in gold, and a long drink at the fountain of youth.

The only thing that *was* understandable in this wretched tangle, Forrest realized as he stared at the cottage, was his lusty response to her extraordinary charms. And while that attraction might be understandable, its intensity was still shocking. He was not a man given to deep, intense stirrings of any sort.

That evening, when the cottage was filled with the rosy light of sunset, Forrest and his uncle sat down to eat and again asked Tamsin to join them. Warily, she approached the table. But when Forrest offered her a bowl containing a steaming, lumpy liquid, she drew back.

"It smells like something ... dead," she said, wrinkling her nose.

Forrest put down his spoon and leveled a sardonic stare at her. "I apologize for the cuisine, your grace, but this bit of sparrow stew is all—"

"Sparrow?" she gasped. "You mean, there is a sparrow in there?"

"Strictly speaking, no. It's quail," he responded tightly. "Don't tell me you dislike quail."

"I like quail very much ... alive." She pushed back the bowl and looked a bit queasy. "I'll just have a sip of dew and a bit of nectar, thank you."

Forrest dropped his spoon in his bowl and swallowed hard. "Nectar?"

"Or just wheat kernels. Or even a few pine nuts." She felt the weight of their stares. "All right ... roots. Just give me a clover root and I'll be happy."

"That's what you eat?" he demanded, his tolerance wearing thin. "When you're hungry you just go out and pull up a clover root?"

"We don't use fire to burn our food, like you. And we certainly don't eat other creatures," she said with a shiver, glancing toward the cook pot. "We don't worry about food—we eat whatever is available. Are you sure you don't have any walnuts or acorns? Or how about just plain pollen?"

He seized on her mention of a food he recognized. "You spoke of wheat. Well, bread is just baked wheat. Have some." He tore a chunk from the round loaf.

"What is in it?" she demanded, eyeing it suspiciously.

"Wheat flour, yeast, salt ... no *creatures*, I assure you," he said irritably.

She accepted, sniffed it, and tested it against her tongue. Deciding it was edible, she pulled off a piece and popped it in her mouth. It was surprisingly tasty. As soon as she had devoured it, he thrust a larger piece into her hands. When she looked up, her cheeks were so stuffed that she looked like a chipmunk. He handed her a cup of water and she swallowed hard, took a sip, then swallowed again.

"Slow down," Forrest cautioned. "How about some honey to go on that bread?"

"Honey? You have *honey*?" Her heart stopped. Her eyes widened. "Where?"

Forrest left the table to rummage about in the shelves and came back with a small crock. She watched him open it and dip a spoonful of precious golden liquid onto a piece of bread. When he held it out to her, she couldn't speak, her mouth was watering so. Quivering with awe, she closed her eyes, and sank her teeth into it. A visible shudder of ecstasy radiated through her.

She had another piece, then another, and still another. Her whole frame quivered with delight each time she took a bite. It was several minutes before she came to her senses and realized she was sitting cross-legged in the middle of the table, staring gluttonously into a dwindling honey pot. When she looked up, Forrest's strange expression caused an inexplicable flush of heat in her cheeks.

"We don't get honey very often," she explained, sensing that she had trespassed some boundary of human conduct. "The bees are nearly as big as we are, and they're so ill tempered and always on guard at their hives. Honey is our favorite food, you know." Her eyes drifted longingly to the crock. "But we never get to have it unless a bear or badger wrecks a bee tree and the honey spills out. That's when we pick berries and, with the honey, make ambrosia. Then we have a feast and a special dance . . . and all the young sprites and nymphs head for the lilies. . . ."

She slid one finger around the sides of the crock, then licked the gooey sweetness from it. "It tastes even better than I remembered," she said, with a groan and a blissful smile. "It's magic."

She was the magic, Forrest thought, watching her

with a hunger that rivaled her own, savoring her unthinkable pose and her impish appearance. Clad in his oversized clothes, surrounded by a cloud of white-blond hair, and sitting cross-legged on the tabletop . . . she could indeed have been a quixotic fairy. He'd never seen a grown woman behave in such an outlandish manner, yet her total lack of regard for etiquette wasn't in the least offensive. He found himself staring raptly as she licked her fingers . . . those long, luxurious strokes of her tongue . . . those shivers of unabashed delight. He'd never known a woman to take such physical pleasure from food. His thoughts began to run wild with imaginings of how her mouth would taste just now . . . soft and fragrant, saturated with honey . . . and how she would react to the more volatile stimulation of a kiss.

Grovenor's voice banished those unworthy musings. "Never seen the like . . . sittin' on a table, eating honey with her fingers. That's a fairy lass for you." The old man had been watching him watch Tamsin. "I warn you, boy, that twitchit is trouble. Got magic in her fingers, lies on her lips, and female tricks in her eyes."

"I have not," Tamsin protested, sliding from the tabletop. A calculating glint appeared in her eye, and she wriggled her fingers at the old man. He shrank back so sharply that he nearly toppled from his stool. "My fingers are just fingers. It's a fairy's wings that contain her magic." She leaned closer to him, causing him to lurch to his feet. "Give me back my wings, old man, and I'll show you what they can do."

Grovenor fidgeted and paced, deciding.

"Wait just a minute." Forrest was around the table in an instant, sending her skittering back several steps. "Earlier you said you had no magic, that your

wings weren't fully grown . . . or some such thing."
He folded his arms across his chest and looked
down his nose at her.

"Sure enough, you did!" Grovenor blurted out,
rescued by Forrest's memory for details. "It's a fairy
trick, that's what. See here, you little twitchit, I ain't
fallin' for your shams and flamming." He squared
his shoulders and smoothed his coat. "I'll be takin'
to my bed now, and when I wake up"—he shook a
gnarled finger at her—"it had better be in my own
palace."

Forrest watched his uncle stride into his sleeping
room, and gave a groan of frustration. The old
man's delusions were as entrenched and persistent
as young Tamsin's. Forrest had a brief and dismal
vision of himself trying to explain all this to a
country-bred constable, over his uncle's mad pro-
testations. Fairies and wings and wishes and
abduction of a defenseless young female—even
without the more titillating elements of nakedness
and beauty, it would still make one hell of a scandal. And in the wake of Forrest's public jilting, the
last thing he needed was to be linked to a debacle
involving insanity, licentiousness, and the meta-
physical! He was going to have to resolve this
mess on his own!

When he turned to Tamsin, he found her staring
at the door with a scowl of uncertainty. "Come,
Tamsin"—he tried to exert a bit of civility—"I'll
show you where you'll sleep."

Deep in the night, Forrest tossed and turned on
his pallet by the hearth. His sleep was disturbed by
fitful images of white-blond hair, shapely legs, and
petulant lips covered with honey. He had given his
bed in the loft to Tamsin and had reserved only two
blankets for himself to soften the hard floor. Fatigue

had dragged him into restless sleep, and when the noise reached his ears, it took a few moments for it to register. The creak of hinges finally penetrated his mind, startling him awake. A blast of cool air surged across the floor, then all was still and dark again.

He sprang up, his heart pounding, and stared at the cottage door. Someone had gone outside. Tamsin! He rushed upstairs to the loft and by the meager light coming through the small window, found her bed empty.

She had waited for him and his uncle to fall asleep, then waltzed right past him. He raced back downstairs, fumbling with his braces, hopping on one foot then the other while trying to tie his shoes. He didn't have time for a coat; he had to catch her before she got too far into the forest and was lost. Praying she had the sense to stay on or near the path, he rushed outside. Despite the heat generated by his running, the chilled night air quickly cooled the fine cotton shirt he wore. All he could think about was how icy and lifeless she had been when his uncle brought her home the night before.

The forest thickened and the deepening leaf canopy filtered the moonlight so that the path was dappled in a silver glow. Around him were the night sounds of the forest . . . the trickling-water sound of leaves stirring overhead, the hoot of distant owls, and the dull thud of his own footfalls. He strained to see and occasionally stopped to listen. Was she fleeing into the forest? Had she taken this path? Just as he was about to give in to doubt, he spotted something lying in the middle of the path ahead.

Reaching it, he found it was a heap of cloth and held it up in the patchy light. His own trousers. They were proof she had come this way. He raced down the narrowing path. When he came to what appeared to be a fork in the path, he groaned with frustration and halted. The sight of something bright lying on one of the paths ahead helped him choose, and he soon found himself holding the shirt he had given her to wear. She was out here naked, in the chill and rising damp.

He pressed on with his lungs burning and his brow beaded with icy sweat, until he came to a small, stump-littered clearing. He paused to survey the spot and glimpsed something in motion, off to one side. It was sleek, softly curved, silvery—*her*! He ducked into the undergrowth, and crept steadily from tree to tree, stalking her as she searched for something in the grass.

"Argo? Hespera? Vandross? Melanchor? Are you there? Please come out—it's me!" Tamsin called softly. "Artemis? Talia? Don't you know me?"

When she heard no response, she stooped and ran her hands through the tall growth, looking for the trampled rings that were left in the grass after a fairy dance. If this was the right meadow, she should certainly find one. But nothing seemed familiar, and she straightened and looked around the clearing, comparing what she saw with what she remembered of where her band lived. Her home had seemed much larger and she didn't remember these stumps. Then it occurred to her that humans always had difficulty seeing fairies. Now that she was as big as a human, perhaps she would have trouble also.

A branch snapped behind her and she turned as quickly as her size-slowed reflexes allowed. Out of the tree shadows, a human figure lunged straight at her. In an instant, that blur of light and dark and onrushing heat coalesced. Forrest! Before she could bolt, his hands closed on her arms and brought her up short.

"Nooo!" She squirmed frantically, but he

wrapped an arm around her waist and hoisted her off her feet. "Put me down!"

"So you can run away again? Not on a bet." He carried her wriggling form toward the trees at the far edge of the clearing. "What in heaven's name do you think you're doing—running stark naked about the countryside in the dead of night?"

"I had to get away—I had to look for my home!" Where his arm was clamped tightly around her, she felt intense heat rushing through her body. "Ohhh— let go—your hands feel like fire!"

"Only because you feel like ice." He stopped at the edge of the trees and set her on her feet at the base of a craggy old oak. "Stay here." And he moved a few steps away to retrieve something from a nearby bush. Recovering, she started to dart away, but Forrest Reed was fast for a human. In a twinkle, she found herself pinned against a tree trunk by his very determined body. Breathing hard, he held up his shirt in one hand. "Put it on."

"Please let me go," she said, going perfectly still.

"I do not intend to spend another night rubbing life back into your frozen hide! I damn near got a case of frostbite. Put it on, or I'll do it for you."

It took a moment for the words to register in her mind. He had warmed her with his hands. She looked at the hand that held the shirt, remembering the sight of it . . . the long, supple fingers, their sinewy flexing, the warmth that radiated from them. It was the heat of his hands that had caused her to grow. The thought worked a spell on her.

Her senses opened. Suddenly she could feel the rhythm of his heart as it thudded against her breast, the heat that poured through his clothes, and the powerful tension in his body as it strained toward her. Her skin was tingling and there was a puddle of warmth in her middle that grew with each second he remained against her.

"You're cold, Tamsin," he said, staring down into her eyes.

"Fairies are always cold," she said softly, staring up into his. "I was perfectly fine until you warmed me and made me grow. That must be why it hurts when you touch me. . . . "

"That's the most preposterous thing I've ever heard." He swallowed hard, struggling to keep his gaze from drifting lower. "I'm touching you now. Are you in pain?"

As they stood there, bodies touching, eyes engaged, she felt his heat transforming into tantalizing ripples of pleasure that spread all through her, awakening every part of her to his presence.

"No," she said in a wondering whisper. "Your body isn't as hot as your hands."

"Oh?" He raised his other hand and brought it to her shoulder, where it hovered just above her skin for a long moment. She could feel its heat, an inch away . . . gentle, radiant heat, permeating her skin. "Does this hurt?"

It felt wonderful. And wicked. So deliciously wicked. She shouldn't enjoy it like this, she thought. It would probably get her into mountains of trouble. When she shook her head, he lowered his hand to her shoulder. She flinched and gasped at the fiery sensation. He drew away, but after a moment's confusion, he took a deep breath and laid his hand back on her bare shoulder.

Once the initial shock of his touch had passed, the fire in her skin damped and the ripples of pleasure she had felt collected into a torrent of sensual delight, flowing through her, engulfing her senses, sweeping away all resistance. Her anxiety receded, replaced by a new tension of expectation. Instantly, he dropped the clothes he held and lowered his other hand to her other shoulder. Her tension melted into a sigh as the wave of discomfort passed, and her body softened, welcoming his touch.

He watched her eyes as the shadows and moonlight danced across her face. He felt the warming, the surrender of her body against his, and knew he should end that contact. He should button her delectable charms out of sight, and pretend he had never run his hands along her smooth shoulders, never felt her cool breasts molding against his ribs. But—Lord!—she was soft and sweet and her eyes were full of sensual wonder, the same overpowering sense of discovery he himself was feeling. There, in the moonlight, with the perfume of the moist earth filling his senses and the urgency of spring pulsing in his blood, it wasn't possible to resist his hunger for sensual contact with her.

The night slowly claimed him. The soft, enveloping darkness was another world, another lifetime, and in its thrall he became another man. The tensions coiled inside him loosened as wave after wave of perception bathed his starved senses.

The silvery glow of her hair in the darkness, the glistening of her eyes, the honeyed fragrance of her breath; together they intoxicated him. Reeling with the effects of her presence, he lowered his head toward her mouth. She whimpered in alarm, but he was too close and too enmeshed in anticipation to stop.

When his mouth touched hers, they both felt the fire dancing through their lips . . . hot, quixotic, unexpected . . . painfully sweet. He felt her shock in the stiffness of her response; it matched his own confusion. But quickly the fire subsided, leaving a sinuous burning that could only be soothed by stronger contact. Tilting his head, he fitted his mouth to hers, seeking out the curves and moist slopes that he had long since explored with his eyes. She was so warm and soft that he couldn't help sinking his arms around her, pulling her closer, covering her bare back with his hands.

A sultry fog rose at the edges of her senses, preventing the intrusion of reason. All she could think or feel was that marvelous heat and the startling feeling of his mouth caressing hers. On impulse, she laid her hands on his sides and slid them to his back. He was lean and hard and for some reason that pleased her. It was some time before she felt him pulling away.

Forrest had a devil of a time focusing his eyes and an even worse time jarring his wits back into operation. He was a single vibrating mass of nerves and impulses . . . all of which seemed to be out of his control. His blood was roaring in his head, his loins were heavy and aching, his mouth burned, and he felt a little drunk. The sight of Tamsin's dazed face brought him partway to his senses. He stumbled back and the sight of her bare breasts gave the rest of his mental functions a swift boot.

"I-I must beg your forgiveness. I have never . . . not in my entire life . . . " He stammered like a schoolboy and dropped his eyes in horror. His gaze fell on the shirt on the ground and he picked it up and drew it around her shoulders. "Here, put this on." As she pushed her arms into the sleeves, he could see she was trembling. Ye gods—what had he done? She had already been driven to the brink of sanity, and here he was pressing himself upon her. It was unforgivable!

Feeling like the lowest cad who ever lived, he helped her button her shirt, slip the trousers back on, and draw the braces up. Embarrassment froze his jaw shut as he led her back to the path. He didn't know where to begin to make it right; he'd never done anything so rash and impulsive in his life.

"Forrest . . ." It was the first time she had spoken his name and it sent an involuntary shiver through him. He paused to look at her. "I honestly can't do any magic. If I could grant your old uncle's wishes, I would, just so I could be free again. Please . . . all I want is to go back home."

In her light eyes, oddly luminous in the moonlight, he glimpsed longing, confusion, and not a little fear. The sight roused his fiercest protective instincts.

"I'll see you get home, Tamsin, I promise you. Come back to the cottage with me tonight and tomorrow I will help you look for your family. I didn't mean to . . . impose upon you. Despite my unthinkable behavior toward you just now, I am a gentleman." He looked down at his hand on her wrist and released her. "I won't touch you again, I swear it."

Tamsin scarcely heard his apology, and wouldn't have thought much about it if she had, for fairies never apologized. Her mind was occupied with other things—his promise to help her find her home, the feel of his lips on hers, and the trembling hungers she was experiencing. And among those strange and wonderful cravings was a rising need for more heat . . . any heat. She was suddenly shivering. It felt like a hot chill, only the other extreme; she was *cold!*

Wrapping her arms around her middle, she felt her teeth begin to chatter and her shoulders begin to quake. By the time they reached the broadening of the path, she was shivering so violently she could scarcely walk. She had never felt anything like it in her life. She wanted Forrest to put his arms around her, to feel his body against hers again, to curl up against his heat. But he had just sworn not to touch her again.

"Cold?" he said. She didn't know whether she

nodded or whether it was just her trembling that made it seem so. Either way, Forrest stepped closer and brushed her cold cheek with his hand. "Lord— you're freezing!"

In a moment he unbuttoned his shirt, pulled it off, and settled it around her shoulders. The warmth of him that still clung to the shirt felt wonderful, and for the moment, she didn't think any farther than that. Fairies seldom did things for others; they had so few needs they couldn't satisfy for themselves, it wasn't necessary. It wasn't until they went on and she stole curious looks at his bare torso that she realized he had folded his arms, just as she had earlier. The thought surprised her: *he was cold*. Why would he give up his shirt to warm her if he was cold?

By the time they made it back to the cottage, they were both chilled to the bone. Forrest stoked the fire in the hearth, took back his shirt, and set about rubbing her bare feet. In the warmth, fatigued from the day's exertions, she grew languid and then drowsy. When Forrest called her name and she didn't respond, he gathered her into his arms and carried her up the loft stairs to her bed.

3

Uncle Grovenor was greatly annoyed, the next morning, to find himself still a grizzled old man, still poor, and still residing in a tumbledown cottage at the edge of a fairy-infested wood. He glowered and rumbled and shook his fist at Tamsin. But she maintained, even by the light of a second day, that she could fulfill his wishes only if he gave back her wings. Declaring that it was some sort of fairy trick, he refused to do so until he got his wishes. Which put them at a total stalemate.

To escape both the tension and the thrall settling over his senses, Forrest made himself presentable and rode into the nearby village of Waincote, hoping to learn the identity of Tamsin's family and gauge how much trouble he and his uncle would face when they returned her to them. He purchased some ready-made garments, slippers, and hair combs from the local shopkeeper and, while selecting his purchases, casually asked if there had been any excitement in the village of late. The disappearance of a rare beauty like Tamsin would surely create a stir in so small a place, he reasoned. But to his surprise, the shopkeeper only sighed and glanced at his dusty cash box.

"There ain't been no excitement in Waincote since they come through recruitin' for the Crusades," he said dolefully.

Desperate for information, Forrest stopped by the local inn and, over coffee and sweet buns, introduced himself and made a similar inquiry. The tavernkeeper proved a jovial, talkative sort who was forthcoming with local gossip—none of which included missing heiresses, runaway daughters, or delusional beauties given to roaming naked through the forest at night.

It was both reassuring and unsettling, for if Tamsin wasn't from the village and no one in the area had reported her missing, who could she be? Forrest pondered that question all the way back to the cottage, but when he opened the door and spotted her huddled on the woodpile with her knees drawn up and her pale hair swirled around her, he felt a guilty relief that she hadn't proved to be a local squire's daughter. She looked impossibly delicate and ethereal in those rough surroundings, and for one tantalizing instant, he had a vision of her with delicate wings and snowflake eyes . . . dancing through moonlit forests and meadows white with frost. . . .

"There you are." His uncle shuffled into his line of sight, carrying an iron skillet that was steaming with something edible. The old man looked him over, then broke into an I-told-you-so grin. "Didn't find her fam'ly, did you?"

"There didn't seem to be any report of a missing girl in the area," Forrest said, recovering control of his meandering thoughts. "But that doesn't mean anything. Her family could be farther away. Or perhaps they've decided to handle it with extreme discretion. A young girl's reputation is a fragile thing, easily bruised." He lifted the packages in his hands. "I did purchase some clothing." He held the paper-wrapped garments out to her. "After we've eaten, I'd like you to put them on."

"*More* clothes?" she said, holding the shirt she wore away from her body with a wince. "But I can't wear any more—I'm about to smother under these!"

Forrest realized she was serious. She was either the most gifted liar or the most pathetically deluded creature he had ever encountered. Either way, he had no business staring at her bare feet and ankles like this. . . .

"You don't wear them *in addition to*," he said, thrusting the package into her hands. "You wear them *in place of*." When she just stared at the package, he untied the string and peeled back the brown wrapping paper. "You can put them on in there." He pointed to his uncle's sleeping room.

She disappeared into the chamber, and as Forrest sat down to eat, he discovered that his uncle had made food for just himself. With a huff of disgust,

Forrest got up and set about fixing something for himself and Tamsin to eat. When the door opened, minutes later, she hung back in the shadows. As he coaxed her forward into the light, Forrest understood why. The blouse hung askew on her bare shoulders; the petticoat was twisted atop her skirt; the skirt hung about her waist, unfastened; and she had the stockings on her arms.

"Good God," Forrest said.

"That's a fairy lass for you—wild as a March hare—" Uncle Grovenor burst into laughter and Tamsin looked down at herself with a tremulous smile.

"This is not the slightest bit amusing, young lady. Now get back in there and arrange your clothing properly." Forrest bustled her back into the sleeping room, but as he turned to go, she grabbed his arm and looked up at him in confusion.

"I wasn't trying to make a joke. I just didn't know how to . . . " After a moment, the distress in her huge blue eyes made him admit she might not be teasing or just being perverse; she really might not recall how the things were meant to be worn. Sobered by that possibility, he showed her how to layer the camisole and petticoat under the blouse and skirt, and helped her start the first stocking rolling up her leg. Then, clearing his tightened throat, he gave her a warning glare and withdrew.

Her seemingly genuine confusion over women's garments and the worry he had glimpsed in her eyes stole his appetite as he waited for her to dress. If she couldn't manage something as simple as clothing, her mental state was far worse than he had imagined. It was imperative that he return her to the bosom of her family as soon as possible. What she needed was something to jog her memory. He determined to take her for a walk along the forest path down which she had led him the night before, hoping she might see something along the way to spark her recollection.

It was some time before she emerged looking presentable. He still had to help her with her hooks and eyes and buttons, and to convince her that slippers were absolutely necessary if she were to go walking outside.

"Outside?" She looked up at him with new hope.

"I said I would help you look for your family, and I'm a man of my word."

"Here—you can't take her outside!" Uncle Grovenor declared, rising through a haze of pipe smoke. "She'll get away! I won't let her go a step 'til I get my three wishes!"

"Don't be absurd, Uncle," Forrest said, taking her by the elbow and steering her out the door. "I promised . . . and I'll be with her the entire time."

Tamsin was blinded by brightness the instant she stepped out into the noonday sun. Never in her life had she experienced anything as overwhelming as the full, unabated light of Old Sol. She blinked and shielded her eyes, torn between her desire for the forest and the comparative comfort of the cottage's dim interior.

"What is it? What's the matter?" Forrest asked.

"It's just so bright. I hadn't imagined . . . " She rubbed her burning eyes and tried to look up at him. Liquid welled in her eyes the way it did when she got pollen directly in them. Forrest shoved his handkerchief in her hands and led her toward the edge of the trees. Once in the shade, she was able to wipe the tears away and look about her. What she saw astonished her.

"The trees!" she cried, turning around and around, staring at the bushes, grass, and up at the trees overhead. "They're so different in the sunlight." She ran along the path, reaching up to touch the leaves that overhung the way. Laughing delightedly, she picked a sun-warmed leaf from a small oak and held it near her face, smelling it, running her fingers over it. Abruptly she turned to Forrest. "What color is this?"

He was taken aback. "Green, of course."

"Green. It's beautiful!" Her smile turned into a bubbling laugh. "I've never seen *green* before—not really. We come out by night and the trees look silver and blue and shadowy. Purple—I've seen purple—and the last lingering red of the sky after Old Sol is safely down. But until now, I've never seen the forest by day!" She hurried down the path, sometimes on her tiptoes, sometimes bending to the ground—looking high and low as she rushed to take it all in. She studied the vines trailing through the leaf litter on the woodland floor, caressed the rough bark and the soft moss that grew on the trees, then tripped on a root and fell onto her knees.

When he ran to help her up, she was clutching a woodland violet. "A violet." She looked up at him, her cheeks flushed, her eyes glowing like patches of midsummer sky. "Do you call it that, too?"

He was speechless; all he could do was nod.

He pulled her to her feet, and she rushed from one side of the path to the other, stroking leaves and pushing aside the shrubby growth to discover the wildflowers below. Windflowers and coltsfoot, wild hyacinth and sweet clover; beeches, ashes, and oaks . . . she had to know the names, the colors, and the words that expressed their smells and fragrances. In all his life, he had never witnessed such joy.

As she explored her new world, her eyes gradually grew accustomed to the light. The forest she knew and loved came alive to her in a new way. The wild hyacinths were a soft, velvety blue, the primroses a rich, creamy yellow, and the bracts of ash blossoms were a tender, new green. Soon she was able to gaze up through the trees at the sky itself. The contrast of the verdant leaves and the pristine blue held her entranced for a time, then she closed her eyes and breathed in deeply. The grasses smelled moist and new, the earth damp, the old leaves musky, and the green herbs tangy.

Her vision, hearing, smell, touch . . . every sense was sharpened and humming with excitation. She wanted to experience it all; to hold it, to wrap herself in it, to let it seep through every inch of her being.

Forrest couldn't take his eyes from her as she rushed into the woods with the raw sensory hunger of an unbridled child. Delight swirled around her like a cloud as she picked wildflowers and scooped up dry leaves and threw them into the air, sending them showering around her. It was as if she was the only person in the world. Eve discovering Eden.

Gradually, the sinuous grace of her movements caused a sympathetic loosening of his tightly held frame. As he followed her rambling course, his stride became more fluid and his shoulders swayed with a subtle new sense of the physical. He drew in each breath a little deeper and saw his surroundings with greater clarity and sensitivity. She brought her woodland treasures to him for naming, and he began to see it all afresh himself, through her discovery.

The sun beat down on the trees overhead as they rambled on and on, across the clearing where he had found her the previous night, and still farther into the woods. She came to walk with him along the path. In the easy silence, she grew acutely aware of her skirts brushing her legs and the movement of her blouse over her breasts. Each step heightened her awareness of her changing body and reminded her she was also awakening to an inner world of sensation that had not been a part of her fairy existence.

"Do you feel what I feel?" she asked, overcome with curiosity. When he paused on the narrow path, she halted and looked back at him. "Everything is so rich and beautiful. Does it make your nose tingle and your eyes feel like they're melting and your fingers itch to touch things?"

"Sometimes," he said quietly, trying to make himself concentrate on why he had brought her here in the first place.

"I never guessed there could be so many lovely colors and smells and textures. Everything in your world is so . . . strong on the senses, so powerful, so . . ."

"Vivid?" he supplied. And because he was as curious about the mystery of her as she seemed to be about the forest, he said, "Tell me about your home and your family."

She smiled wistfully and buried her nose in the flowers she had gathered. "It's always cool and dark and very lovely in its own way. Dewdrops glisten in spring and summer and frost paints lovely patterns on everything in autumn and winter. And it's always merry. We come out just after sunset and look for food and dance and sometimes sit for a story-feast, which is when the elders tell the tales of our folk and of the humans." She stopped and turned to him.

"I thought your hair was as dark as night, but it has an odd reddish glint to it in the sunlight. And your eyes are the colors of the forest itself . . . green and brown mixed with snatches of sunlight." She realized she was staring, but couldn't deny herself the pleasure of looking at him from such close range.

"And your hair is so light," he said softly, afraid

to move lest he betray the intense yearning welling in him. "Right now it looks like sun-kissed snow. I've never seen anything like it."

"You would if you could see the rest of our band. We all have hair this color. And light eyes. And we never get cold, so we don't wear garments like you do." The warmth of him curled and eddied on the air between them, teasing her senses. "The male fairies— sprites—grow beards as they get older. The nymphs—female fairies—grow longer hair and develop a few more curves in their bodies." She looked down at herself, seeming a little dismayed. "Nothing like this, however." She prodded one breast experimentally, scowled, and looked up at him. "Do all human women have these?"

His throat seemed paralyzed for a moment. "They do." His words came out oddly strained. "I believe it is considered a desirable trait."

"It is? Well, it seems to me that they just get in the way—"

"*Tamsin*," he said on a groan, abruptly striking off down the path. "Tell me more. You said you live in a meadow and that you don't plant or reap or spin or weave. It sounds like your family doesn't work." He wondered if that was a clue that they were gentry or just lazy. "What do they do all day?"

"All night, you mean?" she said, hurrying to keep up. "We have fun, of course. We sing and dance and make merry—we all know a lifetime's worth of songs and rhymes. And we count stars and keep track of the seasons. The younger fairies have foot and flying races, train lightning bugs, catch rides on moths, and play tricks on humans. . . . " When he turned a narrow eye on her, she felt her face heat. "That's what got me into trouble. I wanted to snatch a whisker from your uncle's chin and I got too close. He's quick for a human. You are, too."

She frowned and started off again, at a quick pace. "I was quick, too. The quickest fairy in my band. Now I move like a caterpillar on a frosty rock . . . and these skirts you make me wear are partly to blame." She cast him a suspicious look from the corner of her eye. "Are you sure all human women wear them? Or do you just make *me* wear them to slow me down?"

He laughed. "All humans wear clothes, Tamsin," he informed her. "And women wear skirts—at least in civilized countries." He glimpsed a sunny, open area along the path ahead and pointed to it. "I think we're coming to a meadow you might want to investigate."

She came instantly alert, following his gaze with rising excitement. Then she balled her skirts up and out of the way and went running down the path.

When he reached the clearing, he saw her standing in the midst of a meadow full of new spring grasses and early wildflowers. Her face was turned toward the sun and her arms were open wide to embrace the warmth and vitality of the day. He halted at the edge of the glen and watched her turn broad circles and make slow, sensuous pirouettes.

A hot flare of desire shot up his body as she shed her blouse and stepped out of her skirt, wriggling her half-bare shoulders and spinning so that her petticoat furled around her. For that moment she was indeed a woodland nymph, a creature bred of pure light and beauty. His mouth dried, his eyes burned as he stared, unblinking. When she raised the camisole and began pulling it over her head, something inside him launched him into motion.

"Tamsin! What in heaven's name are you doing?" he demanded, running toward her. She turned to him with the camisole half-off, her eyes wide with surprise. "Good God—don't you know that some one—anyone from the village—could happen along that path just now and see you?"

"But it's wonderful," she said, dancing away from his censuring hand. "I can feel the sun . . . like the prick of little quills that melt once they slip inside my skin. Haven't you ever felt it?"

He snatched up her discarded garments. "Tamsin, you cannot just take off your clothes whenever, wherever you please." He pointed to the camisole. "Put that back on!"

She let it fall back into place and watched him come to her, his eyes burning, his body bristling with tension. She sensed that he was trying not to look at her half-clad body, and that his irritation had to do with his desire to do that very thing. An odd sort of pleasure bloomed in her as she looked down at her womanly shape. She must not be too hideous if he wanted to look at her.

When she glanced up, he was standing a pace away, as stiff as a post, holding her garments out to her. His expression was tight and forbidding, but there was a trace of something else in his earthen eyes . . . something empty, something wanting, something that recalled to her the sadness she felt for her home.

"Have you ever felt the sun on your bare body, Forrest Reed?" she asked, ignoring the garments.

"Of course not," he said tersely, shoving them toward her again.

"Have you ever danced without clothes in a sun-drenched meadow? Or lain on a carpet of new violets and watched the clouds drifting past overhead?"

"No." A muscle jumped in his jaw as he clenched his teeth.

"Have you ever worn garments made of rose petals? or gotten drunk on the sight of a new moon? or danced by moonlight to just the music of the stars and the beat of your own heart?"

He didn't move his head, but the tightness around his eyes answered for him.

"Have you ever stood under a bluebell and been showered with sweet, sticky pollen so that you were covered with a layer of gold?" Her voice softened and lowered as she searched the tumult in his face. "Have you ever caught a ride on a nighthawk's back and soared so high you could almost touch the man in the moon?" The hollowness in his eyes seemed to deepen. "Have you ever lain among the sleek, fragrant lilies with your favorite female and made pleasure all night long?" The shake of his head was barely perceptible, but she saw it.

"No? Then what have you done, Forrest Reed?" she whispered.

If she had searched the world, she couldn't have found words with a sharper edge to his heart than that simple question.

He felt suddenly stripped of his defenses . . . vulnerable in a way he had never been before. What had he done? What pleasure had he taken in life . . . or given? There he stood, with his dull and stolid self exposed to the dazzling creature whose vibrance and joy at being alive took his breath. He had never danced in a meadow, naked or otherwise. He had never lain in a field of wildflowers or whiled away an afternoon watching clouds or even gotten roaring drunk and planted a facer on some obnoxious wretch who insulted the queen. Even as a child, he had spent his time in dogged productivity, bending every waking moment toward diligently proving himself. There had been no time for frivolities, no time for the extravagances of joy and surprise and pleasure. There had been only duty, sobriety, and cool approbation from a household of formidably perfect forebears.

With startling clarity, she saw through that breach in his inner wall. Behind his guarded face and hard-set jaw she glimpsed a well of sadness. Something poignant and nameless stirred to life inside her, an overpowering urge to touch him, to dispel that unhappiness. But she had no idea how to go about cheering someone. Fairies never bothered about one another's feelings; a bit of bruised pride or a tremble of annoyance was generally the worst that befell them. All she knew was what made her happy. In the midst of that meadow, under that torrent of sunlight, she reached for his coat.

As it slid over his shoulders, he halted her hands with his.

"Don't you want to feel the sun, Forrest Reed? Don't you want to lie with me in the grass and watch the clouds sail the sea above?" she whispered.

He had never wanted anything more in his entire life. He wanted just once to experience unrestricted and unsanctioned pleasure, to feel the boundless joy he glimpsed in her. He wanted, however briefly, to step out of the dark, narrow cocoon life had spun about him—to let out the man trapped inside it.

With his gaze resting on hers, he abandoned himself to the promise in her eyes and let his hands drop to his sides. She tossed his coat onto the ground and began, however clumsily, to work the buttons of his vest and his shirt. As she pulled his clothes from him, a light appeared in her eyes . . . the same glow they developed when discovering butterflies and blossoming periwinkles.

It was as if he shed a whole life, a whole other being, as she tugged his shirt from him and threw it aside. Self-consciously, he crossed his arms over his chest and she read that gesture with a sympathetic smile. She dragged his arms away and let her gaze travel up his tight stomach, study the light furring on his chest, and linger wonderingly on the taut mounds that sloped and spread across his shoulders.

"Why, you're beautiful," she said with artless delight. The glow in her eyes made him know it was no empty flattery. "Why would you ever want to cover yourself up with clothes?"

He made a rumbling sound that gradually grew into a full chuckle. "God, the things you say to me. . . . " His chest seemed to redden and when she looked up, his face was crimson. She liked the effect. It was so warm, so *human*.

"Feel it—the sun!" she said, turning her face up to it. "See how warm it is . . . how it touches you all over, like a caress."

He *did* feel it. It *was* like a caress. And if he closed his eyes, he could imagine it was her hand and that it reached all the way into his thawing heart. He didn't resist when she took him by the wrist and pulled him into motion.

She led him around the meadow, stopping here and there to whirl about with her arms extended. After a bit of coaxing, he tried it and found it made him as dizzy as a coot. But when she laughed and urged him on, he found himself smiling sheepishly and trying again. Each time it got a little better, and soon the world spun by in a brilliant blur of green and gold and warmth and life.

When he finally stopped, the one point in his world that wasn't careening was Tamsin. She pulled him along with her as she ran, picked flowers, watched butterflies, and stood listening to the birds with her eyes closed. Through her wonder he began to discover the beauty that was crammed into even the smallest and most unassuming corners of nature.

After a while she located a knoll covered with new

grass and pulled him down on it with her. They lay side by side, drenched with warm sun, watching meadowlarks swooping overhead. She told him of the night birds that fairies dreaded and those which were known to be friendly. Then she described some of the members of her band by name and by nature. Stories came tumbling out; outrageous, amusing, and astonishing tales of a world far different from his own. As her vivid descriptions unfolded, he began to picture her make-believe world ... the cool palette of the night's colors, the silver rays of the full moon, the ephemeral lace of frost in autumn, the drone of the sultry summer nights, the exhilaration of winged flight.

He raised onto one elbow to watch her face as she spoke. The soft redolence of new grass and damp earth filled his head and wound its way into his blood. Lying there in the grass, her sun-gilded hair spread around her, her shoulders and breasts bare beneath the thin muslin, her face aglow ... she was earth and passion personified. He touched her cheek and trailed his hand down her nose, across her lips, along her throat.

She opened her eyes to find him looking at her with a strange new heat in his gaze. His fingertips were leaving a trail of heat down the center of her chest and across her garment. Oddly, the cloth did not inhibit her sensation, only changed it as his fingers glided across her breast and traced tantalizing circles around its tightly budded tip. It was a purposeful, knowing touch, meant to stimulate.

A low flame ignited in her taut nipple, like nothing she'd ever felt before. It both burned and itched ... demanding a firmer touch to soothe it. As she shifted her shoulders, he sensed what she wanted and spread his hand over her burning flesh, closing his fingers gently around her. But his touch only drove the flame inward, sending it skittering along her nerves, trickling through her body to places she hadn't realized existed within her. Suddenly her whole body was alive and clamoring for the feel of his big, warm hands.

The memory of the night rose in her as his mouth descended on hers, and she wrapped her arms around his shoulders, claiming him and the wild storm of sensation that engulfed her.

Nothing in her fairy world had prepared her for this full and devastating assault upon her senses. Fairy pleasures were a cool, pale reflection of that which she now experienced in the human world. Every motion, every touch contained the intensity of a hundred fairy caresses. Her whole body began to tremble with both anticipation, desire, and a trace of fear. His hands slid with exquisite tenderness over her breasts, her waist, her hips, her thighs, and soon, there wasn't a part of her that wasn't sighing with both satisfaction and desire. She moaned softly against his mouth and his echo of response hummed through her head and heart.

He found the sensitive area at the side of her neck and felt her shiver with response as he nibbled along it to her ear. Closing his eyes, he brushed her hair back, suckled her earlobe, and swirled her ear with his tongue. She squirmed and giggled as she tried to remain still, wanting that intimate contact and yet scarcely able to bear it.

"It tickles," she gasped, trying not to disrupt those delicious feelings.

"It does, does it?" he murmured into her ear, so that she giggled again. "It's an old human trick. Very effective." His tongue probed the curve of her ear and an odd sensation surfaced in his mind, causing him to open his eyes.

The pale pink and perfect ear he had been nibbling came to a gentle but unmistakable *point*. He stared at it, his eyes widening. As the impact of it washed through him, he tried not to move or do anything that would alarm Tamsin. But she felt the reaction building in his body and pushed him back to look at him. The shock in his expression caused a corresponding tension in her.

"What happened?" she asked, biting her lip. "Did I do something wrong?"

"No," he uttered, telling himself it could be just a coincidence. A lot of people were born with an odd ear or finger or mark on their skin. She turned her head toward him and he saw the lower half of her other ear. On impulse, he swept back her hair, and found himself looking at another delicate and shockingly pointed ear. It was no oddity of birth; it was a matched set!

"What is the matter, Forrest?" she demanded, watching him sit up and back, staring at her. Anxiety gripped her and she sat up, too. "Tell me."

"Your ears, they're . . . " He made a pinching motion with his thumb and finger.

"Pointed?" She smiled with relief. "Of course they are, I'm a fairy. And yours are rounded." She reached up to stroke the top of his ear. "From what I've seen, it's the only real difference between us and humans." Then she looked down at her changed body and felt her face heat strangely. "Every other difference seems to be just a matter of size . . . or proportion. We fairies don't have so many unwieldy curves and bumps. But then, our skin and our bodies aren't nearly as sensitive, either." She shivered, then looked up at him through her lashes and ran a finger over the still-tingling tip of her breast. "You know, I think I like the way these feel. They may be worth the trouble they cause getting in the way, after all."

"Tamsin!" Forrest gave a short, astonished laugh,

unsure whether he should be outraged or amused. She had such an irreverent way of looking at things . . . a knack for reducing things to their simplest and most unpretentious terms. In her eyes he could see the reflection of the bright meadow, the fascinating promise of the world beyond, and the irresistible joy that permeated every fiber of her being as she encountered them. For a moment, he could almost believe she was a fairy . . . that she had magic in her fingers and enchantment in her eyes . . . that she danced with Jack Frost on cold nights and rode soaring nighthawks past the face of the moon.

"Who are you?" he asked quietly, stroking her cheek.

"I'm Tamsin," she said just as softly. "For good or for ill, I've told you the truth, Forrest Reed. All I want to do is—" She halted and looked down.

"Go home. You want to go home, to your meadow," he supplied.

She thought about it for a moment. Home. Of course, she wanted to go back to her meadow, her folk. But now she also wanted . . . She looked up at him and her eyes caught on his mouth. She wanted to feel all the marvelous things Forrest made her feel. And she couldn't do both.

"Would you kiss me again?" she said, looking urgently into his face.

It wasn't right or proper. She wasn't in possession of her full faculties and he wasn't in possession of even a small portion of his self-control. But there was nothing he wanted more than the feel of her warm, fragrant mouth beneath his. And so he kissed her . . . softly, drawing her to him . . . then harder, wrapping her in his arms.

4

Grovenor came charging down the path, his coat flapping and his brow knitted with righteous indignation. He knew every meadow in those woods and by late afternoon had already visited half of them ... searching for his know-it-all nephew and his uncooperative fairy prize. When he spotted the patch of bright sun ahead, he quickened his step to a near run. And as the path emerged from the trees, he stumbled to a halt, scouring the landscape and settling with growing horror on the spectacle of Forrest and his stubborn little fairy on their knees in the middle of the meadow ... pressed tighter together than pages in a book and kissing for all they were worth!

"Forrest Tredwell Reed!" He was halfway across the clearing when the couple broke apart and Forrest lurched to his feet. "What in hell's fire do you think you're doin', boy?" Grovenor demanded as he stopped a few paces away, holding his side. "Have you lost every last scrap of your wits ... kissin' a fairy lass? Don't you know if you give in to her wiles, she'll steal your soul? That's what fairies do, boy. They take human hearts for trinkets." He jabbed a gnarled finger at Tamsin, who scowled and shrank behind Forrest's shoulder. "And Lord knows how many hearts that fancy little piece already has on a string!"

"Uncle, this is none of your affair," Forrest declared, with as much dignity as he could muster while standing half-naked in the middle of an open field. He brought a hand up to shield himself from the old man's burning stare, but the movement only drew attention to his shirtless chest. The old man scrutinized Forrest's bare shoulders, Tamsin's camisole and petticoat, and the pair's kiss-reddened lips, and he groaned aloud, as if in pain.

Seizing Forrest and dragging him a distance away, he turned their backs to Tamsin. "Ye didn't *know* 'er yet, did you? In the biblical way, I mean," he demanded. Forrest tried to pull away, but Grovenor held on. "Didn't take 'er to yer loins, did you?"

"Of course not!" Forrest said, reddening at the thought of just how far things might have gone if his uncle hadn't arrived.

"That's a mercy," Grovenor said with relief. Then he shot a warning glare at Forrest. "Listen, boy, no human can bed a fairy without losin' his heart. You'd be hers forever after . . . pinin' for her the rest of your days . . . wanderin' the woods by night, callin' her name. You got to keep yer wits about you, boy . . . an' keep yer breeches buttoned tight."

Forrest stared speechlessly at the wild-eyed old man. Grovenor Tredwell was a walking, breathing lesson in the perils that awaited those who fell into the clutches of demon rum, he realized. The combination of his uncle's continual immersion in strong drink and self-imposed isolation had finally sent him over the edge. And it was a sad comment on his own behavior that drink-maddened old Grovenor was lecturing *him* on prudence and restraint!

With his conscience aflame, he jerked his arm free and strode back to retrieve his clothing. As he and Tamsin dressed, the sight of her lowered eyes and trembling hands afflicted him. How could he have taken advantage of her distracted and vulnerable state? She clearly wasn't responsible. And that meant he would have to be doubly so. With each step they took on the path back to Grovenor's cottage, he vowed anew to protect her from his uncle's irrational demands, from his own weakness for her, and from her own irresistible discovery of her desires.

When they reached the cottage Forrest thought to ask Tamsin if anything about the meadow had looked familiar. She shook her head. "I didn't see a valley of lilies or a fairy ring in the grass. And there is always a fairy ring after we dance." He released the breath he had been holding and, with a defiant glance at Grovenor, declared that they would try again tomorrow.

As the evening drew on, Grovenor's thirst grew and he became agitated in the extreme. He generally spent his nights at the village tavern, guzzling his way to the bottom of a tankard of ale or a bottle of rum. He licked his parched lips and thought of that pale golden brew . . . then saw the looks that passed between his nephew and his reluctant captive and made himself think of the misfortune that might befall if he left them alone together. He paced and snorted and complained about the supper Forrest assembled.

Forrest handed him an iron skillet and told him to do better. After a long, heated stare, Grovenor snatched the pan and set to work. When they sat down to eat, the food was surprisingly tasty. It was the first time Grovenor had done anything for anyone except himself in years.

The next day, they traipsed along woodland paths, through vales and along stream banks, looking for Tamsin's meadow. Grovenor had refused to allow them to go without him, and since he claimed to know every foot of the forest for miles around, Forrest reluctantly agreed.

It might have been an enjoyable outing, except for Grovenor's incessant reminders of Tamsin's obligation to provide him with a palace, a fortune, and a second youth, and the fact that he insisted on bringing Boxer with him. The hound raced around the woods, digging, barking, and generally disrupting the sylvan serenity. Worse, he watched Tamsin with canine fascination and took every opportunity to investigate her at closer range. She had to stay on guard and within reach of Forrest's protection. Grovenor observed her reaction to the dog with vengeful satisfaction, knowing that she wouldn't try to escape if there was a chance that Boxer would come after her.

Under those less than auspicious circumstances, they located several small timber clearings and another meadow, none of which looked familiar to Tamsin. As each location failed to yield a fabled "fairy ring" in the grass or to stir her memory otherwise, Tamsin sank farther into silence. To draw her out, Foorrest asked questions about her home and volunteered information about human ways—especially marriageable young ladies—and about the world at large. Whenever they got too close or touched, Grovenor inserted himself between them and gave Forrest a warning look.

It was probably just as well that Grovenor behaved so possessively, Forrest told himself when they returned to the cottage that evening. He had virtually no resistance to Tamsin's charms. But when Grovenor began to complain again about the food, Forrest couldn't stop himself from suggesting the old man hie himself back to the tavern and stuff himself in a rum barrel.

Tamsin felt a compelling urge to do something about the sparks flying between Forrest and the old man. It was a curious impulse, for fairies didn't usually concern themselves with others' altercations. Live and let live—that was the fairy way. But when she saw them coming nose-to-nose, chins set and fists clenched, she bounded up from her seat on the settle.

"I'll fix the food," she declared, before she had given thought to what her offer entailed. Both men stared at her as if she had lost her mind, and she frowned, puzzled herself. "Well, I've watched both of you, and I think I could do it."

Shamed by her willingness, they grudgingly agreed to each prepare part of the supper. As they worked, she tagged along and asked questions about human food and the ways it was produced. Grains, fruits, vegetables, and even roots, she could understand, but animal products simply boggled her mind.

"Let me see if I understand," she said as she sat at the table later, staring at a brick of pungent cheese. "You steal milk from a big, hairy, dirty cow. Then you scrape off the thick scum that forms on the top . . . you put the rest in a crock and let it sit until it curdles. Then you squeeze it dry and pack it away in dark holes in the ground until it gets ever so stinky. And then you eat it."

"That pretty much sums it up," Forrest said, cutting off a slab of pale yellow cheese and taking a bite.

She made an incredulous face. "That's the second most disgusting thing I've ever heard. Second only to eating floating bits of dead quail."

"Then I don't suppose you're ready to hear what the French branch of humankind do with snails," Forrest said with a grin.

"They eat snails?" She choked on a mouthful of bread. "But some of my best friends are snails!"

Grovenor and Forrest both howled.

Culinary differences aside, they spent a relatively peaceable night and resumed their search for Tamsin's meadow the next morning. Midday, Tamsin stood in the last secluded meadow in that half of the county and sighed with indecision. It seemed a bit familiar, but she couldn't be sure whether it seemed similar to her home or just to all the other clearings she had seen of late. By the time they returned home, she was feeling panicky.

She was becoming so entrenched in the human world with its intensity and sensation that her memories of her fairy world were beginning to have a distant and unreal quality to them. She stood in the cottage doorway, thinking of all she had seen and felt . . . pleasure, embarrassment, the need to please another, the desire to help and to learn and to give something of herself. She thought of sunlight and honey and of clothes riding softly against her body. She thought of the new tastes and smells and colors . . . and of the stories Forrest had told her of the world outside the woods she called home. There was so much more to learn and to explore in the human world. And heaven help her, she wanted to learn more, do more, experience more.

She tried not to let it, but the thought came anyway: Now that she had seen and been a part of this big, vibrant human world, how could she possibly give it up?

Forrest watched her distress as she wrestled with her thoughts and he realized it was time to take more drastic measures toward recovering her identity. He decided to escort her into the village the next morning and introduce her to some of the local folk. Perhaps she would see someone she recognized, or perhaps someone would recognize her. It went against his every impulse—voluntarily risking the possibility that he might have to turn her over to a family of total strangers—but he knew it was the right and decent thing to do.

Through the long night that followed, he reviewed their time together, trying to set the memories forever in his mind. And the next morning, as he helped brush her hair and pin it up with the combs he had bought, he was devastated by the thought that by evening she might be back with her family, and he might not see her or her lovely hair ever again.

The village of Waincote was a sleepy, picturesque collection of old stone and half-timbered dwellings, built along a wide main street. There were not more than forty or so houses, a town hall and a mill, a mercantile, a tavern, a bakery, a smithy, and a fortresslike stone church that dated from the time of Charles I. From atop a rise overlooking the village, the houses and their neat little gardens looked like children's blocks lined up in wobbly rows. A lush green line through the heart of the village proved to be a meandering stream with banks lined with trees and spring greenery.

To Tamsin it seemed like a treasure trove, filled with wonders and curiosities waiting to be discovered. Not even a harrowing welcome from a select committee of the local hounds was enough to dim her enthusiasm. Her heart beat fast as Forrest walked her down the dusty main thoroughfare and explained what the various buildings and houses were, and the tasks the various merchants and tradesmen performed for the people of the village.

She stared unabashedly at the cottages and shop fronts and the people going in and out of them. "All these people are your clan? They don't look very much like you."

"No, they're not my clan. In fact, they're not a *clan*

at all . . . nor a single band of humans." He laughed and placed her hand in the crook of his elbow, trapping it there to pull her discreetly along. "They come from many different families."

"Families?" she said, ogling a fellow with carrot red hair. "What's that?"

Forrest paused to look at her, and again found the same artless curiosity that never failed to both disarm and worry him. She honestly didn't seem to recall the basic unit of all human society. "A family is a group of people who are related to one another, either by blood—like parents and their children—or by marriage—like men and women who marry. Indeed, that's usually how it gets started: a man and woman marry and live together and they have children."

"Babies, you mean?" she asked, suddenly all attention. When he nodded, a light appeared in her face. "So men and women do this 'marry' to get babies?"

"Actually they marry in order to live together in the same house and share the same bed . . . and babies just usually factor into the equation somewhere along the line."

Her eyes flew wide. It had never occurred to her that he might already be bound to a woman somewhere. The thought was reflected in her face well before it came out her mouth: "Did you marry with someone? Do you have babies?"

"No." He straightened and looked around them uncomfortably, adding on impulse, "Not that I haven't tried." He pointed down the street. "We'll start there."

Forrest took her first to the mercantile, where she touched and sniffed and fondled the merchandise until the shopkeeper stared at her with bewilderment, but no recognition. Then he escorted her to the tavern and introduced her to the tavernkeeper, whom he had met a few days before. Again, no recognition. The miller, several village matrons, the village carpenter, and even the vicar greeted them and politely exchanged introductions . . . with no more than admiring glances for the lovely young woman with the white-blond hair and stunning blue eyes.

Scrutinizing the villagers' reaction to her, Forrest didn't know whether to be heartened or dismayed. For a moment he wondered if her plain clothing might have kept her from being recognized. But as he covertly assessed her demure white blouse and dark wool skirt, he decided that not even the dowdiest of clothes could disguise her beauty. She would be unforgettable wearing a burlap bag. He was left with the conclusion that she simply wasn't from Waincote or anywhere in the vicinity.

They were ready to leave the village when Tamsin stopped in the middle of a sentence and in the middle of the main street to stare at a white-haired woman who had just emerged from the mercantile shop. The old woman was hatless, which in itself was odd for a village matron, and her bountiful hair shone in the sunlight. As she paused to shift the shopping basket on her arm, Tamsin stiffened with recognition, then bolted toward her.

"Aunt Clytie?" she called excitedly.

The woman turned to face Tamsin with a shocked look. Tamsin halted breathlessly in front of her and searched both her memory and the old woman's gently lined and bespectacled face.

"Aunt Clytie—it is you—it has to be! Don't you know me?" She jiggled her hands anxiously, desperate to touch the old woman and make sure she was real. "It's me—Tamsin—your niece!"

Forrest arrived at their side just as the old woman drew back and sputtered with confusion. "I-I beg your pardon, young woman. I haven't the slightest notion what you are talking about."

"You're my Aunt Clytie—remember—from the band in the meadow. You used to tell us stories and teach us to dance with all of the other fa—"

"Your aunt?" The old lady seemed taken aback and glanced around them. "I fear you are mistaken, miss. To my recollection, I've never set eyes on you in my life."

"B-but Aunt Clytie, it's me—and I have to talk to you." Tamsin wrung her hands then seized the handle of the old lady's basket. "See? Our hair is exactly the same color—"

"Madam please—I beg your indulgence." Forrest intervened, wrapping an arm around Tamsin to pull her back a pace, then interposing himself between them. "I am Forrest Reed, of the London law firm of Sterling, Torrence, Darcy, and Reed. I am visiting my uncle, Grovenor Tredwell, who has a cottage at the edge of the forest. Fate has temporarily cast this young woman, Tamsin, into my uncle's charge. You see, some days ago, she suffered a terrible mishap, and since then she has been unable to recall her name or anything about her family. I implore you, if you know her identity or the whereabouts of her home, please tell us."

He held his breath as the old lady straightened her spectacles and employed them to give Tamsin a good looking over. What she saw knitted her brow into a fine web of lines and she shook her head sadly.

"Lost her memory?" The old woman clucked her tongue. "Poor, lovely creature. I wish I could help you, sir. But truly, I don't know who she is, or where her family might be found." Then she addressed Tamsin. "I am sorry about your misfortune, young woman, but I am not your 'Aunt Clytie.' My name is Cleona Harris and I have lived in this village for many years." She reached out to touch Tamsin's hand reassuringly. "I wish you well, my dear. Such a dreadful thing to lose one's memories." A sad smile appeared on her gentle face. "At my age, memories are the most precious things one has."

Forrest thanked her and tipped his hat as she went on her way. They watched her walk down the lane, then Forrest glanced about them and ushered Tamsin into the lane, heading in the opposite direction. When they reached the edge of the village, he found her looking utterly dispirited.

"I'm sorry, Tamsin," he said, slipping an arm about her waist to support her.

"It was her, I know it was," she declared softly. "But she didn't recognize me. Why?" She looked up at him. "Have I changed so much? Am I so horrible?"

"No, sweetheart," he said, tightening his arm in as much of an embrace as he dared give her. "You're beautiful. She just wasn't who you thought she was. Perhaps you have an Aunt Clytie who looks something like her. It's a stroke of luck if you've remembered that. Can you remember anything more?"

She pushed against him to put space between them and scowled at him. "You still think I'm daft. Well, I'm not. Aunt Clytie used to be a fairy, just like me. She was my aunt and she taught me dances and songs, just like the other elders." She halted and looked back down the slope to the village. "And she was the one who told me about human hea—"

His fingers on her lips stopped her, and when she looked up he had a "solicitor" glint in his eye and grim determination in the set of his jaw. "Tamsin, you have to stop thinking and talking about such stuff. Mrs. Harris is not your fairy aunt. You heard her; she's lived here all her life. And if you go about accusing people of being escaped fairies, people really will think you are daft! Enough of this fairy talk. I'll hear no more of it! It's time you began to deal with the world as it is, misfortunes and all." He took her by the hand to pull her along, but she jerked free.

"You don't believe me at all, do you? You think I've made it all up." The accusation in her beautiful eyes wrenched his heart. "You've never believed me. And you never will." When he didn't deny it, she tucked her arms tightly around her waist and walked on with her head lowered.

He watched the rounding of her shoulders and the forlorn dragging of her skirt tail, and released a heavy sigh. What was he going to do with her?

When Uncle Grovenor learned of the encounter with Cleona Harris, he laughed and said he wished he'd been there to see it. Tamsin didn't see the humor in it, and refused to speak to either of them for the rest of the evening. As the evening fire was lighted, Forrest made several overtures to Tamsin, hoping to put the strain behind them. Each time, she gave him a baleful, accusing look and turned away. Grovenor watched between them and felt a tug of dismay that the boy seemed to be suffering on account of her withdrawal. An air of injury mixed with cold disdain was an old female recipe for male torture, he knew, and it was doubly effective when employed by a fairy.

When Forrest stepped outside to put his horse into the pole shed for the night, Grovenor followed him.

"I told you, boy, don't go wearin' yer heart on yer sleeve," he said earnestly, taking Forrest by the arm. "She'll take it and break it before you can say 'Jack Sauce.' "

Forrest's silence and the deepening look of misery

on his face jolted Grovenor and he released Forrest as if afraid of being contaminated. "It's already too late, ain't it? She already got to you." He drew a deep, ragged breath. "Sly little twitchit. Well, there's nothing for it now except to keep as far from her as ye can. And whatever you do, boy, don't go slakin' your thirst at her trough."

"Why, you—" Forrest seized Grovenor by the shirt, thrusting his face into the old man's grizzled countenance. Then with a growl that was part fury, part frustration, he abruptly released his uncle. "Mind your own damned business." And he strode off to cool his temper in the night air.

The next afternoon, Grovenor went off into the woods, ostensibly to pick mushrooms, and Forrest decided to bathe in the stream that ran through the woods, since Grovenor didn't have a tub and he needed time and solitude to do some thinking. After some deliberation, they decided to leave Tamsin alone in the cottage, with Boxer standing guard outside.

For a time, she busied herself with glancing at a few aged picture books and journals Grovenor had tucked away in the loft. But she soon grew tired of looking at them without anyone to interpret them for her. Thinking of Forrest, she grew restless and warm and began to develop an ache in her stomach. Telling herself it was probably just hunger, she went downstairs and stood beside the pantry shelves, looking at the pots and deciding to do something about it. If Forrest and his disagreeable old uncle could cook food to eat, so could she.

She stoked the fire to a blaze, and mixed flour, dried apples, and some of the oil they kept in a crock. She settled a frying pan over the iron grate in the hearth and poured in the lumpy batter, as she had seen old Grovenor do several times. But the fire was too high. A flame traveled up some oil that had dribbled down the side of the pan, and soon the contents of the pan were ablaze. Horrified, she bashed at the flames with a spoon, but it was no good. In a panic she tipped the pan over into the coals and her lone attempt at "cooking" went up in flames. The cottage quickly filled with smoke from the burning food and sent her reeling for the door.

Coughing and wiping her stinging eyes as she stumbled into the weedy yard, she scarcely noticed the beady brown eyes trained on her . . . or the erect ears . . . or the quivering nose. When she looked up, Boxer was bearing down on her at a run and her heart stopped. A second later, she snatched up her skirts and ran for the only haven she knew—the woods.

She made it to the first rank of trees just ahead of his gaping jaws, and managed to grab a low-hanging branch, jump, and boost herself up. She didn't stop climbing until she was at least ten feet off the ground. Boxer tried to race up the tree after her, but quickly dropped back to all fours and pranced back and forth . . . barking and baying as if he had treed some rare game.

She hung on to the trunk, feeling dizzy and breathless and weak with relief. But after a few moments she realized she was stuck there, with treacherous old Boxer at her feet, until either Forrest or Uncle Grovenor returned. She lowered herself to a seat on a limb, dusted the bark from her skirt, and tried to sooth her scraped hands. Just as she was settling in for a long wait, she heard someone calling her name.

"Tamsin!"

She looked down, then around her, seeing no one. The voice wasn't Uncle Grovenor's or Forrest's.

When it came again she realized it had a feminine pitch. She changed position and looked down again through the leaves, and there was a patch of white bobbing around in the limbs below.

"Tamsin! Are you there, little nymph?" came the voice from a now recognizable white head. Tamsin's jaw dropped as the climber paused and located her through the leaves with a smile. It was the woman from the village, climbing up into the tree after her.

"You!" Tamsin blinked and rubbed her eyes. "It *is* you! Oh, I knew it was you, Aunt Clytie!" she cried, her heart soaring with happiness. And as quickly as they could manage it, balancing on branches, they gave each other a huge, joyful hug.

"But why didn't you say something in the village yesterday?" Tamsin asked, as her lingering hurt surfaced. "I knew it was you, but you claimed not even to know me."

"I am sorry about that. I had to, Tamsin, dear," Clytie said, settling on a secure limb opposite her. "It's of the utmost importance that no one know of our . . . origins. People have such strange and awful notions about fairies that if you or anyone else spread it about that I used to be one—well, they would probably think I was a mad old woman and lock me up somewhere."

"You mean no one knows you are—*were* a fairy?" Then the full import of what Clytie had said struck Tamsin and she gasped. "You mean you're not a fairy anymore?"

Her aunt shook her head with a rueful smile. "Not anymore, I'm afraid. I'm as human as anyone else in the village." She gave Tamsin a thorough looking-over. "And you are too, unless I miss my guess. Or you will be, soon."

"I am?" Tamsin tightened her grip on the tree as the shock of the thought caused her to sway. *Human*.

"What do you mean: I will be soon? Am I really turning into a human?"

Clytie nodded. "You got caught by a human, no doubt. That's the way it always starts." When Tamsin nodded, Aunt Clytie smiled. "It's the heat that does it, you know. The more they touch you, the more you grow . . . until you're a full human size. Who was it that caught you, the young man you were with yesterday?"

"No, it was his uncle, Grovenor," Tamsin said. "The cranky old toad thinks I can make wishes come true and he refuses to give me back my wings until I grant his three wishes."

"See there!" Clytie nodded and shook a righteous finger. "That's exactly what I mean by humans having ridiculous notions about—" She halted and cocked her head quizzically. "He did *what* to your wings?"

"Pulled them off and hid them. And he won't give them back."

Clytie began to laugh so hard that she nearly fell off her perch. "Oh, no, dear. He didn't pull off your wings. You've still got them. You simply grew around them."

"I did?" Tamsin twisted and arched her back to see over her shoulder. "Then where are they? I can't see or feel them."

"They're there," Clytie said, taking her hand. "Here, feel this." She turned her back and placed Tamsin's hand on what on a regular human would be a shoulder blade. "Feel that bony ridge? That is the outer ridge of our wings. I know because I was awake when I began to change, and I saw them disappearing into my back as I grew." She smiled softly. "Our wings are still there, Tamsin. And always will be. There will always be a fairy self inside us . . . no matter how human we become."

No matter how human we become. Tamsin smiled wistfully. "Tell me, Auntie, can we go home?"

Clytie sighed and patted her hands. "We can, though it's not an easy thing and can only be done on the first full moon after we've changed. All this growing and stretching is quite a strain on the body, and to have to shrink again . . . it would be very hard." She looked off through the leaves. "If you decide to go back, you must know that it's final, and must be sure that it is what you want to do."

"How would I do it if I decide it's what I want?" Tamsin asked in hushed tones.

"You have to go back to the meadow and find the great circle and join the dance . . . during the next full moon. The only magic we truly have is in the dance . . . and in the dust of our wings. The others can shower you with their dust to make it easier, but it's up to you to dance yourself small again." She searched her niece's uncertain expression. "Do you really want to go back?"

"I—" Tamsin looked down. "I don't know. At first I did, but now . . . "

Clytie read a great deal in the faint pink that came into Tamsin's cheeks. "Ahhh. So it's the man, is it?"

Tamsin would have protested, but the look of understanding in her aunt's face stopped her. She blushed fiercely. "How did you know?"

"Why do you think I stayed? It was a man, of course. A lovely man. A man who warmed and loved me. I married him and had four babies with him. They're all grown now and have lives of their own. My husband died three years ago and it's hard to go on without him. But I wouldn't change all that happened, even if I could." She roused from her memories and grasped Tamsin's hands. "But you must decide for yourself. We all had to."

"*We all?* You mean there are more of us?"

"A few. Brindal, now Brian the Baker, fell in love with a human girl when she came to bathe in our stream one night. And there is Deirdre, wife of the miller, and of course, there's old Rosemount." She laughed. "I think he fell in love with fire as much as he did Matilda. He became the village blacksmith." Tamsin's jaw dropped.

"Rosemount? Hespera's Uncle Rosemount?"

"The very one. Hespera has been scaring the children for years with that awful story." Clytie sighed. "But it has its uses. It keeps young fairies from getting too close to humans and getting into real trouble."

They sat for a few moments, enjoying the silence, then a noise came from below and Clytie stirred and declared that she had to leave. She hugged Tamsin and began to climb down. She was halfway down before Tamsin heard the low, menacing growl and remembered Boxer.

"Auntie—wait! There's a dog—" Frantically she began to climb down as well, calling to warn her aunt. But before Tamsin's horrified gaze, the old lady dropped gracefully to the earth, straight into the big hound's path. "*Auntie!*"

Clytie stood motionless, seeming frozen as the hound slowed and crouched, getting ready to spring. But when Boxer came within heart-stopping range, Clytie planted her hands on her hips and gave him a stare that caused him to halt in his tracks.

"You wretched little beast," she declared, looking him straight in the eye. "Growl at me, will you? Just who do you think you're dealing with?" And before Tamsin's widened eyes, she lunged at the dog and gave him a sharp rap on the end of his nose.

Boxer drew back in confusion. She gave him a second good smack on the nose, for good measure, and he yelped, then tucked his tail and ran. With a pleased laugh, Clytie looked up through the branches to Tamsin's shocked face.

"If you decide to stay a human, my dear, you'll have to learn to deal with dogs. It beats me what humans see in the awful creatures." With a wink and a merry wave, she slipped off through the woods, bound for the village.

When Tamsin climbed down out of the tree, she watched old Boxer coming for her and stood her ground exactly as Clytie had done . . . except that her heart was beating in her throat. By the time Forrest returned to the cottage, there was a much-changed relationship between Tamsin and the dog. When he asked what had happened, Tamsin looked at Boxer with a secretive smile and announced:

"I just discovered I have a knack for dealing with dogs."

Tamsin's fear of canines wasn't all that had changed in a few hours, Forrest learned that evening. As they sat at the supper table, eating a meal that Tamsin had helped prepare, she pinned Grovenor with a sharp look and took him to task.

"You lied to me, Whiskers," she said calmly.

Grovenor lowered his spoon. "I don't know what you mean."

"My wings—you said you'd give them back to me. But you can't because you don't have them. You never did."

"Well, I . . . I . . . "

"Lying is a low and despicable thing, Grovenor Tredwell. I told you the truth: I don't have any wish magic. But if I did, I certainly wouldn't give any wishes to you. You know, you could stand to take a lesson or two from your nephew in that regard. He might not believe I'm a fairy, but at least he's never lied to me." She glanced at Forrest, whose expression was warming by the moment. "I appreciate your honesty, Forrest. And someday, I hope to make you appreciate mine.''

That night, as Tamsin bade Forrest good sleep and climbed the steps to the loft, her thoughts were awhirl. She had a choice to make, one that would shape the rest of her life for good or for ill. And that choice was between two worlds; one cool and familiar and utterly predictable, and the other warm and vibrant and sometimes frightening. As she settled into her narrow bed and watched the moonlight streaming in through the small window, she understood that as much as she loved the enthralling sensations, wonders, and discoveries of the human world, her choice would ultimately depend on just one thing: Forrest Reed.

She would be content to stay in the human world if she knew Forrest wanted her, if she knew she could live with him and be his mate and the partner of his life. Aunt Clytie had married a human and had children with him. Though the exact processes for such events were still something of a mystery to her, she understood that they had to do with the powerful feelings Forrest caused in her body and with the pleasures and intimacy they shared. It was enough for her to know she wanted him.

But did Forrest want her? Or did he think of her as a hopelessly deluded young woman who only needed his help? She had to know. And in the depths of the night, in the quiet of her bed, she recalled the heady warmth of his kisses and the sweet urgency of his body straining against hers, and she understood that there was only one way to find out.

5

The next morning, bright and early, Tamsin asked Forrest to teach her to read. "If I'm stuck being a human, then I may as well learn the things humans have to learn."

Forrest found it incredible that she had forgotten something so fundamental as reading, but he decided to humor her. He searched out old books and magazines in the loft and soon discovered he had to begin with the very basics, the alphabet. She worked diligently at it and by early afternoon was able to recognize all of the letters and the sounds they made. It would have amazed him . . . if he didn't believe she was simply recovering knowledge she already had.

Grovenor sat watching them with his arms folded and his face frowning, growing thirstier and more annoyed with each "W-X-Y and Z." The incessant repetition finally drove him to his feet and, once there, he grabbed his hat and declared he was going into the village. With a meaningful look at Forrest, he announced he would be back by nightfall and departed, with Boxer trotting at his heels.

Tamsin and Forrest halted their lessons for luncheon, and when they resumed, Tamsin made it a point to "happen upon" a picture she had seen before in one of the books . . . a landscape portraying a high mountain meadow. She gasped and held up the book, staring at the picture as if struck to the very heart by something about it.

"What is it?" Forrest asked.

"It's . . . it's . . . " She closed her eyes and squinted, as if focusing all her energy on some mental process. "It's so close. I can almost remember . . . "

"Remember what?" He came to the edge of his seat, leaning toward her, searching her face as she agonized with the effort of recollection. "What is it? What do you remember?" He glanced at the picture. "Mountains? A field? A house?"

She nodded with her eyes still closed, then lowered the book. "A meadow." She opened her eyes suddenly. "I remember the meadow now! One of the ones we saw—the one near the stream! Oh, Forrest, I have to go there—I have to see it!"

In moments they were out the door and on the path into the woods. At his insistence she periodically closed her eyes to try to recall more. But her "recollections" always came back to that meadow, and it was soon clear to Forrest that the answers to the puzzle of who she was and what had happened to her would only be unlocked with whatever key that little patch of ground might provide.

They soon passed the wood-clearing where he had caught her that first night, then came to the meadow where they had whiled away that wondrous afternoon. In search of the key to her memory, they pressed on, crossing a stream on a fallen log, scrambling up a hillock, then leaving the beaten path to search the deer trails old Grovenor had shown them.

It was early evening when they reached the meadow and she began to explore with genuine eagerness. Stopping to listen, she could hear the stream in the distance, and after a time she located an outcropping of rock that once had seemed as big as a mountain to her. The grasses were higher than she had expected, and that gave everything a different appearance. Slowly, she reoriented and took her bearings, walking back and forth, blending her fairy recollections with her new human perspective. After a time, she came to the far edge of the meadow, where, in the dense shade, she spotted a wide, inviting bed of lilies of the valley . . . in full bloom.

And she knew beyond all doubt that she was home.

"The lilies!" she cried, picking her way carefully to the middle of that bed of glossy emerald leaves. "This is it . . . my home. This is where my band lives, Forrest, I'm certain of it."

His heart sank. "Still *fairies*, Tamsin? I thought you were remembering your real family, your *real* life."

"But this is my real family, my real life," she said, coming toward him. "And I can prove it. If this is my home, then there will be a fairy ring in the grass, somewhere over there, in front of that small mound and beside that huge log." She smiled in a way that made his body feel as if it had been stroked. "Go look. See for yourself."

His common sense screamed for him to refuse, to turn on his heel and take her straight back to the cottage. She was obviously beyond his help and he was obviously out of his depth in dealing with her. He should have admitted it that first day and gone for a physician or to the local vicar for help. But it was too late now. He was in well over his head, and the proof was the fact that he was doing exactly what she asked.

Intending to show both her and himself that there was no fairy ring, he followed her gaze across the meadow. Methodically and with all the care that had marked his years as a scrupulous and trustworthy solicitor, he strode from side to side, moving the grasses with his feet and occasionally bending to examine things more carefully.

Under the edge of the trees he spotted the mound

she spoke of, and soon located the log off to one side. As he approached them, he noticed an abrupt end to the taller grass and looked down. There, at his feet, was a circular ring of well-trampled and withered grass, nearly three feet in diameter. He stood staring at it with slow-dawning recognition, unable to move or speak.

"Did you find it?" she said breathlessly, rushing to join him. She looked down at it with a beaming face. "There it is. I knew it was here."

Indeed, it was just as she had said. A ring. A *fairy ring* in the grass. He looked up to find her taking down her hair and shaking it around her shoulders with a triumphant smile.

"There is a bit of trampled grass, I admit," he said thickly, "but it could have been made by anything. An animal or some plant blight," he said, trying to explain it to himself. "Sometimes grass roots get eaten by moles and give an odd appearance above ground . . . or lightning strikes and runs along under the ground . . . "

"It is *not* caused by blight or moles or lightning," she said in soft but determined tones. "It's caused by dancing feet. My feet. I danced here, again and again, with my folk." She raised her chin and narrowed her eyes. "Forrest, this is where I grew up and learned to fly and sing and dance and tell stories. . . . And I can prove it."

He read the flint in her resolve and sensed that the time to settle it once and for all had finally come. "How?"

"Stay with me, here, into the night," she said, sliding closer, looking up at him with an expression that was part invitation, part challenge. "When the moon shines, my folk will come out to dance. You'll see them with your own two eyes."

Stay with her, here . . . in this beautiful, flower-strewn meadow . . . watching the sun go down and the moon rise. But when he looked into her up-turned face and her summer sky eyes, he knew he was no match for the combined persuasions of her irresistible charm and his overwhelming desire for her. If they stayed, things were certain to get more complicated.

If they stayed, he realized, there was also a chance he could prove to her, once and for all, that there was no fairy band. And with any luck, tomorrow morning they could finally get on with the healing of her mind and heart . . . and finding her rightful place in the real world.

Tamsin sensed the arguments, for and against, being weighed in his mind. She could read every careful and responsible thought he was having. And she experienced an overpowering feeling of warmth for him. He was so logical and solid . . . so *human*.

In the end, it was not the logic or the hope of reason, or the possible proof of anything that decided his mind. It was the inexpressible tenderness in her eyes and the irresistible promise of feeling between them. His rigid shoulders melted under her warm gaze and he nodded.

"Very well. I'll give you this night, in this meadow, to prove that you're a fairy."

She burst into a smile that radiated through every pore in her body. She positively glowed as she slipped her hand through his and drew him along.

"What are you doing?" He resisted halfheartedly. "Where are we going?"

"To the stream," she said. When he insisted on knowing why, she laughed and gave him a flirtatious look. "It will be a while before the sun goes down. How long has it been, Forrest Reed, since you frolicked in a stream?"

"Never."

"*Never* is too long," she decreed, tugging on his hand to start him moving again.

Before long they were at the grassy bank of a small, clear stream that tumbled over a channel of rocks. She coaxed him out of his shoes and stockings and knelt by his feet to roll up his trouser legs. He watched her removing her shoes and stockings, and felt a ripple of sensual interest slide through his body. He stiffened, fighting it, but was too late. When she hiked up her skirts and tucked them into her waist, baring her long, elegant legs, not even the bracing cold of the stream could quell the heat rising in him.

She teased and played, splashing about, and began to tell him outrageous tales of vain and greedy trout who came to bad ends and of turtle wars that went on for eons because the messengers carrying the news of surrender were too slow. She regaled him with stories of bats who jousted like champions of old in the skies overhead; of tricks ferrets played on badgers, over and over, without the badgers ever getting wise; and of nearsighted hedgehogs who injured themselves in courting mishaps. She was regal and mischievous and comical. By turns, she actually became plodding turtles, chittering rodents, and impassioned hedgehogs.

He laughed as he watched her performing for his delight, and he felt his heart opening wider as he fell deeper under her spell. And in that moment, with the setting sun splattering the sky with color, he honestly didn't care what tomorrow brought. He only wanted this time with her.

When the water finally got too cold, she retreated up the bank to her shoes and plopped down beside them, declaring that it was his turn to tell her some stories.

The chill that slowly claimed him had nothing to

do with the freezing water swirling around his shins. *Stories.* He had none. He couldn't even recall any from his childhood. "Fairy stories" weren't permitted in his nursery and schoolroom; they weren't considered "improving" for a young boy's developing mind. He honestly hadn't thought about it until now . . . now when he needed a fairy tale or an amusing story, now when he wanted to give the girl he loved something to make her smile.

Never in his life had he felt so plain and dull and lacking . . . or so deeply and painfully ashamed.

"I—I would rather listen to you," he said, with a new stiffness in his tone. There was tension in his movements as he stepped out of the water and walked up the bank.

She watched him balancing on first one leg, then the other, as he unrolled his trousers and used them to dry his legs. Then he began to pull on his stockings and shoes, methodically, mechanically. He was locking himself away from her.

"Come, now. Just one story." She pushed to her feet and swayed toward him, letting her skirts down and smoothing them into place. "You laughed at mine; you owe me one in return. Fair is fair, Forrest Reed."

"I fail to see how my laughing at your stories places me in your debt," he uttered, kneeling to avoid her and jerking the laces of his shoes. "I know of no law that says a man must repay in kind every bit of laughter he manages to enjoy."

She studied his reddening ears and the stubborn set of his mouth. "Well then . . . it doesn't have to be a funny story. Tell me a story of any kind. I know . . . tell me about a princess and a dragon." She sank onto the grass beside him and tried to intercept his gaze. He wouldn't allow it and shifted away from her to tie his other shoe.

"I am afraid I haven't a dragon story to my name," he said tersely. "Nor a princess story . . . nor a young-man-goes-to-sea story . . . much less anything about cute little animals doing absurd things to one another."

"That's ridiculous," she said, alarmed at the way her plan to coax him into revealing and acting on his feelings was failing so miserably. "Everybody has stories—even humans."

"Well, not *this* human!" he ground out. His face came up red and his eyes were burning like hot coals. The shock in her expression spurred him to lash out again, in the painful expectation that if he told the truth, it would build a barrier between them that would protect them both.

"I don't have any stories because I don't have any imagination," he declared. "I never have had. I cannot dance except by numbers, I cannot make social small talk past 'lovely weather we're having,' and I haven't got a single story to my name. I am, in short, the dullest and most boring man on the face of the earth. I am so insipid, in fact, that my fiancée couldn't bear the thought of spending her life with me and threw me over not long ago." Seeing the flicker of confusion in her eyes, he gritted his teeth and made it excruciatingly clear: "The woman I was going to marry, *the incomparable Adele Barstow*, refused to have me . . . said I was as dull as ditchwater, as stiff as a shirtboard, and an insufferable dry stick."

He leaned close, bringing his heated, hard-set face within an inch of hers. She could almost hear the crackle of the flame in his eyes.

"And you know what?" he said grimly. "She was *right*."

In the second that followed, he waited for her to flinch, to gasp, to withdraw, or just to wilt in the face of his pugnacious dreariness. He saw her hands coming up and braced himself, expecting a shove or a resounding slap. What he got was a great deal worse.

She took his face squarely between her hands and *kissed* him. Full on the mouth. Lips soft and insistent. Tongue sleek and stroking. As if she had been waiting days for it. And when he came to his senses and tried to pull away, she wouldn't let him.

She held him there, on his hands and knees, his head caught in her possessive embrace, and his mouth captive to the irresistible hunger and persuasion of hers. She caressed and licked and nibbled and stroked his lips . . . drawing the hurt and shame from him as if they were poison. And when she sank back onto the grass, she took him with her.

His body melted over hers, heated and softened like his heart . . . warm clay awaiting her hands. Somewhere in the press of lips and the shift and rasp of bodies, he felt her touch on his heart, and it was as if she had dragged a magic wand across his soul. Inch by wondrous inch, he was reborn. And he began to return the joy and passion she had just given him.

His lips began to weave a tactile spell on hers, back and forth, stroking, laving, nipping. His hands began to move over her body . . . soothing, fondling, raking, gliding . . . varying each stroke, creating new sensations for her with each motion. It was like music played along her skin so that its echoes penetrated her sinews and resonated in the deepest core of her. And to that complex symphony of movement he gradually added the undulations of his body against hers . . . finding her sensitive hollows, grazing her tingling mounds, moving over and against her like a loving tide.

"Now," she said, dragging her mouth from his

and locking her fingers in his soft hair to make him look at her. "No man who makes pleasures like this can ever be called dull or uninteresting, my big, hot human." She looked into his eyes. "You have stories inside you and I'll prove it to you. Stories start with pieces. Tell me . . . who is the stingiest man you know?"

He sighed against her cheek and, because he couldn't deny her anything at that moment, reached deep inside him for that recollection. "I suppose that would be a banker I know named Cordell Frick. He's so tight he won't sneeze for fear of giving someone his cold."

"And who is the greediest woman?" she wanted to know, her eyes twinkling. He thought a moment. "I suppose that honor would have to go to Mariette DuPont . . . they've reserved a whole section in the churchyard for her dear departed husbands. Her motto seems to be: *no cash too cold, no husband too old.*"

"And what happened when Cordell and Mariette got married?"

"Married?" he said, nibbling the side of her neck. "They're not married."

She smiled. "No, but wouldn't it be fun if they were? And in your mind they can be. In your mind you can make anything happen. Tell me . . . "

Halfway through the story he spun from the whole cloth of his mind—surprising himself with inventive turns of phrase and diabolical twists of plot—he found himself lying on the ground beside her, grinning. And she was laughing. Suddenly he understood that she was teaching him, freeing him. She must have read his mind just then, for she sobered and looked at him with pleasure-filled eyes.

"I had to learn, too . . . we all have to learn to tell stories. Our elders tell them to us as children and we begin by telling them to one another, practicing. Eventually, we begin to make up our own stories."

"I never had stories," he said, shifting his gaze to some place long ago and far away. Her heart ached as echoes of old pain crept into his voice and face. "I never heard them. And I suppose there was no one to retell them to if I had." He shook his head at whatever he was seeing in the distant past and returned to the present and her sympathetic gaze. "There were no fairies in my world."

"Well, there is one now, Forrest Reed," she said, sitting up. "Me. And I think it's long past time for you to have a little magic." She rolled onto her knees before him and shook her hair around her. It was then, seeing her hair shimmering like liquid silver, that he realized night had fallen and the moon was rising over the tree tops. He sat up too, thinking that there was more than a little magic in her laugh, in her looks, and in her loving. She could make him believe almost anything in the moonlight, even that there was hope for a hopelessly dull and unimaginative solicitor.

"I told you fairies have a small bit of magic, and that our magic is in our wings," she said. "Actually it is *on* our wings. A fine powder collects on them over time—dust and old dew and who knows what. If we rake it off and blow it in a creature's eyes, we create all sorts of wonderful sights and sounds. Want to see?"

He nodded, going along with her make-believe, knowing that the truest magic in the world was what was occurring in his blood as he watched her rise to her feet and begin to unbutton her blouse. He knew he should stop her, but the best he could do was to ask her what she thought she was doing.

"I cannot reach my wings with all these clothes on," she said, swaying back toward the meadow, dropping her blouse along the way. By the time he shot to his feet, she was standing in full moonlight, her camisole in her hand. Her thick hair streamed over her shoulders like a cloak and shortly, he saw her skirts sliding down her legs. She stepped over them and came to him wearing nothing but a bewitching smile.

Putting her hand behind her back, she raked her shoulder blade as if it were one of her wings, then she brought her hand up between them and gently blew from her palm into his face. The puff of warm breath made his eyes close in reflex action.

When he opened them again, he saw moonlight radiating from her hair like a halo. Looking up, he could see a vivid, multicolored rainbow around the moon, and when he looked down he saw dew glistening like tiny diamonds on the grass at his feet. He choked out an astonished laugh.

"What is this? Some kind of trick?" He rubbed his eyes and looked again. He saw rainbows and sparkles all around and Tamsin's eyes glistening as she laughed.

"Of course. An old fairy trick. Effective, eh?"

He was speechless. He held his hands up and they seemed to be gilded along the edges. It was like looking at the entire world through a many-sided crystal . . . all prismatics and rainbows and incidental light. He felt something tugging at his coat and knew it was she. He let her pull it from him, then his vest and shirt. The feel of trousers sliding startled him back to his senses and he whirled to find her standing behind him with a wondering look on her face.

"Your back!" She made him turn partway so she could see it again, and she ran her fingers down his shoulder blades. "Forrest, there are wings inside you somewhere—I can feel the edges of them!"

He threw back his head and began to laugh . . . a wonderful booming mirth. Pulling her to him, he wrapped her in his arms so that she could share the soul-massaging vibration of his laughter. "So you think I'm a fairy too, now? Well, maybe I am tonight. Maybe I'll dance naked in the moonlight. Maybe I'll fly across the face of the moon. Or maybe I'll just love you with all the passion and the joy my body holds . . . for I do love you with all that is in my heart."

She pushed back in his arms. "What did you say?" The hopeful tumult of her desire for him was visible in her face.

"I believe I just said, 'I love you,' Tamsin," he said. "I know it makes no sense. I tried not to let it happen. But God help me—I've never been happier in my life than I am at this moment. I love you, Tamsin Whoever-you-are. And I don't care if you're a fairy or a madwoman or an agent of France. I want you . . . with every part of my dull, uninspiring, prosaic being."

"Oh, Forrest," she said softly, a strange tangle of emotions welling in her. This was what she had wanted, needed to hear. It was what she had brought him here to learn. He wanted her. In that moment, in the meadow where she had lived and grown as a child of nature, her decision to remain in the human world was made. She blinked and blinked again, having difficulty clearing the haze from her vision.

"I love you, too."

Joy erupted between them as he took her in his arms and whirled her around and around. Then, because it was the best way she knew to express joy, she stayed in his arms and with her hands on his waist began to move, pulling him into a slow, sweet spiral of movement that gradually widened and broadened.

Reading her movements in her eyes, he followed . . . self-consciously at first, then more smoothly, letting the subtle rhythms of the deepening night invade his blood and sinew, letting his heart lead him. He took her skill, her grace and gave back his strength, his willingness, and his need. In wide, sweeping arcs they circled the meadow, waltzing in moon-silvered splendor. And in the dance, the joining of their pleasure and their hearts was completed. They moved and became as one.

The moon crested the sky as they completed the circle and came to rest in the middle of the bed of lilies, kissing deeply, sharing breath and pulse and the preludes of passion. She lay back on the glossy leaves, luxuriating in the familiar perfume that had always meant pleasure to her, knowing that hereafter, it would always mean Forrest to her. She absorbed the warmth of his hands, collected the nuances of his movements, then returned them to him with loving ministrations of her own.

Their bodies gleamed in the dappled moonlight as they kissed and caressed with slow, sinuous motions. And in joining their bodies they joined all nature in the cyclic movements of love and creation. It was a discovery, a fulfillment, a breathtaking glimpse of paradise on earth. Their moans of pleasure stirred the leaves and ruffled the grasses and found resonance in the fertile earth itself.

Afterward, they curled in each other's arms, sharing warmth and words and kisses of comfort filled with promise. And when they slept, the benevolent old trees overhead sheltered them from the cool sigh of the night breeze and kept gentle watch over their newborn love.

* * *

The effects of the night magic carried into the next morning, surrounding them even as they shivered into their garments and washed their faces in the cold stream. Forrest straightened his shoulders and his coat, feeling the enchantment still swirling through his blood. And when he helped Tamsin tidy her hair and catch it up with combs, he saw strands of iridescent light in it.

Yet, he was fully back to his senses in other ways. He looked at the meadow as they paused at the head of the path. "There was no fairy dance, Tamsin," he said a bit ruefully.

"Are you quite sure?" she said with a twinkle in her eye.

He thought a moment, then laughed. "No, I suppose not."

He didn't fully understand what had happened to him, but explanations didn't seem to matter anymore. What was clear was that it had produced a lingering effect. His stride was more relaxed and assured, his body seemed to work effortlessly, and pulsing through his veins and coiled in his sinews was a new sense of vitality and enjoyment of life.

When they returned to Grovenor's cottage, the old man stared at them, speechless. The glow of their faces and their new physical ease with each other made it clear that something momentous had happened. It didn't take a mind reader to know what that something was.

His nephew, he realized with horror, was a changed man. Forrest hummed as he shaved that morning, smiled constantly, and whistled as he set about making them a meal. There was a new lightness in his step, a new sway in his shoulders, and a fierce glow in his eyes. All through their midday meal, Forrest couldn't stop talking. Story after story came tumbling out, as if they had been bottled up inside him for years. His gestures were broad and expansive, and the magnetism in his countenance held Grovenor so spellbound that for a time he forgot to eat.

And the fairy lass—there was a change in her as well. Tamsin seemed blissfully happy and was rosy from head to toes. Her skirts swished as she walked, her movements were no longer quick and coltish, but strong and womanly, and she radiated satisfaction . . . especially when her gaze turned on Forrest. She listened to his every word, caressed him openly with her eyes, and couldn't wait to be near him, even just to help clear away the supper dishes. Grovenor had never seen a more beautiful creature in his life.

Or a more dangerous one, he realized, coming out of his trance.

"See here, ye—the both of ye!" he declared, standing in the middle of the cottage, hoisting his trousers determinedly about his waist. "I can see what's happened—it's plain as the nose on my face. But I'm here to tell ye, yer in for heartache, sure enough. Ye danced—an' now ye'll pay for it. Mark my word."

Forrest answered with an expression that contained both pity and indulgence, then turned back to the dishes and Tamsin's smile. Seeing that his lecture went unheeded, Grovenor went from worried to indignant. "It ain't right. It just ain't right," he said, stomping out and calling Boxer to accompany him into the woods. But the dog just stood, watching between him and Tamsin and Forrest, who came to the doorway. When Boxer trotted back to squeeze between Forrest's trouser leg and Tamsin's skirts, Grovenor muttered a curse at the dog's betrayal and disappeared into the trees.

For the next two days, bliss and misery dwelled side by side in Grovenor Tredwell's cottage. Tamsin and Forrest spent every waking moment together, walking hand in hand, sharing reading lessons, doing simple chores, and exploring every blissful aspect of their burgeoning new love. Grovenor watched each day until he could bear it no longer, then hied himself into the woods. But even there, images of their happiness haunted him, and in the solitude they began slowly to work a softening in his calcified heart.

Tamsin rose early on the third morning of her new life, helped to prepare breakfast, then saw Forrest off to the village on his horse. He had decided it was time they enlarged her wardrobe, so that she would be presentable when he began to introduce her in the village and accustom her to life among her "fellow humans." She declined to accompany him, preferring to spend time in the woods . . . intending to pick gooseberries and prepare Forrest a sweet surprise for supper that evening.

Setting off, she relished using her new senses in her old home. She found the thicket and nibbled as she picked berries, enjoying every scent, every sunbeam. Midday, as the warmth grew, she stretched out on a huge, moss-covered rock and like a contented kitten, drifted off to sleep.

Forrest arrived at the cottage just after noon with an armful of bundles containing every garment which might fit Tamsin, that the shop in Waincote had stocked. It wasn't a wardrobe befitting the wealth and status she would someday enjoy as his wife, but he thought it would do until they returned to London and she could choose the finest silks and velvets money could buy.

He called for her, looked inside and outside the cottage, and even checked the nearby trees. Boxer was gone as well and he guessed that Tamsin must have gone for a walk. Intent on surprising her, he opened several of the packages and spread out their contents on her bed in the loft. Then he removed his coat and vest and prepared a meal. He was just sitting down to eat when he heard footsteps and hurried out the door to greet her.

But it wasn't footsteps at all; it was the thudding hooves of a cart horse on the grassy road. And in the cart, peering out at him from beneath a large, exquisitely feathered yellow hat, was a pair of extravagant brown eyes he had never expected to see again.

6

"Hello, Forrest," Adele Barstow said with a perfect blend of audacity and contrition. When the cart stopped, she extended her gloved hand to him, anticipating that he would help her down. For a moment he stood frozen, staring at her beautiful face, framed as always in a dramatic swirl of dark hair. "Aren't you going to even help me down?" she said, taking her lip between her teeth as if his lack of manners had somehow wounded her.

He put down the cart steps and helped her descend. She held on to his hand while she dismissed the driver with a reminder to return for her in an hour. As the cart jostled back down the lane, she turned to look up at him through her long, dark lashes.

"What are you doing here, Adele?" he said thickly, catching the drift of her perfume.

"They told me you had come to look after your uncle," she said in carefully modulated tones. "I've been in agony, Forrest, waiting for you to return to London. Please don't be angry that I've come. I just couldn't stay away another minute. I had to see you ... to ... " She stopped and drew back, reading in his expression that she was moving too quickly. She halted with a smile that in earlier days might have passed for modest, and looked around. "Aren't you going to invite me in?"

Against his better judgment, he escorted her inside and offered her a seat on the settle. She glanced at the sooty fireplace, scarred puncheon floor, and frayed rug, and couldn't hide her distaste. So, cleverly, she decided to use it.

"Oh, Forrest, this is where you're staying? It's so small and drab and menial."

"It's my uncle's cottage. He's a poor man."

"But *you're* not," she said, as if expecting confirmation of her assertion. She got none. "Oh, my darling, to think that I may have driven you to such an estate." She halted and took a breath, visibly bracing herself for something difficult. "I cannot bear to think of you here, suffering ... on account of me."

"I am getting along well enough, Adele," he said, watching her lift her buttercup yellow silk dress to avoid contact with the floor. When he again waved her to a seat on the settle, she steeled herself and sat down gingerly. Her hat banged against the high back of the seat and she quickly removed it. For Forrest's benefit, she exaggerated the bend of her waist and the languorous smoothing of her hair. Every motion was calculated for effect, each part of her appearance was designed to appeal to him ... the loose way she had pinned her hair, the yellow she knew was his favorite color, the hint of red on her lips that spoke of a judicious use of cosmetics.

He offered her refreshment, but she declined and patted the bench beside her. When he merely folded his arms and leaned against the rough stone fireplace, she retreated into a litany about her arduous journey and the cramped little inn along the London Road, where she and her aunt had taken rooms. As she talked, she appraised him with an eye that had little of the contrite or of the demure young maiden about it.

She measured his shoulders; she hadn't recalled them being so wide. She visually ruffled his hair and traced his finely chiseled features; they seemed stronger, somehow. She didn't recall his relaxed manliness of stance, or the strong, sinewy appearance of his hands. And she certainly didn't recall his eyes being so intense and direct . . . so deliciously male in their assessment of her.

"What are you really doing here, Adele?" he finally asked, when her stream of distracting chatter began to run dry.

"I've come to ask your forgiveness, Forrest." Her chin quivered slightly and she raised her head to stop it . . . not, however, before she was certain he had seen it. "We have so much in common, you and I . . . common friends, common tastes and goals." She let out a nervous-sounding sigh. "And I miss you so terribly. Haven't you felt it, too? Haven't you, too, longed for those quiet moments alone in the carriage . . . like the night of the Athertons' ball?" She quickly lowered her eyes, her lashes fluttered, and she appeared transported by the memory to the verge of some illicit ecstasy.

Forrest watched in fascination, seeing with new eyes the artifice beneath the charms that had once held him in such thrall. Were they remembering the same carriage ride? The night of the Athertons' ball she had allowed him one long, wet kiss in the carriage and a hasty caress of her bodice. She had left him scorched with frustration and the feeling that he had just been rewarded for not tripping over his feet during the closing waltz. Her dark eyes now seemed flat and unreadable, her wit and her hair both lusterless, and her well-tutored voice and exaggerated femininity left him oddly cold.

She rose and swayed toward him, telling him with her eyes what she had come to say. She wanted him back.

"What happened to the dashing captain, Adele?" he said calmly.

"I was a little fool . . . snatching hopelessly at moonbeams, distracted by polished boots and glittering braid. He dazzled and confused me, and I— silly, fickle creature that I was—abandoned the one true love of my life. It didn't take long for me to come to my senses. And, oh, Forrest, my first thoughts were of you."

"Were they indeed?" he said softly. "Wondering if my fortune was still intact? I take it the amusing captain rather overstated his prospects, and when you learned the truth, you had already charted your course with his."

She stiffened briefly, gauging the level of his anger. "Yes, yes," she said bitterly, deciding on a more candid approach, "it's true. He lied to me, the beast. I was utterly humiliated. And I suppose you think it was only fair, seeing how horrible I was to you. But I've learned a terrible lesson and I am desperate to put it behind me . . . behind us." Just how desperate he could guess from the fact that only a fortnight after jilting him cruelly, she had swallowed her pride and come running to the end of nowhere to get him to take her back. Now she edged closer, gazing up at him with a provocative look that invited him to take whatever he wanted of her as the price of her forgiveness.

"Us? You believe there is still an 'us'?" he said, lowering his arms and gazing into the eyes that had once encompassed his aspirations in life. "Tell me, Adele, what would you want with a shirtboard . . . a dull bit of ditchwater?"

"You're determined to punish me, I see—throwing my words back in my face." Her eyes glowed brighter as they flitted over his fiercely assured mien. She had never seen him like this before. In the silence, her body migrated toward his. "Very well, then punish me," she said huskily. "But when you do . . . remember that *this* will be waiting for you at the end of your revenge."

She pressed her voluptuously curved body fully against his and pulled his head down to plant a kiss on his mouth.

It was cool and faintly pleasurable, he thought. He allowed it and examined it, wanting to know what it was like, needing to test his desires, needing to feel the full extent of both his power and his freedom from her.

Tamsin had realized she was late the moment she awakened and saw that the sun was beginning to lower through the trees overhead. She had wasted precious time looking for Boxer, then finally had started home without him. She had still hoped to arrive in time to surprise Forrest. As she approached the open cottage door, she heard voices and halted, looking at the berries in her basket and hurrying with them to the bench under the window. She could leave them outside, and if it was just Grovenor talking to himself again, she could retrieve them. . . .

But the high, narrow window was open and she

caught the sound of a woman's voice. A woman in Grovenor's cottage? Then she heard Forrest's voice saying the woman's name: Adelaide or Ada or ... Her eyes flew wide with recollection. *Adele*. The woman Forrest had meant to marry was named Adele. What was *she* doing here?

Stealthily, she climbed up onto the bench and peered through the window. In the dim interior she spotted Forrest by the fireplace. A woman rose from the settle and approached him, leaning close, then closer. Tamsin could scarcely make out their words over the frantic beating of her own heart.

"... determined to punish me ... remember this ..."

And as Tamsin watched with burning eyes, the woman pulled Forrest into her arms and kissed him, full on the mouth. Tamsin's jaw dropped and her knees went suddenly boneless. She kept expecting that any moment he would push her away, but the woman continued to kiss him. And when she reached for his arms and urged them around her waist, his hands moved slowly up her back.

She saw the woman draw back and heard her throaty laugh that carried a note of triumph. "My, you've learned a thing or two. Been practicing with the local farmers' daughters?" The hussy made a sultry 'tsk'ing sound and pulled Forrest into yet another kiss that seemed to go on and on. Tamsin couldn't understand why he was allowing her to kiss him or why he seemed to be kissing her back. The sight caused a painful squeezing sensation in the middle of her chest and she made fists and bit her lip as she fought to overcome it.

"You see what you've been missing?" Adele said, pulling back from his mouth. "We were meant to be together, Forrest. This proves it."

"It does?" she heard Forrest say in a slightly ragged voice.

"Can you doubt it? Come back to London with me," she said. "Now. Today. We can be married in only two days, if we get a special license, and we can honeymoon abroad until . . . until it is time to make a graceful return and resume our lives in London." Forrest stared at her with smoldering eyes and she wriggled seductively against him with a provocative whimper. "What's happened to you, Forrest? You've changed. You're so hard, so . . . passionate. You never used to kiss me with such force or . . . " She paused to read his expression.

"What is it? A woman?" She laughed and minced away from him. "Don't tell me some little country mouse has captured your heart in less than a fortnight." She smiled, as if the prospect amused her.

"No, I won't tell you that," he said with an edge that she ignored. She turned from him and swayed toward the door, giving it a shove that sent it shut with a bang . . . causing Tamsin to start and shrink back to avoid being seen.

That door seemed to have slammed on her very heart. There was an ache in her chest that sent rivulets of pain running through her in all directions. Her eyes burned and her throat felt as if it was being squeezed as she turned back and saw Adele unbuttoning her bodice, peeling it down her arms, baring her shoulders to him.

"Darling . . . your little dairymaid doesn't have anything to equal this." Adele laughed wickedly. "Come and let me show you what you can do with it."

Through a stinging blur of tears and misery, Tamsin made out Adele's arms snaking around Forrest's shoulders and her mouth reaching for his. She closed her eyes and leaned back against the side of the cottage. Her heart pounded wildly, painfully, and, like a wounded doe, her first impulse was to run.

She stumbled off the bench, picked up her skirts, and headed straight for the forest. She raced along the paths until her sides hurt, her lungs burned, and her legs ached. Leaving the trail, wanting to lose herself in the woods, she plunged blindly through underbrush, then ran along narrow trails made by animals in the woods. She pushed on and on, until she was too winded to continue and she stumbled and fell.

Forrest's woman had come back to him. She had kissed him and used her feminine wiles to tempt him. And he had kissed her back and touched her the way he had once touched Tamsin: with gentleness and passion.

She lay crumpled on the trail amongst the fallen leaves, scalding tears burning down her cheeks. Her fingers trembled as she touched her lips and thought of his hot, sweet kisses. How could he press his lips to hers and declare he loved her, then do the same to another woman?

Ah, but this was not just any woman. It was the woman he had wanted long before he encountered a troublesome fairy nymph who threw her heart at him. This "Adele" was a woman of his world: a woman who knew about fine clothes and the parties and balls he talked about, a woman who understood carriages and servants and how to eat with five forks. She was a human whose body and heart were full of natural warmth. What chance did Tamsin have against such a desirable human creature?

She was only a changeling fairy who wanted desperately to be a human . . . and to love a man.

She felt small and drab and more than a little worthless. What could Forrest Reed ever see in her to love? She had lived her whole life in a small

meadow and its surrounding forest, telling silly stories, racing tadpoles, and singing and dancing. Her
playmates had been the little, ordinary, insignificant
things of earth: birds and fireflies, snails and cater-
pillars. Until a week ago, she had never even worn
clothes!

What made her think he would marry her and live
with her? He had never spoken of marriage, and she,
not knowing all that was involved, had not wanted
to speak of it to him. But she had hoped, believed
after the last three days, that she could stay with him
always . . . that they would have a future together.

A crushing pain went through her chest as memories of their last days crowded in on her. Forrest
had said he loved her, and every word and deed had
made her believe it. She had watched him open his
heart and let out the sprite locked inside him. Yet he
kissed Adele and let her steal his future . . . and
Tamsin's future with him. She closed her eyes and
again saw Adele removing her clothes.

*Don't tell me some little country mouse has captured
your heart*, Adele had said. And he'd replied that he
wouldn't.

Tamsin had never truly had his heart, and that
was the most killing thing of all.

He would go away with his "Adele." He would
leave her all alone.

There was only one thing she could do. She had
to find her meadow and wait for nightfall. Tonight
would be the first night of the full moon. Her folk
would come out to dance, and she would dance with
them. With any luck, she would leave the human
world far behind . . . all but the memory of one human's heat and the way it had shriveled her heart.

*   *   *

Forrest had suffered just enough of Adele's third kiss to know he never wanted to see or touch her again. He broke it off and set her back, telling her she was wrong, that his "dairymaid" was something to behold, something wonderful. She was livid. She stomped and wheedled and wept and seduced ... using language she had certainly not learned over afternoon tea or in a charity sewing circle. But he coolly handed her the bodice she had discarded, asked her to forgive him for not inviting her to his upcoming nuptials, and hustled her out the door.

She really had thought him a hopeless dolt, he realized, expecting him to take her back and rescue her reputation ... which must be in a shambles indeed for her to press him for a two-day marriage ... by special license, no less. He was free, he realized. Free of Adele and of the constraints of his old self, free to make a new life with Tamsin. He couldn't wait for her to return, so he could scoop her up in his arms, whirl her around, and sink, body and soul, into her honeyed kiss.

Taking a deep breath, feeling at peace with himself and with the world, he strolled back to the shed to brush down his horse. He was so pleasantly absorbed in his own thoughts that he missed seeing the basket of berries on the bench beside the cottage door.

When Tamsin didn't return that afternoon, Forrest went to look for her, checking her favorite places in the nearby woods. Having no luck, he returned to the cabin and while he paced and waited, Uncle Grovenor returned. The old man agreed to stay at the cottage and keep Tamsin there if she returned, while Forrest ranged farther in the woods, searching for her.

As night fell, Forrest returned once more to the

cottage, feeling worn and worried, and not a little annoyed with her for being so impulsive and unpredictable. He collapsed on the bench by the dim glow of the open door Grovenor came rushing out to see if he had found her. As Forrest described the places he had searched, Boxer emerged from the darkening woods and loped over to greet them. First Grovenor, then Forrest snapped at him and pushed him away as he jumped on them. Undaunted, the hound bounded up onto the bench and nosed around in the basket of berries. When Grovenor gave him a swat and ordered him down, the dog tipped the basket over onto Forrest.

"What—" Forrest brushed at his trousers, then realized what had spilled and picked up a handful of the berries. "Where did these come from?"

"*Her*, most likely. She asked about that thicket of gooseberries just this mornin'. I told her not to go pickin' the bushes bare."

Forrest's eyes widened. "This wasn't here when I came home. She must have returned after I got back from the village. Then why didn't she say something?" The suspicion formed: "My old fiancée came today and she must have seen her . . . seen us together." For one horrifying moment, the tension of that sexually charged encounter revisited him. The feel of Adele's avid lips devouring his fanned through his senses, and suddenly he knew why Tamsin had fled. "Adele threw herself at me . . . kissed me and tried to get me to take her back . . . talked of marriage . . . God knows what Tamsin must have thought!" He grabbed his uncle by the shoulders. "I've got to find her!"

Grovenor saw the panic in his nephew's face and knew the trouble he had dreaded had finally come. He grabbed Forrest's sleeve as he turned away.

"Let her go, boy," he pleaded. "She's nothing but

trouble. She's fey—they all are. Don't ye see? Fairies don't know right from wrong and they don't care. She's got yer heart . . . that's all she wants." Forrest tried to pull away, but he held on tightly and shouted down Forrest's protests.

"The little twitchit's flown straight back to her band! It's the full of the moon . . . they'll be dancin' . . . no doubt, celebratin' th' takin' of yer heart. Leave 'er go, boy. Yer better off without 'er."

The old man's words struck him in a vulnerable place. The full of the moon . . . where else would she go when she was hurting? Her meadow . . . her adopted *home*. Without another word, he broke free of the old man's grip and went running into the woods. It was night and the forest seemed like one thick, forbidding tangle as he ran down the narrow path. God knew how he would find his way along those half-hidden deer trails in the dark, but he had to try. He had to find her . . . if it took all night, every night, for the rest of his life.

The moon took forever to rise over Tamsin's meadow. She arrived well before sunset, exhausted and heartsick, and after a moment's respite, went down to the stream to cool her puffy eyes and tear-reddened skin. Once there, she found herself standing on the bank, staring at the flattened grass where she and Forrest had lain together in a blissful haze of sensual discovery. The ache in her chest strengthened and spread, invading her stomach and her loins.

She wrapped her arms tightly around her body and felt tears welling in her eyes again. She had never been so miserable in her life. This heartache was a new and horrible experience. She had never felt real pain before now; fairies never had to deal with such things. And she understood for the first time that the intense joys of the daylit world were but one side of human life. There was also pain and despair, betrayal and disappointment . . . all of which she seemed to have discovered in the past few hours.

It would be a great relief, she thought, to give up this awful, oppressive sensitivity that opened her to the worst of life as well as the best. She dried her face on her skirt and trudged back to the meadow to wait for the moon.

A red haze washed the sky and gradually the light drained, leaving only purples, then darkening blues. Her heart beat wildly as she knelt by the lilies and watched for her people to arrive. It was some time before the moon appeared. Shadows engulfed the edge of the meadow, near the mound and log, and, as the darkness deepened, she watched fireflies taking to the wing and knew it would not be long now.

Then she saw a twinkle . . . a tiny flash of brightness in the distance. Creeping across the meadow toward the mound, she dropped to her knees and parted the tall grass. There they were . . . small flashes of moon-brightened white that she knew to be hair and flutters of iridescence . . . wings flashing in the soft glow of the moon. But she couldn't quite focus on them and realized with dismay that this was probably what humans saw when they looked at fairies . . . blurs and flashes of light . . . there and gone. Concentrating, knowing just where to look and what to look for, she leaned closer and managed to bring them into focus as they cavorted around the ring.

Then one of the elders spotted her and called out a warning to the others. In an instant they were fleeing back toward the mound. Tamsin called out to them in as quick and high a voice as she could. A few of the elders, who had more experience with humans, understood her and halted warily.

"Argo? Hespera? It's me, Tamsin! Please—don't you know me?" As she leaned closer, they gasped and shrank with fright. Frantically, she tore the combs from her hair and let it tumble down her shoulders. It was the badge of her kinship with them and gradually they began to recognize her.

"Tamsin? Is that you?" Argo called, venturing closer. "By Minerva's Hair!" He winced. "You look terrible—like a human! What's happened to you?"

"Oh, Argo—I was captured by a human and got too warm and I grew," she said with a catch in her throat. "Please, I want to come home . . . I want to be part of the band again. But I need your help!"

There was a wild buzzing as the others gathered around Argo and stared at Tamsin, pointing at her eyes and her pinkish skin, her reddened lips and lumpy, human-esque body. After consulting Hespera and several of the others, the leader of the band came forward.

"You want to dance with us, then," he said.

"Yes. I want to dance with you. If you let me into the circle, I'll dance and slowly shrink to my former size."

"And if we let you come back to us, do you give your word to be a dutiful and respectful fairy and listen to your elders? No more dallying with humans, no more flying off on your own?"

"I promise."

There was more consultation, and Argo came back to her with their decision. "We'll let you into the circle . . . we'll help you. We'll have to make the circle wider. . . . Are you sure you remember how to dance?"

"Yes, oh, yes, I remember," she said, her eyes filling with tears.

Soon the circle was re-scribed in the grass, en-

larged to accommodate her. She removed her blouse
and skirt so that they wouldn't get in the way. And
she stepped inside their circle and closed her eyes.
The night breeze carried the faint strains of their
song and the rhythm of their moving feet upward
to her. She took a deep breath and began to move.
The motions felt awkward at first, for they had been
designed for frames that were smaller and more ag-
ile than a human form. But she squeezed her eyes
tight and concentrated harder. She swayed and un-
dulated, finding her beat in the joined pulse of their
hearts. The night music filled her head as of old, and
she pirouetted gracefully again and again. Then in
the final movements, she bent to the ground and
reached to the sky, again and again, symbolically
joining the sources of a fairy's joy and sustenance
. . . Earth and Sky.

Her skin began to burn as her body gave up its
heat and slowly, ever so gradually, she began to
shrink. She could feel it, could sense it. In that moment she became a living flame, filled with fire and
pain. It hurt her to continue, yet she could not allow
herself to stop. Biting her lip, she danced with all the
more fury, shedding her borrowed heat, letting it
float into the cool, forgiving night, carrying away her
heartache.

After that first painful rush of heat, her skin
cooled and paled and when she opened her eyes
some time later, she realized she was just more than
half of her former size. At her back she felt a familiar
flutter and looked back to see her reemerging wings.
Aunt Clytie had been right! Her human clothes now
lay around her in a limp pool and she wriggled her
shoulders and let the garments slide down her body
as she swayed and danced. She was returning to the
elfin slimness of her old fairy self. Her hips were

narrowing, her breasts were getting smaller . . . she was losing her soft, womanly form.

The sight brought her to a halt and she ran cold hands over her still warm breasts and down her straightening sides. She should have been pleased by the transformation; it was what she had come to do. Instead, she felt an overwhelming grief for the loss of her woman-self. Never again would she feel the soft warming of passion in her body or the sweet glide of sensation in loving. Never again would she celebrate the exquisite sensitivity of her senses, the tumultuous store of new emotions and urges, or the sweet and heartrending possibilities of love.

Her eyes filled with tears and in the midst of the bright fairy circle, in the midst of the dancing and the prospect of endless gaiety, she sank to her knees and began to weep.

"What's happening to her?" one of her band shouted, pointing.

"What's wrong with her eyes? They're raining . . ."

"No!" Argo declared, waving his arms to quell the rising horror of the band. "Those are tears. She is weeping."

Tears. They crept closer, staring at the hot rivulets running down her cheeks. They reached out to touch the drops that had splashed onto her bare knees, and drew back as if scorched. Fairies never cried; not one in a score of them had ever seen tears. "What do we do?" they wanted to know. Frantically, they began to try to cheer her, reminding her of what fun they would have when she was fairy-sized again. They tried telling her silly stories and making chipmunk and cricket faces . . . all to no avail. Her tears just fell all the harder, splashing, bathing her with their salty heat and halting her return to fairy size.

The human half of her heart was breaking and, try as they might, her fairy folk could do nothing about it.

Forrest was blind in the inky gloom of night in the deep woods. He was lost, and despite a vague and increasing sense of urgency, he could not make sense of his location or direction. Despair filled him as he thought of her in the meadow, alone, hurting, bewildered by what she had seen and thought she had seen.

He had to find her tonight. He didn't for a moment believe that she was a fairy, that her pointed ears, silvery blond hair, and extraordinary blue eyes were anything but rare human beauty. But the occasional glimpse of the full moon overhead never failed to send a quiver of anxiety through him, and he understood that there was a part of him that was not so convinced by logic and human pride.

Her people danced by the light of the moon, Grovenor said, and she had undoubtedly gone back to them. Now those words formed the core of a growing and irrational fear in him. What if it were true? What if there was any substance at all to her charming and admittedly haunting stories. What if there were elements—*beings*—that he couldn't see or fully explain? And worse—what if he never saw her again?

Uncle Grovenor's dire prediction might well come true. He would wander the forest by night, searching, yearning.

Ahead, he glimpsed moonlight through the forest and rallied his flagging spirits to plunge ahead. He burst from the trees into a meadow, and recognized it as her meadow . . . which for one night had been their private paradise. It took a moment to orient himself and recover his breath. Then as he recalled the events of that night and started across the meadow, searching the darkness, he spotted a strange blue-white glow to one side, in the grass. He headed for it with his heart in his throat.

It was a circle of light, and as he approached, what he saw made him stop dead. Sitting in the midst of that light on her knees was Tamsin, weeping. She was as naked as the day his uncle found her and she stood no taller than a three-year-old child!

He stared, unable to believe his eyes. He rubbed his face savagely and shook himself, but the vision remained. Tamsin . . . half the size she'd been . . . with her pale hair swirled around her and what appeared to be a pair of feathery, iridescent wings peeking over her shoulder.

For a minute he thought he would faint.

Or perhaps he was already unconscious and lying somewhere by the side of a path . . . suffering mad delusions. But the very fact that he thought of that possibility disproved it, and he was left with the evidence of his senses. His Tamsin was . . . a *fairy*.

"Tamsin!" he called to her and began to run. But she looked up, startled, and sprang up amidst a flurry of trembling light—like the glow of jittery fireflies—that seemed an expression of her fear and distress. He stopped short, afraid that she would bolt if he came much closer. And as he stared at her he caught fleeting glimpses of other wings and other tiny, cool blue forms that bore a striking resemblance to Tamsin, only much smaller. Their lightning quick movements kept him from focusing on any one of them for long, but in an astonishingly short time he realized he could see more of them . . . they were all around her.

"Tamsin!" he called to her again. "What are you doing? What is happening to you?"

"Don't listen to the human, Tamsin!" she heard Argo cry, flying near her head. "Stop your ears! Keep dancing! Our circle of light will keep him at bay long enough—dance!"

She did begin to dance, one step, another, then another. But her eyes kept darting outside the circle, toward the darkness, where she could just make out his features. A painful longing went through her at the sight of him, but close on the heels of that terrifying sensation came a soothing, restful wave of pleasure that he had come. He had made the journey through the night. He had called her name again.

Her folk called to her to dance . . . to forget the human . . . to remember who she was and what she must do.

Forrest sensed what was happening, though he could not see it all, and tried to go to her, to take her out of there. But when he came within a few feet of the circle he found it difficult to move and soon was standing still, unable to lift his arms or reach through that light to touch her. Alarm shook him as he watched her turn away from him, listening to her folk, hearing their cries.

"Tamsin . . . please, listen to me. I don't know what you saw this afternoon, but you must give me a chance to explain. Adele came to ask me to marry her, but I sent her away. I don't want her, Tamsin, I want you!" He saw the graceful weaving of her body and, as she turned, the tears streaming down her face. It hit him that she was shrinking as she danced, and icy terror gripped his heart. He was losing her—she was slipping from his world!

"Tamsin!" he cried, with all the fear and passion in his heart. "Don't do this! Please stop—don't leave me. Tamsin, I love you! I love you with everything in me, and I know you love me!"

Tamsin's folk managed to interpret what he said

and it sent delicious trills of both panic and excitement through them. They danced all the harder in order to hold him at bay, caught her up in their ring, moving closer and closer to their fairy mound as they literally danced her away from him. And as he stood frozen, watching, he called out to her again and again, "I love you, Tamsin—I love you!"

Tamsin's fairy folk began to laugh and congratulate her on stealing away her first human heart.

"Such big, slow-witted creatures, humans!" they cried. "Ugly pink bodies with hair all over them. Don't even look at the hideous creature, Tamsin! A paltry race—humans—they cannot dance, cannot fly, and cannot resist the lure of a fairy! Look at him—dull and slow, like a dimwitted old mole! He thinks he's in love!"

Then one young sprite began to mimic Forrest's declaration: "Ooooh . . . 'I love you, Tamsin. Please don't leave, Tamsin' . . . " And others took it up, laughing. " 'I love you, Tamsin! I love you Tamsin!' "

Their taunts echoed in her ears, drowning out his voice, becoming all she could hear. But there was still warmth in her heart, and it was in that stubborn bit of humanness, that defiant and clinging bit of heat, that his words found a lodging. Suddenly their taunts became his pleas. *I love you. Don't leave me.* And she halted, listening for Forrest's voice. Beneath the high tones of her folk's derision came the low, sweet vibrations that were his call to love.

And she did look back.

Through the brightness, she could see him, his arms outstretched, his heart in his eyes. The memory of his warmth, of her passion, of the joy of her marvelous human feelings came flooding back, warming her chilled frame. He had chosen her over the human woman. He *did* love her. Her heart raced as her head filled with echoes of her own voice: *I love you, too.*

Tears rolled down her cheeks as she looked around her. And she knew she'd made her decision. The joy and wonder of his love had enlarged her heart; it could never be content to shrink again into the cool, pale shadows of the fairy world. Whatever happened, she must explore and experience all that she could . . . as a human woman, her heart filled with love.

She turned a smile of great joy on her people, then ran through the circle, breaking through the cordon of light that separated her from her beloved Forrest. She staggered for a moment, then regained her feet and ran on, her arms outstretched and her heart full, growing with each step she took.

Forrest swept her up into his arms, marveling at her changing size but too filled with joy and relief to do more than hold her.

"Warm me, Forrest," she said, reaching for his lips. And as his heat surrounded and suffused her, she gradually returned to her full human size. When their kiss ended, he was all but staggering with her weight.

She shivered and sighed as he carried her to a familiar spot in the grass and, by the light of the grinning moon, did as she requested. He covered her with his hands, his body . . . and warmed her with his love and the low, sweet flame of human passion. Afterward, as they lay wrapped in his coat, replete and glowing, he looked down into her luminous eyes and saw in them the endless delights that lay ahead for him. "What a lucky man I am," he whispered, smiling.

"Indeed you are," she said, nuzzling his chest. "You're the only human on earth who won't eve have to worry about flies in his house, mice in his grain, or slugs in his garden."

He gave a short, surprised laugh. "I won't?"

She grinned up at him. "I know every one of their tricks. Lucky you."

"Ummm . . . lucky me. They were right, you know. You did steal my heart."

"Ummm . . . clever me," she said, luxuriating in the warmth that wound through her, all the way to her very toes. "But as you—*WE*—humans say: Fair is fair. You stole mine first, Forrest Reed. You with your hot hands, soft lips . . . and *honey*."

He laughed roundly and pulled her closer, resting his cheek on top of her head.

"I don't have the faintest idea how I'm going to explain your ears to my parents."

The next morning, when Forrest and Tamsin arrived at the cottage, they received a fierce dressing-down from a freshly shaved and parson-sober Uncle Grovenor. "It's a disgrace, I tell you. A scandal—and I won't have no part of it!" he declared hotly. "Look at the pair of you. Unnatural—that's what it is!"

"Not anymore," Forrest said, holding Tamsin tight against his side. "Officially, as of this date, she is no longer a fairy. Henceforth and forevermore, she is Tamsin . . . Tamsin . . . " He tried to think of a temporary name, one that would serve until she became Tamsin Reed. She beat him to it.

"Harris, I'm Tamsin Harris. And my aunt, Cleona Harris, lives near here . . . in the village of Waincote."

"Tamsin? You can't possibly claim—"

"Oh, she's my aunt, all right." She grinned. "And I think when you ask her this time, she'll be pleased to admit it."

"Holy Mother—" Grovenor swore, but without much heat. It just wasn't humanly possible to see their happiness and not feel a little better about love and the human race in general. "Next thing ye'll be sayin' you're goin' to marry the little twitchit and settle down with her!" he said, as if it was the worst thing he could imagine.

"Clever old devil. You're right. That *is* the next thing I'll be saying." Forrest turned Tamsin by the shoulders and went down on one knee before her. "Miss Tamsin Harris, would you do me the honor of becoming my wife . . . as soon as it can decently be arranged?"

She rolled her eyes and gave him a look of impish calculation. "I will . . . on the condition that you grant me three wishes, handsome human." And over Grovenor's gasp and mutters of outrage, she laid out her demands.

"I want a home near this very forest. I want you to promise to dance with me whenever, wherever I choose." Her mischievous grin melted into a warm, loving smile as she placed her arms around his neck. "And I want to feel the warmth of your touch every night . . . for the rest of our lives."

Betina Krahn

BETINA KRAHN's fascination with fairies began at the tender age of six, when her parents took her to see the animated Walt Disney version of the story *Peter Pan*. Peter was a *boy* and annoying, and Wendy was too much of a goody-two-shoes. But Tinkerbell ... there was a character with whom she could identify ... a female with an attitude, even in the fifties! Since then, Betina has loved and collected fairy lore. It is something of a disappointment to her that outside of books and the silver screen, she has never encountered a real fairy. She is, however, willing to be open-minded. Having seen a number of "fairy rings" in the grass of her front lawn over the years, she is still hopeful that someday they may prove to be more than ordinary "turf fungus."

The parameters and details of the fairy world in "A Touch of Warmth" are purely a product of Betina's fertile imagination. And that same imagination has led her to write a number of award winning books, including *Caught in the Act*, *Behind Closed Doors*, *My Warrior's Heart*, *The Princess and the Barbarian*, and currently, *The Last Bachelor*.

Sweet Cream and Irish Whiskey

Glenda Sanders

1
A Rude Awakening Brings Hope To Dannyboy

"Ooo-eeeiii!" Clasping his palms against his ears, Danny O'Shea sprang into a sitting position. Such infernal noise! It was enough to raise the dead.

Danny laughed at his own witticism. *Raise the dead—ah, that was a ripe one, Dannyboy.*

Lowering his palms, he cocked his head, listening, trying to sort one noise from another. Begad, what was this racket that had roused him?

Footsteps. On the stage—on the very stage itself! He rubbed his hands in delighted contemplation. It bore immediate investigation. Concentrating on the sounds, he floated in the direction from which they came.

Ooomf! Musha, but the bloody wall had never offered so much resistance. He had to strain through it, slow as a snail. How long had he been sleeping to be so dense he couldn't pass through wood with the ease of water through a sieve?

He floated ever closer to those who'd disturbed his peace, hovering somewhat nearer to the boards than to the high ceiling, another sign of density. The humans, two women, were just right of center stage. The younger of the two was curiously examining something on the floor.

Danny eased closer, hoping to glean what these intruders were about.

"Here it is!" the comely lass said excitedly, kneeling, touching the stain with her fingertips. "The spot where my great-great-uncle fell and hit his head. See, Rosie, his blood spilled into a perfect likeness of Ireland."

Great-great-uncle? Musha! Danny dived toward her, intent on getting a look at the woman's face. When he did, the shock almost sent him plummeting to the floor. A touch more red in the hair and green in the eyes and she'd be the exact double of his baby sister, Maggie. It could be none other than Maggie's great-granddaughter before him in the flesh. His very own great-great-niece, as fresh and pretty as morning sunshine.

Rosie crossed herself urgently. "It's unnatural, that's what. Your grandfather, God rest his sainted soul, was wrong to show ye such a thing, Miss Emily. There's no good to come from the morbid fascination with the blood of a dead man."

"Not just any dead man," Emily said. "The blood of Dannyboy O'Shea, the Irish Amadan."

Her adoration flowed like sweet nectar over Danny's spirit.

"*Amadan* is right. A fool he was, stealing a kiss and having to go running onto the stage so fast he lost his footing."

"The story that he was late coming onto the stage because he was kissing a woman in the wings has never been confirmed," Emily said.

Never confirmed? Danny fumed. *Ah, but he remembered the lass and the kiss so well!*

"You know how wild tales grow up around the untimely death of a famous person," Emily continued. "The story doubtless has taken on some embellishment since 1834, for all that the stain hasn' faded in the thirty-eight years since then. He slipped and fell, cracking his head open on a table. The part about the kiss and the woman offstage is probably a total fabrication."

A fabrication indeed! Danny thought, outraged. *Marie, the colleen's name was, and as sweet an armful as ever a man held.*

"Oh, and it's all that famous he was?" Rosie said.

"Famous enough that Mr. P. T. Barnum tried to buy these boards from my grandfather for display in his museum of curiosities," Emily said.

P. T. Barnum? Danny thought. *Who was P. T. Barnum?*

"To go with his two-headed calf and his bearded lady!" Rosie quipped with an impudent cackle.

A two-headed calf? Danny regarded the plump matron with narrowed eyes. *Such a lovely Irish lilt to her tongue, pretty as any he'd ever heard, but mean-spirited she was!*

"Audiences were enchanted by Dannyboy O'Shea," Emily said. "The house was always full when he performed."

Ah. Much better. The girl has good sense, and a modicum of respect for the dead.

Rising, Emily looked out over the rows of empty seats. Oh, she was a fine figure of a woman in her pretty green dress; just like her great-grandmother, who'd had all of Philadelphia at her feet.

"This theater," she said, with such passion that Danny reeled with the throbbing of it, "the theater he built, will be full again. We'll fill these empty seats, and laughter will echo from these walls just as it did when Dannyboy O'Shea walked these boards as the Irish fool."

Fill the seats? Danny rubbed his hands together with glee. This lovely, bright child so like his sister was going to reopen the theater! Was this, at long last, his chance to finish the performance interrupted by his ill-timed death?

Rosie harrumphed. "Aye, Miss Emily, you've got your heart set on it, and I've no doubt you'll do it or die in the trying, just to prove to your father you can."

Emily's strong emotional reaction to the mention of her father screeched over what had once been Danny's nervous system, knocking him back several feet and very nearly sending him into a spin.

"I shall take great pleasure in sending him tickets to our opening night," Emily admitted, her voice weighted by irony.

"Ye've your work cut out for you before you open this place," Rosie said. "A good Irishman could plant potatoes in the dust settled on those seats you're so anxious to fill."

"Then we'd best get on with our survey of what needs to be done," Emily said. "The workmen will be here within the hour and I want to have at least a partial list prepared so we may put them to work immediately. Then I shall begin organizing my office so that I may greet our new manager with at least a token appearance of organization when he arrives this afternoon."

2
Mr. Ruskin Makes
An Entrance

It had been nine years since the War Between the States had forced the Irish Playhouse to close its doors. The building was in disrepair, the ancient playbills posted on its front faded to illegibility, the sign marking it as the Irish Playhouse weathered and worn. All over, there was a look of decay and neglect about the building that indicated it had too long been unoccupied and unappreciated.

Even the stone eagles guarding the building from their rooftop perches at either corner appeared tired and weary of their duty. But in spite of the building's disrepair, Gilford Ruskin's heart throbbed at the sight of it, throbbed with the thrill of an actor in anticipation of a stage and the joy of a man on the verge of realizing a dream.

He had never been to the Irish Playhouse, but so intimately had he studied its history in preparation for this visit that he passed through the door with a sensation of homecoming; he paused in the lobby to pay mental homage to the memory of Dannyboy O'Shea, a legend in life after building this theater in 1830 and an even larger legend after dying on its stage four years later.

The doors to the auditorium were propped open.

Inside, half a dozen workmen were as busy as ants, sweeping, hammering, and scraping. The stage was small, but expeditiously arranged, quite workable. Instinct lured Gilford toward it, although he stopped short of actually mounting the short bank of steps that would have placed him on the boards. It might seem presumptuous of him if he were found there without invitation or authorization. Still, he could not suppress his excitement over the prospect of eventually mounting those steps and traversing that stage in a succession of leading roles.

Manager of a dramatic company! In a city renowned for its theaters, and in a theater with such a rich history—never would he have believed such an opportunity would open to him so unexpectedly. He held the letter bearing the signature of E. M. Charlton, Owner and Proprietor of the Irish Theater, Philadelphia, in his coat pocket, touching it from time to time to reassure himself of its existence. The inquiry had come through a referral from a younger cousin he adored but would have thought too frivolous to have close connections to any serious business interests.

Gilford did not recognize the name Charlton. His study of the theater's history had gone only through its last renovation in 1858 and its closing five years later during the War Between the States. Then it had still been under the ownership of Dannyboy O'Shea's nephew, Nigel Throckmorton Lindsay. Lindsay had since died, so reason thus dictated that E. M. Charlton was either an heir or had bought the theater from the estate.

Gilford didn't really care who E. M. Charlton was or how he had acquired the theater or what Charlton's connection was to his cousin Elsbeth. He was too delighted by the prospect of leaving a walking gentleman position in a small but prestigious company in New York to assume the post of manager/

principal actor in a new company to fret over such meaningless details.

"Do you have business here, sir?" one of the workmen asked.

"I'm looking for Mister Charlton," Gilford replied.

"*Mister* Charlton?"

"Mister E. M. Charlton," Gilford clarified.

The workman scratched his chin thoughtfully and appeared more perplexed than ever.

"E. M. Charlton. The owner," Gilford reiterated.

"The owner's in the office off the lobby," the man said, with an inexplicable grin.

Gilford nodded a thank-you and returned to the lobby where, in his anxiety over the impending interview, he had overlooked the narrow doorway that opened into an office. Approaching the doorway, he discovered a young woman seated behind a desk and surrounded by crates that dwarfed her. Engrossed in a stack of papers she appeared to be sorting, she did not notice him immediately.

He cleared his throat and she looked up with a ready smile. She was quite stunning, with large, bright eyes and hair the exact color of the chestnut pony that had been his particular favorite as a child. Despite his preoccupation with the business which had brought him to this place, he found himself studying the graceful curves of her full mouth with uncommon concentration.

"Hello," she said, her rich voice giving the greeting far too much familiarity.

"I'm to meet Mr. Charlton at two," Gilford said, stiffening his spine a bit against the seductive distraction she provided.

A sly grin did amazing things—intriguing things—to her mouth as she pondered the information. "Mr. Charlton?"

"E. M. Charlton," he said. *Was the man a phantom?*

Had no one heard of him? He stiffened his spine another degree and said authoritatively, "I am looking for the owner of this theater."

"You are looking *at* the owner of this theater," she said with fully as much authority as he'd been able to muster. "I am E. M. Charlton."

"You?" Gilford sputtered, losing a bit of the starch in his spine. "*You* are E. M. Charlton?"

She smiled disarmingly. "Emily Marie. Elsbeth's friend. Do you not recall meeting me at your aunt's house?"

"No," Gilford said. "I'm sorry. I don't. You must be mistaken. I most assuredly would have remembered—"

"The intervening years have fogged your memory," Emily said. "You and your friend entertained us with a reenactment of one of your Hasty Pudding Club mock trials."

"Why, that was immediately after graduation," Gilford said. "We had just received our commissions. That was . . . eight years ago at least. Elsbeth and her friend were just children."

Again that intriguing grin claimed her mouth. "That is probably true, although we fancied ourselves quite grown-up. You and your friend were dashing in your uniforms, with your officer's stripes."

Gilford smiled drolly. "We were full of ourselves, marching off to war to show those Johnny Rebs the error of their ways."

He was still dashing, Emily thought. Every bit as tall as she remembered and all the more handsome for the maturity the intervening years had brought.

"Elsbeth told me about your forming a performing company of soldiers to entertain the troops, and later about your years abroad, touring European the

aters. When I decided to reopen the theater and realized that I needed an actor/manager to form a
company, I immediately queried Elsbeth regarding
your current address."

3
Miss Emily Hires A
Manager And Mr. Ruskin
Has Lustful Thoughts

W*h-wh-what?* Danny jerked awake to a keen
sensation of falling. He'd been dozing atop a
stack of crates in Emily's office, away from the infernal hammering and scraping in the auditorium.
In truth, he might have chosen this sanctuary even
without the noise, for he had grown fond of his sister's great-grandchild. Her pleasant disposition
soothed him. The sound of her voice was musical.
She smelled of flowers and fresh air, a welcome contrast to the mustiness of this old building that had
been his monument in life, his mausoleum in death.

As he scrambled in midair for his bearing, he was
knocked for a jolt by the sound, quite unanticipated,
of a deep male voice. *So Miss Emily's manager had
arrived!*

Easily righting himself now that he was fully alert,
he floated up to the ceiling and hovered, scrutinizing
the man curiously. *So this was the man who would
bring drama back to the stage of the Irish Playhouse.*

If looks were a measure, he certainly had leading

man potential. Tall and lean, he carried his well-cut clothes with a certain negligence, as though he considered them utilitarian rather than decorative. His face was handsome, his features saved from perfection by a fine network of squint lines around his eyes and a certain firmness in the set of his jaw that suggested a healthy skepticism. An understated elegance in his stance held the promise of grace in his movements.

"Would you consider it brash of me to inquire how you came to own this theater?" he asked.

His elocution was perfect, his voice a rich baritone which would project well, his words finely formed but tainted with a trace of upper-class Bostonian influence.

Saints preserve us, he'll be wanting to open with Hamlet! Danny thought. He did not dwell on it, though, as he concentrated on the conversation below.

"I inherited it," Emily replied.

"Have you any familiarity with the theater?"

"Aside from owning it?" she asked, lifting her chin in challenge.

Bravo, Emily! Danny thought delightedly. Despite her non-Irish blood, the child had the O'Shea spirit.

"I meant no offense," Gilford said coolly. "But this situation seems to me most irregular."

"I inherited a theater and would like to turn it into a profitable venture. You would not find that so irregular if I were a man."

"You, Miss Charlton," he said, with an indulgent smile, "are most assuredly *not* a man."

Oh, excellent! Danny thought. A subtle lift of brow, a wry intonation. He had said so much, with such an economy of words. The lad had talent.

Emily bristled, and Danny experienced her outrage as a shrill screech that made him clamp his hands over his ears. *These mortals and their emotions*

"I am Nigel Lindsay's only heir," Emily said. "Grandson or granddaughter is of little relevance."

"My dear Miss Charlton," Gilford said, with a charming smile; "it is not a factor so easily ignored as you believe."

Something charged the air as he spoke, a strange energy. It came to Danny as something akin to music, a peculiar, persistent hum that piqued his curiosity. He let his hands slide away from his ears and cocked his head, concentrating. *Saints preserve us— so that's what it was!*

His eyes narrowed as he cast a menacing glare toward Gilford. *Lust after me baby sister's great-granddaughter, will ye?* Well, Dannyboy O'Shea hadn't been dead so long he couldn't remember what the company of a pretty, sweet-smelling colleen like Miss Emily could do to a man. But this upstart had best be showing the proper respect, or he'd have the wrath of a great-great-Irish-uncle's ghost to contend with!

Emily squared her shoulders. "You ask if I have a familiarity with the theater. With *this* theater, I have an intimate familiarity. I am descended from the blood that stains her stage. I could have left her boarded up and empty, but I chose to bring her back to life because in doing so, I bring life back to my grandfather and the uncle whose memory was so dear to him."

"Your ambition is more nostalgic than pragmatic, I fear. A woman running a theater—"

"Laura Keene was successful in New York and Mrs. Drew has done an exemplary job with the Arch Street Theater here."

"But they are actresses. Miss Keene studied in London, and Mrs. Drew has been on stages her entire life. Do you know what it means to run a theater?"

"It means I must hire an actor/manager who knows what must be done and how to do it," she said archly. "I am in the position of questioning *your* credentials, Mr. Ruskin, not the other way around."

Danny rubbed his hands together gleefully. *How quick she was, and so spirited, like his sister.*

"Your point is well taken," Gilford said.

"I have read your list of credits and the reviews you submitted," Emily said. "They, along with Elsbeth's high regard for you, have convinced me that you could do the job I am offering."

"I am gratified by your confidence," Gilford said drolly.

"The question now becomes whether you are interested in the job."

"There is scarce an actor in the world who would not seize the opportunity to be actor/manager of a company. A Philadelphia theater with such a renowned history as the Irish Playhouse—"

"I think it prudent to inform you that my plans for the theater may not be as lofty as you assume. There are theaters enough in this town to serve those who would discuss Hamlet's moral dilemma or the treachery of Lady Macbeth. My great-great-uncle built the Irish Playhouse for the masses. He was the clown, the comedian. I wish to pursue that tradition. Comedy, farce, melodrama, music, and dance."

"To be frank, Miss Charlton, comedy, farce, and melodrama are not what came to mind. The last time the theater was open—"

"It was a legitimate house. My grandfather regretted the decision to make it so to his dying day. The war was only an excuse to close it. Attendance was never better than mediocre. My grandfather told me more than once that if he'd only had the strength and will left in him to reopen the Irish Playhouse, he would not make the same mistake again."

Her voice had grown soft with endearment as she spoke of her grandfather. "He could have sold this place, but he refused all offers. He meant for me to have it. I think he knew I would reopen it."

"It is unconventional for a woman of your background to undertake an entrepreneurial challenge," Gilford said. "Is your father as sympathetic to your ambition as your grandfather?"

She laughed bitterly. "My father's ambitions for me were of a different strain, especially since my grandfather's death."

"A fortuitous marriage?"

Emily bristled. Again her outrage shrilled through Danny's nervous system. "The fortuity of a situation is often dependent on interpretation," she said sharply.

Gilford grinned cockily. "As bad as that?"

"I do not wish to discuss my personal life," Emily said. "You take a liberty in your speculation."

"I most humbly beg your pardon for my untoward familiarity, Miss Charlton," he said, mocking her with his formality.

For a moment, Miss Emily's mouth hardened in vexation, but if Danny's nervous system was any barometer, her ire at Mr. Ruskin's shenanigans was not severe. In fact, there was a tinkling aspect to her reaction, a quality both delicate and sweet, and quite female. Danny had not heard such before, in life or death. Very quickly, the tinkling was gone, replaced by a low drum of determination.

"Would you find working for a woman offensive?" she asked, with renewed resolve to be about theater business.

"Not if she were a reasonable woman," Gilford replied.

Emily pondered his reply. "And what do you consider reasonable, Mr. Ruskin?"

"Only that she has a brain and does not shy away from using it."

"Then may I assume that you consider me reasonable?"

"It seems quite reasonable to prefer the adventure of opening a theater to a marriage that is fortuitous only in someone else's interpretation." He grinned charmingly. "Of course, I have had a lifelong passion for all things theatrical, so what seems reasonable to me might not seem so to the father of a respectable young woman from New York."

A passion for all things theatrical, is it? That's not the sum of what you've a passion for, laddy! Danny thought, as a fresh hum of lust drifted up to rattle him. The young man had a look in his eye that made him bear watching.

"The job," Miss Emily said with authority, "is to assemble a company for the production of comedies, farce, and melodrama. You would be given a budget and have full authority over casting, rehearsals, and supervision of stage sets and properties, and a voice in the larger matter of selection of plays. You would be answerable to me in all issues regarding the theater, and if you accept this position, you are never to speak familiarly of my father or his ill-conceived plans for me again."

"I am in a quandary, Miss Charlton. Should I bow thusly—?" He gave an exaggerated bow, spreading one arm across his waist and extending the other full length. "Or should I salute"—he clicked his heels together and snapped his flattened hand to his brow—"as I saluted my commanders while in the army?"

He ignored her pique at his antics—which was no pique at all, but a reoccurrence of the melodic tinkle.

"In any event," he assured her, "I wish to have the job."

"You are content to produce comedy, farce, and melodrama?"

"There can be excellence in any performance. The Irish Playhouse will become known for the quality of its productions no matter what our fare."

"The job is yours then, Mr. Ruskin. I trust you will make good your prediction. If you wish to get started, you might begin by acquainting yourself with the stage and backstage areas. You'll want to convert one of the rooms into an office."

"At the rear of the theater?" he asked.

"This office is hardly large enough for the both of us."

"I see," he replied petulantly. "And must I use the back door as well?"

"Come now, Mr. Ruskin—you must not put so much store in the placement of an office. The backstage location will be convenient to the stage, where you will spend most of your time, and the front office is convenient for me. It is a *reasonable* arrangement, wouldn't you agree?"

Gilford's outrage reached Danny as a roar, like that of a locomotive. But within the roar was a hum of desire so powerful it knocked Danny upward with its force. Danny sympathized with the lad's plight. Such a pretty face, set in an intractable pout, surely was capable of confusing even the most logical of men, especially combined, as it was, with a quick wit and large, lively eyes.

Danny rubbed his hands together gleefully. Things were not going to be dull around the Irish Playhouse with these two underfoot! Not dull at all. Nothing like a bit of lust in the air to perk up the spirits of an old ghost.

The spirits of an old ghost! Danny thought with a self-satisfied chuckle. *Another good one, Dannyboy. You're full of them today.*

Ruskin's spine was as rigid as a steel rod. "Naturally I am anxious to have a look at the stage."

"I'll accompany you," Emily said. "My appearance from time to time will discourage the workers from dallying."

4

Rosie Is Rudely Awakened And Dannyboy Seizes An Opportunity

Dust stirred by the workmen hung heavily in the air and made traversing the auditorium unpleasant for Danny. He was still dense following his long rest, and the clouds of grit scratched and irritated him.

Although the noise of the workers remained bothersome, the high ceiling above the stage provided more hospitable hovering places from which Danny could observe the humans below.

With Miss Emily at his side, Ruskin made a thorough and careful inspection of the boards and the wings, pausing from time to time to comment on a particular feature. His instinctual thespian's excitement over being on a stage vibrated upward, taking Dannyboy back to his mortal days. How well he remembered the exhilaration of playing to an audience, feeding on their adulation, the relentless drive to make a character come alive in their minds.

Had he not been so driven to make the Irish Amadan live for his audiences, had he not poured such energy and concentration into his portrayal of the lovable fool, he would not be earthbound now, destined to haunt the theater he had built until he could finish the performance that had been disrupted by his accidental death.

A confused soul, he was, having died while portraying the character so beloved by his public. In the passion of performance, Dannyboy O'Shea, the human being, had become the Irish Amadan. So who had died when he fell and cracked his head—Dannyboy, or the Irish Amadan? Actor, or character?

The Irish Amadan was naught but the manufacture of a talented writer's imagination, and had no soul; but so much soul had Dannyboy poured into him that only part of Danny's soul had gone with him into death. Until he could finish his interrupted performance and reclaim the portion of his soul he'd left behind in the part, he was doomed to this not-quite-human state, absorbing the emotions of living beings like a sponge sucking in liquid, yet incapable of feeling anything of his own beyond the nostalgic memory of his mortal life and the yearning to reassemble his soul and go on to a righteous death.

In nearly forty years of ghostdom, he had honed his skills of perception to an impressive level. Though he could not read specific thoughts, he could discern and identify most emotions and moods. Confined to the scene of his death and longing for the eternal rest due a mortal man after a life fully—if not morally or piously—lived, he sensed in the latest arrivals the prospect of rescue from his plight.

These two young people had the energy and passion of youth; the lad reminded him of himself at that age, full of vigor and a love for the theater; and the girl, so like his beloved sister, shared his long departed sister's beauty and wit.

The lass was his blood kin; the lad shared his love of the theater. They were the key to his deliverance, Danny was sure. He had only to persuade them to stage a production of *The Irish Amadan* so that he could finish his performance.

The Irish Amadan. The Irish Amadan. The Irish Amadan. He concentrated fiercely, repeating the name over and over as he studied the humans for any sign of receptivity to his thoughts.

Miss Emily suddenly grew still and cocked her head slightly, as if listening for something she wasn't quite sure she had heard.

"I beg your pardon?" she said.

Ruskin looked up from the ropes he'd been inspecting and testing. "My pardon?"

"Did you say something?"

"No," he said, shaking his head for emphasis.

"I thought—" She hesitated oddly. "I must have been mistaken."

He smiled. "Perhaps you were hearing echoes of past performances."

"My great-great-uncle Danny, cavorting about as the Irish Amadan?"

"I would gladly lay down coins for a chance to see Dannyboy O'Shea play the Irish fool."

It's working! Danny thought triumphantly, and resumed his silent chant.

"Would you like a look at Philadelphia's most famous bloodstain?" Emily asked.

"Philadelphia's most famous bloodstain," Ruskin repeated distractedly.

"The spot where my uncle fell, and his head wound—I'm surprised you have not heard of it," Emily said, as if suddenly realizing that he might think a discussion of a bodily injury an indelicate topic of conversation.

"Of course I've heard of it," Ruskin said. "Dan

nyboy O'Shea's blood stains the boards in the shape of Ireland, impossible to remove. I've just never heard it referred to in that way. Philadelphia's most famous bloodstain. It is a good turn of phrase, Miss Charlton. It could be useful in our playbills and advertising. We could make it our slogan: The Irish Playhouse—Home of the Most Famous Bloodstain in Philadelphia."

"It has a certain morbid fascination guaranteed to pique the interest of the public," Emily agreed. "At the same time, it refers to the theater's long history—"

"And gives the Irish Playhouse a certain venerableness that is missing in many theaters with a similar repertoire," Gilford said. "And—"

He was cut off by a bloodcurdling scream coming from behind the stage.

"Rosie!" Emily cried, already at a run, fighting her full skirts. "My nurse was napping on a cot we found in one of the rooms."

My cot? Danny thought with a sting of resentment. He considered the presence of the old nurse in his bed usurpative. But the scream had been real, and Miss Emily's alarm was genuine, so Danny trailed after the humans to see what the problem was.

A series of loud thunks and a string of invectives succeeded the scream. As Emily and Mr. Ruskin rounded the backdrops, a huge rat raced toward them, pursued by Rosie, who was brandishing a broom with the mien of a plundering pirate with a broadsword. Wild-eyed, her gray hair spreading in all directions like Medusa's snakes, she appeared witchlike as she lowered the straws upon the spine of the wayward rat. "Sit on my very chest, would ye?" she ranted, reverting to her heavy Irish accent in her rage. "Brazen as the very devil, ye are!"

Her aim was true, but the blow had little effect on

the fleeing rodent, save to urge him to greater speed in his retreat into a crevice along the floorboard. Rosie let loose a growl of frustration. "If I but had a good branch of blackthorn, that devil would be dead."

Miss Emily spread her arm across Rosie's shoulders. "Calm down, now, Rosie. Come and sit on the cot a while."

Rosie? Danny thought. *Rosie!* Bedad, it was little Rosie, the nurse his nephew had hired to care for his baby daughter after his wife took a fever and passed on tragically. Rosie had been no more than a slip of a lass then, and here she was, sixty years old if she was a day.

"Woke me up, he did, sittin' on me very chest," Rosie said. "Staring at me, he was. Sizing up my nose for his lunch, no doubt."

"We'll borrow one of Aunt Minny's house cats," Emily said. Along with her grandfather's house, she'd inherited a great aunt with an elderly spinster's fondness for cats. Recalling the largest and feistiest of the lot, Emily concluded, "I daresay Kilkenney'll make short work of him."

"Oh, aye," Rosie agreed. "That beast would take on an elephant if given the chance. Couldn't be any meaner if he'd just stepped off the boat from Kilkenney."

Emily had guided the aging Irishwoman to the cot. "I'll fetch you some water."

"I've me flask in my pocket," Rosie said. "It'll do. There's nothing better than a tot of good Irish whiskey to soothe a person's nerves."

Miss Emily pouted, as if she was disinclined to agree, but refrained from arguing as the nurse pulled the flask from her pocket and lifted it to her lips with trembling fingers.

Irish whiskey! Begad! Danny could almost feel the

liquor burning its way down his throat as he watched the woman. He neither ate nor drank in his earthbound state, but he could well remember the taste and pleasure of a good stiff drink. Perhaps if he concentrated, he might divine some of the pleasure of it from Rosie.

"You must rest now," Miss Emily ordered, as Rosie recapped the flask.

Mellowed by the liquor, Rosie lay back on the cot and released a ragged sigh. Then, unexpectedly, she cackled. "It wasn't the first rat I've chased with a broom in recent months."

"Or the first time a rat's deserved worse than he was given," Miss Emily said bitterly.

"Aye," came the soft sigh of agreement. "T'would have been a great justice served in showing Mr. Reginald Green the unfriendly end of a blackthorn shillelagh."

Danny sensed Miss Emily's dark scorn at the mention of the man's name and noted the amusement curving Ruskin's lips as the lad observed the lovely pout and flattering blush that colored the lass's face. But Danny couldn't dwell over this bit of romantic drama. He had business to attend to. He'd had a sudden inspiration. Now if he could just remember where he'd put the script—

Emily stood next to the cot until Rosie began snoring softly. Turning to Mr. Ruskin, she whispered, "She is feisty, but quite frail, I'm afraid. I fear for her health. She has spells of weakness from time to time."

"She has been in your service many years?"

Emily nodded. "And my mother's before me. My grandfather hired her after my grandmother's unexpected death. She is like family."

Mr. Ruskin extended his elbow. "Shall we leave her in peace and look over the other rooms?"

Emily put her hand lightly on his arm. "There's no gas in this part of the building yet. We'll need a lamp. Take the one from the table."

They walked together to the next room, where long racks held garments of every size and description, and hats of every type hung on pegs along the wall. Holding the lamp high, Mr. Ruskin touched a black waistcoat which hung at the end of one rack with his free hand. "Our villain will be well outfitted."

"Can it be?" Emily mused aloud, as a flash of green caught her eye. Reaching for the garment that had attracted her attention, she removed it from the rack and held it in the light of the lamp. She turned to Mr. Ruskin. "It is the costume Danny O'Shea wore in *The Irish Amadan.*"

"Are you sure?"

"There can be no mistake. My grandfather showed it to me many times."

"A man surely would look a fool in that," Mr. Ruskin admitted. "And only an Irishman would wear that shade of green."

"Suggestive of a leprechaun," Emily replied. "He ordered it so."

"These will have to be inventoried and put in some sort of order," Mr. Ruskin said. "That way we'll not be buying anything we have on hand or searching for something we know we've seen but cannot find at the opportune moment."

"Perhaps Rosie can help," Emily suggested. "She insists on accompanying me to the theater, and she wants to be useful."

"There'll be plenty of work to go around."

The next room was a catchall for small props and other miscellany. Emily was forced close to Mr. Ruskin, her wide skirts a nuisance as they wove their way to the center of the cluttered room.

"My skirt is caught," she said, and gasped as Mr. Ruskin held the lamp in her direction and the glow of the wick landed on the glass eyes and vicious teeth of a mounted tiger. She laughed with relief as she realized what had "captured" her.

"A central character in some production, no doubt," she said, carefully freeing the lace edging on a flounce of her skirt from where it had snagged on the cat's front teeth.

Mr. Ruskin held the lantern above the cat's face as she worked and said dryly, "I've known leading ladies with similar temperaments."

"Have you anyone in mind for leading lady of the company?" Emily asked.

"I have a dear friend, Marjorie Angersoll, who has been walking lady in another troop for some time. Her husband, Bertram, is an excellent heavy. If they will make the move, I'd like to offer Marjorie the leading lady position. Married couples help stabilize a company—provided, of course, they are on speaking terms."

"Will Bertram take kindly to his wife in a leading role while he remains in a lesser one?"

"I believe he will be pleased for her," Mr. Ruskin said. "He does not aspire to a leading man role— why would he? He's too large and rugged to play a leading man convincingly, and he excels in the role of heavy."

From the rear of the room, there came a crashing noise. Startled, Emily jumped, unconsciously grabbing Mr. Ruskin's arm for support. "What was that?"

"Probably another of our rodent friends," Mr. Ruskin said and, as if on cue, a mouse skittered between them.

Emily drew closer to her protector as a shiver crawled up her spine. "I shall not return to this place without one of my great-aunt's cats in tow."

Although the mouse was well gone, it did not immediately occur to Emily to draw away from Mr. Ruskin. His strength and superior size comforted her, as did his warmth, and the subtle bay rum scent about him, which reminded her of her grandfather. Indeed, as she stood there, so near to him, her hands curved over his arm, it seemed to her almost as though he were growing warmer, his presence compelling her closer.

Above them, Danny clamped his hands over his ears. A bloody cacophony, that's what it was. Ruskin's lust humming, and that tinkling, happy female sound, loud as a harp choir.

That tinkling female sound! Saints preserve us all! Danny realized suddenly what it was. He peered down at his baby sister's great-granddaughter with the disapproving scowl of a prudish old uncle. And she such a sweet thing, too. It was trouble abrewing, or he wasn't Irish. Trouble abrewing! But for the moment, he had a more important matter than his great-great-niece's virtue to deal with.

He concentrated once more on his immediate business, chanting silently: *The Irish Amadan. Investigate the crash. Pick up the script! Investigate. Find the script!*

Ruskin cleared his throat. "Perhaps, Miss Charlton, we should see what the little pest disturbed."

"Perhaps, Mr. Ruskin, since we'll be working so closely together, you should call me Emily."

Oh, quit the blasted tinkling and look for the damned script! Danny thought in exasperation.

"In that case," Ruskin said, his hum of lust becoming a virtual roar that pinned Danny against the ceiling with its force, "you must call me Gil—short for Gilford."

The devil crack the legs under you if you don't pick up

SWEET CREAM AND IRISH WHISKEY 219

the script! Danny ranted in a furor of impatience.

The commotion below ceased immediately.

"We . . . uh, had better see what the crash was," Emily said. Holding his gaze with her own, she added, with the inflection of an endearment, "Gil."

"I fear it may be necessary," Gil said, "for you to let go of my arm."

"Oh!" Emily said, nonplussed. She withdrew her hands.

Danny slapped his forehead. *Saints preserve us! The lass is in love! And the lad is equally besotted.*

Nevertheless, they were making their way toward the back of the room, getting closer to the script with each step.

"A crate toppled," Ruskin said, holding the lamp over the splintered crate and its scattered contents.

"No mouse could have pushed off anything that big, surely," Emily said.

"It must have been tottering on the brink," Ruskin said, kneeling. "These look like scripts."

"*The Irish Amadan*!" Emily read excitedly. "Do you suppose it's one of the copies used during the original production?"

"It certainly looks ancient enough," Ruskin said, picking it up and giving it a cursory examination before handing it to Emily.

She opened it and gasped in delight. "There are changes handwritten in the margins." She tucked it under her arm before helping Ruskin gather the remaining scripts into a neat stack. "I must read it!"

"I should like to read it, too," Ruskin said, passing the lamp to Emily so that he could collect the remains of the busted crate and set them aside. "I should like to see for myself what made the *Irish Amadan* character so enduring."

"Dannyboy O'Shea's interpretation made the character memorable," Emily said.

"Since the opportunity to see Dannyboy O'Shea portray the Irish Amadan is long gone, I shall have to content myself with searching for the essence of the character within the text."

5

Miss Emily And Mr. Ruskin Make An Important Decision

Gilford Ruskin did not often feast on forbidden fruit. He was neither a seducer of innocents nor a luster after other men's wives. He took care of his man's needs in ways both morally and socially accepted, with an occasional rich, older widow or nubile and accommodating chambermaid. He had engaged briefly in an affair with an actress whose devotion had ended along with the run of the play in which they'd been cast opposite each other as young lovers. She had gone on to a new affair with another actor, leaving him to nurse a broken heart and emerge from his heartache wiser and with a certain cynicism where women were concerned.

To Gilford Ruskin, Miss Emily Charlton presented an enigma of the most vexing sort. She was a gentlewoman of good breeding; she was also unconventional, venturing forth into entrepreneurship of a major theater with rare courage. Bright, witty, and spunked up beyond her own best interests, she was rebellious and determined, but her precocity made her vulnerable.

In Miss Emily Charlton's presence, Gilford Ruskin felt strongly protective. The innocence and naïveté buried within her shell of rebellion and determination appealed to his manly need to keep safe the weaker, fairer sex. He gloried, like a proud parent, in her successful dealings with the various tradesmen who came into the theater, for she was a shrewd negotiator and demanding patron. But he would have hesitated not in the least in inflicting physical damage on anyone he suspected of taking advantage of her.

As an employee, he respected her acumen.

As a man, he desired her beyond all reason. He was obsessed with her and he knew it, and he fought the obsession, fought it with the desperate temerity of a drunkard fighting the longing for liquor, of the addict fighting the need of opium. And like the drunkard and the addict, he fought in vain, for he was lost to her, heart and soul.

Still, he determined not to act on his desire. He had control and moral backbone enough not to seduce an innocent, and pride enough not to seduce the woman who offered to him his chance for recognition within the theater. He would not have it said of Gilford Ruskin that he was a leading man through the benefit of the boudoir.

Nor would he have it whispered that he was after Miss Emily Charlton's considerable inheritance. He had money enough from his mother's side of the family to keep him comfortable, and he had not, so far, been disinherited by his father.

His eldest son status, his degree from Harvard, and his distinguished service as an officer during the war had, so far, counterbalanced, in his family's eyes, his distasteful and inappropriate passion for the theater. If he distinguished himself as a manager and leading man—and if he did so without the taint of suggestion of having seduced his way to recognition—he had hopes that his family might yet accept his avocation, and that he might be considered a curiosity of society rather than a social pariah.

So it was that he shored his resolve to resist the charms of Miss Emily Charlton before every encounter with her. But his resolve softened like wax in her presence, just as more physical parts of him hardened to steel.

On the morning he returned the script of *The Irish Amadan* to her, he found her at her desk with Kilkenney, the scruffy orange tabby tomcat commissioned to rid the theater of rodents, sprawled across the blotter on her desk. He tried without success to ignore the delicacy of her hands as she stroked the purring tomcat, the voluptuousness of her mouth as she smiled, the music in her voice as she greeted him.

Wha . . . wha . . . wha . . . what! Danny woke abruptly. *That again!* The poor lad was going to wear himself out if he kept this up. All hum and no action, he was. All this lusting and he had yet to kiss the lass!

"Did you read it?" Emily said, and when Danny caught sight of the script in Ruskin's hand, he instantly forgot the issue of Ruskin's unresolved lust. This could be what he'd been waiting for!

"Quite carefully," Ruskin said. "Just as you asked."

"What did you think?"

"It's an excellent example of its kind. There's genius in the characterization of the Irish fool, and much humor in the story. I can see how, with the proper execution, it could enchant audiences."

The cat, purring loudly, rolled onto his back in ecstasy as Emily kneaded the thick fur on his chest.

Ruskin broke into a cold sweat and idly pulled at his collar.

"Remember the idea about our slogan?" Emily asked. "The Most Famous Bloodstain in Philadelphia?"

"Certainly."

"Mightn't we play on it even more strongly if we made *The Irish Amadan* our premiere production?"

Saints be praised! Danny thought, rubbing his hands in glee. Such a good lass, she was! So bright! So ingenious! He could be proud to call her kin.

"I suppose we could," Ruskin said, with a pronounced lack of enthusiasm.

"You are hesitant," Emily observed.

Hesitant? If the lad were any colder on the idea they'd need overcoats to stay warm. Ruskin's resistance drifted up to Danny as a low, churlish whirr.

"I laughed aloud while reading it," Emily said. "I smiled. If the script is that strong, the production surely could not fail to entertain. We could do it as a tribute to Dannyboy O'Shea, open on the anniversary of his death."

'Atta girl! Tell him, lass! Danny cheered, hovering close above her head so as not to miss a single word.

"To be frank," Ruskin said, "*The Irish Amadan* is not the play in which I would choose to debut as leading man of a new company. The part of the fool is appealing, but different from the way I would introduce my talent to Philadelphia, and the part of the young lover is too bland to be memorable."

"A revival of *The Irish Amadan* on the anniversary of Danny O'Shea's death would be certain to get us coverage in the papers."

Ruskin, his face stony, remained silent.

"I must consider the theater above all else," Emily said curtly. "*The Irish Amadan* may not be the most advantageous forum for your talent, but it will be a successful production, and as manager, you will benefit from that success. Once the theater is established you will be able to select plays that will allow you to show off your talent to best advantage."

Well said! Danny thought.

A frown had settled on Ruskin's face. "I try not to fall victim to the vanity which afflicts so many of my peers," he said. "But I am as human and as ambitious as the next man. Naturally I had hoped to select a part which would help establish me as a leading man."

"The part of the Irish fool—"

"Shall always belong to your great-great-uncle," Ruskin said. "I would be a usurper."

"The Irish Playhouse will always belong to him, too," Emily said. "I feel strongly that we should pay homage to him before moving into a new era, when a new leading man shall emerge as a major talent."

Ruskin was silent for a long, thoughtful moment, then sighed. "Emily, if I should ever find myself on trial for my life, I shall trust my case to your defense."

6

The Irishman Enters On Cue

"**I** have received good news from New York," Gil announced.

She was, Emily realized as she looked up at him from the announcement she was drafting, every bit as taken with Gilford Ruskin now as she had been when his cousin had introduced him to her when she'd been a mere girl and he a vastly romantic figure in his dress uniform with officer's stripes and epaulets. Framed by the door of her office, a more mature Gilford appeared as befittingly dashing as a leading man should. He wore fitted black pantaloons and a white tailored shirt open at the neck. His golden hair, parted crisply, fell in negligent waves over his forehead, suggesting a rebelliousness of spirit.

His smile of pleasure softened his expressive mouth and lent sparkle to his deep blue eyes, and his gaze warmed her in a way that was mysterious and grand. "From your friends, Marjorie and Bertram?" she asked.

"Yes. They have agreed to join our company."

"That is good news indeed."

"They must finish a production at their current theater, which means they will not arrive until the first of the month. That should pose no real inconvenience, since their roles in *The Irish Amadan* will be small. We can post them a script so they can learn their lines, and have one of our walking men or walking women fill in for them at the early rehearsals."

"I have been working on this announcement for the papers. Would you read it?"

He stepped behind her desk and read over her shoulder. "What's this word?" he asked, leaning for a closer look.

"Convenience," she said, suddenly aware of his warmth.

"Oh. I thought it was two wor—" His voice trailed off as Emily turned her head.

Whatever he was saying lost its significance when Emily discovered his face only inches from hers. Suddenly the air was fragrant with bay rum. Emily felt her face flame as her gaze settled on his mouth, moving inexorably nearer to hers. Her lips parted slightly in anticipation of the first touch.

From a great distance, or so it seemed, came the sound of a throat being cleared. Emily and Gil jerked their heads apart guiltily, turning in the direction of the disruption and staring at the source as if jarred from a trance.

"Top of the morning to ye," said the gentleman who'd cleared his throat. Crossing an arm over his waist, he bowed dramatically, then straightened. "I'm at yer service."

The visitor was of medium height, about sixty years old and slightly potbellied, with snow-white hair that waved wildly down to the bottom of his ears from a center part. He was dressed in knee breeches and a peculiar jacket of green wool felt.

Still slightly slow-witted from the spell of the kiss lost to them, Emily and Gil exchanged perplexed expressions before turning their attention back to the odd man.

"At our service in what way?" Gil asked. "Tell us at once who you are, and what business you have here."

The visitor snorted softly, as though dismissing the question as superfluous. "My business is the play, m'lad. You're producing *The Irish Amadan*, are ye not?"

"Why, yes, but—"

"Then where else would I be? The minute I heard—"

"Where did you hear?"

"Word gets around, lad. Ye're putting up notices, aren't ye?"

"The notices are still at the printer's."

The odd little man continued as if Gil had not spoken. "The minute I heard, I said to meself, 'Danny—

that's my name you see—Danny, it's off to the Irish Playhouse for you, to offer your assistance.' "

"What type of assistance?" Emily asked.

"Why, with the play, of course. Know it inside and out, I do. Backwards and forwards. Up and down. Side to side. Every line and every gag. There's not a living soul on this fine earth who knows it better than I, and that's the God's sweet truth."

"Come now, sir—" Gil began.

"Oh, it's fine to be hearing a lad with so much respect for his elders. Fine, indeed. But we'll have none of this 'sir' business. No, that won't do at all. I'm Danny. Just Danny, although some may call me Dannyboy."

"How is it that you came to know this play so well?" Emily asked.

"How do I know it? Why, haven't I been performing in it for most of me life? May the devil blister me if it's not true! The Irish fool is the part I was born to play. Who better than an Irishman with no better sense than to go into the theater?"

"You've played the title role in *The Irish Amadan?*" Emily asked.

"Where is it you're supposed to have played this part?" Gil interjected suspiciously.

"Oh, here and there."

"Here and there," Gil repeated cynically.

"Must you be so suspicious?" Emily said, her tone censuring. "The man has come to help us."

Gil's expression was grave as he turned to her. "Don't you see what he's about? He has no familiarity with this play unless he saw it in his youth! There hasn't been a production of *The Irish Amadan* on this continent for years. Decades. He's simply come to try for the part." He turned to the visitor. "Your initiative is admirable, sir, but the part has already been cast."

"Been cast?" Danny said. "How can it be cast when ye haven't even posted the notices?"

"Well, if you must know," Gil said tartly, "I am going to play the part."

"You?" Danny was outraged. "Why, you're not even Irish, lad! And you're much too handsome for the role."

"He has a point," Emily said.

Gil's jaw dropped. Recovering, he snapped it shut and turned to Emily with a scowl. "The man is obviously deranged. Look at him! An escaped lunatic, for all we know. Trying to tell me how to run—"

"He looks like the perfect Irish fool to me," Emily said. "If he's gone to this much trouble, you might at least let him read for the part."

"The part is cast!" Gil persisted.

Emily stood. "Mister—"

"Danny," the Irishman reminded her.

"Danny," Emily amended. "I would very much like to speak to Mr. Ruskin privately. Would you mind stepping out of my office for a few minutes?"

" 'There be none of Beauty's daughter/ With a magic like thee;/ And like music on the waters/ Is thy sweet voice to me,' " Danny quoted, with another deep bow. "Your every wish is my command, lass."

He exited with a smooth stride. Emily closed the door and turned to Gil, who was regarding her with a thunderous scowl.

As soon as the door was closed behind him, Danny gratefully dissolved. Saints above, he'd forgotten how exhausting it was to materialize. Appreciating the buoyancy of his spirit state, he leapt through the wall and hovered over the mortals who might very well be deciding his destiny. The very air in which he floated was a miasma of their emotions, so confused he couldn't sort one from another

"How dare you!" Ruskin said. "How dare you challenge me in front of an actor? Casting is my venue. I have full authority."

"You demand reason of me," Emily said. "I must demand it of you as well."

"Reason?" he retorted with a smirk. "What is reasonable about letting a man of questionable ability and background read for a part that is already cast?"

"And what is reasonable about your insisting on playing a part that might be better played by someone else?"

"Better played?"

"The man looks the part!" Emily persisted.

"Looks are purely superficial. A good actor makes an audience see beyond the superficial to the character within." He made a strange, wounded sound. "Have you so little confidence in my talent that you would favor a derelict off the street?"

"I would not favor him as leading man or as manager of the company. I merely suggest that you let him read. Your list of actors required for the company includes an eccentric comedian, does it not? Might he not qualify for that?"

"Then let him apply according to our instructions, at the specified day and time. His sham tactics are an insult. We cannot afford to encourage such unethical ploys."

"We cannot afford to think of anything above the welfare of the theater," Emily said. "If he has a familiarity with the role—"

"He can have no familiarity with the role. The play has not been produced!"

Danny clamped his hands flat against his ears and groaned. If his fate for all eternity did not rest on the shoulders of these silly humans, he'd gladly retire to his cot. Such a ruckus the lad's anger and frustration created! And the lass's mix of emotions was a shrill cacophony, so confused and contradictory that he could not pick one from another. Oh, he would not be a female for anything, not even the chance for eternal rest!

"Perhaps he saw it as a child. Perhaps he came upon an old script and took a fancy to the story. What harm to let him read? If his claim of familiarity is a sham, as you believe, it will be quickly obvious. If not, and he is convincing in the role, where can the harm be?"

"The title role is cast!"

"In stone?" Emily challenged.

Ruskin rolled his eyes. "Do not accuse me of intractability because I make a decision!"

"It's quite an abrupt decision to be so final!" Emily snapped. "When last we spoke, you were undecided whether you would play the fool or take the role of the besotted young lover."

Ruskin sucked in a deep draught of air. His mouth hardened into a line and a muscle in his clenched jaw twitched from strain as he formed a reply. His words were taut with control as he finally replied, "Miss Charlton, I fear I may be destined to play the fool as long as I remain at the Irish Playhouse."

"Don't be absurd!" she said. "It is but one play, the first of many to be performed here. The part of the young lover is a significant one, and your good looks will be an asset in it."

Ruskin's features softened as he looked down at her fingers, curved imploringly over his forearm. "Do you find me as good-looking as all that?"

"I think you are quite the handsomest man I've ever seen," she said. Her eyes, golden brown and flecked with the green of her Irish ancestry, confirmed her sincerity.

Aw! Not that foolishness again! Danny thought exasperatedly as the hum of Ruskin's lust and the harpish trill of Emily's desire became nearly deafening. *There's more pressing business at hand.*

"You mustn't tell a man such things, Emily," Ruskin said, with the sternness of a man losing control.

Slipping hopelessly under the spell of her charm, the lad was, Danny decided. *Hopelessly.*

"I don't see why not," Emily said. "You asked me a question. I merely answered it. Men are forever telling women how beautiful they are when they don't mean a word of it. I don't see the problem in telling the truth."

"But such an admission from a woman could inspire the baser instincts in a man."

"Not nearly so quickly as the prospects of a sizable dowry," Emily countered caustically. "In any event, I would expect a gentleman of your character to overcome his baser instincts where a lady is concerned."

Oh, Emily, if only ye knew! Danny thought. *Ye stir the lad's baser instincts more than ye realize.*

"Unfortunately," Emily continued, "not all men professing to be gentlemen share your integrity."

"I have only to recall the plight of such a man to bolster my integrity," Ruskin replied drolly. "I should not want to find myself at the unfriendly end of Rosie's broom."

Emily's mouth twitched in resistance before yielding a smile, which he answered in kind.

The play! Danny thought, waving his fist in a fit of frustration. *Quit this infernal sparking and think of the play!* Randy as hares, they were! And glad he was that he had no such silly human sentiment left to him.

At last, after a long silence during which their smiles mellowed, Emily seemed to absorb his message. "We are off the subject," she said. "Our peculiar Irish gentleman is outside, awaiting a decision."

Good lass! Danny thought. *Bring him back to business!*

Emily frowned—quite prettily. She drew in a breath and released it in a sigh of resignation. "Actually, he awaits *your* decision. It *is* a question of casting, and, therefore, the decision is yours."

Danny slapped his hand over his face and groaned. *No, lass, don't throw it in his corner. The lad's vanity is at stake.*

"I only hope," she continued, "that you will consider the matter fairly and come to a reasonable decision."

Saints be praised! Danny thought, delighted. *The lass is shrewd.* A reasonable decision. *No wonder Ruskin was frowning—the poor lad couldn't refuse without looking like a nincompoop.*

"We'll hear him read," Ruskin said, grating the words through his teeth.

7

Rosie Gets A Fright

They opened the door to find the lobby empty.

"Perhaps he reconsidered," Emily said.

Gil chortled aloud at the notion. "Highly unlikely, after all the trouble he took to show up in costume."

"You were rude to him."

"Rude? The man was a fraud. I called his bluff. That's not likely to deter an actor set on a part. My guess is that we'll find him on the stage—"

" 'Musha! Lad. Ye're takin' it all to heart. It's a draught of *poteen* ye're needin—' " The lines from the play, delivered in a beautifully brogued baritone, drifted in from the auditorium.

Gil allowed himself a smug lift of an eyebrow as he tilted his head in the direction of the door leading into the auditorium and extended his arm in invitation. "Shall we catch the rest of this performance?"

For several minutes they watched the Irishman's flawless depiction of the Irish fool. He paced back and forth, speaking to an imaginary young man, pausing for the line that no one delivered, then coming back with the proper retort, as if the cue had been given him. His timing was perfect, his elocution excellent, his movements graceful, his accent authentic. He looked, sounded, and moved like the Irish fool.

Emily stole a glance at Gil and discovered him transfixed by the Irishman's performance, excited by it as only a true lover of great theater could be. She had feared he would give the Irishman half an ear and throw him out, but obviously he was awed by the actor's skill.

"So," she said softly, "you'll play the young lover."

"A role well suited for someone so deucedly handsome, is it not?" Gil replied with an endearing grin.

Emily's lips curved into a fetching smile before she turned her attention back to the Irishman on stage. Caught up in his portrayal of the Irish fool, she did not see Rosie step onto the stage until the maid gasped loudly. By the time Emily and Gil turned their heads to see who was there, the elderly woman was crossing herself. "Saints preserve us, it's himself!" she said, and then sank to the floor.

Emily and Gil took off at a sprint. Reaching Rosie's limp form, Emily knelt and pressed her ear to the old woman's chest. Relieved to hear a faint but steady heartbeat, she looked at Gil. "She's just fainted." Tears brightened her eyes as she cradled the old woman's head in her lap, stroking her silver hair.

"Should I fetch a glass of water?" Gil asked.

Emily shook her head. "She prefers whiskey. She'll have a tot as soon as she comes to."

Danny had joined them. "Is she—?"

"Merely fainted," Gil said. "I don't think she was expecting to encounter the Irish Amadan on the stage just yet."

A low moan drew their attention to Rosie, who was regaining consciousness. She mumbled incoherently for a moment then, spying Danny, let loose a discordant scream.

Emily hugged her fiercely, trying to still her. "Sh-h-h-h. You've had a fright."

"It's himself!" Rosie said, staring wild-eyed at Danny. "It's Dannyboy O'Shea, back from the grave."

"Oh, it's not Danny O'Shea, Rosie. It's only an actor, come to read for the part of the Irish fool."

Unable to peel her gaze from Danny's face, Rosie took several deep breaths in rapid succession.

"You *must* calm yourself," Emily insisted.

"He's the spitting image of Dannyboy O'Shea," Rosie said.

Danny bowed gallantly. "Danny O . . . 'Dowd at your service."

"He's in costume," Emily said. "That explains the resemblance to the old portraits we have."

"Portraits?" Rosie said. "I saw Dannyboy with me own eyes many times. Sure, and didn't he come visiting yer own grandfather when your dear mother,

God rest her soul, was but a wee thing. Always spoiling her with peppermint candies, he was, and saying how much she looked like his poor dead sister. Would I be forgetting such a famous man's face?"

She raised herself to a sitting position, bracing herself with one elbow.

"Slowly now," Emily ordered.

"I've no need of mollycoddling," Rosie said. "A tot of whiskey will put me to rights." She slipped her hand into her pocket and brought out her flask.

Staring at the old woman's shaking hand, Emily let her drink, then turned to the men. "We must get her to a comfortable place so she can rest."

Over Rosie's spirited protests they led her to the cot backstage. Emily sat beside the cot, as much to make certain Rosie rested as to keep her company, while the men retreated to afford them privacy.

"Ye're making too big a fuss," Rosie said. "It's devil's business to be lying abed in the middle of the day!"

"You fainted, Rosie," Emily said.

"Aye. And so would you, if ye thought ye'd seen a ghost!"

"Is this Danny O'Dowd so very like my great-great-uncle?"

"Oh, aye, Miss Emily. Even the voice is the same. I couldn't believe me ears when I heard him, and went to see for meself. It was himself, I was sure of it."

"That is quite a coincidence," Emily said thoughtfully. She didn't believe for a moment that Danny O'Shea had come back from the grave, of course; Rosie was superstitious and excitable and had not seen Danny O'Shea in nearly forty years, and then perhaps only a few times. But if Danny O'Dowd looked and sounded enough like Dannyboy O'Shea to convince someone who'd seen her great-great-uncle that Dannyboy O'Shea was back on the stage at the Irish Playhouse, perhaps the resemblance between the two men could be used to advantage. She would have to mention it to Gil.

8
Emily's Troubling Reflections

Emily sat in the center of the auditorium watching Gil and Danny exchange lines. Gil held a script, reading the part of the young lover. Danny spoke his lines from memory, never missing a cue. But there was more in his performance than an accurate recitation of lines. He was immersed in the character; actor and character were one and the same, in a single person.

Gil was convincing, too, although not yet as deep into his role of the young lover. Oh, but he looked the part—dashing, handsome, and virile enough to make a woman's heart sing. And sing Emily's heart did, just as it had the first time she'd seen him, in the parlor of her best friend's home. She'd been only a young girl then, and late that night, when she and Elsbeth should have been sleeping but instead were exchanging secrets the way young girls are wont to do, Emily had confided to Elsbeth in a whisper that she was in love with the handsome Captain Ruskin.

How long ago that seemed! And how it hurt to remember what it was like to be so filled with romantic notions. She'd been so naive, too naive even to suspect that she would, through her inheritance, become a commodity for her father to barter.

Her grandfather's death had altered her life irreversibly, changing her from debutante to heiress. The aura of wealth had descended over her like a dark veil. Her inheritance had roused the greed in people, and she had learned, almost overnight, how quickly and thoroughly people were corrupted by the scent of money.

Men had come in hopes of winning her hand and the purse that came with it. Her father, under the guise of protecting her, had sifted through the prospective suitors and settled on the one who could do him the most benefit: Reginald Green, an altogether disagreeable man—overbearing, vain, vapid, insufferably boring, and intolerably stupid.

She had rebuked him, her father had championed him, and therein had begun a battle of wills that had ended with the most bitter revelation of all: her father had married her mother not for love, but for the Lindsay family connection and fortune. Ironically, that fortune had been denied him by the mischance of having his wife die before she could inherit the wealth from her father, and having his father-in-law live long enough for Emily to reach her majority before becoming his heir.

In a moment of high conflict, her father had confessed his bitterness over the failure of his marriage to produce the wealth he'd anticipated. She owed him this marriage, he'd insisted, for he'd long yearned to see the Charltons and the Greens linked by marriage.

At Emily's first threat of moving to Philadelphia and reopening the theater her grandfather had left her if her father didn't relent on his insistence that she marry Reginald Green, whom she abhorred, her father had berated her. The final, crushing blow had been delivered when he cursed the Irish taint in the Lindsay blood, a peculiarity of her great-grandfather's highly improper love match with an Irish woman whose beauty had made her the sensation of Philadelphia society at the height of her brother's fame. The taint, as he referred to it, had been responsible for certain common qualities in his wife which, he feared, had been perpetuated in his daughter.

In desperation, her father had arranged for Green to catch Emily alone, intent on dishonoring her so she would have no choice but to marry him. But they had not counted on Emily's fierce resistance or Rosie's savage broom. By the time Emily's father returned to the house, expecting to find his daughter humbled and compliant, his daughter and Rosie were en route to Philadelphia.

So here she sat in the theater she owned, an heiress, rebel entrepreneur, and social pariah. Estranged from her father, missing her grandfather, living in a house with a great aunt for whom she'd never felt any particular affection, she had only Rosie to cling to—Rosie and the theater, which had become the focus of her attention.

Refusing to dwell on the melancholy aspects of her life, Emily blinked back tears, sniffed, thrust up her chin defiantly, rose, and withdrew to her office. There was much to consider since the arrival of the newest member of the Irish Theater company. If they could but exploit his resemblance to Dannyboy O'Shea and link it with the revival of *The Irish Amadan*, all of Philadelphia would be clamoring for tickets to the Irish Playhouse.

9

A Moment Of Bliss

An hour or so after leaving the auditorium, Emily heard Gil and Danny in the lobby. Within minutes, Gil appeared at her office door. "I've hired him," he said.

Emily nodded thoughtfully, looked down at the draft of the announcement she planned to send to the papers, and then back at Gil. "Did he tell you any more about himself—where he came from, or where he's performed?"

Gil's mouth hardened as he considered the question. "Only that he is originally from County Galway, and did some theater in London."

"The same as Dannyboy O'Shea," Emily mused aloud.

Dematerialized once again, Danny floated in to observe.

"I still do not trust him entirely," Ruskin said.

"He knows the play," Emily said. "He was thoroughly convincing."

"That much is true," Ruskin conceded. "But there's a strong odor to his story."

The lad is going to be trouble.

"Does it matter so much where he came from if his performance is good?"

Good point, lass.

239

"Once the curtain is up, nothing matters but the performance."

Now ye're talking sense, lad.

"I suppose he's not the first man to write himself an advantageous personal history," Ruskin added with a resigned sigh.

Advantageous personal history, is it? Danny thought, outraged. *Gospel truth it was, every bloody word of it!*

"You are quite cynical, Mr. Ruskin," Emily observed.

"I have been around enough theaters to know these types," he replied, and smiled mischievously. "You may discover that not all actors share my sterling character any more than they share my extraordinary handsomeness."

Oh, and he's humble as well as brilliant.

Emily frowned. "I fear I shall live to regret that bit of flattery."

"Most likely," Ruskin said. "But I hope you never lose the spontaneity that enabled you to speak your mind. That would be a great pity. A great pity, indeed."

Their eyes met as he spoke, and Emily felt that remote contact almost as a physical thing, for she saw something in his eyes that matched something that dwelled within her, an undeniable yearning. Warmth passed through her, accompanied by a sensation of such exhilaration that she found it difficult to sit in the chair as though nothing extraordinary were happening.

Emily searched for something to say, and finally reverted to the safe topic of theater business, sharing her ideas about exploiting Danny O'Dowd's resemblance to Dannyboy O'Shea. "If we could but get people talking about the coincidence, we might interest a journalist in the fact that we are staging *The Irish Amadan.*"

"Yes-s-s," Gil said thoughtfully. "The right word

of mouth in the right quarters might serve us well. Our production would pique the interest not only of serious theater patrons, who would concern themselves with the history of the Irish Playhouse, but also of those just out for an evening of farce."

"So how do we begin?" Emily asked.

"With Rosie."

"Rosie?"

"Are there servants in your house she might tell about mistaking Danny O'Dowd for Danny O'Shea?"

Emily grinned. "I'm sure with a little coaxing Rosie could be persuaded to repeat her blood-freezer of a tale."

"Everyone to whom she relates the tale must be advised that it is to be kept in strictest confidence. That will assure that it will circulate with the swiftness of an epidemic."

"You are quite outrageous," Emily said, but a smile undermined the sternness of the remark.

"And you are astute to see so quickly how we could exploit the theater's history through our peculiar friend," Gil countered. "If he shows up for rehearsals and isn't prone to the Irishman's curse of the whiskey bottle and doesn't freeze in front of an audience, then we're lucky to have him."

Freeze in front an audience? Dannyboy O'Shea? Why I was walking the boards in front of audiences before yer father was even a grawl! The lad had gone too far this time! In a burst of temper, Danny grabbed a massive spiderweb from the corner of the room and dropped it over Ruskin's head. It billowed down and settled over his head, matting his hair and clinging to his skin.

"What the—?" Ruskin said, clawing at the sticky web in a panic.

Emily ran around her desk to offer assistance, wiping at the fine silk threads with her fingertips, trying to roll it off his skin. "I don't see any spiders," she said reassuringly.

"They're probably crawling down my spine," Ruskin said, rolling his shoulders.

"That was the queerest draft," Emily said. "It was almost as if—" Words failed her as she realized how near she was to him, that she was touching him in an intimate way. In a single rush of awareness, she noted the roughness of a day's growth of whiskers under her fingers, the warmth of his flesh, the scents of bay rum and wilting starch and something male and disturbing and wonderfully exciting.

Aggghhh! Danny thought, as the humming and trilling recommenced. *Not that again! Those two are going to set the building ablaze with all this nonsense.* Having heard what he needed to hear, he floated from the office, through the auditorium, across the stage and into the wardrobe room, where he could curl up in a stack of discarded clothing and recover his strength. Visibility was draining.

Suddenly, Gil's hands were on Emily's waist. She felt them there, hot and strong and strangely reassuring, and realized she didn't mind them there at all. Her heart pounded wildly as his face moved nearer and nearer. At the first teasing brush of his mouth on hers, a whisper-soft gasp escaped her lips, leaving them lightly parted. And then the devastating gentleness of that tender contact gave way to an imposing urgency as his mouth pressed more firmly. His lips were soft, slightly moist, and . . . clever.

Oh, how cleverly they moved, thrilling her with sensations she could never have imagined and yet had been waiting for her entire lifetime. It was the magic and madness of which the poets spoke, but now, experiencing it, falling under the magical spell, she realized that no words could adequately describe this splendor.

Gil felt the same splendor. Her beauty captivated him. Her wit and spirit intrigued him. Her very innocence sparked in him a primitive urge to possess her in a way no man ever had or ever could again. He'd tried to resist her, but with her fingers on his cheeks and the scent of her hair in his nostrils and the frank adoration in her eyes as she'd met his gaze, he'd been drawn into a tempest of temptation that proved stronger than his most determined resistance.

Her sweetness inflamed his senses, stirring his lust; her softness terrified him in the way it drove him both to protect and possess her. He had kissed many women, on many occasions. The physical sensations were not new to him, but this fierce need to protect was, as was the intensity of his desire for her. Perhaps the very knowledge that he should resist her made her all the more irresistible. Whatever it was about Miss Emily Charlton that stirred his ardor to such a pitch, Gil found himself reluctant to end the kiss. Upon forcing himself to take his hands away from her waist, he suffered a devastating sense of loss and regret.

He took another step away from her, guiding her hands from his face.

His eyes did not leave her, however. She was clearly dazed from the effects of the kiss, her cheeks flushed, her lips swollen. She opened her eyes slowly and smiled with such an expression of wonder that Gil had to exercise an iron will not to pull her back into his arms.

Unable to continue looking at her, he turned his head—by chance, in the direction of the door.

"You needn't look over your shoulder for a falling broom," Emily said. "Rosie is backstage, sleeping soundly." She reached up to pluck a small patch of web still clinging to his hair.

Gil trapped her wrist and pulled her hand away. "Emily."

He had meant to explain, with extreme tact and consideration for her feminine pride, the inappropriateness of their having kissed. To take the blame, to beg her forgiveness and assure her that there would be no recurrence. But her face was still flushed, her eyes full of guileless adoration. Her expression still held the wonder of a woman's first true kiss.

So instead of words, the only sound to emerge from his throat was an unintelligible growl of frustration, and instead of a lecture, Miss Emily Charlton received her second true kiss—more thorough, more enduring, more ardent and demanding than the first.

10
Rosie's Suspicions Are Confirmed

A few days later, Danny plopped down on the pile of clothing in the corner of the wardrobe room with a weary sigh of relief. Musha, but all this visibility was wearing on a soul! A quick nap in his spirit state would refresh him.

Relaxing, he closed his eyes and allowed himself to fade slowly. He was but a translucent, shadowy figure, near to sleep, when he heard a gasp.

His eyes jerked open—to the sight of Rosie staring at him from between the clothes racks.

"Saints preserve us, it *is* you!" she said. "Danny-boy O'Shea, back from the grave."

With an aggrieved frown, Danny forced himself to become visible. "Aye, Rosie, there's no use trying to deny it now. Ye've found me out."

"It's no surprise," she sniped smugly. "I knew ye'd been kissing the Blarney stone when you said your name was O'Dowd."

"Ye're not afraid of me, then? Like ye was the other day?"

"It's surprised I was to be seein' ye is all," Rosie replied. "It's quite a shock to meet a dead man."

"I'd be obliged to ye if ye didn't tell anyone."

"Not if ye'll tell me what brings ye back from the grave."

"It's me soul, Rosie. It's confused. I died in the middle of a performance, ye see, so part of me soul stayed behind as the Irish fool. I've only to play the part once more and exit as Dannyboy O'Shea to put me soul back together. It's almost forty years I've waited for this chance, and if I don't do it now, there's no telling how long it'll be before I get another chance. So I'd appreciate you keeping my secret until after I've gone on."

"Aye. I'll keep your secret for ye," Rosie said. "Miss Emily's done had me *colloguing* like a *blatherskite* with the other staff about mistaking you—or Mr. O'Dowd, that is—for a ghost. But if I start talking about confused souls, Miss Emily's likely to put me in me bed with a cloth on me head. The lass worries about me so."

"Aye. A fine colleen she is, and the spitting image of me baby sister. Ye've done a good job with her, Rosie." He shook his head slowly. "Dear little Rosie. I remember when me nephew hired you to take care of me sister's grandbaby. Just a slip of a lass you were. And now ye're all grown up and fubsy, a fine figure of a woman."

"I'm an old woman, and that's the truth of it," Rosie said. "And not too far from where ye'll be going when you finish yer play."

Danny gasped. "Rosie, no! Ye mustn't talk that way!"

"Oh, but it's true," she said. "There's nothing to be gained by trying to deny it. It's me heart, ye see."

"Oh," Danny said morosely. "It's like that, is it?"

"Aye. It's not so bad for me. I've had a good, long life. It's Miss Emily that concerns me."

"Miss Emily?"

"Oh, aye. Poor lass. I'm the only one she has left, with her mother in her grave all these years and her Grandfather Lindsay gone this year."

"What of her father?"

Rosie sniffed indignantly. "Her father! Now there's a piece of work. Looked down his nose at the Irish, he did, and forbade her from mentioning her Irish blood."

"No!" Danny said, outraged.

"Sorry as it is, it's the gospel truth," Rosie lamented. "Himself was going to marry her off to a *bosthoon*, but Miss Emily wouldn't stand for it. So here we are in Philadelphia, and when I'm gone, she'll have no one."

"The lad?" he asked. "He seems smitten with her."

"Oh, I was hoping. She's smitten enough with him. Ye should have heard her. 'Oh, Rosie,' she says, 'he kissed me, and it was glorious. It was quite the most extraordinary experience.' She talked that way for an hour, and never once grew tired of the telling of it."

"Has she had a change of heart?"

"Not Miss Emily," Rosie said. "No, it's the lad

He's gone and broken her heart. He's proud, ye see, and he doesn't think it's fitting to be romancing his boss."

"No!"

"Aye. The lad's set on making his reputation on his talent alone. He won't stand for people saying he got his managership any other way."

Danny shook his head. "It's a perplexing predicament. A perplexing predicament."

Rosie shook her head, too, sharing his dismay. "Such a shame, it is, and so cruelly unfair. When her grandfather died, the men came buzzing around her like flies on a melon rind. After her money, ye see, and she held them all in contempt for their greed. And now she's gone and fallen in love with a man who won't court her because of the very thing that drew the others. It's a cruel twist of fate, I tell ye. A cruel twist."

"It's only his pride that stands in his way," Danny said. "Perhaps with some persuasion—"

"Oh, I'd like to see it before I die," Rosie said. "I'm so tired, ye see, but I can't bear leaving her so alone. If I but knew he'd be there to care for her, I could go without the burden of it on my mind."

Danny winked broadly. "The boy just needs to have his eyes opened, is all."

"Oh, if you could—"

"I'll do what I can," Danny promised. "But I fear Miss Emily is the only one who can open his eyes."

11

Dannyboy Plays Matchmaker

Danny had to wait days for an opportunity to catch Mr. Ruskin and Miss Emily together alone.

They were avoiding each other. That was the way of it, and the tension between them was as thick as molasses. Danny wasn't as sensitive to emotion in his corporeal state as in his spirit state, but a man only needed eyes to see that they puffed up like cornered cats when they came within sight of each other.

Danny took that to mean that they were thinking about kissing each other. Aye, but there was nothing harder on a man than wanting to kiss a woman, and thinking about kissing a woman, and not kissing her. Hell on earth, it was for a strapping healthy lad like Mr. Ruskin.

With the arrival of a long line of actors and actresses wanting to read for the company, and the workmen still cleaning and patching, and painters working on sets, the theater had grown chaotic. Danny had to give the lad credit. He was coordinating it all well, keeping peace in the lines and putting everyone to work. Very authoritative, the lad was. Even Miss Emily was wielding a paintbrush on the backdrops, although she'd volunteered—actually, insisted, which had only made Mr. Ruskin scowl all the more.

Danny had caught the lad ogling her as she worked, always with that scowl of frustration on his face. Oh, the lad was ripe as a red apple for a bit of persuasion and eye-opening!

Danny's chance came early on a Thursday morning, when the theater was still relatively empty. Miss Emily was in her office, reviewing proofs the printer had sent over. Mr. Ruskin had been in and out of the office he'd set up backstage, going back and forth to the stage to check on worrisome details.

Danny perched himself on the stage, confident that he'd intercept any attempt of Mr. Ruskin's to see Miss Emily. He was rewarded in less than an hour, when Mr. Ruskin strode forth from the wings, crossed the stage, and headed down the aisle toward the lobby with the grim countenance of a man with distasteful business to attend to.

Though her office door was open, he knocked before entering. Danny floated through the wall to hover above them.

"I've prepared a list of positions I believe we should fill," Ruskin said. "Beyond the slots already filled, there are six additional, four male and two female."

Emily skimmed the list he'd put in front of her. "The response to our advertisements was very good," she observed dryly.

"I've had a good look at what's available and have asked the most promising of our applicants to return for a second reading. Two of them, I'm sure I'll hire, unless their encore readings disappoint. Others will have to compete for the roles that are open. I should be able to compile a final list by day's end."

Oh, the expression on Emily's face! If Danny had seen it once, he'd seen it a thousand times, and it was enough to throw fear into the heart of any reasonable man, alive or dead. The mouth, set in a pout. The nose, tilted a bit too high. The chin, thrust defiantly. Danny could not help feeling a stab of pity for the lad upon whom such a look fell.

"You do excellent work, Mr. Ruskin," she said, and Danny decided that she must be thinking about kissing Mr. Ruskin for her manner to be so formal or her tone to be so brittle.

A muscle twitched in Ruskin's jaw as he acknowledged the compliment with a stiff nod. "I should like to begin offering jobs tomorrow," he said. "You have given me a budget for staff. Am I free to allocate that sum at my discretion, or must I submit a budget of proposed allocations for your approval prior to making my offers?"

"You have full authority over the hiring and negotiation of the players," Emily retorted. "That includes setting the salaries within the budget you've been allotted."

"Very well then. I shall set appointments in the order of strength of preference, in case I have to make adjustments to my estimates in order to get the players I really want. When the negotiations are complete, I'll submit a full report."

"I would expect nothing less from my manager," she said sharply. "After all, you've made it abundantly clear that you are aware of my status as owner."

She was thinking about kissing him, all right, Danny decided. The tinkling was beginning, and Mr. Ruskin had been humming ever since he'd entered the room.

The lustful vibrations rose to almost unbearable levels as they stared at each other from across the desk in the tense silence.

"If there's nothing further," Ruskin said finally.

"I'm sure there's nothing," Emily snapped.

"Then I shall retire to my office and put my notes in order before the actors arrive."

Oh no, lad, ye won't! Danny thought. *Enough of this nonsense! I've only to get the two of ye close enough together—*

Lowering himself to the floor behind Emily's chair, he gave the leg a good swift kick. The chair collapsed, and Emily went with it, screeching in surprise.

The lad was at her side in a flash. "Emily? Are you—?"

Emily had recovered from the surprise and gave him a quelling look, but it was too late. His hands were already on her, cupping her elbows to assist her up from the floor, where she and the chair had landed in an ignoble heap. Danny had to clamp his hands over his ears to block the concert of all their pent-up yearning as her expression softened, and the concern on the lad's face changed into a different kind of tenderness.

"Oh," Emily said as he guided her to her feet, never losing eye contact with her.

"Emily," he said, pleading for mercy that was not in her power to give, for the strength of resistance she was powerless to supply him.

"Gil," she replied, as her hands came to rest on his chest.

Danny slowly floated away as nature took over. Despite the caterwauling of their mingled desires, there was sweetness enough in their kiss to make a man nostalgic for his youth! Such passion. Such intensity.

Aye, he told himself as he materialized in the lobby and guarded the door, so as to intercept anyone who might disturb them, *it's a good piece of work ye've done, Dannyboy. A good piece of work.*

Not wishing the two young mortals disturbed, he

took a sentry position in the lobby, steering the actors who'd been invited for a second reading into the auditorium through the door at the opposite end of the lobby.

12
The Bitter With The Sweet

The world was spinning crazily, but Emily did not care. She closed her eyes against the dizzying effects of Gil's closeness and slipped her arms around his neck, hugging him fiercely while his mouth—clever as always—covered hers and performed magic. It must be magic—what else would explain this marvelous tingling that burned through her? This feeling that she might float away if he were not holding her so firmly against him?

His tongue passed over her lips. Startled, she gasped, then surrendered to the glory of sensation as Gil took advantage of her mouth being open to sample its secrets.

She pressed closer to his warmth, his hardness. Her knees grew so weak that it seemed she might collapse if her arms were not around him. She wanted . . . she knew not what. Something greater and sweeter, something thrilling and fulfilling. Something only Gil could make her yearn for, and only Gil could grant her.

Oh, he must surely feel it, too. His body was heating, his heart racing as he held her. There was a desperation and recklessness in the way his mouth probed hers, an impatience in the way he anchored her against him as though trying to fuse them into a single entity. Surely he would realize now that this was meant to be.

But, suddenly, with an animal-like growl, Gil tore his mouth from hers, and pried her arms from around his neck. He stepped back, abandoning her, leaving her breathless and hopelessly confused.

"This will not do!" he said, as if accusing her of something grievous. Anger contorted his beautiful features.

Tears stung Emily's eyes. What had she done to deserve his scorn? She wanted him, body and soul— was her regard for him so repugnant that he should fling it in her face?

"Do you not feel it too?" she asked. "This force pulling us together?"

Feel it? Gil was flabbergasted. Was she so blind that she did not see that he was fighting against that force with every shred of resistance in his body? So naïve that she could not recognize the passion she roused in him? So innocent that she did not know how sexual yearning could drive a man near to madness?

"We have been through this before, Emily. There can be nothing between us beyond our alliance as owner and manager, and without hope of more, such intimacy is most improper."

"Improper?" she repeated. "What do you care about propriety? If you wished to be proper, you would not defy convention by seeking a career on the stage. If you cared about propriety, your objection would be my reputation, not my ownership of the theater. It is only your vanity that forbids a personal alliance with me!"

"My reputation as an actor—"

"Oh, you are loathsome!" Emily said. "Loathsome

and conceited! Because of pride you deny us both the pleasure of . . . of—"

"You know not even of what you speak!"

"I would have you teach me."

Gil froze. "You torture me with such talk," he said. "And I fear you are too innocent even to realize it."

"Do you loathe my innocence so much?"

Gil regarded her for a long moment, studying her face, still flushed from their kiss; her lips, still bruised by the greed of his mouth on them. "Yes, Emily. I loathe your innocence. I loathe it because it demands strength from me. I cannot marry you and I will not ruin you, so I am condemned to the hell of wanting you while knowing I cannot have you."

"It is only your pride that condemns you," she said, and exhaled a weary sigh. "And condemns me as well."

After an awkward silence, Gil said stiffly, "I was wrong to kiss you, Emily, but your eagerness undermines my willpower. It would help if, in the future, you would not be so . . . agreeable to kissing me."

Emily's frustration gave way to rage. "You may be assured, Mister Ruskin, that you will never again find me in the least agreeable to kissing you!"

"You needn't overdramatize. I merely ask that you restrain yourself from—" How was he to finish the sentence? Melting in his arms when he touched her? Tasting like heaven? Setting him aflame with his desire for her?

"Restrain myself?" Emily shouted. "There'll be no need for restraint!" She hurled a blotter at him. "I'd sooner kiss a jackass!"

Gil dodged the blotter handily, but as he righted himself, a bottle of ink caught him in mid chest. He stared incredulously at the black ink spread across the front of his shirt, then he turned a furious scowl on Emily. "I have actors coming to read. How am I to explain—"

"Tell them it is proof of the Irish temper of the great-grandniece of Dannyboy O'Shea!" Emily said. "And now I suggest that you remove yourself from my sight. The only thing left to throw is the letter opener, and it's very sharp. One famous bloodstain is quite enough for any theater."

13
Dannyboy Advises Miss Emily On The Nature Of Men

"No, no, no!" Gil thundered. "This fence cannot go this far upstage. Do you want our Danny to trip over it and bust his head the way Dannyboy O'Shea did?"

"No, sir!" Charlie said. "I'm sorry, Gil." As the youngest member of the company, the boy spent most of his time as stagehand and errand boy—and, when the situation demanded it, taking the brunt of Gil's ill temper.

In the wings, Marjorie, the leading lady, observed, "Gil's been in her office again."

"He's going to wind up marrying her or murdering her," her husband, Bertram, agreed.

"Let's hope he marries her. If he strangles her, they'll hang him and close the theater, and we'll be out looking for work," Marjorie said.

"Either way, we'll fall victim to his foul temper until he decides which it's to be."

"Especially poor Charlie," Marjorie said. "Gil's been tough on the boy ever since he caught the two of them with their heads together."

"Poor Charlie," Bertram agreed. "He was only asking Miss Emily's advice on how to woo the taproom keeper's daughter."

Marjorie harrumphed in exasperation. "Gil is a madman where she's concerned. It's like trying to tiptoe past a hornet's nest to be around him."

Danny, who'd been observing Gil's browbeating of the young actor, listened with interest to the exchange between his fellow actors, wishing he knew how to bring the lad and lass together. Since the day Gil had stormed out of Emily's office with ink staining his shirt, there'd been no peace between the two of them. The lad had grown churlish and volatile, the lass sullen and withdrawn. Wearing their hearts on their sleeves, they were, and thinking no one could see what was gnawing at them.

Danny sighed. Time was running out. Opening night was less than a week away, and they were still at odds.

"Marjorie!" Gil called. "Let's go through the scene in the garden. And Bertram, pay attention. You've missed your cue every time we've been through it."

Marjorie gave Bertram a small shrug and walked onto the stage.

"Danny!"

"Aye, Gil, I'm moving to me position."

"No. Your lines are fine. Charlie can read them. I want you to go out into the seats and see how the scene looks from there."

"Whatever ye want, lad," Danny said.

As he left the stage and moved into the auditorium, he spied Emily sitting near the rear of the theater, looking as though someone had piled the weight of the world on her shoulders.

He went to her. "Do ye mind if I sit with ye, Miss Emily?"

Her face brightened briefly. "Please do."

The actors were just a few lines into the scene before Marjorie got her tongue twisted and broke into giggles at the way she'd botched the line.

Gil threw up his hands. "All right. Let's start over."

"Will we have a good show, Danny?" Emily asked, as Marjorie moved back into position to begin the scene again.

"Oh, aye, Miss Emily. Gil knows what he's doing. He's good."

Emily sniffed disdainfully. "He's a beast!"

"So it's like that, is it?" Danny said. "Is it anything ye can tell an old man about?"

Her chin quivered as she thrust it up in defiance. "I do not understand men at all," she said. "They are the most unreasonable creatures."

"Sure, lass," Danny agreed. "It's the gospel truth. Especially when it comes to women."

"Or money," she said, with a sniff.

"Oh, aye. Money'll do it, too. Turn a perfectly reasonable man into a fool, same as a woman's face."

"Or pride."

"Oh, aye. Pride can be a fearful thing in a man."

A tear slid down Emily's cheek, and she fought valiantly not to shed another. It was enough to break an uncle's heart.

"He's not immune to your charm," Danny said consolingly. "I've seen him looking at ye."

"He finds me pleasing enough," she said. "It's the theater that's the problem. So long as I own it, and so long as he's leading man, he wants nothing to do with me. He fears everyone would attribute his success to his . . . romantic alliance.''

"Oh, it's a dilemma for a proud man," he agreed. "A dilemma."

Emily's chin quivered again. "This theater is my legacy. It came to me from my grandfather, and to him from an uncle he dearly loved. I'll not give it up for a man who doesn't have the courage to love me in spite of my owning it."

"That's the spirit, lass. A man with no more backbone than that doesn't deserve the love of a fine woman such as yerself."

"It's quite unfair. I left New York to get away from men who wanted to marry me for my inheritance, only to meet a man who shuns me because of it. So I shall have the theater and be miserable."

"Well now, that depends, lass. That depends."

"On what?"

"On whether ye're willing to fight for what ye want."

"I'll not go chasing after him!" she said.

"Well now, there's chasing, and there's . . . convincing."

"Convincing?"

"Aye. The lad likes ye well enough. It seems to me it's just a matter of convincing him that a soft woman is a better companion than pride."

"Mr. O'Dowd!" Her eyes were round as saucers.

"I mean no disrespect by speaking frankly, Miss Emily, but if ye want to win a man, ye need to think like a man. There's never been a man yet who could understand the way a woman thinks, and that's the gospel truth of it."

Hesitantly, she asked, "How would I—?"

"Well now, there's many a father would tell his daughter that no man will buy a cow if he can get the milk for free. Oh, I've embarrassed ye, lass. I'm sorry."

"No," she said, swallowing for composure. "Please do go on, Danny."

"It seems to me if I wanted to sell a man a cow, it's not the milk, but a taste of the cream I'd be giving him." He nodded. "Aye. A taste of sweet cream."

Emily's face turned bright red. "You've been most frank with me, Danny, and I shall consider your advice very seriously."

"Aye. Ye're a bright lass. Think on it a while."

14
Sweet Cream And Irish Whiskey

"**D**anny!" Charlie said, running into the wings from backstage. "It's Rosie. She needs to see you."

"Rosie?"

"She says it's urgent," Charlie replied.

Danny virtually ran to the wardrobe room. "Rosie, what is it? Is it yer heart?"

"Oh, and sure it's me heart, sure enough! It's abreakin', Danny. Atearin' into tiny pieces. And it's all on yer account."

She grabbed a broom propped against the wall in the corner and waved it menacingly, finally bringing it down in a blow that would have struck Danny soundly had he not adroitly jumped back. Undeterred, she brought the weapon up again for another close brush with Danny's person.

"Aiii, Rosie, what are ye doing, making a man jump around like a fish out of water? If ye keep this up, I'll have to make meself disappear."

Another close strike.

"Rosie, ye mustn't get yerself so worked up! Remember yer heart!"

Rosie gave a cackle of derision. "Me heart's breaking and it's all because of you."

"Aw, Rosie, put the bloomin' broom down and tell me what's got ye so worked up."

Like a wind-up toy that had lost its tension, Rosie slowly lowered the broom. "It's Miss Emily. She's—" Rosie burst into tears, but backed away when Danny reached to console her. "Don't ye come near me, ye . . . ye blackguard. Ye traitor. It's all yer fault."

Infernal woman! "What's all my fault. Quit the blathering and boo-hooing and tell me what's wrong with Miss Emily."

"It's her virtue," Rosie said. "And her such a sweet, innocent thing. She doesn't know what she's doing, the ramifications— She's gone and sent for Mr. Ruskin, and they're going to be all alone. Oh-h-h, and it's all yer fault."

"My fault?"

"Aye. And didn't you tell her that to sell a man a cow, she must give him a taste of the cream?"

"That I did, and sound advice it was, too."

Rosie sniffed. "Well, she's taken it to heart, that one. She's sent for Mr. Ruskin, and she said for me to tell you that she's going to let him taste the cream. They're going to be all alone in that garden, what with the servants off and her great-aunt off playing whist, and not a soul to chaperon them. Oh, it's tragic, Danny. Tragic. A sweet young lass like Miss Emily."

"Oh, but it's not tragic, Rosie. Don't ye see? This

is good news. The two couldn't go on the way they've been these past weeks, all pent up and ready to explode. They're in love, and they've been denying themselves."

Rosie dissolved into fresh sobs. "Such a sweet lass. So innocent."

Danny draped an arm across her shoulders. "Aye, but he's a good lad and he loves her. He'll come around and do the right thing by her, wait and see."

Rosie cried harder. "Just a lass she is. Just a little girl."

"Aw, Rosie, ye're naive. She's a woman, fully grown. She has a woman's needs."

"A woman's needs!" Rosie repeated, and broke into renewed sobs.

"Ye don't understand the way it is with men and women, Rosie. You were but a bairn yerself when ye went to work for me nephew, and ye've been with little girls ever since. It's a natural thing."

"Don't understand?" Rosie protested, suddenly infuriated out of her tears. "So ye're thinking I don't understand what it is to love a man, to be loved, are ye? Well, ye obviously don't know about Mr. Timothy O'Hanlan or ye wouldn't be saying such a thing about me."

"Mr. Timothy O'Hanlan?"

"Aye. Me dear Timmy. Such a handsome lad, he was. He was head groom in Mr. Lindsay's stables. A fine hand with a horse he had, that one. And handsome as the very devil. And don't ye be thinking that he didn't teach me what it was to be a woman, for all that we had only a horse blanket thrown over a bed of sweet hay spread in a stall in the stables."

A beatific smile transformed her face as she recalled the splendor. "*Musha*, it was grand." The smile faded slowly, to be replaced by a scowl as she turned back to Danny. "So don't ye be telling me I don't know what's about to happen in that garden."

"And knowing, would ye deny her that pleasure?" Danny challenged.

"It's different for a lass like Miss Emily. She's a reputation to consider. If she's to make a suitable marriage—"

"Aw, Rosie, don't ye see—she's too unconventional to make a suitable marriage. She wants to marry for love. Mr. Ruskin's a fine man, and he's the man she loves. And he's as unconventional as she is. They're a perfect match. He has only to let go of his stubborn pride."

"But what if he doesn't? Her heart'll be broken even worse than before."

"Like yours was, by Mr. Timothy O'Hanlon?"

"Aye," she said. "Off to Virginia he went, to work with the finest Thoroughbreds in the land. Miss Emily's mother was still just a *bairn* at the time and still dependent upon me. I could not leave her. And he would not stay. Off to chase a dream, he went."

"But you have the memories."

"Oh, aye," Rosie agreed. "The sweet, sweet memories."

"And if Mr. Ruskin doesn't do the right thing, at least Miss Emily will have the memories."

"Aye," Rosie said, and exhaled a weary sigh. "But it's not easy to think on. She'll always be that wee babe I rocked in me arms." Reaching into her pocket, she withdrew her flask. "A good tot of Irish whiskey should ease me mind a bit. Will ye have one with me?"

"I cannot, not while I'm visible. Oh, but it would be grand to taste it again. I wonder, would ye mind so much if I disappeared? If I concentrate, I might be able to taste it along with you."

"Well, it's most peculiar, but I suppose, if it's the only way—"

"Aye. And a joy it would be to taste Irish whiskey again. Ye'll not be alarmed now, when I start to fade, will ye?"

"Oh, no. Not if ye've warned me," Rosie said, raising the flask in a salute. "*Slainté* to ye, Danny O'Shea."

"And to Miss Emily and Mr. Ruskin," Danny said, closing his eyes and concentrating on her taste buds as she took a deep draught.

15
An Artful Seduction

"**M**iss Emily's waiting for you in the garden," the maid said crisply. "Just follow that pathway, and you'll reach a clearing soon enough."

Gil nodded.

"She'll have to show you out later," the maid called after him. "I'm off for my afternoon."

Gil did not find that tidbit of information reassuring. Intent on finding out what Emily was up to with her peculiar written summons, he followed the path with grim determination. Whatever could she be thinking to order him here when there was so much at the theater that required his attention?

The path fed into a grotto-like area walled by vine-covered trellises. The vines were past their season, but a few random blossoms remained, and here and there a late climbing rose offered a spot of color. But it was not the roses Gil noticed, but Emily, seated on a plaid blanket with the full skirts of her pale blue dress billowing around her like a cloud and the midday sun glowing gold in her hair.

She held a tablet in her lap and was sketching, with great concentration, a likeness of one of the cherubs in the statue at the center of the clearing. Next to her was spread a picnic—wine, a loaf of bread, fruit, a small wheel of cheese.

Thinking it best to remain as formal as possible under the circumstances, he greeted her with, "Miss Charlton."

She looked up as though surprised to see him. "Mr. Ruskin. Do please join me." She patted the blanket beside her.

"This is highly irregular," Gil said, moving near the blanket, but making no move to sit down.

"You've been working much too hard," she said. "The theater is a center of chaos. Actors, journalists, set painters—everyone racing about. It's not at all conducive to agreeable digestion. Come, relax, have an unhurried meal. It may be the last moment's peace you realize until after the show opens tomorrow night."

Frowning, Gil sat down. "This is unwise, Emily, and quite improper. We've no chaperon."

"Do you fear me so much that you cannot take a meal with me without the protection of a chaperon?" she said. "I'm not as formidable as all that."

"You are quite the most formidable person I have ever known, and you have topped yourself this time," he said, with heartfelt sincerity. "I fear it's far more than a meal you wish to engage me in. But if you must know, it's myself I don't trust. It's obvious what you're about."

"You do rattle on, Mr. Ruskin," Emily said. "And you flatter yourself. This is merely a quiet celebration of our anticipated success. Please, open the wine. It's an excellent year. My grandfather was a connoisseur. I would have opened it myself, but I'm useless with the corks.''

Gil picked up the corkscrew and worked it into the stopper. The cork yielded with a healthy pop, and he served their glasses.

Emily took a sip, and then a deep breath, sighing as she savored the robust flavor. "Ah. Yes. It's excellent.'' She held up her goblet. "Let us toast our opening night and the longevity of the Irish Playhouse.''

Frowning, Gil raised his glass. He doubted the wisdom of taking liquor when he was already drunk with desire for her, but he could hardly refuse to drink to the success of the theater. "To the Irish Playhouse,'' he said.

The last word lodged in his throat as she smiled. Her lips were still moist from her first sip of wine, and as he swallowed his first draught, he fancied that it was her mouth he tasted. He fought for a modicum of control. "Your note suggested some sort of urgency,'' he said firmly. "Otherwise, I would not have left the theater when there's so much to be done there.''

"The theater will be there when you return, and you'll go at the tasks with renewed enthusiasm when you're refreshed,'' she said. "Do slice yourself an apple. They're slightly tart and excellent with the cheese.''

Because it was easier than arguing with her, Gil reached for an apple and a small paring knife, thinking drolly that the woman was totally unaware of the danger she courted in arming him when she was purposefully whipping him into a state of unbearable frustration.

"This is folly,'' he complained. "Pure folly to be

sitting in a garden slicing apples while there's work to be done."

"Where's the harm in a little celebration? We've worked so very hard and—oh, Gil, it's so exciting! Every seat sold!"

"You have judicious gossip and a scandalously titillating newspaper column to thank for that."

Emily giggled. "Yes! Isn't it delicious? Our strategy worked!"

"Yes," Gil agreed. "And now that we've drawn in the curious masses, we must see to it that we do not disappoint them."

"How could we disappoint them? The show is grand, grander than any I've ever seen. Danny is remarkable, and you are—" Fixing her gaze with his, she sighed languidly. "You are quite the most splendid young lover that ever walked the boards."

Gil came near to choking on the chunk of apple he was swallowing. "You are less than objective, I fear."

"Oh, much less," she agreed, her eyes large and limpid and adoring.

Gil cleared his throat meaningfully then took a fresh bite of apple.

"I love this garden," Emily said. "The house is old and drafty, and there's commerce on every corner around it, so I'd sell it or have it torn down if not for my great-aunt. She's lived here for thirty years and wouldn't know what to do with herself anywhere else. But I would miss the garden. I have always found it soothing to come here when I am frazzled. I thought perhaps it would have the same effect on you."

Gil chuckled. "Am I supposed to be frazzled?"

"Oh, of course. Everyone knows it. Even the actors have mentioned your churlishness."

"Churlish, am I? That's the thanks a man gets

when he insists on hard work. They're a talented lot, but lazy to a fault. And it's not to frazzlement they attribute my bad humor."

"Whatever else could it be?" Emily asked sweetly.

Gil frowned. "They are not blind, and certainly not naive, Emily. It is obvious to them all that I . . . that you . . . that you and I—"

Emily lifted an eyebrow. "That you and I what?"

"That there is a strain between us!" Gil said, irritated at being forced to put the obvious into words.

"A strain!" Emily said, imbuing the words with heavy irony. "How preposterous a notion! Where would they get such an idea when we have so fine an understanding between us?"

"Of which understanding do you speak?" Gil asked, dreading the answer.

"Why—that you desire me, but do not wish to kiss me under any circumstances, and that I desire you, but would sooner be kissed by a jackass."

"Is that so?" Gil asked, nettled by her cheekiness.

"Oh, quite," Emily said, with a haughty tilt of her chin.

Gil knew as well as he knew his own name that it was not so at all. She was doing everything she could possibly do to goad him into kissing her. A jackass, indeed! Why, she was lucky he didn't kiss her exactly the way she wanted!

"I suppose that's why you invited me here without a chaperon," he challenged.

"A mere accident of timing," Emily said blithely. "Tomorrow is opening night, so today was our last chance. I cannot help it if Aunt Minny is off playing whist and the servants have the afternoon."

"And why you ply me with wine."

"I merely wanted to toast our opening."

Gil found himself moving involuntarily but inexorably closer to her. "And why you're wearing that blue dress—"

Emily shrugged. "There's nothing special about this dress. Would you have me greet you with no dress at all?"

Gil thrust his face inches from hers and shook from the strain of restraining himself from touching her. "Must you ask, Emily? Can't you tell? I would have you under me with no clothes at all! I would feast on the sight of you and fill my hands with the soft fullness of your flesh! I would taste the sweetness of your breasts and bury myself in you!"

Having expended some of his pent-up frustration and embarrassed himself in the process, he backed away from her. "If I weren't such a gentleman—"

Emily sighed dismally and looked deeply into his eyes. "I fear I wish you less a gentleman and more a man, because where you're concerned, I would prefer to be less a lady and more a woman."

Desire for her, combined with tender regard, overwhelmed him. Though he knew he was courting danger, he cradled her cheek with his fingers. "Do you know what you're suggesting?"

"I would have you show me," she said. "Here. And now." Her eyes remained locked with his unflinchingly. "If you don't, you are more a fool than a gentleman, for I love you with all my heart, and I have never offered my love to a man before."

She clutched the front of his shirt. "Oh, Gil, is it so important what people think? Does it matter who owns the theater when we can work together to make it a success? You won't be wearing the deed to the theater with my name on it when you step onto the stage. Your talent will speak for itself."

"Emily—" The name rushed forth.

"Oh, Gil. Why must you have so much pride when I have none at all where you're concerned?

know in my heart that we are meant to be together. You know it, too, and yet you fight it. Why must you fight it so?"

He slid his hands into her hair, sending hairpins flying as he massaged her luxuriant locks between his fingers, then lowered his mouth to brush hers softly before replying, "I can't even remember why I tried."

The next kiss was longer, more ardent, more demanding, and when he lifted his lips from hers, Emily opened her eyes to discover that her vision was blurred.

"I am trembling from the need of you," he said.

"Then why do you hesitate? I, too, am trembling."

"Consider this carefully, Emily. Once given, the gift you offer is irretrievable."

"It will be yours to keep," she said, stroking his cheek with her fingertips. "And the giving of it will be sweeter because I have entrusted it to you alone. I would hope that would make it dearer to you in the taking."

"It will be taken in love," he said. Gathering her into his arms, he lowered her onto the blanket and kissed her, slowly and thoroughly.

The drawn-out seduction of her mouth made her restless for more. Bereft when his mouth drew away from hers, she was soon enthralled by the new sensation of his lips, still moist, moving over her neck and down, finally settling on her throat in the hollow above the bodice of her dress. His hands warmed her ribs through her clothing while, deep inside her, another warmth spread slowly through her.

"What am I to do?" she entreated breathlessly, for it seemed that too many wondrous things were happening at once.

Gil propped himself on one elbow and looked

down at her. His expression grew tender as he studied her face. Such awe and eagerness and apprehension in her eyes—the deflowering of a virgin carried with it such imposing responsibilities!

"What do you know of this?" he mused aloud. "And what must I tell you to prepare you? There will be a moment of pain when your virginity is breached. I would spare you that if it were possible, but I cannot, anymore than a king can spare his queen, or the poorest tradesman his bride. Instead, I give you my pledge that I will be gentle, and that I shall feel the pain as keenly in my heart as you will feel it in your secret place."

Her eyes spoke eloquently of her love for him. "If I had thought otherwise, I would not have entrusted the deed to you."

He dipped his head to kiss her eyelids, then smiled reassuringly. "The act of lovemaking is the same for all, yet it is different for every couple who lie down together. You need not fear it, though at times it may seem fearsome. You need only to accept the pleasure and I will take my pleasure in yours."

He tugged his shirttail from his pants, guided her hand beneath them, and pressed it, palm side down, against his ribs. He closed his eyes, and sighed softly before opening them again. "The feel of your hands on my flesh both soothes and excites me. Do not shy away from touching me. Your soft hands can bring me only pleasure."

He worked the buttons and laces of her bodice and chemise until the tops of her breasts were exposed. A subtle flush spread over her chest and rose to her cheeks. "There is no need for embarrassment when I look at you, for the differences between your body and mine fascinate me, and your beauty in itself excites me."

He kissed, then tasted, the smooth skin he'd exposed until she drew in a ragged breath. "You need not fear expressing yourself," he told her, "for the sounds you make will drive me. Your arousal will stimulate me, and your desire for me will feed my desire for you."

He removed his coat, grabbed the tails of his shirt, and heaved it over his head and set it aside, then lay down next to her, insinuating his arm beneath her neck to cradle it. "Come, let me hold you. Slide your hands over my back, and let me feel your cheek against my chest a while. And when we're ready, we'll explore the mysteries and majesty of making love."

Emily gratefully shifted into his arms and settled with a sigh. Oh, but it was glorious to be here with him this way. The hair on his chest was coarse against her cheek, the muscles of his back smooth and firm under her hands. Somewhere in the back of her mind she thought she should be self-conscious because he was undressing her, but she couldn't seem to find shame, only a strange and exhilarating excitement as his fingers deftly dealt with buttons and laces and reverently pushed them aside.

After baring her breasts, he admired them unhurriedly, and his appreciative gaze sent heat coiling through her again. Rolling slightly, he pulled her under him and covered her mouth with his own as his chest pressed fully against her breasts. Oh, the bliss! How could she have imagined this sweetness, this heat, this glorious fullness as his mouth plundered hers and their bodies touched? She had wished for this splendor without suspecting how grand it would be.

He made love to her slowly, gently, thoroughly. There was never a moment when she feared his touch, only the intensity of sensations new to her, each more splendid than the last. The roughness of his palms produced a delicious friction on her skin. His warm breath fanned over kiss-moistened skin, scorching with almost unbearable pleasure. The warm, wet magic of his mouth drawing on her breast made her whimper aloud with the need for something wild and dangerous.

Gil's breathing grew deep and ragged, and his skin dampened with his own driving need. Emily's heart raced, and it seemed the very blood in her veins carried the fire of passion and desire. Though she had only the vaguest notion of what was happening to him, she could feel, through their remaining clothing, the heat gathering in him and the hardness of his body as it pressed into hers.

Instinctively, her body responded with a heat of its own. She grew restless and arched beneath him, straining for something unknown to her, something she could neither name nor define, something she had never experienced but yearned for with a terrifying intensity.

With vexing effort but determination, he worked at undressing her, casting aside her petticoats in one toss and, finally, her skirt, leaving her the modesty of her drawers while he stood and, with his back to her, removed his own clothing.

The sight of his body mesmerized her. Emily stared at his broad back, admiring the way the muscles worked as he moved. His backside was beautiful, his buttocks muscular and firm. He turned slowly, watching her face as his swollen organ came into her view. She gasped slightly and he forced a smile as she stared at him, her face a study of concentration, awe, and apprehension.

Kneeling next to her, he lifted her hand and guided her fingers around him. "It is but flesh," he said. "Though swollen with the desire for you, it is yet simply flesh. Do you feel it quake in awe of your touch?"

Emily drew her hand away, and her eyes betrayed an innocence that defied her precocity and natural sensuality. Settling next to her, he stroked the length of her arms soothingly until she gentled, then he rained a trail of kisses over her shoulders, to her neck and on to her mouth for a probing kiss.

He stroked her body, moving gradually lower, until he encountered the top of her drawers and loosened the ribbon that bound them around her waist. He peeled them from her, feeling her flesh quiver beneath his knuckles as he guided them down her legs. She was so lovely, her skin smooth and flawless and pale as cream.

He forced himself to be patient as he drew her into his arms for a deep kiss; she embraced him and clung to him as if to let go of him would be to forfeit her life. She moaned as he cradled her, and drew in a sharp, ragged breath as his finger glided into her moist recess. Her tightness surprised him, excited him. This was to be his gift, offered to him and no other.

She was malleable as sculptors' clay as he urged her knees apart, and settled his legs between her, and his erection brushed her sensitive flesh.

Her arms, looped over his shoulders, convulsed around him, anchoring his chest to hers as she emitted a low, guttural, pleading moan. Gil trembled with his need to bury himself in her and claim the release her soft body promised.

Poising himself at the narrow opening, he kissed her eyelids, then whispered, "It is time, Emily. I'll try to be gentle."

She grimaced involuntarily as he pressed against her barrier.

"There is no other way," he whispered regretfully.

Emily clung to him, worrying his back with her fingers. He tried again to breach her virginity and froze as she drew in a steeling breath.

"Emily," he said.

"Claim me," she said, closing her eyes and bracing herself. *This cannot be right,* she thought frantically as his hardness strained painfully against her, but even as she cried out from the pain as he finally claimed the gift she had given to him, she knew that she was nearer to quelling the urgent longing consuming her.

He stilled within her and cradled her in his arms, placing tiny, fleeting kisses over her face. But when his mouth fused over hers, she shifted restlessly under him, urging him to move.

Emily did not try to make sense of what was happening, but simply gave herself up to the terrifying intensity and the frantic quest for release from this preemptive yearning that burned within her. Gil moved inside her, and it seemed to her that he stoked the fire consuming her until she thought she might die of it. And then, quite suddenly, release came in waves so forceful and unexpected that she convulsed against him and cried out.

She felt as though she'd toppled from a high cliff and, instead of falling, soared with the freedom of an eagle. She wondered if it was the same for Gil, and suspected it was as he thrust hard into her and then shuddered, wrapping his arms around her and hugging her close, his breathing as erratic as hers, his heart beating so strongly that she could discern its rhythm within his chest.

For a timeless interval, they were quiet, still except for their labored breathing. And then she said his name on a sigh.

"Are you—?" he began, but she quelled his concern.

"I am mystified," she said. "Never did I suspect— oh, is it always so . . . *glorious* between men and women?"

"We are especially compatible," he said. "Emily—"

She regarded him with wide, inquisitive eyes still filled with the wonder of their lovemaking.

"Words fail me," he said. "There is no way to express—"

"I am quite speechless, too," Emily said, and snuggled closer to him with a sigh of contentment.

16
Opening Night And
A Farewell Performance

"Look at them, Rosie," Danny said. "They have the glow of young love about them."

"Aye," Rosie said. "It's as plain as the noses on their faces, and them thinking no one has eyes enough to see or sense enough to know what they're seeing!"

Gil and Emily were standing in the wings. Gil was in costume, and Emily was adjusting the flounce of his cravat.

The entire backstage was abuzz with activity, actors scurrying about in various stages of dress suffering various symptoms of opening night nerves. Bertram, who had proved to be as big and burly as Gil had described him, was walking the floor and wringing his hands.

"Rosie!" The distressed cry came from Marjorie, who was getting into costume for her first scene as the young innocent. Spying Rosie approaching, she said, "Thank goodness! This waist must be let out. I simply cannot breathe." She fanned her hand frantically in front of her face and drew in a labored breath. "Oh, I simply cannot breathe back here. The air is too scarce."

Bertram paused in mid-stride. "There's nothing wrong with the air, Marjorie. It's your nerves."

"Don't be ridiculous," Marjorie answered, as Bertram resumed his pacing. "I don't suffer nerves at all."

"Rosie had better be quick with her needle," Gil said, consulting his pocket watch. "Curtain is in twelve minutes."

"I'd better go lend a hand," Emily said. "I'm very concerned about Rosie. She's been working much too hard. She has an ashen look about her, but I can't make her slow down."

"I'll go have another peek at the audience," Gil said.

"Do they seem a friendly crowd?" Emily asked, joining Gil a few minutes later.

"Not a rotten tomato among them," Gil quipped, moving over slightly so she could see through the slit in the curtain. Her shoulder pressed his as she craned her neck for the best vantage point, and they looked at each other and smiled the knowing smile of lovers before she turned her gaze back to the audience.

"You were not long in the wardrobe room," Gil observed.

"There was plenty of extra seam to be let out," Emily replied. "Rosie has things well in hand. We could not be sewing on the same bodice at the same time."

Consulting his watch again, Gil said, "Five minutes. I'll cue the piano player and then rouse the actors." He reached for her hand. "Are you ready, Miss Charlton?"

Emily sighed. "It's not an easy thought, speaking to so many people at once."

"Just pretend this is a lovely party and they're all your guests," he said. "It's not so far from the true situation."

"Paying guests," she said, with a grin, and tried not to think about having to stand before this crowd.

The piano player, who'd been awaiting his signal, began playing a lively march and, satisfied that his order had been carried out on that front, Gil gave Emily's hand a reassuring squeeze. "Now for the actors."

He was gone but a minute before Danny joined her for a glimpse of the audience. "Oh, it's a fine crowd. A fine crowd," he said. "I see but one seat empty."

"The aisle seat on the fourth row," Emily said. "I sent the ticket for that seat to my father. He'll not show up."

"Are ye so sure of that, lass?"

"Yes," Emily said flatly. "Quite sure. But I have the satisfaction of having sent it."

"Is there no hope for peace between ye?" Danny asked sympathetically.

"No. But I do not wish to think about my father tonight." She stepped back a bit and put her hands on Danny's shoulders. "Let me look at you, Danny. Why, you're grand!"

The green jacket, sponged and pressed, might have been tailor-made for him. And with his crisp white shirt, stiff collar, fancy cravat, and plaid pants, he looked every inch the Irish Amadan. His white hair had been oiled and shone even in the pale light of the wings.

His stage nerves took the form of exhilaration rather than agitation or apprehension. From his manner, it seemed he could hardly wait to make his entrance. He rubbed his hands together, releasing excess energy. "It's a pretty sight ye are tonight in that yellow dress, Miss Emily. Ne'er have I seen a prettier theater owner. It's enough to make an old man nostalgic for his youth."

"You're quite the flatterer," Emily said, flushing becomingly with the compliment.

"Oh, aye. Quite a ladies' man I was in me day. But there's no need for exaggeration where ye're concerned, and that's the truth of it, Miss Emily. Why, it's fair to glowing you are. I take it Mr. Ruskin has acquired a taste for cream."

Emily blushed scarlet.

"Oh, come, lass! There's no need to be coy about it once you've done it. It's not as though it ain't obvious. Why, Mr. Ruskin's doing everything but licking his whiskers, and looking happier than a fat dairy cat."

"Oh, but— No one must know!" she said. "No one but us, until the Irish Playhouse is a success and he's made his name."

"Oh, but it's only me, Dannyboy, ye're talking to. It's yer own business, and I'm not one to be spreading other people's secrets about. It's only that I'm happy for ye that I mention it."

Emily threw her arms around his neck for a hug. "I have you to thank for the advice and courage, Danny. Thank you a million times over. It's even more than I'd hoped for."

"Oh, don't ye be getting all sentimental on me. But as long as we're thanking each other, I want to thank ye for giving me this chance. It means more to me than ye know to be playing the Amadan again. More than ye know."

Emily fancied that she saw a tear glisten in his eye as she pulled away from him.

"Not so quick, lass. Here, pretend I'm yer uncle and give me a *pogue* for luck."

"A *pogue*?" she asked.

"A kiss, lass. What kind of Irishwoman do ye claim to be that ye don't know what a *pogue* is?"

Laughing, Emily pressed a kiss on his cheek.

Gil arrived, watch in hand. "One minute! Are you ready, Emily?"

She responded with a dubious nod.

"How about you, Danny?" Gil asked.

Danny smoothed the lapel of his jacket and took in a breath that swelled his chest. "Aye, lad. Readier than ye know."

Gil snapped his watch closed and thrust it into the pocket of his brocade waistcoat. "Then let's cue the piano player for a fanfare." He took Emily's hands and said her name.

"Oh, don't fret so over her," Danny fussed. "She's a smart lass. She'll do fine."

Gil grinned self-consciously. "Opening night nerves," he said.

"Well, don't ye be a worrying about the play, either, lad. The audience'll love it, or my name isn't Dannyboy O'—" He cut off the last of his name abruptly.

Gil shook his head and laughed softly. Danny had agreed to Emily's wild scheme to shorten his name to the enigmatic O' to help fuel the speculation over his uncanny resemblance to Dannyboy O'Shea. The ploy had worked to their benefit quite nicely, but Gil still found it somewhat suspicious that an actor would forfeit his name in such a way. Still, if the play were a big success, the speculation would probably continue to the point that someone would uncover his true identity.

"There's the fanfare," Gil said, instantly alert. He dropped a kiss on Emily's cheek and squeezed her hands before releasing them. "You're on."

Addressing the audience was not nearly so difficult as Emily had anticipated. With the glare of the foot lamps, the auditorium was but a blur, so she could not see the faces to fear them. With a smile still lingering on her lips, she exited much relieved as the piano player launched into the ditty that would eventually cue Danny's entrance.

But a single look at Gil's face quelled her smile instantly. "What is it?"

Gil cupped her elbows, as if to brace her. "It's Rosie, Emily. She's collapsed."

"Rosie!" Emily took off at a dead run. She found her nurse, her maid, her confidante, her friend stretched out on the cot. Marjorie, in full costume, was at the bedside.

Emily knew at once that Rosie was gravely ill. Her face was ashen and blue, and she was uncannily still. Her chest hardly moved as she breathed.

"Oh, Rosie," Emily said, kneeling beside the cot and taking the old woman's frail hand.

Marjorie gave an apologetic shrug. "My cue is in less than three minutes."

"Go on," Emily said. "I'll stay with her. But find Charlie and send him in at once." Charlie had only one small part toward the end of the show. As a utility, he did whatever was needed backstage.

Rosie opened her eyes to reveal what little life was left in her within their depths. "Miss Emily!" she said, trying to push up into a sitting position.

"Sh-h-h," Emily said. "You'll wear yourself out When Charlie gets—Oh, Charlie! Thank goodness That reporter who did the column, Mr. Franklin, i in an aisle seat near the rear of the auditorium. He seems to know everyone in town. Fetch him and ask if he knows of a doctor in the house. If not, we'll send for one."

"There's no need to fuss," Rosie said, her voice tremulous from the exertion of speaking. "There's no use in it. Just move me cot to the wings so I can watch Danny perform."

It was nonsense, of course, but Emily didn't challenge her for fear of bringing on another collapse. "Oh, Rosie, you've been a mother to me, and I've let you work yourself to this. We'll get you home and hire a nurse and you'll be fine again after a long rest."

"Hush, child! It's useless and we both know it. Just let me watch Danny's performance. I always wanted to see it, from the first time I met him in yer grandfather's house."

"You're confused," Emily said, her heart breaking. "It's Danny O'Dowd, not Danny O'Shea."

Rosie gave a mirthless cackle of a laugh. "Aw, lass, ye don't see what's before yer very eyes. He's Danny O'Shea, all right, back from the grave to finish his performance so he can put his soul to rest. I'll be going with him, so ye might as well let me watch."

"Rosie, don't talk so," Emily sobbed.

"Don't go carrying on, lass," Rosie replied. "I'm an old woman, and I'm dreadful tired."

Emily saw the old woman's lined face as if for the first time and realized that it was true. She'd been so blind, so self-centered! She'd always thought the woman immortal, indefatigable. "Oh, Rosie, I need you so much."

"Oh, lass, I'll be leaving ye. It's me only regret. But Mr. Ruskin will look after ye right enough. If ye'll just have Bertram move the cot around, we can watch Danny together."

It was but a small request after so many years of service. To move a cot so that she might see the play into which she'd poured her last waning strength. "I'll fetch Bertram," Emily said.

She found him easily enough, still pacing the floor in circles. His first entrance was not until the end of the first act.

He moved the cot, Rosie and all, to the wings, where she had a perfect view. Gil had just made his first entrance and, as the soon-to-be-besotted young man, was just noticing Marjorie, as the fair country girl. Danny, as the Irish Fool, was observing the scene and commenting to the audience, a droll, omniscient narrator.

"Oh, but he's a fine actor," Rosie said. "It's easy to see how his soul could become confused. There's so much of Danny in the fool, and the fool in Danny."

Emily let her rattle on without challenging her, attributing her delusions to her illness and an infatuation with Danny. Yes, it had been obvious that the old woman was taken with him. They'd spent much time together doing wardrobe work. Even Rosie's speech had grown to reflect their closeness, reverting to the heavy Irish of her youth.

Charlie returned with the reporter and a middle-aged gentleman—a doctor, Emily assumed, from his dark coat and the leather bag he carried. After nodding a greeting, the doctor immediately produced a stethoscope from his bag and pressed it to Rosie's chest, listening with an expression of grave concern. He checked her wrist for a pulse as well, and looked at her fingertips.

Finally he rose, folded his stethoscope back into his bag, and motioned for Emily to join him further offstage, where they could talk more conveniently.

"There is nothing to be done for her," he said.

"She wants to watch the show."

The doctor shrugged. "Where is the harm, if it makes her happy? She'll be lucky to last to the final act. She'd probably not even make it to a hospital, and there'd be no use in it, anyway. Her heart is wearing out a little with every beat."

A little of Emily was dying along with Rosie, but Emily realized suddenly as she sat next to the cot and took Rosie's hand, that a lot of the old woman would live on through her. She'd done so much to shape Emily's life, had been such a steadfast advocate. *Oh, Rosie, why did I have to realize so late how much you mean to me?*

Contrary to the doctor's prediction, Rosie did make it through to the end of the play. She was weak, but alert. "Listen to the audience clap, lass. They love him."

From the level of the applause, it was a good guess that the audience loved the play in its entirety. Each of the players received a thunderous accolade from the audience, from whom their performances had earned a steady succession of laughs throughout the evening. The actors jubilantly bowed their way through several curtain calls.

Finally, exhilarated and exhausted, the players filed offstage. Marjorie whizzed past with an exuberant, "Thank God!" Bertram trailed closely behind her. Charlie also filed past on his way backstage.

Danny went immediately to kneel beside the cot. As he reached for Rosie's hand, Gil offered his hand to Emily to assist her up. She moved readily into his comforting embrace, grateful for the support his strength offered, burrowing her cheek against his broad chest and sliding her arms around his waist.

"Ye did it, Dannyboy," Rosie said, with the last of

her strength. "Ye finished the performance. Now ye can put yer soul back together."

"Aye, Rosie. And ye're coming with me, I see."

"Aye. If ye don't mind. I've no one to greet me there, and I've never been good at finding me way around strange places, so it would be a comfort to tag along with ye."

"Aye, Rosie. Let's be on our way."

Rosie heaved a labored breath and then went limp, her head rolling to one side to reveal a beatific smile that would remain there through eternity.

Bereft, Emily turned her face into Gil's chest and sobbed.

His heart breaking for her, Gil comforted her as best he could, stroking her back. He was quite in love with her, he realized, as she clung to him for consolation. He'd known he was lost from the moment she'd manipulated him into letting Danny read for the title role, and he'd been falling ever more hopelessly into that fool's state ever since. That she loved him he doubted not one bit, for she had shown him as much in giving herself to him. Of all her attributes, he admired her courage perhaps most of all.

His concerns about people thinking he was romancing his way to lead roles seemed silly now. What did it matter what people thought? He and Emily would be partners, working together to make the theater a success. His personal triumphs or lack thereof on the stage would rely on his performances in front of audiences, and he'd been a fool to think otherwise.

It was not the moment to declare himself and ask for her hand, but the right time would come soon. For now, he would see her through her grief, comfort her, and offer her his strength to lean on.

17
A Mysterious Exit

Emily awoke to a shower of kisses over her face. Opening one eye, she saw nothing but newsprint. "What?" she murmured. "Gil?"

The newspaper slipped away to reveal Gil's smiling countenance. "We have made the columns again, Mrs. Ruskin."

Emily pushed up into a sitting position, gathering pillows between her back and the headboard of the bed. "Our columnist friend again?"

"Yes. Announcing the marriage of Miss Emily Charlton, owner of the Irish Playhouse, to Mr. Gilford Ruskin, actor/manager of the same."

"So quickly!" Emily said, picking up the newspaper. "We are married on Friday, and it is news on Sunday."

"You are Nigel Lindsay's heir," he said. "You can hardly expect anonymity in Philadelphia."

"Not when I marry Philadelphia's most prominent leading man," she teased.

"Most *notorious* leading man, you mean," he corrected.

"Oh, Gil—see how he describes you: 'A vastly talented actor who will surely emerge as a moving force in American theater, particularly in Philadelphia.'"

"Read on," Gil said drolly. "He reviews the entire history of the theater, including Danny's mysterious disappearance on opening night."

"Again?" Emily skimmed the rest of the column and sighed. "Yes. I see what you mean. Every bit of it. 'Eye witnesses, including this humble columnist and esteemed local physician Dr. Lucas Smythe, continue to insist that the actor who'd just portrayed the title role in the theater's revival of *The Irish Amadan* simply faded from view in the theater wings following the death of Miss Rosie Woldy, lifelong nurse to Mrs. Ruskin (née: Charlton), with whom he was reported to have a close personal friendship.' "

She read on in silence, then looked at Gil from over the top of the paper. "Our friend of the quill is still insisting that, although he saw it with his own eyes, it was a stage hoax of some kind."

Gil sniffed disdainfully. "As if we could make a man dissolve into thin air."

" 'Rumors persist that the enigmatic Irishman who portrayed the Irish fool in the opening night performance was none other than the ghost of Irish Playhouse founder Danny O'Shea, who died following a fall during a performance in 1834. But this humble columnist still feels the disappearance is naught but a theatrical trick of epic proportions conceived to sell tickets,' " Emily read.

"Oh, but listen, Gil—it's not all bad. 'Fortunately, theater patrons suckered in by this elaborate and flawlessly executed stage trick get their money's worth, as the play is thoroughly entertaining, and Mr. Ruskin, though not Irish, performs more than capably in the role first created four decades ago by his bride's ancestor, Dannyboy O'Shea.' "

She set the paper aside with a sigh. "It is a paradox. Either our theater is haunted, which is scandalous, or we have hatched a preposterous plot to sell tickets."

Gil sat down on the bed next to her. "Our refusal to comment fuels the gossip and speculation."

Frustration clouded Emily's expression. "Our denials of a plot would only keep the suspicion alive. And to swear that my great-great-uncle's ghost performed on our opening night would leave us open to ridicule. Better that we leave it an enigma, and let the legend of my ancestor develop as it may."

Gil took her hands in his. "There's little else we can do when the only reasonable explanation of the situation is the most unreasonable one of all."

"He was my great-great-uncle. If we accept that, everything else falls into place—his resemblance to Dannyboy, his familiarity with the play, his stunning performance—"

"If I had not seen him disappear before my very eyes, I would deny the possibility. But he was there as solid as you and I, and then he simply . . . faded. No living being could do that."

Emily drew her hands from Gil's to wrap her arms around his neck and pull him into a hug. "I'm glad I had my face buried in your shirt and did not see it. I prefer to remember his tenderness as he kissed my cheek and assured me that I need not grieve overlong about Rosie because he would take good care of her."

"No one saw him kiss you," Gil said. "Not even I, who was holding you."

"No," she said. "But I felt the brush of his lips next to my ear as surely as I felt your arms about me, and I heard his voice as clearly as I hear yours now. That lovely, lyrical voice with the Irish lilt. It was only afterward that I became aware of the panic that had set in."

"I learned much from him as we worked on the play, yet never realized that I had a master for a mentor."

"And he advised me as a beloved uncle would. Oh, Gil, if not for his counsel, I might not be here with you now. For that, his memory is all the dearer, and I count myself fortunate to have known him."

"What do you mean?" Gil asked.

Emily smiled against his shoulder. "He saw what we refused to accept. If not for his encouragement, I might never have summoned you to the garden."

Gil hugged her fiercely. "Then I am more indebted to him than I knew, for you are dearer to me than life itself."

"Oh, Gil. I love you so much."

"And I you, Mrs. Ruskin," Gil said, between gentle nibbling kisses on her neck. "And now I shall show you just how much."

Above them, hovering near the ceiling, Rosie sighed. "We'd best be leaving them alone now."

"Ye're sure ye've seen enough?" Danny asked. "Remember, we're allowed only one glimpse before we're off to eternity for good."

"Aye," Rosie said. "I've seen enough. They'll be fine now. There's love enough between them to see them through all of life's challenges."

"Oh, aye. That there is, Rosie," Danny replied, as they began their ascent. "That there is. And didn't I tell ye so?"

Glenda Sanders

Before discovering boys—
    And the roller skating rink—
    GLENDA SANDERS spent her Saturday evenings
with the witches, ghosts, vampires, monsters, and
werewolves in the scary movies on the late, late
show.

Today, Glenda likes to combine the thrills and
sighs of a good love story with the chills and goose-
bumps of those eery late night tales by combining
ghosts and romance.

"Sweet Cream and Irish Whiskey" marks the his-
torical debut of this award-winning contemporary
author.

Shadow's Bend

Jodi Thomas

October, 1994.
Over twenty-five years of loving you, Tom.
If I love you every day of this lifetime
and into the next,
it still won't be enough.

1

Chicago, Illinois
1902

"**S**top talking to the furniture, Jamie!" Inez's voice was probably heard through the walls of the shop and to the street below. "I swear to Moses you treat each stick in this store like we adopted it instead of bought the thing for resell."

Jamie didn't answer. There was no use trying to explain to Inez how every piece of used furniture had a personality . . . such as the Victorian rocker she now dusted. The original red damask was starting to fade and the walnut might be cracked in a few spots, but the chair stood proudly against time and misuse.

"Mrs. Murphy told me this rocker is just like the one Lincoln sat in the night he was shot." Jamie touched the back of the piece and it seemed to nod in agreement. "The chair must have rocked forward with the shot and backward with the president's weight as soundlessly as this one does."

"That's just what I mean, dear sister." Inez never failed to make the words "dear sister" sound like a curse. "You're driving away what few customers we have with such talk." Though the same height, Inez was twice Jamie's width, yet she still felt the need to yell like a child proving a point. "Last week I heard you tell a couple you feel like the Chippendale easy chair hugs you when you sit down. You're . . . "

The front door's creaking silenced Inez in a blink. Her puckered face spread wrinkles toward her ears in a broad smile as she turned to greet their first customer of the day.

A ragged old lady, wet with rain and out of breath from climbing the front steps, hobbled into the store. Her back was so bent, her gaze was focused permanently on the ground. She carried a worn carpetbag filled with trinkets she was afraid to leave in her tiny apartment two doors down.

"Morning, Mrs. Murphy."

"Mrs. Murphy," Inez snapped as she turned toward the stairs. "Come sit a spell." Her invitation was as insincere as her sister's had been welcoming.

"Why, thank you, girl." Mrs. Murphy removed one of her many layers of coats and lowered herself into the rocker Jamie had just dusted. "I love this chair. I think I'll sit down for a few minutes and warm myself. Winter's coming."

"It usually does about this time of year," Inez mumbled from the landing.

"I'll turn up the heater." Jamie patted the old woman's shoulder. She didn't mind Mrs. Murphy's company, especially since it kept Inez upstairs in the apartment they shared. Jamie had tried all her life to love her half sister, but some folks were like cheap wood. No matter how much you polished them, they didn't have many endearing qualities.

"Quilts," Mrs. Murphy said as she rocked. "I've told you before, child, you'd sell more rockers if you carried lap quilts to go with them."

"Yes, ma'am," Jamie answered, watching the old dear fall asleep. Mrs. Murphy had given her the same advice every winter for five years. Jamie had even made some quilts, but she'd sold them in the church bazaar so the money she earned wouldn't mix with the store's.

Jamie lifted her duster. She loved mothering all the slightly used merchandise. That's why she'd insisted the store be named "Aging Treasures" and not "Second hand Store." To her, each item had a story to tell. She smiled as she dusted the many drawers of the high chiffonier behind the counter. Its warped mirror always seemed to wink at her in greeting. A lifetime of treasures must have been hidden in the chest.

As the door blew open again, the sudden gust of wind pulled her from her daydreams. An old man fought to close out the frigid air. Mrs. Murphy wiggled without waking and settled deeper into the rocker's red covering.

The stranger moved in silent strides toward Jamie. He was tall and willow-thin, with a slight limp that pride corrected almost completely. The icy rain glistened off the shoulders of his oiled duster and wide-brimmed hat, making him sparkle in the light. If she were guessing by his clothes, she'd say he belonged more to Texas or Wyoming than Chicago.

"May I help you?" Jamie moved around the desk, wanting a closer look at the stranger. He smelled of winter, of campfires and leather . . . of a freedom she'd never known.

"I hope so." His voice cracked with age. "I've been looking for this place all morning."

She studied him closely. His face was crisscrossed

with wrinkles from a life spent in the sun. A thin white scar crossed from cheek to chin, making Jamie curious about the adventures he'd lived. The scar seemed more to add character than to disfigure. She sensed a wealth of experiences, a life lived and not merely watched.

"I'm looking for Jamie Edwards. That's you, isn't it, young lady?" He politely removed his hat, revealing silver-white hair and eyes the blue of a summer sky.

"Yes, sir." She fought the sudden urge to brush a strand of his damp hair back into place. He reminded her of a century-old painting by a master, not handsome but haunting.

He smiled without surprise at her answer. "You're the one I've come to see. I've something here you'll be wanting to look at."

The old cowboy lifted an odd-shaped set of saddlebags from beneath his coat. "This is one of the satchels used by the Pony Express over forty years ago. For all I know, it may be the last one left. I've traveled a long way to let you have a look at it."

Hesitantly, Jamie took the cold pair of bags. The leather warmed in her hands, giving slightly to her touch as if in welcome. "I've heard of these, but I didn't think any of them still existed. When the Civil War broke out and the Pony Express was disbanded . . ."

"This one made it," he interrupted as his hand followed hers along the leather, deepening the imprint of her fingers. "They were made special, with mail pouches to hold the letters evenly and double straps to tie to the saddle. My guess is most of them were carried into the war, both as Reb and Yankee gear."

Jamie tried to focus on the satchel instead of the scarred old hand twisted slightly with age. For once in her life she found a person more interesting than an object. Perhaps they'd talk later; for now, he'd come to sell.

The bags had been well cared for over the years and looked almost new. She could imagine all the important messages carried cross-country in such a satchel. This was a treasure she must have for the shop, but it would cost far more than the petty cash she kept in the drawer.

Looking up at the old man, she noticed he was watching her closely, as if trying to memorize her features. "I have to check with my sister about the price." Though she hated to say it, she knew that if she bought one more thing without asking Inez, she'd endure days of her sister's endless complaining.

The old cowboy placed his hand over hers. "Whatever you think is fair, Jamie. I brought the saddlebags for you."

Knowing she should be offended by his boldness, she challenged him with a stare. But his eyes were deeply earnest, as though he'd traveled half a world to give her the satchel. "I'll only be a minute." Jamie pulled her hand away from his touch and lifted the bags.

She could feel his gaze as she climbed the stairs. He was old, maybe seventy, but he had the power to make her feel more alive than ever before. Jamie was afraid to think what he might have done to her temperature if he had been thirty or forty years younger. No one in her life ever touched her so, and she could still feel the warmth of his hand on hers.

Pushing her feelings aside, she opened the door to the shared living quarters. The rooms were dark and cluttered with furniture. Inez's possessions occupied almost all the available space. Jamie wasn't sure if her sister liked owning things or merely wanted to claim every extra inch from floor to ceiling as hers. Her various collections were poorly kept and unorganized.

She had rows of teapots of all shapes and sizes, now so dusty the china looked gray. Inez also kept stacks of dolls and piles of dried flower arrangements long past any usefulness. She'd rigged poorly built shelves to hold salt and pepper shakers.

Moving around a rack covered with men's hats, Jamie stepped over a small bookend collection. She wanted to finish her talk with Inez and return to the man in the shop.

As always, Inez insisted on offering far less than the saddlebags' worth. Jamie argued for several minutes but finally gave in. She would name the amount Inez suggested and when the old man refused, she could always offer more.

Inez was still lecturing when Jamie threaded her way back through the parlor. Her sister disliked bargaining with the public herself but she never hesitated to evaluate the results of Jamie's efforts.

When Jamie returned downstairs, the cowboy was gone. At first she thought he might be sitting in one of the many chairs or browsing in a remote corner. But he seemed to have disappeared, leaving only the coldness of winter behind. In his coming and going, he hadn't even awakened Mrs. Murphy, who still slept soundly in the rocker she'd never be able to afford.

Jamie hugged the saddlebags and wished it were spring. What had he said? *I brought the bags to you, Jamie.* As if he wasn't there to sell something at all, but only to give her his treasure. In her entire life she could never remember anyone giving her something so nice.

"How much did you have to pay?" Inez yelled from the landing above.

Hesitating, Jamie moved out of sight and pretended not to hear. If she told her sister the truth about the bags, Inez would have them for sale at a bargain price within the hour.

"How much?" Inez's voice rattled Mrs. Murphy from her sleep.

"He said he'd think about the offer," Jamie lied.

Inez marched halfway down the stairs. "Well, he'd best not take too long, or we'll charge him rent. You did get his name?"

"I . . ."

"I swear to Moses, Jamie. You're as dumb as you are plain. It's no wonder few men come courting at your door. Headache or no, I'd best be down in the shop every minute, for you've no sense for business."

Without answering, Jamie moved around the store looking for a place to hang the saddlebags. She'd like to pretend the old man had brought them just for her. Maybe he wasn't as handsome as he must have been forty years ago, but he'd looked at her as though she were the shop's only treasure.

Inez was wrong about the number of men who'd come to court. Several, not few. But none had been willing to fight their way past Inez or wanted the widowed, older sister as part of Jamie's dowry. Jamie might have demanded her freedom, had any of her suitors looked at her with half the warmth the old man's gaze had held.

All day Jamie kept returning to the saddlebags hanging out of Inez's line of vision. Jamie took great care to oil the leather and clean the buckles properly. She couldn't rid herself of the image of a rider traveling at top speed across the country with the bags flopping behind his saddle.

The Chicago wind blew colder as day darkened into night. Huge snowflakes plinked against the window, making lacy designs. As the weather worsened, Jamie knew the old man wouldn't be coming back to retrieve his property and she'd have another day to enjoy her fantasies about the saddlebags.

With a heave of frustration, Inez slammed the books closed. "It was a waste of time even to open the shop today."

"We did have the old gentleman." Jamie tried to sound cheery.

"One customer and he only wanted to sell something. I don't call that much of a day. I'm going to put the water on for tea. You lock up." Inez climbed the stairs. "And don't forget to put the 'closed' sign in the window."

Inez was too far up the stairs to see Jamie mouth her last words. In the five years they'd lived together, Inez had said the same thing every night. Jamie never forgot the sign or the door, and Inez never failed to remind her.

Jamie locked up and turned off the lights. The last glimmer of daylight would show her the way to the landing.

In the evening twilight the store looked wonderful and new. None of the worn spots or cracks showed. Mrs. Murphy's Victorian rocker could have been back in an opera box, and the tall clocks stood like polished sentries lining an entire wall. The walnut tables shone, ready for fine china once more. The highboys waited at silent attention for a gentleman or lady to open a drawer and pull out evening gloves.

A shaving stand reflected the light from the street as Jamie moved among the items, saying good night to her world. As she passed them, Jamie patted the saddlebags, her fingers almost a caress.

Something fluttered in answer.

Jamie took a step backward and touched the bags

once more. Again she heard a rattling sound.

Slowly, she lifted one of the leather flaps. Nothing could be in the bags. They hadn't been out of her sight all day. When she pulled the latch free, a sudden tingling sparked across her fingertips, as if she'd collected static.

She jumped back, dropping the bags. A creamy white envelope fluttered from beneath the leather into the shadowy glow of twilight.

Timidly, Jamie lifted the envelope and moved to the lamp beside her desk. "This must be some kind of joke," she whispered. Her hands trembled with more than cold as she pulled out a single piece of paper.

The sheet was onionskin-thin, and it crackled slightly in her fingers as she unfolded it. At the top, written in a bold hand, were the words, *February 27, 1861. Shadow's Bend, Nebraska Station Number 31.*

Jamie moved the thin paper closer to the light. Her hands shook as though she were somehow looking forty years into the past.

"To anyone beyond Shadow's Bend," the letter began.

Holding her breath, Jamie felt she was invading someone's very private mail. How had the letter just appeared in the bag? Could she have missed it when she cleaned the satchel? Was this a trick?

She read on. *I know no one will ever read this, but I have to write. The isolation of this station is playing tricks on my mind, and I fear for my own sanity. A rider passes every other day, stopping only long enough to change horses and down a dipper of water. The drumming of my loneliness pounds through my body with every waking hour.*

"Jamie!" Inez's voice shattered the silence. "Aren't you finished yet!"

Hurriedly, Jamie folded the letter back into the envelope and replaced it in the saddlebag. "I'm coming!" she shouted toward the stairs.

All through dinner the letter filled her thoughts, but Jamie couldn't bring herself to tell Inez about her find. She wasn't sure how her sister would react, but somehow the letter would never be as precious to Jamie once Inez handled it. She even thought briefly that Inez might have penned the note as a joke, but a wisp of humor had never breathed through Inez's body.

Scolding herself, Jamie did the dishes without even bothering to ask for her sister's help. *I'm being selfish about the letter,* Jamie thought. But hadn't the old man said the bags were for her? When had anything been just hers? Their father had married Jamie's mother when Inez was almost grown. When the new wife became pregnant within a year, Inez rebelled and married the first boy foolish enough to ask for her hand. He'd been rough and quick-tempered. Jamie heard her father say once that the boy had died before Inez's third anniversary and "good riddance to trouble he was." Inez had no choice but to move back home. Jamie's mother was ill with the second pregnancy, and neither she nor the baby survived the birth.

Jamie's earliest memories were of Inez making fun of everything she did. By the time Jamie was old enough to go out with a young man, Inez convinced her it would be a waste of time. Their father's illness snuffed out any hope she'd had of going to parties or dances. When he died, Inez had already planned what they would do with the money he left and Jamie, in her youth, had simply followed. She felt she had nothing of her own except a small purse of coins she'd kept well hidden. Most of her clothes were cut down from Inez's old garments and all the profits from the store went into Inez's hands.

But the letter, Jamie thought, *the letter is mine. If it exists, of course.* She'd only seen it for a few seconds in the dying light. What if she'd only imagined touching the paper? By bedtime, she had half convinced herself that the letter had only been her imagination playing tricks on her. Tricks that included an ancient life-scarred cowboy. Hadn't Inez told her often enough that she lived more in daydreams than in reality?

"Good night." Jamie pulled off her apron. "I think I'll turn in early."

"Might as well," Inez answered. "For all the company you've been tonight I could just as soon have talked to that cat of yours. It'll probably be hours before I'm able to sleep. But don't give a thought to staying up with me."

Jamie reached and scratched Winchester's ears. "I don't think I can tonight." She yawned loudly and lifted the cat into her arms. The one fight she'd won with Inez after their father died, was over the cat. The one thing she wouldn't give up. Inez ranted and screamed for days, but in the end, Winchester stayed.

Without another word, Jamie slipped into her room and dressed for bed. She knew Inez wouldn't remain awake long. Her sister liked to play a game of acting as though she stayed up late or rose early, but Jamie had long ago learned that she exaggerated.

Sitting by the tiny stove in her bedroom, Jamie brushed her hair. Her father used to enjoy seeing her hair down. He called it a waterfall of sunshine. But no one except the mirror had seen its length for years. She was almost twenty-five and had never felt a lover's caress or heard a low voice whisper her name in passion. "The drumming of my loneliness," she repeated from the letter.

A smile touched her lips as she glanced around

her room. Even after all the years of living here, most of her things still lined the walls in crates. She always thought of this place as temporary and not her home, but now dust covered the boxes. Even though she wasn't alone, she sympathized with how the writer of the letter must feel, for her isolation sometimes seemed complete.

"Like believing I saw a letter," Jamie said aloud, tiptoeing across to the door and peeking out. No light showed from beneath Inez's door. She had gone to bed.

"Quiet now, Winchester," Jamie whispered to the cat. "We're going back downstairs."

Winchester showed no interest in following her when Jamie slipped from the room and crossed the living area to the staircase. She carefully lowered her weight onto each step so as not to make a sound. Jamie couldn't contain a giggle as she thought of Inez running out of her room with her hair in rag curlers and their father's old Patterson Colt in her chubby fingers. She might not fight an intruder, but she'd do a good job of frightening him to death.

Jamie reached the bottom without any sign of Inez. She didn't need the light; she knew where everything was.

When she touched the Pony Express saddlebags, a slight shock coursed through her once more. The tingle passed along her arm and swept her body, doubling her excitement.

Carefully, she carried the bags to the back of the store and lit a tiny lamp. The woman who had sold it to them had sworn it had belonged to one of Napoleon's generals. The light would be blocked from both the landing and the windows by all the high-backed Rhode Island dining chairs they'd collected from an estate sale last year.

Reaching into the bag, Jamie cried softly with

pleasure as her fingers touched the envelope. "It wasn't my imagination," she whispered as she pulled the paper into the light.

Curling her feet beneath her in the chair, she leaned close to the lamp and unfolded the single sheet of paper.

The date was still there, February 27, 1861. *Someone wrote this letter forty-one years ago,* Jamie thought. *How is it possible that I'm the first to find it?*

She glanced over the opening paragraph she'd seen earlier and read the second. *I swear this station must be the most isolated spot between St. Joseph and Fort Laramie. I wish I'd never left Texas, but when the Pony Express offered to buy a hundred of my horses if I'd sign on for a year as a station agent, I thought the offer too good to refuse.*

That was before I saw Shadow's Bend. The cabin sits beneath a solitary cliff which is the only rise in the earth from horizon to horizon. All winter I've been listening to the wind, thinking I'd go out of my mind if it didn't stop.

The Indians around here call the low moan that the wind makes a death howl, and truly I do feel half-dead. I get through the day taking care of the horses and working on a new windmill design I might use back home someday, but at night I'd give all I own just to feel the weight of another person lying beside me.

Tonight I couldn't take the loneliness any longer. I'm planning to finish this letter and put it in the extra saddlebag by the barn door. It won't go anywhere, but at least I can pretend there is someone out there who gives a damn if Adam Shelton is alive or dead.

Jamie pressed the letter against her chest and fought down the tears. "I care," she whispered.

2

By the time Jamie finished, her hands and feet were so cold they no longer had any feeling in them. But she'd done the only thing she could do. She'd written to Adam Shelton.

She knew it was crazy, and Inez would probably have her committed to the state hospital if she found out, but Jamie felt compelled to answer the cry she'd read. Silently, she sealed the single page of writing paper into one of the store's brown envelopes and slipped it into the other half of the saddlebags. Then she carefully replaced Adam's letter.

The letter was simple and to the point. *Dear Mr. Shelton. Someone does care. We may be separated by miles and time, but I know the loneliness you feel, for it eats away at my heart every day.*

She'd gone on to describe her life. Somehow putting the words on paper made her days seem much more lonely than Jamie usually thought of them as being. Even as she climbed the stairs and crawled into bed, she couldn't stop thinking of Adam. He was alone, too. As alone as she.

In what seemed only minutes, Inez yelled at her to get up. Though the day was dark and stormy, somehow Jamie's spirits were bright. She spent the morning smiling every time she passed the saddlebags, knowing two letters were inside. Two secret letters written by people who wanted someone, even if it were an imaginary person. But her man was real, she reasoned. Or at least he had been forty years ago. Adam Shelton had written the words of his heart, and his feelings were as real today as they had been when he'd slipped the note into the bag.

Inez kept Jamie busy doing inventory, and she didn't have a chance to look over her letter again. The next day was Sunday, and there was no time for dreaming. Sunday was Jamie's only day away from the store and she took full advantage of it. She sang in the choir for early service, then helped cook a huge lunch the church provided its elderly members. In the hours between services, she visited friends who were always reluctant to call on her at the store.

All through the afternoon Jamie watched for the old man who'd brought the saddlebags, but he wasn't among the aging who filed into the church for a meal or the people she passed in the neighborhood. She'd known he wouldn't be. She'd never seen him before, and she guessed she'd never see him again.

After evening service, Jamie returned home in time to cook supper.

A week passed before Jamie had an opportunity to look in the saddlebags again. Inez finally took an afternoon off to visit an old school friend, leaving Jamie alone to mind the store.

As soon as Inez turned the corner, Jamie lifted her new treasure down from the hook. She couldn't wait to read Adam's letter once more and see if she remembered every word correctly.

She slipped her hand into one side of the bag, expecting to feel either her letter or Adam's. The compartment was empty. Panic danced in her blood. Had she only imagined the writings from a week ago?

Or had Inez found the letters? Right now her sister might be sharing them with her friend, Mary Beth, and Mary Beth's hawklike brother, Raymond. The three were probably laughing at what a fool little Jamie was.

Mary Beth would probably say, "And to think she snubbed my Raymond in favor of an invisible man from the past. The poor child will never marry."

Jamie flipped the saddlebags over. She hadn't snubbed Raymond. She'd run like all hell was after her. He was a man whose only personality dwelled in the stories his sister told of him. He had huge eyes and a long, pointed nose. Jamie would swear she'd never seen him blink, much less show any emotion.

Shoving her hand into the other pouch, she prayed that at least one of the letters remained. Two envelopes met her touch.

Pulling them out slowly, she wondered how she could have been so sure she'd placed the notes in separate compartments.

But the envelopes she pulled were both the creamy white transparency of Adam's first letter. The outside of one was dated as before—February 27, 1861—but the other was marked March 4, 1861.

Jamie couldn't keep her hands from trembling as she opened the second dispatch.

No heading greeted her, only the words:

Yesterday I decided to remove my foolish writing from the bag before I accidentally switched it with one of the bags in use. When I reached in, my letter was missing and a brown envelope had taken its place.

Jamie dropped everything and covered her mouth to stop the scream escaping her lips. It was impossible! His letter might have been left in the bag fo all these years, but how could her letter have traveled back in time?

She crumpled to the floor beside the satchel, her heart pounding so loudly that her ears throbbed. This could not be! Slowly, she lifted the second message once more.

Jamie, I'm not sure how your letter came to me from a far-off place like Chicago, but I'm glad you've written. I'm placing this letter in the pouch in hopes more mail will pass through.

Perhaps I should call you Miss Edwards, since we've never been formally introduced, but I've thought of you every moment since I found your letter, and in my mind I call you Jamie. I think I know you from what you've written and from what I feel. If I may be so bold? I know you brought sunshine to my life, therefore you must be beautiful. And proud, judging from the way you don't blame anyone for your loneliness. Jamie, I'd guess your weakness is numbers, for you missed the correct date on your letterhead by forty-one years.

Jamie laughed as tears rolled down her face. She gathered things about Mr. Adam Shelton also. For one, he was stubborn and used to thinking himself right. She read on:

I wish you could see this land. Winter's almost over and March has truly come in like a lion. The only time the wind seems to die is at sunset. What beautiful sunsets I could show you. The sun doesn't just go down in a quiet death, but spreads out across the horizon in miles of fire. When that passes, the horizon turns soft shades of pink and yellow, but the clouds above still reflect the dying sun's colors, as if banking the warmth for tomorrow's fire. I wish you were here to see just one.

Respectfully yours,

Adam Shelton

Jamie folded the letter and pressed it against her heart. "Respectfully yours," she whispered.

The rest of the day passed in a haze. Inez returned, rambling on about the fun she'd had spending the afternoon with Mary Beth and Raymond. She rehashed all their conversations, including how they'd laughed about Jamie's daydreaming.

Jamie only half listened to Inez. She'd heard all the words before. Her thoughts remained on Adam. He'd said he'd show her the sunsets, as if it were possible.

"Are you hearing a word I'm saying?" Inez pulled Jamie back to their conversation. "I swear I don't know what's to become of me if you go completely mad, Jamie. Perhaps I should go after Raymond myself instead of pestering him to court you. I've sung your praises so often, Mary Beth is teasing me about being a canary."

Jamie fought to hide her anger. "Oh, please don't tell him I'm interested in him. I could never care for a man like Raymond."

"And why not?" Inez took offense. "He's honest and sober. You could do a great deal worse, believe me, I know. I've never overburdened you with my marriage problems because, after all, my husband died and it's wrong to speak ill of the dead. But it was beyond hell."

Straightening, Inez seemed to push the past behind her. "If you married Raymond, we could furnish the attic, and you two could live above us."

"Us?" Jamie sensed a plot.

"Mary Beth and I would live here, of course. We're older. You wouldn't expect us to climb two flights of stairs." She raised an eyebrow at Jamie. "I swear, 'dear sister,' sometimes you can be so selfish. Raymond could help you run the store. Why, this afternoon you should have heard some of his splendid suggestions. With his ideas we'd be making twice the money in no time."

"I won't hear of it!" Jamie stood, almost knocking the tea service from the table.

"Oh, you'll hear of it, girl!" Inez shouted back. "Haven't I always known what's best for you? Well, I still do. If we don't act, in a few years you'll be past the marrying age. Virgins aren't like wine, you know. They don't improve with age. I'm not planning to hurry you, but in the end you'll marry Raymond and make everyone happy."

"Everyone but me!" Jamie ran for the door. "I'll not marry him."

"Where do you think you're going?" Inez shouted.

"I've work to do downstairs." Jamie fought for control. Getting mad and yelling at Inez never did any good. In the end it only solidified her sister's determination.

"Well, don't expect me to do these dishes. I've had a long day."

Jamie barely heard the words. She ran downstairs and grabbed the saddlebags. Moving in almost total darkness, she crossed the store to her favorite Chippendale chair. The huge wings and arms seemed to cuddle her as she closed her eyes and wished she were at Shadow's Bend with Adam.

Why couldn't he have lived today? She'd have

written and begged to visit him. He'd understand.
Somehow she knew he would. "Adam would have
told me to come to him," Jamie whispered to the
faded upholstery. "If he were real, he'd care about
my happiness. I'd take all the money I've saved and
go to him."

As sleep overtook her, she imagined what the sunset must be like on the open plains, with nothing to
block the view. She could see the house Adam had
described nestled in the earth's sudden jutting of
cliffs. The cold wind caught her hair and pulled it
free of pins as she stood in the tall grass a hundred
yards from the house and corral. She couldn't find
Adam in her dream; then she realized she had no
picture of what he looked like.

All the tall clocks were striking midnight when
Jamie awoke and turned on a light. The need to
write to Adam was greater than any hunger she'd
ever felt. As silently as possible, she moved to the
desk and penned her second letter. She told him of
her sister's plot to make her marry and of her dream
of standing outside Shadow's Bend. Boldly, she
asked him to describe himself.

On the last inch of the page she tried to explain
how she'd found his letters and how in her world it
really was 1902. Whatever magic connected them,
the letters reached out to cross not only space but
also time.

The sun was almost up when she stuffed her
brown envelope into the bag and went up to bed.
Again she dreamed of standing on the open plains
staring out at the Pony Express station.

A week passed before an answer came. Jamie
checked the saddlebags every day. Seven mornings
without an answer, then three creamy envelopes
tumbled from the bag. Jamie snatched them up and

ran to the attic, shouting to Inez about needing something from storage.

The half-finished attic was the only room Inez never entered. Damp and dusty, with evidence of rodents in the corners, the room was only large enough to be a small bedroom. Jamie couldn't imagine sharing such a tiny space with Raymond. Inez seemed to have dropped the idea of their marriage for a while. Maybe it was because all week Jamie had been going down to work early and staying late.

Jamie sat on a box by the one window and unfolded the third letter, dated March 11, 1861.

Across the top of the page, the bold handwriting said simply:

Spring has come to Shadow's Bend and its name is Jamie. I never believed in magic until I found your letter.

Jamie couldn't help but laugh. If she had brought a fraction of the joy to Adam's life that he had brought to hers, there really was magic in these letters.

You asked what I look like. How does a man describe himself to a woman? I'm too big to be a Pony Express rider and old enough at thirty to know better. I'm from Texas, and some men say that's all that needs to be told about a personality. I wouldn't call myself handsome, but I don't frighten small children when I pass. My mother was half-Mexican so I have her dark hair (which is in need of cutting), but my eyes are blue.

I was married once in '52, when I was just big enough to think myself a man. We bought land in West Texas and started raising horses.

The first winter my Margaret caught cold. It moved into her lungs. There was nothing I could do to save her. After that winter the ranch kept growing, but my heart stopped. There's been no woman in my thoughts since Margaret . . . until you, Jamie.

I don't need to ask what you look like. I saw you walking on the plains in front of my cabin a week ago. You were wearing dark blue and your hair was blowing in the wind. Hair the color of sunshine. I don't know how such a thing happened, but come back again. I watch the horizon every evening and wait.

Jamie let out a cry and almost dropped the letter. How could such a thing be? How could he have seen her?

"Jamie!" Inez's voice shouted from below. "Are you all right up there?"

"I . . . " Jamie's mind whirled. "I thought I saw a rat."

"Well, I wouldn't be surprised," Inez grumbled from below. "I've suggested ten times you clean that place up. If you'd get the attic in shape, you could move all those boxes out of your room. I swear to Moses, I don't know how you get around in that bedroom of yours."

Jamie folded the letter and placed it back in the satchel. "He saw me," she whispered. "Adam saw me."

3

While a week of quiet days passed, Adam was never far from Jamie's thoughts. Somehow he'd seen her, and she couldn't wait to find out if she'd dream of going to him once more. In the slow days of managing the store's few customers and dusting endlessly, she waited. The time had to be right for dreaming. A quiet night. Undisturbed. She waited and planned.

It took every ounce of her patience to sit with Inez after dinner each evening and talk of nothing. At last, one night the older woman decided to turn in early.

Jamie watched Inez close her bedroom door. As her sister's room darkened, Jamie ran to the wardrobe and searched for something to wear. But all her dresses looked the same, worn and old. Even her Sunday best was frayed at the cuffs and a serviceable black. She couldn't wear black to meet Adam, even in a dream. All the stockings were darned and patched, her shoes were scuffed, and she didn't own a decent hat. Jamie plopped down on the bed in frustration. She'd finally met a man worth knowing, if only in her mind, and she had nothing to wear.

Winchester jumped up on the bed and rubbed against her, purring loudly. "You don't care how I look, do you old friend?" she whispered to the cat. Jamie smiled slowly. "And my guess is if Adam really is a man worth knowing, he won't either. I can't miss my one chance to dream of him again for lack of an outfit."

She slipped into her best pair of darned stockings and her only church shoes. Making a blind choice, she drew one of the many drab dresses from the wardrobe and slipped it over her plain cotton petticoats.

The shop stood as silent as a church on Monday evening as Jamie tiptoed downstairs. The streetlamp's glow spotlighted a couch made of deep cherrywood and tattered tapestry. The huge claw-and-ball feet made the couch seem like a crouched beast waiting in the shadows.

Moving to the old Chippendale chair, Jamie curled up in it as she had a week ago when she'd dreamed of going to Shadow's Bend. The aging arms of the chair cradled her, protecting her.

Closing her eyes, Jamie pictured the cabin in her mind, the corral, the cliff, the sunset. Slowly the scene cleared before her. Again the wind caught her hair and pulled it free of pins. Now the wind was warmer, with a whisper of spring. She smelled new grass and soil heated from a day in the sun.

Jamie's world in Chicago slipped away, and she once more stood before Adam's cabin.

From the darkness of the barn came a man, tall and lean. He walked with his head down, into the wind. His leather chaps flapped around powerful legs, and his chambray shirt molded against his arms and chest. Just before he reached the path to the cabin, he turned slightly and looked toward Jamie. For a long moment he just stood watching her then he removed his hat and stared.

She raised her fingertips to her mouth, hiding her smile. Adam Shelton was a fine-looking man, and she saw him as clearly as if he were real. His black hair curled around his collar. Disbelief, then pleasure, altered his stance.

"You're back!" he cried as he broke into a run toward her. "Jamie!"

His size, his sudden nearness, frightened her, and she took a step backward. Caring for a man by mail was one thing, but having him before her was quite another.

The moment she retreated, he slowed his pace. He stopped several feet away with only the knee-high grass between them. "I didn't mean to scare you, miss." His smile was broad and honest. "I guess I've thought of you so much, it seems like I've known you for a while. I've about worn my eyes out watching for a glimpse of you again."

Lowering her hands, Jamie forced her fingers to uncoil. "I know. All I've thought of this week was coming back," she whispered. "I feel that somehow you're a part of me, maybe a part that's always been there, but I never knew it. You're taller than I imagined you'd be."

"And you're beautiful," he whispered more to himself than her. "I've tried to picture you close up, but I never guessed you'd be so lovely."

A hint of a grin widened her lips. "Sorry to learn of your poor vision, Adam Shelton, but I know very well I'm plain."

Adam laughed. "There must be no mirrors in Chicago, for you are truly a wonder, Jamie Edwards."

She decided she'd been right about him not noticing her worn clothes. "Are we both dreaming now?"

"I don't know." He moved a foot closer. "I don't care as long as you're here. I've longed for the sound of your laughter. Sometimes I've even thought I could hear it carried on the wind all the way from Chicago."

"My sister would think me mad." She didn't add

that there was very little she laughed about.

"Then we'll be mad together. I'm afraid to question too deeply how you came here. I only know I was on the point of not caring if I saw another sunrise when I received your letter."

"Oh, no, Adam, don't ever think that." She reached out and almost touched his arm before pulling away. She'd never even considered touching a stranger so boldly before. But he wasn't a stranger. He was her Adam. The man she'd been talking to in her mind for days. The man who halved her loneliness by sharing his thoughts in letters.

"You've called me Adam twice." He ran his hands along his pants and took a step nearer. "Does that mean you wouldn't mind my calling you Jamie?"

"I wouldn't mind," she answered, liking the way her name sounded in his slow Texas drawl. "If we're going to be in each other's dreams, we might as well be on a first name basis."

Adam's voice was so low she wasn't sure she heard the words. "I need to touch you, Jamie."

"What?"

He stepped so close she could feel the warmth of him beside her. "I need to know you're with me and not just a ghost haunting both my sleeping and waking hours. I have to know you're real."

Jamie raised her hand and placed her fingers, feather-light, over his heart. "I know what you mean about being afraid to believe. But you seem quite solid." Her hand alighted on his shoulder. "More solid than anyone I've ever touched, I think."

He moved an inch toward her, but she pulled her hand away and stepped back again. Adam hesitated, not wanting to frighten her, but afraid she'd disappear if he didn't hold on to her. "Jamie," he whispered as she lowered her lashes.

"Jamie," he said again, not knowing what to do

How could he explain that she'd been in his every thought, every dream for two weeks? He'd read her letters so many times they were worn out from being refolded into his pocket.

After an endless moment, she looked up at him. "Don't just touch me . . . hold me, Adam. Hold me tight."

In one swift movement she was in his embrace, and he was crushing her against him. He lifted her off the ground and swung her around in a full circle. His powerful arms were as hard as oak around her, his chest warm, and his heart pounding.

Laughter rumbled between them. "You feel so wonderful, Jamie. I've ached to hold you since the day your first letter came."

Leaning her head back so she could see his eyes, she looked at him closely. No one had ever hugged her so completely. Her father had been frail and, though loving, uncomfortable with displays of affection. In Adam's arms she felt warm all the way to the soles of her feet. There was a wildness about him that awakened her senses. "I think you'd best put me down, Adam, before I faint from lack of air."

Adam lowered her gently and stepped away. "I'm sorry. I guess I'm a little rusty. But you feel so good."

Jamie blushed. She knew hugging a total stranger was improper, but she wished he'd do it again. "You promised to show me the sunset," she managed to say.

He pulled his gloves off and shoved them in his back pocket, then offered his hand. "Shall we?"

Jamie placed her palm in his. It felt so right, as if she'd found the perfect fit. Warm, protective, strong.

They walked across the field to where the rocks formed natural steps to the top of the cliff. He guided her up, carefully shielding her with his open arm without touching her except when she stumbled.

"I'm not used to the country," she explained. "I've been out of Chicago only twice in my life and both times were before I turned ten."

"I've never lived in a town where you couldn't stand in the middle and throw a rock out into the country in any direction. I saw Chicago once when I delivered horses. It looked crowded and dirty."

She smiled up at him. "It's not so bad." She wanted to say she'd like to show him the parks in the spring and the lake in summer, but he'd never belong in the city. He was a man made to live on open land. The wind whipped his midnight hair across his forehead, and Jamie wanted to brush it back. His face was not the smooth handsomeness of a banker or shop owner, but lined from squinting into the sun and rugged from exposure in all sorts of weather. A day's growth of beard brushed his strong jawline.

They reached the top of the hill without saying anything more. The wind blew at full power there, tugging at Jamie's long skirts and almost knocking her over. She felt as if she could see forever in every direction. The barn, cabin, even the windmill, looked small below them, almost like toys in a sandbox.

Adam pulled her in front of him and widened his stance. "You'd best let me block the wind, or I'll be looking for you in the breaks. It's a hundred-foot fall off this side of the cliff."

She felt his warm chest press against her back. When she leaned into him, his arms circled lightly around her waist. Neither spoke, as if by saying nothing they were free to enjoy the intimacy without feeling it improper.

Sun touched the horizon. They watched in silence as the sky put on a magnificent show. Turning from yellow to orange, the sun seemed to melt into the earth. The clouds took on colors bright with day and dark with approaching night. They curtained the dying glow with royal velvet and reflected gold.

As light faded, the wind died down, but Adam didn't move away. Jamie rolled the back of her head slightly against his shoulder until her hair brushed the bottom of his chin. He pulled her closer in answer.

"That was wonderful." She turned slightly, loving the circle of his arms.

Adam couldn't reply. Heaven had just fallen into his grasp. He sensed she was a little afraid of him. After all, he was a stranger who'd only written her. But he was a man, not a dream as she seemed to think, and judging from the way she was moving in his embrace, she was every inch a woman.

"Are you cold?" he finally said.

"No." She curved her hand along his arm where it rested at her waist. "It's November in Chicago and I stay cold most of the time. But here, I feel no chill at all."

Adam knew it couldn't be November in Chicago and March here. He might be far from civilization, but he couldn't be that far.

"Riders say there'll be full war between the states by spring." He didn't want to think of anything except the woman he held, but if he didn't say something, he knew he'd try to kiss her. "If it comes, there'll be no more Pony Express, and this station will be abandoned. Most of the boys are already talking about enlisting."

Jamie swallowed hard, afraid of a war that had passed almost forty years ago. "Would you go?"

"I don't know," Adam answered. "I could supply horses. My ranch in Texas has plenty, and someone would have to break them. But I'd probably enlist."

"And would you join with the North or the South?"

"I'd fight for Texas, if it came to war. I'd rather be in some camp defending any cause than alone again. I've had my fill of eating three meals a day without anyone across the table."

"But the South can't win." Jamie didn't want to think of this strong man being defeated.

"No one wins in war," Adam whispered against her hair. "If I had someone like you in Texas, I'd stay out of the war and raise horses."

"Someone like me?"

"Jamie." Adam's voice was as deep as the evening sky. "You feel so right in my arms. I don't want to frighten you, but I think I could hold you all night like this."

When she sighed softly, he turned her to face him. One hand spread wide across her back, pulling her close against him, while his other hand clutched her hair.

Closing her eyes, she smiled as feelings exploded in her body. She'd seen couples embrace in the park, but she'd had no idea it felt so wonderful. He held her with a strong gentleness that warmed her and made her feel cherished.

Adam's fingers tightened in her hair as he leaned nearer. His chest crushed Jamie's breasts a moment before his mouth covered hers. At first she didn't respond, just let the tidal wave roll over her. His lips pressed hard against hers as his fingers pulled her hair gently back.

A fire sparked deep inside her. A frightening fire that heated her blood and made her heart pound.

Jamie moved her hands up his chest and shoved, but he didn't budge. She tried to pull away from his kiss, but his tongue parted her lips and demanded more than she knew how to give.

Pounding on his chest in panic, Jamie fought to free herself. The perfect dream had become a nightmare. His fingers released her hair and slid beneath her arm to brush the side of her breast.

She jerked her mouth free at the same moment her open palm slapped hard across Adam's face. She'd never been kissed except politely on the cheek. His advance was an assault against all she'd ever known.

For a second he didn't react, but stood frozen, still holding her to him. She watched the fire in his eyes turn to confusion.

"Let me go!"

Adam released her instantly. His face was a collision of shadows. Desire and anger. Need and betrayal. He stood so still he didn't even seem to breathe.

With unsure steps, Jamie backed away, shaking so badly she didn't trust herself to speak. Her perfect man, the man she'd dreamed of for weeks, had attacked her like an animal. She might never have been kissed before, but she knew kisses were supposed to be tender and soft, not hot and savage with open mouths. And no one had ever touched her breast. She could still feel his hand. Even now her flesh throbbed.

"Jamie . . ." Adam's voice was ragged as he tried to control himself. He hadn't meant to kiss her so recklessly. He'd only wanted to taste her lips. But when he'd touched her mouth, the need to drink deep had stolen his control.

"Don't say anything." Jamie took another step backward. "I've never been kissed before." She fought the tears. "I've never been touched like that."

Adam ran his fingers through his hair. He was a fool. He'd frightened her. But how could he apologize when, in truth, he wanted nothing more than to pull her back into his arms? If she hadn't stopped him, he'd have ripped off the rag she called a dress, and made love to her right here on the top of this hill in plain sight of God and everyone within a hundred miles. If there was anyone within a hundred miles. . . .

"I didn't mean to frighten you," he managed to say while his mind screamed that he wanted to crush her to him until they were both wet with passion, drunk on the scent of each other. "I guess I thought that by your age, you'd been kissed a few times. No woman as beautiful as you could still be a virgin."

"Don't call me that!"

"What? A virgin?" Adam stepped toward her. "It's not a sin to be a—"

"No!" Jamie cried, remembering how many times Inez had reminded her that she would always be a virgin.

She took another step backward, but her foot didn't feel earth beneath her heel. She'd passed the edge of the cliff. Frantic, she grabbed at weeds that clung to the rocky edge. The dried plants cut into her palm as they snapped from her grip.

Adam jumped to pull her back, but she was already falling. Falling into the total darkness of the night. She opened her mouth to scream, but her ears filled with the sound of Adam crying her name as she fell farther and farther away.

4

Adam searched 'til dawn looking for Jamie's body, but he found no trace of her. He'd yelled her name so loudly into the night when she'd fallen that he hadn't heard her body strike the rocks. He wasn't sure he'd have remained sane if he'd heard such a sound.

The morning turned from black to gray, but his mood remained the same. Every muscle ached from climbing up and down the cliff, but he couldn't stop looking. She might have survived the fall and rolled into a ravine or been wedged between two rocks. He couldn't rest until he knew she was safe, or dead.

As the sun rose, Adam stood on the spot where she'd stepped off. Nothing. No sign of her. She'd disappeared completely into the night. He couldn't see a scrap of clothing or a drop of blood. Nothing.

He pulled off his gloves and shoved them into his back pocket. His clothes were ripped and torn. Several spots of crimson dotted his arms where he'd collided with rocks during one of his countless journeys over the uneven cliff.

He wiped a dirty sleeve across his face and swore at the dust that made his eyes water. There was no body to mourn. She was only a dream. He'd spent the night searching for a woman who was no more real than the thin vapor clouds along the horizon.

Cramming his hat low, Adam climbed down the

cliff one last time. Without really thinking why, he knew he'd never come to the ridge again to watch the sunset.

When he reached the foot of the cliff he could hear the horses already demanding breakfast, and the cow was an hour past milking. Adam didn't bother stopping at the cabin. He didn't want anything to eat and was too tired to care how he must look. There were chores to be done and a Pony Express rider coming in at ten. After that he planned to find the bottle of whiskey he'd been saving and wash the memory of Jamie from his mind.

He dunked his head in the rain trough by the windmill, then straightened, slinging the water from his hair and wishing he could toss her memory away as easily.

Jamie jerked awake with a violence that almost shook her from the Chippendale chair. She moaned and shook her head as she passed from the shadows of sleep to reality.

"A dream," she whispered, reassuring herself while her blood still pounded. "I dreamed I was falling."

In the silent store, all the furniture seemed to watch over her and set her mind to rest that all was unchanged and normal. The tall clocks ticked against the wall, slowing her heartbeat with their steady rhythm.

Touching her lips, she remembered the dream. It had been so real she could still feel the warmth of his lips on hers. The feel of his arms around her. The panic. The fall.

"Only a dream," she repeated as she stared at the thin cuts in her palm. "Nothing really happened tonight."

Perhaps that was best, for she'd made a fool of herself. She'd allowed him to hug her and hold her hand. She'd had no right to be surprised when he'd kissed her.

But it wasn't real! Jamie tried to make herself believe, yet she could picture the sunset and feel the wind in her hair. The memory of his long, powerful fingers sliding along her breast still made her flesh tingle.

"Jamie!" Inez's sharp voice sounded from the landing. "Are you down here?" Her tone warned Jamie of her half sister's anger.

"I'm over here," Jamie answered, wishing she could move from one floor to another without Inez feeling the need to keep up with her.

"I didn't think I'd have to track you down," Inez complained as she tried to pull a robe two sizes too small around her. "I was almost asleep when I remembered I invited Mary Beth and Raymond to dinner tomorrow night."

Jamie didn't answer. Anything honest she had to say would only cause Inez to yell. She nodded and started upstairs to bed, thinking one day she'd take the little money she'd saved and disappear, leaving Inez to cook for herself and her boring friends. Even the dream of falling was better than having to plan a meal for the Whitneys.

She kept her comments to herself all the next day as she cooked and cleaned. Inez didn't have time to help; she was too busy trying to organize Jamie's future. She still saw her little sister as a child who needed direction.

To Jamie's disappointment, the Whitneys were right on time. Mary Beth waddled in first, her arms cradling plum jelly she'd made years ago and must have vowed to force on people at every opportunity until it was all gone. When she thrust the gift at Inez, Jamie noticed the jar was dusty, and the canning date had been rubbed off.

Raymond walked a step behind his sister. He wore his hat low, shadowing his huge eyes from anyone's view for as long as custom would allow.

Jamie fought the urge to look behind him to see if he could possibly be more than an inch thick. He seemed like a chalk drawing of a man. A character so thin she sometimes thought he was almost transparent.

Inez greeted her friends warmly, but Jamie stood back, hoping they wouldn't notice her. Yet she could feel Raymond watching her. As she took their coats and led them upstairs, she knew he stared. Even as she served the meal, his gaze never left her. He had no need to talk; his sister seemed to enjoy telling everyone what he thought.

As she watched him eating, Jamie couldn't imagine him holding her . . . or kissing her. He ate each bite of food as though it were tasteless, a sentence he'd been committed to for the evening. He even drank the wine Inez had insisted on buying as if it were water.

Almost laughing aloud, she remembered Adam's bold touch. He might be a dream, but he seemed far more real than the man before her. She'd give anything if he could be the one here tonight instead of Raymond. She could almost feel Adam's gaze warming her deep inside.

Forcing herself to stare straight ahead, Jamie looked at the great mirror that hung behind the table. Inez had sworn it made the room look larger, but Jamie thought it served only to double the clutter.

As her gaze focused on the mirror, she could almost see Shadow's Bend before her. Adam stood on the prairie with his legs squarely planted and gloved fists resting at the top of his chaps. His hair was the black of his Latin blood and his eyes the blue of

Texas. He was calling her name in half request, half demand.

"Adam!" Jamie whispered.

"What, dear sister?" Inez leaned toward Jamie, but her attention still focused on something Raymond seemed about to say.

Jamie looked at the other dinner guests. Panic climbed up her spine as she realized she'd rather live in a dream than in any reality that included these people.

"I said," Jamie replied, trying to keep her breathing normal, "Adamsville has a nice look to it for dining room chairs."

Inez waved her hand in frustration, seemingly unaware that her fork was wedged between her chubby fingers. "Pay attention, Jamie. We haven't been talking about furniture for half an hour."

Jamie lowered her gaze and collected the dinner plates. "I'll get the dessert," she mumbled as she hurried toward the kitchen.

As the swinging door closed, she could hear Inez explaining how her "dear sister" was sometimes just too much of a cross to bear. Jamie knew without hearing more that her next topic would be how their father had simply been too old to parent a normal child, and if it hadn't been for Inez's constant guidance, there would be no telling what poor little Jamie would have become.

Jamie set down the plates and closed her eyes. "Poor little Jamie's gone mad," she said, wishing she could return and relive the dream from the night before.

Forcing herself to slice the coconut pie, Jamie tried to remember every detail of the dream. He'd kissed her in a way she didn't know folks kissed. It had been all warm and filled with need. She smiled suddenly. If she had a chance to do it over again, she wasn't sure she'd pull away so quickly. Just once she wished she'd be brave enough to do something other than what was planned for her. And why hadn't she? After all, what did it matter if she were reckless and bold in her dreams?

"Jamie!" Inez shouted. "Do we have dessert?"

Jamie abandoned her daydreaming and carried the four saucers of pie into the tiny dining area.

Inez smiled down at her large slice. "I was beginning to think you'd forgotten dessert." She shoved a bite into her mouth. "The meringue's a little stiff," she announced as she pointed with her fork. "Which I guess befits the soup that was too watery."

Mary Beth Whitney laughed at Inez's humor but only stared at the pie.

"It's coconut," Jamie offered. "I made it fresh today."

Raymond pushed the pie a few inches away. "I don't like coconut. I had it once, and it got between my teeth. Most disagreeable, as I remember."

"I'm not fond of it myself," Mary Beth added, always agreeing with her brother's pointless wisdom. "But I'll be polite and try a bite." She shoved a third of the slice into her mouth and mumbled. "Inez is right. The meringue's been overbeat. Too much cream of tartar. But don't worry, dear, with a little advice I'm sure you'll improve."

Jamie stared at her slice. The dinner had progressed as all dinners with the Whitneys did. She'd done all the cooking, except for the plum jelly no one tasted, and they'd criticized every dish. She'd never endure a marriage to Raymond. She could just imagine hearing him say "I don't like coconut," or "spring'll come soon enough," or any one of the hundred little sayings he seemed to repeat every time she saw him.

"I'll clear the table." Jamie stood without looking

at the other three. She'd been making pies for the elderly every Sunday for years without a complaint. "Since no one likes the pie, I'll save it for Mrs. Murphy."

Inez snorted. "Don't do that. The old woman's like a stray dog. If we start feeding her, she'll never leave. I'd rather see you throw out the pie."

Jamie moved into the kitchen as Inez continued telling the Whitneys about old Mrs. Murphy, who wandered into the store almost every day to sit in a Victorian rocking chair as if it belonged to her. They all agreed the woman should be discouraged. Raymond even offered to drop by next week and toss her out with a hand firm enough to insure she wouldn't return.

Tears bubbled over Jamie's lashes as she carefully wrapped the pie in waxed paper. "I'll save it for Mrs. Murphy." Even the thought of Raymond hurting the old dear's feelings bothered Jamie and she knew she'd have a talk with him if he tried to carry out his plan.

"They might think they can order me around," she mumbled. "But I'll not stand for them bothering Mrs. Murphy."

The image of Adam flashed in her mind. She couldn't see anyone pushing him around or making him bend to their will. He was as strong as she wished she were. After the fool she'd made of herself in her dream, Jamie knew she could never even pretend to visit him again. Even though he'd frightened her, at least she'd felt alive.

"Mary Beth suggested I give you a hand," Raymond said as he stepped into the kitchen. He folded his arms across his thin chest, leaving no doubt that he had no intention of being of any help.

Jamie felt sorry for him for the first time in all the years she'd known Raymond. He was as trapped by his life as she was by hers. In many ways they were the same, both ordered around by sisters. Except he ran a small bookkeeping business by himself and his sister waited on him.

He leaned against the pie safe and stared at her with odd eyes that seemed to open just a little too wide. Jamie wondered briefly if they closed completely even in sleep.

"Raymond." She moved closer, feeling light-headed from the wine. "Have you ever thought of kissing me?"

To her surprise he reddened with anger. "Certainly not! You're not the kind of woman a man would think of doing such a thing with."

"But you've known me for years and you've never even touched my hand."

"I pride myself in touching people as little as possible. Haven't you heard of germs? It's my thesis that everyone would be a great deal more healthy if they endeavored not to come into contact with another person."

Jamie thought of reaching out her hand and touching his arm just to bother him, but she realized she didn't want to feel him anymore than he obviously did her. Adam's hug and kiss might not have been proper, but at least she'd felt alive. With Raymond she might as well be lying in her coffin as his bed for all the warmth he'd shown her.

"Would you like coffee?" She turned away, wishing she'd never even brought up the idea of kissing or touching him.

"I would," he answered. "Only I'll direct you in the proper proportions. Your coffee is far too weak."

Storm clouds gathered, echoing Adam's mood all day. He worked, pushing himself harder than usual trying to shove Jamie from his mind. By mid afternoon, he knew a full gale storm was coming and there were a hundred things that must be done. He pushed his tired body to the limit, welcoming the numbness that came with being too tired to think.

No sunset colored the horizon at nightfall as black clouds boiled across the sky. Huge splats of icy hard rain stung his skin when he closed the barn door and turned to make a run for the house.

He hadn't taken three steps before he noticed that the top pole of the corral fence was down on one side. A quick glance told Adam the bad news. The extra horses were gone, and by morning, with all this lightning, they'd be wild with panic and half-way to Kansas.

Rain blurred his vision as Adam moved over the fence and entered the barn's side door. Judging from the clouds, he had less than ten minutes to find the horses before the wrath of the storm broke and they'd be impossible to round up.

Grabbing a rope from the wall, he didn't bother saddling his roan, but threw the bridle over her ears and shoved the bit into Red's mouth. The old roan was the only mount on the place fast enough to catch the runaways . . . provided she didn't get spooked by the storm.

Adam felt every bone in his body protest as he climbed on Red's back and kicked. The horse bolted into the rain at full speed before they cleared the broken fence. He darted past the half-finished wind-mill looming like the skeleton of a castle tower in the cloud-covered sky. Adam guessed the runaways would be heading south, away from the storm.

His fingers knotted around the reins as the storm worsened. The wind froze rain into his shirt. Thun-der rolled across the land like a runaway train shak-ing the world with its fury. Through flashes he scanned the open plains. No sign of horses. They were too far ahead of him to catch in time.

Lightning struck the prairie only yards ahead of them. Red reared and kicked the air with her front legs, attempting to fight off the storm. The wildness of the wind fired her blood. The animal bolted back toward the barn. Adam heard the crash of wood amid the shatter of thunder. He gave the horse her head. It was madness to try and find anything in the tempest around him.

Lightning outlined the buildings. In the flash Adam realized something was wrong, but he didn't have time to react. Red was at a full run and his hands were too cold to move quickly.

"The windmill," he swore as the horse ran across the path of the falling tower. Pipe and lumber crashed into them with all the force of the storm behind it. A board slammed against Adam's head, and he tumbled from the horse's back. An instant later he heard Red's whinny and knew the horse was also hurt and tumbling to the cold ground. She screamed, an almost human cry, and shook the ground with the force of her fall.

For a long time, Adam lay in the mud with the windmill twisted around him. He couldn't hear Red and guessed she'd broken her neck in the fall. Rain washed away all noise beneath its relentless pounding.

Adam slowly slid his hand along one leg. It didn't feel broken, but the weight of several boards made any movement impossible. He could feel a cut along one thigh, but it wasn't deep. Two huge blades from the windmill's fan pinned his left arm. The metal pie shapes were firmly planted in the ground, imprisoning him.

He jerked to free his arm, but he couldn't get any power behind his pull without first freeing his legs. He couldn't release them without both arms. Wher he wiped the rain from his face, he tasted blood dripping off his forehead.

Rain mixed with crimson and formed a puddle of blood beside his head.

Adam surrendered to the storm. He stopped struggling as he swore into the night. All the isolation and loneliness of this year weighed upon his heart heavier than the rubble across his body.

Loss of blood made his head feel light. After no sleep in two days, he closed his eyes and wanted only rest.

As the last ounce of energy passed from him and Adam slipped into sleep, he whispered the one name that had lightened his soul. "Jamie."

5

Jamie jerked instantly awake, as if someone had called her name sharply in the silence. She looked around her tiny room. Winchester was asleep on a stack of boxes along one wall. The curtains were drawn across the room's only window. The lamp she'd left burning low made the shadows flicker but failed to banish them.

Without stopping to think about the cold, Jamie slipped off the bed and moved from her room. All was silent. She crossed to Inez's door. The sound of her sister's snores came to her even through the wood.

Pulling a quilt around her, Jamie tiptoed down the stairs. The shop was freezing. Inez insisted she could never sleep if the heater were left on, but Jamie always felt a little sorry for all the furniture downstairs in the cold at night. She knew it would be noon tomorrow before the rooms heated up enough to make the air bearable.

She curled into the Chippendale wing-backed chair and closed her eyes. Maybe she wouldn't go back to Adam. Maybe she'd only dream of standing in the warm grass and watching the sunset. But she had to cross time once more and say good-bye to Shadow's Bend.

But as she passed into sleep, only darkness surrounded her. She couldn't see the grass or the barn.

Jamie moved in the blackness and felt rain on her face. The soft, gentle rain that followed a storm. The ground was almost liquid beneath her feet as she moved in blindness. As her vision adjusted, she saw the outline of the cliff, the cabin, the barn, but the windmill was missing.

"Adam," she whispered, sensing something was wrong, very wrong.

"Adam!"

Something brushed her leg and Jamie knelt to feel her way in the darkness. Boards. Cold metal. Hair.

Trembling hands brushed across the back of an animal motionless on the ground. Through the rain she saw the huge horse's outline. Her legs were twisted in unnatural angles and several pieces of lumber lay across the dead roan's back.

Jamie brushed the animal's red mane, her fingers catching in the bridle's leather straps. This had been no wild horse caught in the storm's fury. If there were a bridle, there could have been a rider.

"Adam!" she cried as she moved through the rubble of wood and steel.

No one answered and she knew the hollowness of being totally alone. Rain and mud hampered each step. The boards splintered into her hands as she tried to shove them away.

In the center of the wreckage, she stubbed her toe on something that gave slightly. Kneeling, Jamie forced herself to feel through the darkness. Soft leather gave beneath her touch before she felt muscle. Adam's chaps. Adam's leg.

Afraid to call his name and not receive an answer, Jamie moved her hand along his leg to his waist. Her fingers slid over the wet shirt and pressed gently on his chest. She could feel warmth. He was alive.

"Adam," she whispered as her hands brushed over his face. He didn't answer, but the heat of his blood spread across her fingers as she touched his forehead.

Jamie stood, suddenly wanting to run for help. But where? Hadn't Adam said there was no one within a hundred miles? All her life she'd been only a shout away from others. Someone had always been near. The policeman on the corner, her father, Inez, the neighbors, the shopkeepers on either side of her. But now, when she really needed someone, there was nowhere to turn.

Shoving a board off Adam's leg, Jamie realized that if he were going to live, she must do something fast. Tears mixed with the rain as she lifted the twisted boards piece by piece. Finally, she reached his pinned leg. Hesitantly, her hands traced his side, checking for broken bones. He didn't move ·as she touched him and Jamie feared he might already be dead. If the falling windmill had killed a powerful horse, it might also have claimed a man.

She pulled the wet quilt off her shoulders and placed it over him, hoping to block the rain. Kneeling beside him, Jamie tried to pull Adam's arm from the twisted steel that held him captive.

She wasn't strong enough. Frantically, she clawed

at the wet ground, pushing the mud away from his arm.

An inch at a time the earth gave way to her fight. His hand slid beneath the metal and pulled free.

Exhausted, Jamie knelt beside Adam and cradled his head in her lap. "I can't carry you inside," she cried, knowing his head and leg were still bleeding. "You'll die out here in the rain and there's nothing I can do."

Adam moaned and moved slightly as her fingers touched the wound on his forehead.

"You're alive!" she cried, and leaned close over him.

A muddy hand touched her hair. "Jamie?"

She didn't care that they were both covered in blood and mud. The warmth of his fingers in her hair felt like heaven. "I heard you call my name," she whispered as he slowly tested his strength. "Can you stand?"

Adam rolled to his side. "I think so." He allowed her to help him to his feet, leaning on her shoulder as they struggled through the rain to the cabin. Each time he pulled his right leg, she could feel his body tighten in pain.

The interior was cave black. Adam left her side for a moment. After several strikes on flint, a tiny fire flickered. Within moments the fireplace in one corner came alight.

Jamie looked around the small, orderly cabin. Everything was in place, from the homemade rope bed with its blanket pulled tight, to the four fan-back Windsor chairs arranged around a table covered with books and drawings of wind machines. Jamie moved nearer the fire as she studied Adam's world.

When he rose from kneeling in front of the fireplace and glanced at her, an oath escaped his lips and he lowered his head. Damp hair covered the wound on his forehead, but she could see crimson stains on his shirt from the open cut.

"I'm sorry." Jamie scolded herself for looking at the man's furniture while he continued to bleed. "Let me see about your wounds."

Adam cleared his throat and refused to look at her. "My wounds are nothing." His voice sounded harsh. "You're welcome to wear one of those shirts behind you." He turned and faced the fire. When he spread his arms wide to grip the mantel, she could see tension mold his shoulders.

Jamie looked down at herself in horror. Her cheap wet cotton nightgown clung to her body like thin paint. In one glance he must have seen every curve.

"I'm so sorry," she whispered, and grabbed for a shirt hanging from one of many pegs behind the door.

"You're not going to run away again, are you?" He seemed to be forcing his voice into calmness.

Jamie pulled the warm wool over her head. "No, I don't think so." She struggled into the sleeves. "I'd like to stay long enough to wrap those cuts. I'm not much of a nurse, but it looks like I may be all you have around these parts."

She turned and met his blue eyes watching her. He was doing it again. Standing so still, she wasn't sure he breathed. The fire in his gaze chased her chill away, but in the lines beneath his eyes, she saw the hurt that she must have caused when she'd disappeared and the lack of sleep he had suffered since then.

"I'm sorry," she whispered, knowing fully the pain she must have caused him.

"You've said that three times." He didn't move or smile. He wasn't going to make it easy for her.

Jamie lifted a towel from a shaving stand almost identical to one in her store. Crossing the room to him, she stated the obvious. "You're still dripping blood."

He pulled one of the Windsor chairs away from the table. "It doesn't matter." Sitting, he leaned back, crossing his long legs in front of him. "I didn't mean to frighten you last night, but you didn't stay around long enough to allow me to apologize. Even now I'm afraid not to stare at you lest you vanish the moment I look away. I've tried all forms of logic, but there is no way you can be here, so why was I so upset when you disappeared?"

Jamie tried again to clean the wound. He reluctantly allowed her to press the towel against his forehead. "I don't think I'll vanish so quickly," she said. "As near as I can understand, I'll stay here until I wake up in the chair I'm sleeping in back home."

Adam folded his arms over his chest and watched her as she timidly cleaned the small cut on his forehead. After a few washings the wound stopped bleeding and she stepped back to look at him.

"There's blood on your leg also. You'd best take off those chaps."

Adam smiled and watched as she blushed at her own command. She looked so beautiful with her hair curling all around her shoulders and her still muddy bare feet showing beneath his shirt. Jamie must be determined to drive him to the breaking point by looking so desirable, and yet he knew she would move away if he tried to touch her.

"I need to get the extra horses back." He had to make his mind think of something else besides Jamie.

"Won't they be much easier to find come morning?" Jamie asked. "Right now you need care."

He opened his mouth to disagree, but found it difficult when he knew she was right. He could feel blood running down his leg.

Slowly, he untied his chaps and let the leather, heavy with water, hit the floor. Pulling his shirt from his pants, he then hesitated with his belt half-unbuckled.

Jamie glanced at him from the washstand. "And the pants," she ordered as if she were a mother talking to a stubborn child.

He grumbled but removed first his boots then his pants. Only the length of his shirttail kept her from embarrassment.

When he sat back down in the chair, Jamie knelt beside him. She used a towel to cover most of his leg as she began washing a long thin cut across his flesh about halfway between his knee and hip.

"You'll need to sew it up," he said calmly, as if they were talking about material and not his flesh.

"Me!"

Adam laughed. "You can sew?"

"Of course. I've made countless quilts and sold them. But I've never put a needle into someone's skin."

He reached behind him to the bottom shelf of the pie safe. Pulling out a wooden cigar box and a bottle of whiskey, he offered the box to her. While she rummaged through the box for needle and thread, he downed half the bottle and poured the rest over the wound.

Jamie began her task, pulling the skin closed as she sewed. She didn't stop to meet his eyes as she worked. She wasn't sure she could have done what they both knew must be done if she'd seen the pain she was causing.

When the stitching was finished, Jamie gently washed the blood away.

Adam couldn't force his muscles to relax as he felt her fingers brush his skin. She didn't look up at him and he didn't speak, but slowly his need to be near her outweighed the pain in his leg. When her hands began to circle his leg to wrap the bandage, Adam thought his nerves might explode.

The silence grew, becoming an invisible wall between them. Jamie couldn't keep her hands from shaking while she tied off the bandage. She was glad she'd come when he'd called even though she guessed he would have been fine without her. Somehow he'd have survived alone. He had up till this point.

Her fingers moved over the steely muscle of his leg as she checked the bandage one last time. They were so different. He'd lived alone and was strong enough to do so; she didn't even have the strength to tell her sister no and make Inez believe it. In all Jamie's life she'd never spent more than a few hours without another person within speaking distance, but she'd be willing to bet she was as lonely as Adam.

Lifting the pan she'd used for water, Jamie moved to the washstand. She could hear Adam cross the room. The longer they were silent, the harder it became to speak. He dressed in a clean pair of pants and sat on the edge of the bed to pull his boots back on. She kept busy washing the pan and putting a pot on for tea.

The stove was an even older model than the one she'd used at church, but it looked almost new. She had the water heating in only a few minutes and turned to ask Adam if he'd like her to warm supper for him.

Adam sat upright, leaning his back against the cabin wall. He had one boot on and the other rested beside his open hand.

Jamie moved closer and smiled. Her dream man was sound asleep.

6

Adam came awake slowly, one sense at a time. The wool of a blanket brushed against his chin. A pain throbbed in his leg. The unmistakable aroma of baking apples and fresh biscuits drifted around him. A woman's soft voice sang a song he hadn't heard in years.

Slowly, he opened his eyes, afraid the wonder surrounding him might vanish if he woke too quickly. Jamie stood by the stove. She wore his cream-colored wool shirt and an apron that almost touched the ground. Her feet and legs were completely covered by a pair of dark socks he recognized as his. For a long while he just watched her, enjoying the scene as though it were a work of art.

When she set a bowl on the table, she finally glanced in his direction. A smile brushed her lips, making the muscles around his heart contract.

"You're awake?"

He didn't answer. All he wanted to do was stare at her.

She moved toward him without taking her gaze from his face. "You've been asleep for over an hour and I've had time to think."

He forced himself not to move as she knelt on the rag rug by his bed.

"I don't know how long I'll be here, or if I'll ever come again when I leave, but can we start over as friends for the time we have?"

"Start over?"

Licking her lips, she continued in a speech she must have been rehearsing while he'd been asleep. "I don't mean from the beginning, but maybe from somewhere in the middle. I've never had a man to talk to, and I've a hundred questions I'd like to ask. But you must make me one promise."

Adam didn't need to ask her condition. The bars on this heaven would be that she didn't want him to touch her. She'd made that plain enough on the cliff. Hell, the woman had stepped off a hundred-foot drop just to avoid him. What more proof did he need? "Fair enough," he said, resigning himself to her terms.

"But you haven't asked what the promise is." She laughed and laid her hand over his knee as if her light touch could stop him from taking any action. "I know it may sound funny, but it's very important to me."

The warmth of her touch branded his leg. "The promise?" Maybe she was a witch, he thought, come to make his last days torture.

Jamie's cheeks flushed with color. "I'd like you to promise to taste everything I cook. I know this is only a dream, but there's never been anyone who still had the majority of their teeth who enjoyed my cooking."

Adam had no idea what she was talking about, but she could make mud pies and he'd eat them if she asked him to. "I promise," he said as he slid his fingers over her hand and gently pressed.

She didn't pull away but looked down at their hands and added, "I've also thought about this being a dream and if you're only a vision, I guess everything doesn't have to be proper. I'd like you to teach me things."

"Teach you what things, Jamie?" His fingers moved over her hand, caressing lightly.

"I don't want to be afraid to touch you anymore."
She raised her hand and intertwined her fingers with
his. "No one has ever hugged me, or held me, or
kissed me good night in years. When I was little, my
sister always yelled at me if I did something wrong,
as if she'd be dirtied by laying a hand on me. When
my father was dying I tried to hold his hand and he
pulled away. He was too far into the next world to
even know me."

Adam's fingers tightened slightly as she continued. "The few times friends have touched me it's
always been in brief, impersonal ways. I'm tired of
never feeling the warmth of another person. I'd like
to be nearer to you than arm's length."

"But I might frighten you." Adam's voice was
hard. He'd touched enough people in his life and
lost. Even now he remembered how he'd held his
wife all night after she died, as if he could somehow
refuse to let her go. She'd grown cold and he
couldn't keep her warm. He wasn't sure he wanted
to risk that kind of caring again, even if Jamie was
right and they were only in some kind of strange
shared dream.

"You could go slow and tell me what to expect."
She pulled him to his feet. "I'll vanish if you move
too fast again."

He hesitated, not trusting her words completely.
"Something's happened since you were here last
night. You've changed." He leaned on her as he
moved.

"No, nothing's happened," Jamie answered honestly. Nothing could ever happen to her in her life
back in Chicago. If she was going to taste even a
tiny bit of life, she'd have to do it here in this magic
time. He'd awakened a need in her.

As she led Adam to the end of the table where
she'd moved the books aside and set two places, she

remembered the way Raymond had grown angry when she'd asked him to kiss her.

"Sit down," she ordered gently, "and I'll get the pie out of the oven."

Adam did as she requested. His dark eyebrows pulled together as he watched her closely, wondering what could have changed her in only a few hours.

Jamie carried the pie to the table. "I cooked a stew from the food I found in your cool box and root storage. The apples looked just right for a pie."

Smiling as he silently admired the pie she'd made, Jamie turned back to fetch the two bowls of soup and biscuits.

When she pulled her chair out, he made an effort to stand. Timidly, she touched his shoulder, signaling him to remain seated. They ate without saying a word, but she sensed his enjoyment of the meal with every bite he took.

As she cut the pie, he finally spoke. "That was the best stew I've ever tasted, Jamie. I don't know where you came from, but I don't accept your idea that our meeting is only a dream. Dreams don't fill my stomach and I could never have produced the stew by myself."

"You liked it?"

His gaze caught hers and he realized how important it was to her that he enjoy the simple meal. "I'd ask for another bowl, but I want to save room for pie."

Jamie removed the bowls. When she returned she stood at the end of the table only a few inches from Adam. "What would you say if I asked you to kiss me?"

When he didn't answer, she added, "Would you tell me I'm not the kind of woman you'd think of doing such a thing with?"

Adam still didn't answer and Jamie felt her cheeks warm. "Well?"

"I wouldn't say anything," he finally answered. She didn't notice the death grip he had on the side of the table. "If you asked me to kiss you, I'd do so. And you *are* the kind of woman who's made to be kissed and loved, and cherished, if that's what you're wondering about." He wanted to pull her against him and press his face into the wool shirt that covered her body. But he could never tell her such a thing.

Straightening slightly, Jamie moved to her side of the table. Raymond had made her request sound dirty, but Adam reversed the feelings.

"Are you asking me to kiss you, Jamie?"

"Wouldn't you be afraid of germs?"

"Of what?"

Jamie laughed. "Oh, for a time before germs." She realized he had no idea what she was talking about. She lifted the knife. "How large a piece of pie would you like?"

"Half the pie, if you don't mind," he answered. "It's been a long time since I've had any."

Jamie cut the pie and sat in amazement as he ate every bite. While he finished the meal, he talked of windmills and all the changes he believed they'd make on his ranch in Texas. One minute he was describing the beauty of the land and the next he was telling her about storms so mighty that they would make the one tonight seem insignificant.

He seemed to need the easy talk between them to cool the tension, and she loved listening, learning of a world she'd never see.

When he pushed the empty plate forward, he added, "That was perfect." His blue eyes sparkled with mischief. "I'm hoping you stay around for a while, but if you have to go, could you leave the other half of that pie?"

Jamie swatted him before she checked herself, loving the way he teased her and complimented her at the same time.

Adam held his hands up in surrender and slowly limped away to the safety of the fireplace. He tossed another log on the fire and looked up. "Don't worry with the dishes. I'll do them tomorrow when you're gone." His last words erased the smile from his lips.

Jamie moved the pie to the tin safe above the plate storage and joined him at the fire. No one had ever told her to leave the dishes. "I've enjoyed cooking for you. When I go, a memory will be all I'll need to take with me. It'll make what I have to cook back home easier, knowing someone enjoyed eating it once."

She sat on the small rococo-style sofa that had been placed to one side of the fireplace. "I like your furniture. It's quite a mixture."

Adam didn't want to talk about furniture. He didn't want to talk at all. He felt as if just beyond his sight there was a huge clock ticking, warning him that the minutes with her were slipping by. Forcing himself to take a deep breath, he said, "Every now and then a wagon comes through headed for California. Sometimes they want to trade for horses. I took that sofa and the dining chairs as trade for a team."

"I didn't think you bought them." Jamie ran her hand along the black horsehair upholstery. "This sofa doesn't seem to fit you."

"In truth I've never sat on the thing. I usually read at the table if I have any energy left after dark."

He couldn't help but watch her fingers move over the back of the sofa. She had to be a witch, he thought. She'd feed him, then drive him insane with her play of innocence. If she'd been a real woman, she would have died in the fall last night, and if she were a dream, she couldn't have fed him dinner. He'd never believed in witches and the like, but she was starting to convince him of the possibility.

Her hand shook slightly as she whispered, "I know furniture better than I know people."

"That's the way I feel about horses," Adam replied. "They're much more predictable than the average person. I'd even be willing to bet that, come morning, most of my runaways will be grazing up on that huge patch of early green buffalo grass to the south."

Jamie thought herself on safe ground now. If he could talk of his horses, she could tell how she felt about her furniture. "I can run my hand over the wood of a chair and tell you how much care was taken in making it and how long it will weather."

Adam nodded. "Don't you wish you could do the same with people? Touch them and know what strength they contained?"

The images his words brought to mind silenced them both. Adam turned toward the fire, knelt, and poked at it with an iron. He didn't hear Jamie moving on stocking feet toward him. She was a breath away when he straightened. Her nearness passed through him like a balmy breeze, making him forget everything but that she stood behind him. Hearing the light intake of her breath, smelling the wool of the shirt she wore blended with the damp nightgown which he guessed was still beneath it, awakened all his senses.

Her hand lightly touched his shoulder, but the shock that bolted through him was a lightning strike on his nerves. He didn't move as her fingers pressed into his damp shirt and spread out along his back. Muscles tightened as her fingers drifted across his back to the other shoulder. Adam stood, stretching his arms along the mantel just lower than his head. She moved directly behind him. Her hands traveled slowly along his back to his waist and up again. She seemed timid at first, but when he didn't move, her touch grew bolder.

With a brief caress, she brushed his hair and slid her hand along his arms, exploring every curve. He fought to remain immobile. The enchantment had begun and he was powerless to fight her. When her fingers slipped around him to touch his chest, Adam gave an involuntary jerk.

She backed away and for a moment, he thought she wouldn't continue, but her warm hands pressed once more against his shoulders.

Again her fingers skimmed his chest, and this time he braced himself for the shock of pleasure.

"You're my dream," she whispered as though she owned him body and soul. "*My* dream."

At that moment, Adam wasn't sure she didn't own him. He'd always thought himself a strong, independent man, but he knew he could deny her nothing.

Gripping his shirt, she pulled the buttons free. She spread her hand over his heart and felt it pounding in her palm. When her thumb accidentally brushed his nipple, she felt him shudder and knew the power her touch must have on him.

Jamie grew bolder. After all, he was only a vision. A man she'd made up in her mind. Tomorrow she'd have to go back to the real world, but tonight she'd know what her dream man felt like.

She moved so close behind him that she could feel the heat of his body even through their clothes. Pulling the shirt from his pants, she shoved the material aside so that her hands could run up and down along his ribs. His body was hard and lean, the muscles rippling slightly beneath her touch. Wanting to taste the flesh she felt, Jamie pushed up his shirt in the back and placed her lips on Adam's skin.

He gave a low moan that made her smile and move her lips between his shoulder blades. This man did not think her the kind of woman who should never touch or be touched. His white-knuckled grip on the mantel told her just how dearly he longed to turn around and hold her, but he was forcing himself to be still while she explored.

Her fingers played along the short hair of his chest and moved downward to where his belt barred his body from her search. She pushed his shirt off his shoulders and brushed her cheek against the warm muscles. Moving close against him until her body lightly molded against his, she whispered into his ear, "If I asked you to kiss me . . ."

All barriers shattered around his restraint. Adam twisted to face her and pulled her into his embrace. His fingers moved into her hair as he held her face an inch from his own.

His blue eyes looked deeply into her soul. "Are you afraid of me?" he whispered in a Southern voice low with passion.

"No," she lied.

His grip around her waist loosened slightly. "Then *you* kiss *me*."

With unsteady hands, she cupped his face and stood on tiptoes. Gently she brought her lips to his, feeling the heat of his mouth.

His fist captured a handful of her nightgown and shirt at the base of her back.

She stretched again and pressed her lips to his. This time her body leaned into the wall of his chest. His mouth opened slightly to welcome her playfulness. The warmth of passion spread through her, but this time Jamie didn't run from the feeling. She accepted it as part of being alive.

"Stay with me tonight," Adam whispered.

"Will you hold me and kiss me?"

There was no need to answer her with words. Adam sensed she wanted to be cherished tonight, courted with a gentle embrace and loving kisses. He'd force himself to move slowly, for he'd not risk shattering their shared dream tonight.

7

J amie blinked away the sunlight reflected in the shaving mirror. Almost identical, she thought, only round, not square-framed like Adam's. She was back in Chicago. Judging from the height of the sun, it must be long past breakfast time. Her arms and legs were stiff, but she didn't feel cold. She remembered the warmth of Adam's arms surrounding her all night. As the dream faded, panic coursed through her blood.

She jumped from the chair and grabbed the saddlebags. She took three steps up the stairs before the front door to the shop popped open and Inez's shout outpaced the entering cold. With dread, Jamie turned toward her sister, guessing what was to come.

"There she is! She's not outside as we feared but hiding in the store!" Inez yelled loud enough to shake the walls. "Oh, dear Lord, look at her!"

To Jamie's horror, the Whitneys flanked Inez.

They held Inez between them as all three stared openmouthed at Jamie.

"There's blood on her shirt!" Mary Beth declared and Inez screamed again, duplicating her earlier cry.

Jamie looked down at Adam's wool dress shirt. There *were* a few crimson stains where he'd bled on her and a dusting of flour from a spot the apron hadn't covered. She wanted to smile, wishing that some sign of where he'd touched her showed on the clothes as well. He'd held her in his arms until they'd both fallen asleep cuddled into one end of the sofa.

"It's a man's shirt," Raymond announced with such overwhelming disgust that the two chubby women gasped. "Your sister is wearing a man's clothing."

Both Inez and Mary Beth fanned their hands in front of them as if the room had grown suddenly too hot to endure.

Jamie didn't wait to hear more. She darted upstairs to her bedroom before any of the three thought to follow. She shoved several boxes to block any entry into her room and ran to the mirror inside the door of her wardrobe.

The sight that met her almost frightened a scream from her own lips. She stood looking at a creature she'd never seen. Her hair was wild and free around her, and her lips were lightly swollen and darker than they'd ever been. A pale face looked back at her, but her cheeks glowed with a blush that no amount of powder could hide. Adam's shirt was half-unbuttoned, open just enough to reveal an inch of the swell of her breasts on either side. She remembered how he'd teased her skin by sliding his knuckle along the open slit as he'd kissed her long and tenderly.

Once again, her dream had spilled over into reality. If Adam were only make-believe, how could she be standing before the mirror in his shirt with a light blue mark at her collar bone where he'd tasted her skin?

"Jamie, let us in right this minute!" Inez hammered on the door. "I've already sent for the doctor, so there's no use trying to hide."

Jamie knew she had little time. She jerked off the shirt and stuffed it into a worn carpetbag she kept hidden between boxes beneath her bed. The bag held all her valuables: Jamie's one collection, her father's pocket watch of real gold, a cameo her mother had worn around her throat the day she'd married, money Jamie had saved for years, and now Adam's shirt.

Replacing the bag, Jamie hurriedly scrubbed her face with cold water and slipped into her oldest and plainest dress.

"Open the door!" Inez continued to pound. "If I have to, I'll go down to the corner and get a policeman."

Jamie pulled on her stockings and tied her hair back into a knot. She couldn't help but smile at the memory of Adam playing with her hair for hours, as if he'd never grow tired of it.

"I have Mary Beth and Raymond to testify that you've gone completely mad if you don't open this door right this minute."

Shoving the boxes aside, Jamie turned the knob and tried to straighten to her most proper self.

The trio stepped back as if they'd been slapped. Raymond's forever wide open eyes narrowed slightly. Inez was the first to recover. "Well, at least you had the decency to clothe yourself properly. I've never seen such a display in my life. . . . "

Inez continued talking and the Whitneys comforted her as Jamie made tea. She refused to answer any of their questions. They wouldn't have listened to the answers anyway. They wouldn't have believed.

From the talk Jamie guessed Inez had missed her when breakfast wasn't on the table. Her sister had made a quick search of the place without bothering to look in every corner of the store. Then she had run down the block to fetch Raymond and Mary Beth, more to help with her own plight than to search for Jamie.

"I'm going to talk to the doctor about your behavior right now," Inez said as Jamie moved through the kitchen doorway. "I always thought you were not quite right, but lately I've begun to worry."

"Do you think she's dangerous?" Mary Beth asked.

"No," Inez added quickly, "but I may need some help in taking care of her."

Both women made a kind of humming sound, as if they were tuning their thoughts to the same tone.

Raymond followed Jamie into the kitchen as the two older women continued to plot. He leaned against the counter and folded his arms over his thin chest. "I think I have a right to know where you got that shirt."

"It doesn't matter." Jamie cleaned the dishes. She didn't even want to look at him. "And you have no right at all to know anything about me."

"What about the blood? I demand to know how blood got all over that shirt."

She didn't comment.

"Jamie, I'm talking to you!" Raymond snapped. "Answer me."

"Or what?" Jamie faced him, the last of her calmness stripping away to reveal raw nerves. "Or you'll slap me? That might prove dangerous, Raymond. Don't forget I have germs. Maybe the blood was from the last person who tried to tell me what to do." She couldn't hide her smile at her own bravery.

Raymond looked shocked.

"Maybe I cut him into little pieces and served him up in the giblet gravy we had last time you came to dinner."

Horror drained all color from Raymond's face.

Inez saved the man from Jamie's wrath by opening the kitchen door. "The doctor's here."

"I don't need a doctor," Jamie answered calmly.

Inez wasn't so easily put off. "You'll see him here or at the state hospital, dear sister."

Jamie knew her sister meant to have her way. Inez would carry out her threat. Jamie followed the doctor into the bedroom. For a second before she turned away, Jamie thought she saw a flash of challenge in Inez's stare.

Doctor Abernathy had been treating her all her life and had seen the family through forty years of health and illness. "Unbutton your top a few inches, Jamie, and I'll listen to your heart." He dug in his bag.

"I'm not ill," Jamie insisted as she did as she was told.

Abernathy listened to her heart a moment before asking, "You getting any sleep?"

"Yes." Jamie didn't know if dreaming counted.

"Inez tells me you've been moody and acting crazy. Talking to yourself."

"I probably have been." Jamie blinked as he forced each eye open a bit wider.

"You eating good, girl?"

"I had a bowl of stew only a few hours ago." Jamie heard the mumbling of Inez's denial coming from the other side of the door.

Abernathy rubbed his fingers along her scalp. "Have you fallen lately and hit your head?"

"No, sir." Jamie doubted falling off a cliff in a dream counted.

The old doctor put his instruments back into his bag and moved to the window. Jamie followed. He reached for his pipe and began filling it as he whispered, "You look like your mother did the first time I saw her. She was a beautiful woman. Gentle too."

"Weak?"

"No, gentle. And loving. She loved your daddy even if he was twenty years older than her."

Jamie smiled, wondering how the doctor would feel about Adam. If they were both in 1902, Adam would be over forty years older than her.

The old doctor didn't miss the twinkle in her eyes as Jamie smiled. He glanced at the door and carefully kept his voice low. "I think you've got that rare illness we all pray we'll catch at least once in our lives. You're showing all the signs of being in love."

Jamie opened her mouth to deny it, but she couldn't with any honesty.

"I won't say anything to Inez," Abernathy continued. "That woman spends enough time butting into your business, I'd guess. I can't blame you for not telling her. I know she's tried to be good to you, but she always resented your mother and you for coming into her life."

He lit his pipe and allowed Jamie a moment to think before he continued. "Now she'll resent your leaving to marry."

"I'm planning to leave here anyway."

The doctor looked at her with questioning eyes. There was apparently much he'd like to ask, but he wouldn't pry. "If you ever need it, there's a job at the clinic waiting for you. The pay's not much, but you'd be welcome to live in the wing with the nurses."

"You're not afraid I'm crazy? Don't forget the reason Inez called you."

Abernathy laughed. "You're the kind of crazy we all should be. You're a kind and loving woman, just like your mother."

"Thank you." Jamie hugged the old doctor. "I'll think about that job."

He patted her shoulder. "I'll tell Inez you need complete rest for a day and for no reason should she disturb you. That should help. But leave this house as soon as you can, Jamie. I don't doubt but that that sister of yours will get another doctor who'll see your behavior differently. You're in danger, real danger."

"But she'd never . . . "

"She could and she would," he corrected. "Your sister is losing control of you. I've seen folks do some mighty strange things to keep the upper hand."

He moved toward the door. "Get some rest. I'll drop by in a few days."

When he turned the knob, three eavesdroppers almost fell into the room. They quickly recovered and followed him, asking questions as he descended the stairs.

Jamie lay across her bed. She thought of how Inez had always been there to tell her what to do. Even when Jamie had grown old enough to make up her own mind, she'd usually followed Inez's plans to save arguing. But deep inside Jamie knew that one day she'd have to make a stand. She'd saved what little money she could, for when that day came Jamie knew she'd have to leave with nothing but what she could carry.

Sounds of Inez complaining drifted through the door of Jamie's room. Mary Beth offered to stay and help with the cooking and Raymond said he'd be downstairs. They were moving in, Jamie thought. Step-by-step.

Closing her eyes, she thought of Adam and how warm his arms had felt around her. Maybe the doctor was right. Maybe she was falling in love. But not with a man, with a dream.

The morning passed slowly. Jamie slept soundly for a time before being awakened by Mary Beth yelling through the door that if she wanted any lunch, she'd better come out.

Jamie ignored the invitation.

Mid-afternoon, Raymond pounded on her door. Without waiting to be asked, he entered, dragging the Chippendale wing-back behind him. "We're doing some organizing downstairs. Inez said you'd have a fit if we tossed this out, so you'll have to find a place for it in your room."

"But you have no right . . . "

Raymond frowned at her. "I think I have. I've considered offering marriage to you. Mind you, I haven't made my decision yet, but your sister has promised me full run of the store."

"Well you can stop considering. If the offer were made, I wouldn't marry you."

"We'll discuss it later." Raymond spoke as if he were talking to a child who would grow up soon and see the light. He was closer to Jamie's age than Inez's, but he acted far older.

She didn't want to consider marriage to him at all, but Raymond seemed to take her silence as agreement. He gave a slight, formal bow and left the room. Jamie shoved several boxes against the door as if she could bar him forever.

She tried to relax and go back to Adam, but she couldn't. The movements below and the constant shouting from one floor to the other kept Jamie from being able to sleep.

After several hours, she finally gave up and went downstairs. Inez refused to talk to her except when giving a command, yet she constantly asked Raymond for advice. Jamie did her share of the work and retired early.

When the store and apartment were finally quiet, Jamie tried again to go to Adam. Her dreams were filled with darkness and whispers. She couldn't reach Shadow's Bend.

Similar days passed for a week. Each day Jamie worked and each night she tried to return to Adam. The mornings brought only the sorrow of her world.

Finally, Jamie could stand the days with Inez and her friends no longer. "Tonight will be my last in this room," she whispered as she shoved the boxes to block her door for the night. "I'll be gone tomorrow before Inez wakes."

After pulling the saddlebags from their hiding place beneath the carpetbag under her bed, she curled into the chair. The familiar rustling of letters inside the bags greeted her.

Jamie lifted Adam's letters. She wanted to hold them to her and in some small way feel closer to him. But the bundle was thicker.

Six extra letters tumbled onto her lap. Jamie couldn't keep her hands from trembling as she opened the first, then the second, third, until they all lay open around her.

Adam's bold handwriting had penned the same message on each one:

Jamie, come back to me. Love Adam

Tears streamed down Jamie's face as she folded the letters. "I'm trying," she whispered. Closing her eyes and clenching the saddlebags, Jamie tried one last time to travel back to Shadow's Bend.

*   *   *

The spring storm had vanished, leaving the land around Shadow's Bend newborn. She moved through the wet grass, loving the way the wind played with her hair. The sun was golden and low in the sky as she passed the open door of the cabin and moved toward the barn. Adam had stacked all the lumber from the fallen windmill, but it didn't look as if there were enough unbroken boards to rebuild. She knew without asking how disappointed he must be.

The barn door stood open, but Adam was nowhere in sight. Jamie climbed the ladder to the loft, hoping she could look out over the station and see him. When she stepped in the doorway of the loft, the wind caught her hair and whirled it gently across her face.

"Don't move." Adam's low voice came from the shadows of the loft. "I want to touch the sunlight in your hair. I've wished a hundred times I could see you standing just as you are now."

Jamie smiled as she watched him come toward her. He favored his injured leg, but the cut on his forehead was almost completely healed. He touched her hair, feather-light, and she whispered, "I don't want to go back to my world, Adam. I want to stay here with you. I didn't come to you the first time I tried. I'm afraid next time I might not be able to get to you."

He moved closer. "I don't know how you come or why you go, but I'd give the world if you'd stay. I don't feel alive except when you're here."

She knew he didn't believe that she could be in 1902 and he in 1861, any more than he thought she really came from Chicago to see him. "You've got to believe me," she pleaded as she leaned into the hard wall of his chest.

"Why?" he murmured against her ear. "Would it make any difference? Would you stay if I believed?"

"I don't know. Something keeps pulling me back to Chicago. Just as you and your letters keep drawing me to Shadow's Bend." Suddenly she was silent. Terrified that the next time she was in Chicago she wouldn't be able to get back to him. Frightened that the cross in time might catch up with them and he would be forty years older than she was.

There was only one certainty. Adam was real to her now and she loved him more than she'd ever loved anyone. Tears rolled unchecked down her cheeks. If she couldn't have a lifetime with Adam, at least she'd have tonight.

He turned her in his arms and kissed her tenderly. "Each time you leave, I fear the magic that allows you to be here is disappearing. And each time I see you, I need you more."

They sat in the hay and talked until late, then he offered to cook her dinner. While they ate he asked every detail he could think of about her life in Chicago, even getting her to draw a floor plan of the store and apartment above.

She helped do the dishes then cuddled with him in front of the fire.

"Don't go back tonight," he whispered into her hair.

"I wish I could stay. I wish I could wake up in your arms." She slowly moved her fingers along his arm twined around her waist. "But all we have is a few hours, I fear."

"No." His voice sounded hard and cold. "Fate wouldn't do this to me twice, give me a woman worth holding for a lifetime and take her away just as I realize how badly I need her. I'll come to Chicago and get you."

"It wouldn't work." Jamie knew there would be

no record of her in a Chicago of 1861. She also knew his logical mind wouldn't accept the time travel. Maybe that was for the best. For when she stopped coming to him, he'd think he'd only dreamed of her. Maybe the reason she crossed time was that she believed in him so much. She couldn't demand the same; he had to give it freely.

"I don't want to talk of Chicago anymore," Jamie whispered as her hand moved over his chest. "I need you to hold me."

Adam pulled her close and kissed her with slow, simmering passion. His arms felt so right around her, as if they'd held her in a protective embrace for years.

"Stay with me tonight," he whispered. "Let me love you."

"I'll stay as long as I can and when I go I'll be only half-alive until I come back."

He lifted her and carried her to his bed in the corner of the cabin. As shadows washed the bedroom area in gray, Adam undressed her. There was no time but the present moment, and no place in this world except within his arms.

When he pulled the material away from her breasts, he paused for a long time, only inches above her but so still he seemed made of stone.

"Is something wrong?" The shadows hid his face from her.

"No, something's perfect," he answered as his callused palm lightly curved over her flesh.

Jamie smiled and spread her arms out across the quilt. She arched her back slightly as he finished pulling away her clothes. It crossed her mind briefly that she should be shy, but she loved the way his hands moved over her, warming her with his touch.

He straightened for a moment. She watched as he undressed with only the light of the fireplace outlining his body. As he lowered himself above her, she felt her softness give willingly against him.

In all the years she'd dreamed of loving a man, she'd never thought of the pleasure just his touch would bring her. The soft way his hair tickled across her skin as his mouth moved over her. The rough scratch of a day's growth of beard. The completeness of belonging to him as his chest pressed against her heart.

She'd also never thought of the sounds lovers might make, but now Adam's low words were a music that enchanted her soul. He whispered of his love against her throat and shouted her name when he seemed lost in passion.

Jamie wrapped her arms around him and held tightly. For as long as she stayed with him, she wouldn't go. She'd love Adam enough to last a lifetime.

8

A scream echoed through Jamie's bedroom, tumbling her from Adam's arms to reality in one harsh blow.

"I swear to Moses!" Inez shouted from the doorway where Raymond stood, having managed to shove aside the boxes. "I can bear no more of this insanity!"

Jamie lifted her head and looked toward her sister's voice.

Raymond was as white as new snow. His eyes were wider than Jamie had ever seen them.

Mary Beth sank to the floor in a fainting heap while Inez tried unsuccessfully to hold her up.

For a moment, Jamie couldn't imagine what had upset them so much.

Then she felt the breeze from the other room on her body. All her body!

She looked down to find herself curled up completely nude in the old Chippendale, the warmth of Adam's lovemaking still hot on her flesh. With a frantic leap she jumped toward the bed and yanked the spread around her.

Inez continued to clamor. "I tried to raise her the best I could, but she's too much for me to handle alone. First talking to the furniture, then befriending every stray who passes the door, and now taking off all her clothes in public."

Jamie opened her mouth to remind Inez that her room was hardly public, but Raymond spoke before she could say a word.

"I'll marry her!" he shouted.

"What?" Inez's volume dropped suddenly.

"I said, I'll marry her." He stepped over his sister and pushed Inez aside. "After she's my wife, the craziness will stop."

Inez smiled from behind Raymond, as if she'd planned Jamie's nudity as a trap. "We'd best have the wedding right away." She knelt and tried to pull Mary Beth to her feet. "The sooner the better."

Jamie held the covers close around her. "I'll not marry you."

"Oh, yes, you will, 'dear sister,'" Inez answered. "You'll marry him before the week's out or I'll have you committed to the state hospital. I hear they have a room there where none of the folks wear clothes and they only feed you once a day from a trough. If I can't get Abernathy to sign the papers, I'm sure another doctor will when all three of us tell how you've been acting."

"She won't go to any insane asylum. I'll take care of her," Raymond mumbled, as though he were doing her a great favor by offering.

A cold chill spread through Jamie. The last straw had fallen. Her plan to leave would be carried out. There was no need upsetting Inez with further discussion.

Inez was so concerned with helping Mary Beth straighten her dress that she didn't see Jamie's look of sorrow.

"I'll never marry you," she whispered to Raymond as she moved to her closet and began pulling out her clothes. As soon as it was daylight, she'd leave.

"If you'll all excuse me, I need to get dressed."

To her surprise they all moved away. The women were already planning the small wedding, and Raymond excused himself to work on his new office downstairs.

Jamie collapsed into the chair. She tried to envision Shadow's Bend and return to Adam's arms, but she couldn't focus enough to think. If she didn't marry Raymond, she had no doubt Inez would try to have her committed. The three of them would have the apartment and the shop, no matter what she did. Jamie had to leave now.

She spent the rest of the night writing Adam a letter. Jamie wasn't sure she'd ever be able to go back in time if she left this place and the wonderful old Chippendale. She put the letter in the saddlebags while she packed, but when she looked, it was still there. Somehow the magic had disappeared.

When her room lightened, Jamie finished dressing. She placed the saddlebags beside her carpetbag on her bed and went downstairs to say good-bye to the store.

Everything was stacked and tied into groups for a quick sale. The tall clocks had been hauled off because Mary Beth said the noise gave her a headache. Even Mrs. Murphy's rocking chair had been moved next to the back door to be put out, and the heater had been turned up at Raymond's request.

Knowing she'd have only a few minutes to herself before Raymond and Mary Beth arrived for breakfast, she moved through the store one last time. The shop she'd cared about for five years was gone, replaced by a crowded junk store. No one had dusted or polished any wood for days. The furniture looked like stacks of lumber with little value to anyone. Now the early morning shadows seemed to enlarge the scars and stains, distorting the furniture into ugly, twisted parodies of their former beauty.

The basement door creaked suddenly, setting Jamie's nerves on edge. Raymond moved through the thin porthole from the lower level. His padded coat was missing, revealing his narrow shoulders and scrawny chest.

"What are you doing here?" Jamie asked before she thought to hide.

"What are you doing up?"

"I live here." Jamie tried to control her anger.

"Well, so will I before long. The first thing I'm going to do is replace that heater. No matter how high I turn it, the thing still doesn't give off enough heat. Everything is falling apart in this place, and your sister doesn't even have insurance."

"We were doing fine without you." Hate built inside Jamie.

"Not according to Inez. She says you spent every dime on worthless junk while she had to scrape just to have money for food. If it wasn't for her, you'd have nothing."

Jamie balled her fingers into fists and prepared to attack. A sudden explosion silenced her. The entire house rattled, expanding as though drawing in one last breath before death. The floor beneath her shook and several small pieces of furniture tumbled off their perches. A popping noise came from the door to the basement as window glass shattered behind her.

Jamie stood frozen as the sound increased and bright light shone from the tiny door. It felt as if they'd trapped the sun beneath their store. The room grew hot and the light shone brighter.

"Fire!" Raymond screamed and grabbed the cash box. "Fire!"

He raced for the door. Jamie clutched his sleeve. "We have to get Inez! And find Winchester! And get as much out as we can!"

Raymond jerked frantically at her hand. "No!" he yelled, as if she were asking him to do something disgusting. "No!"

He knocked her down and bolted for the back door. As Jamie's fingers touched the floor, she knew she must move fast.

She ran up the stairs screaming her sister's name. Inez hurried from her room trying to pull on her wrap. "What . . ."

"The heater exploded!" Jamie gasped for air. "We've got to hurry!"

"My collections!" Inez glanced around the room. "I'm not leaving without my collections."

Jamie grabbed a blanket and started throwing dolls into it while Inez ran from place to place trying to decide which of her many dusty, neglected collections were the most valuable.

Their arms loaded, they ran down the stairs. The

shop was smoky now, warning of how little time they had left. As soon as they reached the street, Inez turned to her sister. "Go back in for more, Jamie. I can't lose my collections."

Jamie set her load down and ran back into the house but not for Inez's collections. She had to save the saddlebags. She'd risk dying to hold on to that tiny part of Adam, his letters.

The shop had turned from summer warm to oven hot. Jamie climbed the stairs. She glanced at all the worthless things lying around the living room. The saddlebags were a million times more important than anything. *He gave them to me*, she thought. *The old man brought them to me.* "Adam," she whispered.

As she passed her window, she saw Mrs. Murphy in the alley below. Somehow the aging woman had pulled her wonderful Victorian rocker from the fire and was dragging it down the deserted alley. Winchester sat on the red damask cushion as if he planned never to leave.

"They belong together," Jamie whispered.

"As do we." Adam's voice came from behind her.

Jamie turned and cried out in horror. His clothes were blackened and a gash cut across his cheek. "What happened?"

"When you didn't come to me, I finally ignored logic and tried to come to you. I pictured every inch of the shop you'd described to me. When I came through the passage, the place was on fire. I had a split second to decide if you were somewhere outside with the others or upstairs alone. The stairs were collapsing as I climbed them."

Jamie ran for the door. "Oh, but Adam, we're trapped!"

He pulled her into his arms. "No, I'll lower you out the window, or we can go to Shadow's Bend. But if you do, there will be no coming back."

She could hear the crashing of wood beneath her and knew her furniture was dying an honorable death rather than one of neglect and disgrace. "I've no reason to come back."

"Jamie!" Inez shouted from below the window. "Jamie, throw down my things!"

The noise of the fire drowned out her sister's voice as Jamie took Adam's hand. "Will you promise to hold me?"

"Forever." He touched her lips with a kiss. "I'll never let you go."

The hot pressing air of her room grew warm like the first touch of spring in the morning. Smoke cleared as the soft breeze of Shadow's Bend touched her hair. Jamie could feel the damp grass beneath her feet. Adam lifted her in his arms and held her tightly against him. "Welcome home, Jamie. Welcome home, my love."

Epilogue

"Now, Ryan be careful with that leg! Cole, lower your side into the wagon first. Matt, hold those horses still. If you three break this chair before we get it home to your mother, she'll have you all sleeping in the barn for Christmas."

The youth of fifteen who had stepped from the train platform into the flatbed of the wagon paused and laughed. "Do you think you could slow down on the orders, Pa? The War Between the States has been over for years and we're not a bunch of young

Texas Rangers you're trying to whip into shape to defend the frontier."

"Yeah," added another youth with the same black hair and blue eyes of his brother. "This is just Mom's usual Christmas present. It's not like we don't have a dozen more at the house. Every year you order her the newest model."

Adam Shelton smiled and ran his fingers through graying hair. "I know, but I ordered this one all the way from Kansas City. Jamie's gonna love it."

Brook Shelton slipped her hand into her father's and smiled up at him from waist height. "Well, she says that crazy thing she always says about being glad to see a chair like this one again."

Adam winked at his youngest daughter. "I wouldn't be surprised. You know how good your mother is about dreaming about the way things will be in the future."

He lifted her up onto the wagon seat. "You ride home with Matt in the wagon. The rest of us will lead those new horses. We'll have to make good time in order to be home for supper. Wouldn't want the neighbors eating it all."

Adam forced his stiff leg over his horse. As he settled onto the saddle, he smiled at his sons, who were already starting toward home. He'd been gone from the ranch for only a few hours and already he longed for the sight of Jamie.

When his horse trotted up the drive to the home they shared, he knew she'd be waiting for him on the porch, her arms eager for his welcoming embrace.

She'd crossed time to capture his heart and he'd stepped through fire to win her love. Every day for almost twenty years he'd looked in her eyes and believed in magic.

Jodi Thomas

JODI THOMAS lives in a small town in Texas where folks take their time saying hello and sunsets are endless. A former teacher and crisis counselor, she loves talking with people. Once, while volunteering at the Panhandle Plains Museum, a tourist told her she should read Jodi Thomas' books about Texas and Texans. When Jodi told the woman she was Jodi Thomas, the woman frowned and walked off, probably thinking she'd finally met a Texan telling tall tales.

"Shadow's Bend" is Thomas' first venture into time travel but not her last. She enjoyed having a couple cross time for one another. October thirty-first may be Halloween, but for Thomas it's a romantic time. It marks the anniversary of her first date with her husband. After twenty-five years together and two sons, they still manage a special date on the night when everyone else seems to be thinking of ghosts and goblins.

Avon Romances—
the best in exceptional authors
and unforgettable novels!

MONTANA ANGEL   **Kathleen Harrington**
77059-8/ $4.50 US/ $5.50 Can

EMBRACE THE WILD DAWN   **Selina MacPherson**
77251-5/ $4.50 US/ $5.50 Can

VIKING'S PRIZE   **Tanya Anne Crosby**
77457-7/ $4.50 US/ $5.50 Can

THE LADY AND THE OUTLAW   **Katherine Compton**
77454-2/ $4.50 US/ $5.50 Can

KENTUCKY BRIDE   **Hannah Howell**
77183-7/ $4.50 US/ $5.50 Can

HIGHLAND JEWEL   **Lois Greiman**
77443-7/ $4.50 US/ $5.50 Can

TENDER IS THE TOUCH   **Ana Leigh**
77350-3/ $4.50 US/ $5.50 Can

PROMISE ME HEAVEN   **Connie Brockway**
77550-6/ $4.50 US/ $5.50 Can

A GENTLE TAMING   **Adrienne Day**
77411-9/ $4.50 US/ $5.50 Can

SCANDALOUS   **Sonia Simone**
77496-8/ $4.50 US/ $5.50 Can

America Loves Lindsey!

The Timeless Romances
of #1 Bestselling Author

KEEPER OF THE HEART   77493-3/$5.99 US/$6.99 Can

THE MAGIC OF YOU   75629-3/$5.99 US/$6.99 Can

ANGEL   75628-5/$5.99 US/$6.99 Can

PRISONER OF MY DESIRE   75627-7/$5.99 US/$6.99 Can

ONCE A PRINCESS   75625-0/$5.99 US/$6.99 Can

WARRIOR'S WOMAN   75301-4/$5.99 US/$6.99 Can

MAN OF MY DREAMS   75626-9/$5.99 US/$6.99 Can

SURRENDER MY LOVE   76256-0/$6.50 US/$7.50 Can

Coming Soon

YOU BELONG TO ME   76258-7/$6.50 US/$7.50 Can